The Common Murders

The Common Murders

S J Ridgway

To Mary.

S J Ridgway

2023

ENJOY

BLUE HOUR PUBLISHING
2015 edition

First Printing: 2015
ISBN: 978-1-326-46343-4

Blue Hour Publishing
Whitemoors Road, Stoke Golding
Nuneaton, Warwickshire CV13 6EG

Contents

Acknowledgement

Thank you to everyone who has given their advice and support enabling my first novel to come to fruition; including -

Stuart Gibbon; crime writing consultant. Derek Ridgway and Ivan Szubin; retired police officers. Stephen Booth; crime writer

The Common Murders

CHAPTER ONE

Standing in front of the mirror; my disguise was perfect. No one would ever see the real me. Especially people in London who always averted their eyes from strangers. But if they really looked at me, they would see a young white man with a clear complexion and just a hint of a shadow, looking at them. They would describe me as being around 28 years old, handsome, with blue eyes, and light-brown hair with a fringe swept roguishly to one side. A young businessman from the city, they may think to themselves. And, although my suit was pinstriped, if anyone got close enough to see, it was casual enough to blend in. I was just another young guy about town.

My choice was good as I portrayed the type of man women trusted. The kind, researchers say, women feel comfortable with; slightly boyish, angelic even, but with a masculine air. My voice, although slightly higher pitched than I would have liked, suited the character perfectly. There was nothing threatening about this young man. Women would confide in him. Tell him their secrets, and would walk home with him, and come to no harm. But I needed a suitable name, and after some deliberations, settled on Thomas. So, whenever I put on a disguise, I metamorphosed into Thomas, a calculating stalker and killer; the kind of killer the police found difficult to catch.

And I knew, and therefore Thomas knew, I would never be caught. The disguise would always protect me, or should I say us?

I watched as the woman drank her tea and poked around her plate as if she wasn't interested in the contents. Her auburn hair dangled into her food giving me the impression of curtains draped across a window of a face that didn't really want to be seen. She looked out of place and uncertain of her surroundings. Probably in her mid-twenties, she was slim and dressed in a pristine blue jacket with matching skirt which contrasted to the dull walls and vacant cobwebs in the café.

Finishing her tea and placing the cup on the table, the woman looked furtively around, stood up, donned her coat and headed for the door.

I waited for a couple of seconds before following her. As my feet scudded across the pavement I felt like a missile; armed and ready for action. I could hear my own heart thumping, beating like a drum; a drum of war. And, to me, this was war, my war. The drums beat louder and louder, I couldn't hear anything else, not even my thoughts. As the beat quickened, so did my pace. There was no going back, I was ready to strike; nothing would stop me.

The woman took the path I knew she would take. I ran along a shorter route, enabling me to get further down the lane on the edge of the common well before she arrived.

When I'd visited the spot earlier, I used a different disguise so people would not be able to recognise me. No one would point a finger and shout, 'that's him. That's the man I saw before.' My identity would remain intact—no one would ever know. I hated the thought of being inadvertently caught; especially as my actions were aimed at the very person I loathed more than anyone else in the world. So I only chose women who resembled

Margaret. But it wasn't really them I was getting at; they were just the means to an end. No, I would have to kill and kill again until they pointed the finger at him. He was the perpetrator of the real crime; the crime against me.

The lane was quiet. The spot perfect to carry out the deed without being seen, and there would be no interruptions from mobile phones. I began to wriggle into my disposable overall, knowing that, when the forensic team visited later, they wouldn't find anything, unless I wanted them to. The whole project was going to be carried out like a biological military operation. And even if the woman from the café saw me in the overall, she would probably apologise for disturbing me.

The woman was taking her time walking along the lane. And in the approaching darkness, I was finding it difficult to see as the nearest street light was some distance away. I reasoned that she must be enjoying the cool air and admiring the early autumn colours after the oppressive atmosphere of the café.

Then I imagined she was being watched by hundreds of tiny eyes of creatures waiting in the undergrowth to gather the harvest for another cold winter. They would be annoyed with the intrusion of yet another visitor who delayed their feast at nature's table. But they would have to wait, as I had to, while she finished her final journey.

So far my plan had been carried out with precision timing, but now I was running out of time. I needed an excuse to get her to move faster. Soon it would be too dark to carry out my work. So, instead of waiting without making a sound, I decided to call for help in a high-pitched voice that sounded more like a woman's voice than a man's. At my call I heard the woman's footsteps quicken on the gravel path behind the hedge.

'What's wrong?' she said in a hurried but reassuring voice. 'I'll be there in a minute. Where are you? I can't see you.' She sounded concerned and a little annoyed.

'I'm here, please hurry,' I answered in a voice that was just audible as I quickly covered my overall with the plastic mac I had brought with me. And then I sat perched on a rock with my head down, as if I were in pain.

'What's the matter?' the woman asked as she entered the field and ran towards me—cursing her mobile phone. I kept my head low as she bent down but failed to see the hammer in my hand.

'Please, please help me,' I whimpered.

As soon as she was close enough, I pounced and hit her over the head with such force from the hammer that the first blow felled her. As she lay on the floor groaning. I tore off my mac, pulled the hood of my overall up across my head, and put on my latex gloves. Now I was ready for the real action. The dagger plunged into her warm flesh more times than I could count, as if it had a mind of its own. And as it plunged, I felt the strength that Bates must have felt in the film *Psycho*. I didn't hear voices then, only my own. And of course the music; there was always the music.

I had never experienced such power as I did then. Oh yes, I was in control, and there was no denying it, I liked the feeling. I felt like a God, controlling who should live and who should die. And once I had chosen a victim, they had to die, sooner or later, they had to.

By the time the attack had finished, I ripped open the woman's skirt and pants, and inflicted the last insult on her dead body. As the dark settled in, I walked slowly along the field behind the hedge. Then, carefully peeled off my protective overall and gloves and rammed them into the plastic bag.

My car was so well hidden behind some trees that I nearly missed it. Opening the boot, I dropped the bag in. As I slipped behind the steering wheel and started the engine with a roar, I felt relieved and contented with a job well done.

CHAPTER TWO

Superintendent Cadema Sharma sat at her desk wondering how she was going to handle the murder of a young woman found on Wimbledon Common. Brushing her fingers through her long black hair, and taking another sip of the tepid coffee, she recalled what her predecessor had said.

'Always take the helicopter approach. Rise above each crime and make sure you examine every detail. The last piece of the jigsaw is there somewhere; it's up to you to find it.'

But he didn't stay long enough to teach her more of his ways, as Jim Logan had been killed by a sniper. He had literally used his own philosophy. He stood up at the wrong moment and was shot through the head by the sniper's bullet. No one could have saved him, let alone Cadema, who was only a few metres away, unable to move; knowing if she did, she would become the next victim. She was not afraid. This was the job she had always wanted; working in the Homicide Command of the Metropolitan Police Service, London.

The perpetrator would be caught; they all were when Jim Logan was on a case. But he was dead. She was now the most senior police officer at the scene. Despite this, she had to crouch like a coward, restrained by health and safety protocol, waiting for armed officers to arrive. As other bullets were fired, one sang past, ricocheting off the metal shutters of an empty flat; just missing Sergeant Marriott's head.

'Keep your head down, Sergeant,' Cadema shouted as another bullet hit the concrete of the building behind her. Then, for some reason she could never explain, she heard Jim's calm voice whispering to her. With a surge of energy and courage, she crawled, face down, across the pavement towards the door of the multi-storey car park and entered the building.

It took her a couple of seconds to adjust to the darkness after being in the bright sunlight. Standing in the silence of the evacuated building, she could hear the far-off put-put sound as a rifle was fired again and again. She moved cautiously forward, looking for any movement. As her pounding heart increased, she ran towards the concrete steps. Trancelike she ascended to the seventh floor. As if in a vacuum, there were no sounds or thoughts to warn her of the danger she was in. Moments later, she had reached the door leading to the balcony where the sniper was crouching—loading his rifle. Her eyes quickly scanned the scene. By the store of ammunition, food and drinks around the sniper she realized he intended to stay for a long time; probably until the next day. It was now up to her to stop him before he could shoot anyone else.

The metallic smell of the cordite stung at her nostrils, while her heart seemed to stop as she edged forwards. She took shallow breaths to prevent the fumes from entering her lungs. Then, for a second she was back on the firing range all those years ago. She was anxious then, but not as anxious as she was now.

Despite the chill of the early autumn air, Cadema began to perspire, afraid that she had made a mistake and she would be the sniper's next victim. Then she sensed Jim's presence. He would not let anything happen to her. She would instinctively obey him, not just because of his higher rank, but because she trusted him.

Taking a deep breath, she tiptoed forward and hid behind a pillar. As she peered from behind it, she could see the man much better now. But, silhouetted against the blue sky, she couldn't see his features. *Was he white, black, young or old?* she thought to herself. All she could tell was that he was male, armed and determined to kill; that he stood tall, military-like. She imagined he was sure of himself and always in control. He would be alert and sensitive to every sound, to every shadow. He would work to perfection. He would always be accurate and never miss a target. So here he was, a killing machine on the balcony of life and death. And she—well, she was just a woman, alone and unarmed.

Cadema edged forward along the pillar which blotted the sweat from her back— leaving her feeling cold and clammy. As he turned to crouch and fire again, she heard Jim's voice in her mind, 'go, go, go.'

Lunging forward, she grabbed the man's arm that held the rifle, wrenched it from his grasp, and threw it over the balcony.

But she didn't realise he had a handgun. And, as he turned, she felt the heat stab at her side as the jolt of the bullet felled her. She felt numb, dead, and unable to move, breathe, hear, or think as his heavy hands grabbed at her body. They were rough hands but they searched her with the precision of an experienced police officer. When he left her for dead, her warm blood pooling on the floor, she heard the unmistakable put-put of another rifle.

Lying motionless on the floor, she could feel the pain of the bullet as it travelled around her body; gouging holes into her organs. When it came to a halt, she heard the muffled voices of her colleagues.

'Drop the gun. Put your hands on your head. Turn around slowly.' The commanding voice of authority said calmly but with emphasis on every word.

When four men dressed in black aimed their guns at him, the sniper did as he was told; his body rigid.

'Look directly at me, don't look anywhere else, only at me,' the resolute voice of the police officer said as he moved forward towards the sniper.

'Now. Get down. Keep your eyes on me. Keep looking at me.' When the sniper obeyed, the police officer bent down and rammed the handcuffs onto the sniper's wrists.

'Officer down,' another voice screeched into his network system while the thunder of approaching feet nearly drowned out the wailing sirens of the incident support unit and ambulances.

***

The sirens from the street below Cadema's office jolted her back from the incident. Rubbing her left side, just below the last rib, she cringed at the thought of the sniper's bullet. Her heart quickened as she coughed, leaned forward and took the last sip of her coffee. Since she was deemed fit enough to resume work, this murder on Wimbledon Common was her first serious case. She shook her head—there's no time for procrastination, she thought.

When the body was found, it was obvious the woman had been dead for a few days. Any evidence there might have been, was scattered around, probably by nocturnal animals. After Doctor Julia Lilly, the forensic pathologist, confirmed the victim was probably killed five-days earlier, on the thirty-first of August, Cadema knew the case would be difficult. Her team would need something tangible to focus on, no matter how small. So before heading for the briefing room, she gathered as much information as there was, hoping they would think she was in control of the situation. Even so, at this point, she felt that the situation was controlling her.

Something's missing, she thought. But after shuffling through papers on her desk, and rummaging through her in-tray, she could not find Julia's report. Suppressing the urge to scream, she sat back in her chair, closed her eyes, took several controlled deep breaths, and then gradually opened her eyes again. *Relaxation, that's the key,* she reasoned. Looking out of her third-floor office window, she noticed streaks of grey dribbling down the window pane, and imagined the world was crying with her. But after a quick shake of her head, she sat upright, picked up her phone and pressed the number four button.

'Sorry to trouble you Julia, but have the slides been sent from your autopsy. I need them urgently for my presentation.'

'Hi, yes I think so, but let me check,' Julia's voice sounded as cheerful as ever as Cadema heard the phone being put down, and the muffled voices in the background. 'Yes, Bagley says he sent them first thing on PowerPoint to Sergeant Marriott. He should have received them by now. And he's just sent you the transcript of the slides.'

'That's great. Thanks Julia. Tell Bagley he's a star,' Cadema smiled and put the phone down. Frowning, she wondered why Marriott hadn't told her he had the slides. Despite him being new to the team, he should know she needed to have such informant and not keep it to himself. *I'll have to have a word with him*, she thought as she printed Bagley's transcript, gathered up her notes from the desk and then headed for the briefing room.

***

Cadema could hear the raucous voices of the officers even before she reached the second floor of the police station. As she entered the room all, except Marriott who was getting the PowerPoint projector ready, went quiet. The assembly of officers' resembled party-goers, with shirt buttons undone, and sleeves rolled up. The room matched the theme, with chairs out of sequence, crisp packets on the floor, and several empty plastic coke bottles scattered under foot. *Time to make my presence felt and let the team know what sort of ship I run.*

'What's all this rumpus and mess? The place looks like a pig-sty. I expect my officers to be professional in their work. I hope your sloppy appearance doesn't depict the way you'll be working in my team. Your last boss may have accepted your behaviour, I don't, and you'll have to accept that.' As she spoke, three officers hurried to do up their shirt buttons. Some tidied their hair with their fingers and sat upright. One picked up a waste basket which was filled as it was passed around. 'Good, now let's get on with things.'

Marriott gave two short coughs. 'The projector is ready for you Ma'am,' he said with pride, but with a hint of embarrassment in his voice.

A photograph of a young woman with auburn hair flashed onto the screen.

'Thank you Sergeant. Now I'll give you a brief account of the information I have to date.' Cadema foraged through her notes trying to find the first page. The team sat shuffling their feet, and then crossed their arms as she gathered up her notes into the right order, and coughed. 'Good, so let's get started. Mobiles off, and I'll be grateful if you'll leave your questions until the end.' The nods, and uncrossing of arms gave Cadema the impression that they would comply with her requests.

'This woman is about twenty years old. She was probably killed on the thirty-first of August last. But the body was not found until the fifth of September. As you can see, the back of the skull, photograph number two please Sergeant, has been shattered by a heavy blunt instrument, possibly a hammer. The first blow probably killed her. The whole body photograph,' she nodded to the Sergeant for the next slide, 'shows two deep stab wounds and ten superficial ones on the torso. No weapons have been found. Most of her clothes have been torn away, probably by animals. And there,' she pointed at small brown holes on the legs, 'they are rat bites.'

Cadema noticed two of the younger officers shudder as she spoke. DC Galke looked green and began rubbing his arm. *As if he had been bitten by the rodents*, she thought. *Was he going to be sick?* She didn't think so. He turned his head away from the photograph, and swallowed. Sergeant Marriott only took a glimpse, and then looked at his boss as if he were waiting for further instructions. Cadema's voice echoed round the silent room.

'Doctor Lilly's found some remnants of sperm. But it's so degraded that there's very little chance of obtaining any DNA, even with the use of polymerase chain reaction, which she says could have enhanced even the smallest amounts of it. If any of you want to know more, I'll ask Doctor Lilly to explain it to you.' Cadema hoped the officers hadn't noticed her voice quivering.

She remembered Jim Logan telling her about his experience in the Yorkshire Ripper case. To her, there were similarities with this case. And she didn't want the repeats of that initial investigation. Therefore, to avoid delays she allocated two of her senior officers, Detective Chief Inspector Christine Ryan and Detective Inspector Paul Evans, to each lead a team.

DCI Ryan had been promoted three years ago, just after her colleague was shot in the back by bank robbers. She recovered from the incident quickly and asked to be on Cadema's team. She had been an exemplary officer but Cadema believed that she spent too much time in the gymnasium which accounted for her almost anorexic appearance. Nevertheless, her tall physique and her large green eyes made her appear as strong as her male colleagues, who seemed to enjoy working with her.

DI Evans career had taken a different path. Since his degree entry into the police service, he had been fast-tracked up the ranks. On his ascent he had upset many officers. There were several occasions where he was near to being disciplined, only to be saved by promotion boards. Now, on her team, he had good crime results, but she had heard that he had cut corners to get them. He often used his large frame and his six feet two inch height to intimidate his colleagues, especially the women.

Allocating the two senior officers to specific roles according to their expertise, Cadema expected some resistance as they had their own methods of doing things. Nevertheless, she was in command and needed them to gather the intelligence to inform her decision making and to keep Chief Superintendent Norman Grimes, and the rest of the senior management team, well informed.

'DCI Ryan take your team and try to establish who this woman was. Do the usual media appeal. When you've found out, piece together her last moments.'

'Yes Ma'am,' Ryan answered.

Standing on tiptoe, Cadema searched the sea of faces in front of her. Most of them looked attentive except Evans who had been distracted by someone in the corridor. She ignored him, but made a mental note to talk to him about it later, and continued with her instructions to Ryan.

'We need to see if any similar murders have occurred in other UK areas.' She turned to the rest of the team. 'So let's give HOLMES-two, our expert oracle, including its storage system and cross-referenced database, something to work on. And don't forget, the Actions you will investigate have all been classified as urgent.' The team nodded. They were all familiar with the Home Office Large Major Enquiry System. 'Our office manager will follow the results of these Actions and report directly to me.' John Kasson, nodded in response.

Ryan stood up: 'Yes Ma'am, as soon as we've found the information I'll let you know,' she pointed to her officers in turn and gestured to them to follow her.

'DI Evans,' Cadema's voice echoed across the still room as his head turned towards her. 'You take your team and do another search of the area where the body was found. There must be something we've overlooked and we need to find it.' She noticed the slight twitch of a grimace as he brushed a strand of his brown hair from his face, leaned back in his chair, and folded his arms.

'But Ma'am, it's already been searched twice, and nothing has been found.'

'Nothing? You know I don't believe in nothing. This time will be different; I want you to extend the search outward from the scene and to the roads surrounding the Common.' Evans fidgeted, cleared his throat and then took a sip of water. Cadema was used to this behaviour from him, so ignored it. 'There may be areas that have been disturbed, evidence of a parked car, or tyre tracks perhaps. You know the signs; you've done this kind of work before. So let's get on with it.'

Cadema thought she had managed Paul Evans well and that he understood what she needed him to do. But when he took a deep breath, lifted his shoulders, and stretched his neck, she knew that her five-foot three slender frame was no match for him. And for the first time since her appointment as Senior Investigation Officer, she felt challenged. Not by his stature, as she wouldn't allow herself to be intimidated, but by her lack of experience in dealing with such insubordination.

Paul cleared his throat, instructed his team to carry on with the Actions they had been given, then turned to Cadema: 'Can we go somewhere private, Ma'am?' he asked as his officers left the room.

'Yes, my office.' *What now?* Cadema thought as they walked swiftly up the stairs. The sound of their steps squeaked on the recently polished floor. Entering her office, they stood facing each other.

'What is it Paul?' Cadema didn't blink as she looked into his blue eyes, her stance deliberately confrontational. He looked at his feet, shuffled and coughed.

'Well Ma'am, you know I'm quite capable of identifying the work which needs doing in these situations. God knows, I've had enough experience on the front line in murder investigations. So you didn't have to spell it out, especially in front of my team like that.' His voice rose, as did his head. After wiping his forehead with a tissue he took another deep breath; his voice evened out. 'You can trust me to do the work. And if you don't mind me saying so, I don't think you've really recovered from your ordeal.'

'So you're a doctor now, are you?' she said as she stood with her hands on her hips. 'Well that's no business of yours. Anyway it was God's will.' She felt her heart racing in her chest at having to justify her survival, especially to him of all people. Yes, she was next to Jim when he'd been killed. Yes, she'd received counselling and was now fit to work. She took a couple of even breaths and remained standing in front of him.

'Sorry Ma'am, but it's only an observation…'

'Look Paul, you probably mean well. But let's just forget it and move on. Anyway, I know what you are capable of, but I'm in charge of this investigation and I need to know what my teams are doing on a twenty-four/seven basis. I need to trust them to keep me up to date. How can I report to Chief Superintendent Grimes if I don't know what's going on?'

'Does that mean you don't trust me?' His stance mimicked Cadema's.

'I didn't say that. I know you're an experienced officer and I do need you to head the team; but on my terms.'

'That may well be the case, but I didn't like the way you humiliated me back there.' His neck reddened as he spoke.

'That's your interpretation. Anyway I don't need to justify what I said. And you know very well I've had problems with you in the past. Last time I did say I would keep a closer eye on you in future.' Cadema was almost shouting now.

'But Ma'am, that was ages ago, anyway the crime was solved even though there was some delay with the evidence.'

'"Some delay", you call it. You were lucky I didn't formally discipline you there and then. I gave you the benefit of the doubt instead, hoping you would learn from your behaviour. I hope I'm right.' Her voice softened.

'Yes, you are and I'll prove it to you by telling you what I intend to do during this investigation. Hopefully it meets with your approval.' Cadema ignored his condescending tone.

'Good so let's hear it.'

'Anyway before I continue, can I have twelve officers on my team as the eight I have isn't enough?'

'I'll agree to that in principle, but you'll need to put in a good case. And if I agree, Chief Superintendent Grimes won't be very pleased.'

'I know, but the work has to be done. Besides there's another issue. I don't think it's possible, or necessary to treat the whole Common as a crime scene. It's not practical.'

'What do you mean, not practical. The murderer used the whole Common didn't he? So we must do the same. But yes, I agree we need to be practical. So section it off, grid system, you know the score. When you've done with one grid, move to another. I'll expect you'll find something before you reach the last grid.'

'I'll do my best.'

'You'd better do so. Find what you can, clothing perhaps, a discarded cigarette, a handbag; broken twigs, just find something. The killer may have made mistakes, especially if he worked in the dark.'

'I will do, but it'll take about five days to do it all.'

'That's not good enough, I expect something much before then, especially with more officers. I'll want you finished by day five and your report on my desk on day six, with the results of the Actions entered into HOLMES by then, is that clear?'

'Yes Ma'am.'

'So let's not have any more delays. Don't forget regular updates.' Cadema's voice echoed after him as he marched down the corridor. She smiled to herself, knowing that all her officers would carry out her orders, and hoped her plans would meet with Grimes's approval.

CHAPTER THREE

With the information DCI Ryan had obtained, Cadema hoped to establish whether the murder victim found on Wimbledon Common, was Jane Gaunt. Jane had been reported missing on the second of September by worried flatmates who had not seen her since the thirtieth of August; now Mr and Mrs Gaunt were on their way to identify the body. If it were their daughter, she knew there was nothing she could say to console them.

Since the death of her husband in a car crash over three years ago, Cadema found it difficult to support bereaved people. The death of Jim Logan exacerbated her feelings, so she decided to delegate the task to DI Joanna Johns.

DI Johns was one of the officers she trusted. Despite her inexperience, her reputation, together with her appraisal reports, were excellent. So she decided to give her plenty of opportunities to enhance her knowledge and skills, and subsequently help with her promotion plans.

Cadema picked up the telephone:

'Hello Joanna, will you come to my office.' Cadema spoke in a tone that was more like an order than a question. 'When Mr and Mrs Gaunt arrive I want you to escort them to the mortuary to formally identify our murder victim.'

'Yes, of course Ma'am, I'll be with you in a couple of minutes.'

As soon as she entered the office Cadema noticed the flushed appearance on Joanna's face. Not only that, but as she took gulps of breath and thumped her chest, as if she were trying to cough, Cadema thought she was about to collapse.

'Are you all right?' her voice sounded concerned.

'Too many cigs; and too much paperwork, and not enough exercise Ma'am...' Her voice tailed off as she thumped her chest again.

'You'd better sit down before you fall,' Cadema taunted. 'Anyway, I know this isn't the time,' she took a deep breath. 'But I've been meaning to talk to you about the work you've been doing since you joined the team. Nearly six months isn't it?'

Johns coughed again. 'Yes, next Tuesday to be precise. That's when my first appraisal with you is due. Is there a problem Ma'am?'

'No, not at all. It's just that I don't think the work I've given you since you started here has been as professionally challenging to you as it should have been. And that's my fault.'

She frowned. 'Your fault? But how can it be? Anyway it's no different to what I'm used to.'

'What do you mean by that?'

'Well Ma'am, you may be able to understand, being a woman, and from India,' her breathing improved as she cleared her throat. 'But since I was fast-tracked into the service, and then quickly promoted through the ranks up to inspector, some officers seemed to resent me. *Positive Institutional Discrimination*, I believe it's called. And I've heard rumours saying I was only promoted because I'm black and a woman, and certainly not on merit.'

'I've never heard anything derogatory about you.'

'You wouldn't have, not at your rank. But I assure you the prejudice is there. Not that I can point at anyone, but I know what they believe.'

'Nevertheless, you seem a good officer to me. And from now on you will be getting a diverse range of jobs that will help with your future promotion. So let's forget the rumours for now, they can wait. We need to get back to the Gaunts as they have arrived and are waiting for us.'

***

When Cadema met Mr and Mrs Gaunt, she estimated that they were in their mid-forties. Mr Gaunt appeared a little older than his wife. He dressed formally in a tailored suit and matching tie; *as if he had just come from the office,* she thought, as she watched him brush his brown but greying hair from his forehead. Mrs Gaunt wore a casual dress, flat shoes and carried a shabby brown handbag. Her coy smile revealed brown uneven teeth that were incongruous with her round angelic features and well-groomed auburn hair.

After brief introductions with the couple, and explaining about the procedure, Cadema said she would leave DI Johns to look after them, and then left the room.

'I'm pleased to meet you but so sorry about the circumstances,' Johns said softly as she shook hands with the couple and gave an awkward smile. Leading them into the quiet room, they sat down on the two-seater couch. Mrs Gaunt took a tissue from her handbag and wiped her eyes.

'Sorry,' Mrs Gaunt whispered, 'but this has been such an awful ordeal,' she wiped her eyes again.

'Please don't apologise, I understand and appreciate how you must be feeling.' She took hold of Mrs Gaunt's hand as she spoke. 'I'm here to help you in any way I can. And if you don't want to see the body, then Mr Gaunt can do it on his own if these are your wishes?' She looked up at Mr Gaunt's face. He nodded. But after a few moments of quiet discussion, the couple decided to go together.

They were overcome by grief when they realised that the body was that of their daughter, Jane. Mrs Gaunt had to be helped out of the room. While Mr Gaunt looked pale, his expression motionless.

'I'm so very sorry,' she whispered as she escorted the couple back into the quiet room. 'We'll do all we can to find the killer and bring him to justice,' her voice quivered. Then a knock on the door interrupted what she was about to say. Opening the door, she took the tray of teas from a police constable, placed it on the coffee table, and offered the couple a drink. Mrs Gaunt was unable to take hers as she began to sob into another tissue and then spoke between breaths.

'She was a lovely girl, why someone had to do that to her heaven knows.' She wiped the tears from her face as her husband put his arm around her shoulders and whispered something. Mrs Gaunt continued to sob as she spoke again. 'She had her life in front of her, she did. She was such a lovely baby, and a very pretty young woman. Just returned from New Zealand as part of her gap year from Uni.' Mr Gaunt shook his head slowly and held his wife's hand. 'She was about to finish her last year at the South Bank and get her degree. And she didn't have any boyfriend to get in the way. Art was her passion, so she decided to put her love-life on hold until she'd finished studying.'

Johns offered a smile, or a frown, or a gentle touch of her hand when she thought it was appropriate. The statutory cups of tea seemed to help them relax and talk openly about their daughter. When they decided to leave, transport was arranged to take them to their hotel for the night. As they departed, she assured them that she would be in touch. She then picked up the telephone and called Cadema.

'I thought you would like to know straight away, Ma'am. The Gaunts' have positively identified the body as that of their daughter.'

'That's good at least we know who she is, but I wonder why she was at or near Wimbledon Common.'

'Don't know but they've gone to their hotel. Do you want my report now?' Johns' voice sounded eager.

'Yes of course, bring it to my office as soon as you've done it.'

Johns stood panting outside Cadema's door, took a deep breath and then knocked.

'Come in Joanna,' Cadema looked up from behind her desk as she entered.

After explaining what Mr and Mrs Gaunt had said, and how upset they were, she reiterated what their daughter had said to them:

"If old boyfriends came around, they would still be her friends but nothing more."

'That's interesting, so we could be looking for an old boyfriend who wasn't pleased with that arrangement.'

'I thought that too Ma'am, but when I asked them if they knew of any of their daughter's old boyfriends who might have a grudge against her, they said they couldn't think of any. That all three were such "nice boys" and "would never do such terrible things."'

'That's beside the point, we must have their names, assuming they know them.'

'Yes, but I've left the Gaunts' to get over their initial shock. They'll give me their names tomorrow.'

'Good. So what else is happening tomorrow?'

'They're going home. I said I'd visit them there, so they didn't have to keep repeating the same things to other officers. I'll follow up on the old boyfriends after that.'

'That's good…' Cadema was interrupted by the phone ringing on her desk. Responding to the call, she stood ashen-faced. Then, after a short pause began to speak. 'Yes I understand, I'll organise things right away.' Placing the receiver on its plinth, she shook her head slowly and turned to DI Johns. 'I'm sorry, but I've just been informed that another young woman has been murdered on Wimbledon Common. As you can appreciate, this is now my top priority so I'm afraid the Gaunts' will have to wait. I'll send a uniformed officer to visit them and get the information we need. Anyway, I don't suppose the old boyfriends will have anything to do with her murder.

'No, I think we are now looking for someone quite different, perhaps even a serial killer, who knows?' Cadema shook her head and sighed.

CHAPTER FOUR

The instant I saw her I knew my mundane day was over. I caught her outline in my headlights as I reached Common Road. She was a young woman of about nineteen years old, hitchhiking. The perfect opportunity, I thought. At first I was reluctant to give her a lift, what with her build and the frayed jeans giving me the impression that she could take care of herself. Then, on reflection I began to relish the idea of a challenge. So after driving past her, I turned the car round at the next junction, and drove back on the opposite side of the road. Finally I turned the car around again and drove slowly along the edge of the pavement and stopped the car where she was standing.

'Where are you going at this time of night?' I asked in the most concerned way that I could. My heart accelerated. 'You shouldn't be in a place like this. Can I give you a lift?'

My questions were spoken so quickly that the girl had no time to consider the answers so she spontaneously said:

'Oh yes, please.' She smiled as water dripped from her drenched auburn hair.

Once the girl was in the car she spoke to me as if I were her long lost friend. Indeed, she spoke so much that she didn't give me any chance to question her, or even think what I should do next. I drove on listening to the verbosity of a mouth which barely moved.

'You don't know how pleased I was to see you. Some old guy stopped earlier and gave me a lift but I didn't like the look of him, or the way he looked at me. Gave me the creeps he did. So I told him I was heading for London. So he says "you said you were heading for the Common, so why have you changed your mind?" I said, I hadn't changed it, you just didn't hear what I said. So I told him to let me out so I could go back to London. And you know what; he pulled over and let me out. Just goes to show what an ass-hole he was.' She giggled, giving me the impression that she was pleased with herself. But as she continued on, and on, and on, I tried unsuccessfully to block out the sound of her voice. I couldn't think, I needed her to be quiet so I could plan what I was going to do with her. But with all that talk, it was impossible for me to go on.

'Ha, you've gone quiet. Sorry I do babble on when I'm excited, and I am very excited tonight. You won't believe this, but it's the first time I've hitchhiked. By the way my name is Madeline, what's yours?'

I began to wonder why she was telling me everything; after all I was a stranger to her. And it amused me to think how she would react if I told her she was being kidnapped and about to be murdered. She would not confide in me then, and no doubt she would finally shut up. Nevertheless, I took a deep breath and was about to answer her, but her voice broke into my mind again.

'It's great to get a lift, and practically to the front door. Are you sure I'm not putting you to any trouble, it's such a long way you know. What did you say your name was?'

'I didn't.'

'I'll guess then, I like guessing. The man who gave me a lift early on, well his name was Bernard. Now that's a trustworthy name. I always think of the dog when I hear Bernard. But I didn't trust him. In fact I don't trust many men, especially old ones. He said it was his birthday, the thirteenth of September. Unlucky for some I thought, even though I didn't believe him.'

Her voice went on, but I had stopped listening and began grinding my teeth, something I was always told off about when I was younger. They didn't realise I only did it when I was angry. Madeline, in her naivety, didn't realise this so she was unaware of the danger she was in. I prayed for her to stop but she kept on and on.

'Please don't say anymore,' I screamed inwardly. *'I really don't want to find out who you are, or where you're from. I prefer my victims to be anonymous. I will find it very difficult to kill you if I know who you really are.'* I continued with my internal discourse as I fidgeted and coughed. But Madeline's voice rambled on.

'Anyway I had this set to with a guy when I walked to school one day. He was hiding in the bushes and had his trousers…well, being a man you know what I mean. But my dad sorted him out. Then there was Mike, I liked him but my dad said he was too old for me. So my dad had a word with him and I never sawed him again. But don't get me wrong, I like guys, but only the ones that my dad approves of. I like them to treat me right. Don't you agree that women should be treated right? Do you treat your women right?'

'Yes,' I said too spontaneously, and then tried to show how indifferent I was to her. But I couldn't help thinking about the grammatical mistake she had made, saying sawed, instead of saw. And, at the same time I was concentrating on the traffic which had slowed to a crawling pace.

'That's good. I thought you were a nice guy when we first met. And I'm not forward you know, but I do, for some reason I can't explain, trust you. Okay so I've only had a couple of real boyfriends, but I've never been all the way with them.'

'If you mean you haven't had sex, why didn't you say so?' I said assertively, hoping it would stop her from talking.

'Say what? Sex?' she asked as if she hadn't expected me to be listening or to give such a forward answer. An answer, which I could tell from the way she shuffled in her seat, she was embarrassed by.

'Yes. It is a word that everyone uses nowadays, so you should say what you mean. It takes out the ambiguity if you say what you mean,' I said, then realised that she was becoming even more uncomfortable with the situation.

'Well, well, ambiguity, what a big word. So okay in that case, sex. Now I have said it but I haven't had it and that's that. You understand what I am saying, don't you?' She folded her arms and looked indignant as the traffic moved about five miles an hour.

'Yes, I understand perfectly.' I shook my head instead of nodding it.

'Well I had a friend called Jane.'

Oh for Christ sake don't say she's a lesbian too, I cannot cope with that right now, I thought as the windscreen wipers moved to the rhythm of Madeline's voice.

'Look Madeline, stop telling me about you and your friends, I really don't want to know. When I'm driving I need to concentrate. It's difficult as it is driving at night, and you are making it even more difficult.'

'Sorry,' she folded her arms again. 'I was only trying to keep you company. It must be lonely driving on your own-'specially at night in the countryside. Why haven't you got a radio? Did someone nick it? I had a friend who had her car stolen and when they found it...' I shut my ears to her voice at that point.

When I stopped the car in the lay-by I could see the light drizzle like tiny insects swarming around the tunnel of light formed by the car's headlights.

'Get out of the car Madeline.'

'But we haven't got to where I need to be yet; it's at least another ten miles.'

'Please get out of the car Madeline.' I was assertive and ignored her snivelling voice.

'But.'

'Out.'

'Okay, okay, don't get stroppy. I'll be quiet from now on. But please don't make me get out of the car, I'm soaked enough as it is. Anyway it's too dark for a young girl like me to be out there on my own on a night like this.'

'Get out. Go and hitchhike the rest of the way. I've gone too far. I should have turned off back there.'

'But you said.'

'Never mind what I said. I was wrong, so you'll have to go.'

'But it's lonely here and very dark, can I…'

'No. Get out.'

Madeline sulked as she opened the door and with pleading eyes, which almost made me change my mind, she slid out and banged the door shut.

I couldn't believe that I had chosen such a person. And I hoped I'd have better luck with the next one. But there wasn't going to be a next one that night as I was hungry, tired, and had lost the will to kill. Instead I decided to drive back to London, my home and my bed for sleep which I knew was badly needed.

***

By the time I had walked up the stairs and opened the front door of my flat, I could feel the cold. The central heating needed attention again, but with working and my busy evenings, I couldn't find the time to have it fixed. So I had to wait for the gas fire to heat the living room.

Nevertheless, I was home in my sanctuary from the hassle and bustle of the world outside. A sanctuary from the decadent populous of a city that was doomed to be the cesspit of the world. A place where people ignored one another. Where unseeing eyes looked away when confronted by poverty, or when they glanced at intoxicated homeless bodies curled up in shop doorways. People were locked in their own thoughts, in their own worlds, as they plodded home under the dank blanket which they had created for themselves. So why should anyone care about a few who were murdered?

My microwaved dinner filled me with the warmth I should have had earlier, and after the hot shower and a large glass of brandy, I curled up into my favourite quilt, and fell asleep while watching the usual rubbish on the television. But when I finally went to bed, I couldn't sleep.

Every time I closed my eyes, all I could hear was Madeline's voice echoing in my brain. I wondered if she would ever get the lift she needed and reach her destination. Would others abandon her? And I imagined that, if I were to get in my car and drive back to Common Road, she would still be waiting, bedraggled, at the roadside, waiting for a lift which would never come—a perpetual hitchhiker. I felt like going back, but my bed held me there. And after several hours of self-cross-examination, recriminations, and dreams; I fell asleep exhausted.

It was eight o' clock when the radio-alarm went off, waking me from my tormented sleep. I could hear the faint buzz of words in my ear, but none were audible as I lay there trying to waken my senses as I stretched and yawned. Syllables, then words and finally sentences began to form. The male announcer spoke in an urgent whisper, compelling me to listen. I leaned closer to the radio, waiting for the bad news. Finally it was there, I could hear what was being said.

'The young woman who was found stabbed to death last night has been named as Madeline Belton; a twenty-two year old from Leighton Buzzard. Apparently she was seen hitchhiking along Common Road on her way to her grandparent's home. When she didn't arrive they reported her missing. Her body was found…'

The radio was silenced with a blow from my clenched fist; Thomas had heard enough and so had I. Was that the Madeline Thomas had picked up last night?

I thought how Madeline must have upset another driver who decided to put her out of her misery, or out of his misery. But Thomas had been stupid. Suppose someone had seen him pick the girl up. Suppose his car, my car, our car, had been seen on the CCTV? But, worst of all, I thought of how Thomas had missed a great opportunity, one that he would never have again. Someone else had seen to that, so I hoped the person would soon be caught and then Thomas would be able to see who had been brave enough to kill Madeline.

Thomas knew I was furious with him for not killing Madeline when he had the chance. When I reprimanded him on this, we began to argue as we usually did if things didn't go as planned. And eventually we stopped speaking to each other, which was our way of dealing with problems.

Now I was determined that Thomas would never be caught out again and I made him promise to be more patient and tolerant in the future. And I would make sure he would never miss an opportunity to kill again.

CHAPTER FIVE

Cadema's teams had almost completed the Actions of gathering information on Jane Gaunt's murder when the second body was discovered on Wimbledon Common. The victim, Sophie Millburn, had auburn hair and was found on the eighth September. The perpetrator used the same modus operandi as he had on Jane.

By the fourteenth of September, Cadema was on her way to a third murder scene. Due to the complexity of the investigations, she was happy that DCI Ryan had been given the role of deputy SIO.

Ryan, together with some of Cadema's officers were still continuing their investigations around Sophie Millburn's murder, while others were following up further Actions identified by the office manager.

Uniformed officers, DS Marriott and the CSI team were already at the scene when she stepped out of the car. Crossing under the taped outer cordon, Cadema dressed in forensic clothing then entered the police tent where Madeline Belton's body lay.

'So what do you think, Marriott?'

'Ma'am,' he gave a puzzled look as he flipped open a page of his pocket book. There had not been any time for him to think. He had just taken notes from Doctor Lilly, who managed to reach the scene the same time as the he had. He coughed. 'Looks as if she was killed here; there's no signs of sexual assault, but she's been stabbed many times.'

Cadema moved closer. 'Mm…I see. Any idea on the time of death?'

'It's not quite clear. But Lilly said it was just after midnight today, Ma'am when…'

'Doctor Lilly to you Sergeant, she hasn't studied for years to be disrespected. So don't forget next time.' Cadema moved out of the tent towards Julia, Marriott followed at a distance.

'Hello,' Cadema whispered. it's good to see you.'

'Likewise, but I'd prefer it to be over a glass of wine; not this,' Julia lowered her voice as she looked towards the Sergeant who was examining something on the ground.

'So would I,' Cadema agreed. 'This is the third one now and I'm no further forward. Let's hope this one will lead us to the perpetrator.'

'That may prove difficult,' Julia shook her head. 'Anyway, how's things going with you? I see the old wound is still playing you up.' She nodded to Cadema's side as the Sergeant was called away.

'That's the problem with doctors, there no hiding anything from you. But thanks anyway for your concern.' Cadema flushed but felt relieved no one was around to overhear them. Besides, when people mentioned her injury she had to cope with the flash-backs. 'Can you tell me what's happened here?' she asked as they walked back towards the tent, both with their eyes fixed on the ground.

'Yes, of course I can tell you. Would you like to hear?' she tormented. It was always the same when people didn't ask her direct questions. Cadema should have known better especially since they had been working together for the last five years. But their work always seemed to interfere with the maturity of their friendship. And when people were around, they acted professionally.

'I would like to hear everything from the beginning; please.'

'That's no problem,' Julia said. Then gave an account of what she believed had happened and her rationales for this.

'It started raining at ten thirty yesterday evening, so I know she died after that, as the ground was wet under the body. Therefore she was probably murdered between eleven-thirty and twelve-thirty. There are signs of rigor mortis. She was struck over the head with a fairly sharp object at the junction between the right parietal and occipital lobe of the skull. From the shape of the wound on the scalp, I think the murder weapon is an axe. But I cannot be totally sure at this stage. When I get her to the mortuary, I suspect she died from a cerebral haemorrhage. There is no sign of rape or sexual assault, and the stab wounds all appear to be superficial.'

'Thank you. But in your opinion...'

'I don't give opinions; I only ever give the facts. You should know better than that,' she gave a half smile.

'Okay, sorry. Anyway, do you think this could be the same person who murdered the other victims, or should I be looking for a different perpetrator this time?'

'You're the detective, it's up to you to find out. But when I've done the post mortem, I can tell you the similarities and differences between this murder and the others. Then, as usual, we will have to wait for the CSI's findings and the results of their samples.'

'Yes, let's hope there's no delay this time,' Cadema shrugged as Marriott greeted them with excitement as he pointed to some tyre tracks. Julia moved away.

'That's good Sergeant, so it appears we're looking for a four-by-four. I assume you've asked for moulds?'

'Yes Ma'am. It's all being dealt with.' He shrugged and walked off towards the tent. Cadema moved over to where Julia was changing out of her forensic clothing.

'Before you go Julia, can you tell me if the perpetrator was right or left handed?'

'The wound is on the right side of the skull, so if the killer struck her from behind, which no doubt he or she did, then the killer is probably right handed.'

'Was there any evidence of semen?'

'As far as I can tell there's no evidence. I'll be able to answer that after the PM especially as the other two were left with traces of ejaculate over them. Nevertheless I haven't found any on this body yet.'

'Thanks that means there are some similarities in these cases, but only some. All had auburn hair and were bludgeoned to death; the first two with a hammer, this one with an axe. None were raped but traces of semen were found on the other two, but none, so far, on this one. So it does look as if we might be dealing with different killers. But I'll keep my assumptions on hold at the moment, as the auburn hair is still ringing alarm bells in my mind.'

'I agree, so let's see what I can find.'

'That's great, I'll arrange for the body to be removed so we can get on with searching the area; we might come up with something else. Besides, Madeline Belton's mother will be coming to identify the body. Once that's over, I'll see you at the post-mortem.'

After saying goodbye to Julia, Cadema stood in the open for a while forming her action plan in her mind, then headed for her office.

***

Julia had never liked performing autopsies on murder victims. When she was younger she dreamed of being a professor; leading a team, instead of having to be a team player. The professorship had been lost last year to a young male colleague who had far too little experience but despite this, was promoted above her. She was so angry that she invoked the grievance procedure but decided not to peruse it in case of victimisation. Although the employment law was on her side, she couldn't face being ostracized by her peers, especially having worked with them for so long. Now the job refused to stimulate her intellect, but she was resigned to stay, at least for the time being.

She took an intake of breath when she entered the mortuary that evening to find everyone was gowned-up and waiting for her. After washing her hands and dressing quickly, she stood before her audience.

'Are we all ready?' she scanned the room to check that all six persons were correctly clad, in the statutory green protective clothing, including hat, gloves, masks and overshoes. 'And how come we have so many here, and who are they Brown?' she turned towards the mortuary attendant.

'Oh sorry Doctor Lilly, these are the three students I mentioned to you last week,' he pointed at them in turn as he said their names: 'Sarah, Philip and Benjamin,' they nodded a greeting. 'I thought it was okay to bring them in.'

'It is, I'm sorry, I forgot.'

'And this is Super…'

'I know Superintendent Sharma, and the DS Marriott, I've worked with them enough times,' Julia's voice sounded exasperated, she tutted.

'Yes of course, sorry…' he lowered his head while his body gave an involuntary twitch.

Brown had been with the department for the last three years and at first his work was exemplary. However, recently Julia noticed he was making mistakes and had become irritable when challenged. He fumbled a little, and occasionally had dropped sterile instruments on the floor. When she reprimanded him, he lowered his head and moved about the mortuary with an ape-like gait. Now he seemed less tolerant towards her, as if he were just waiting for the right moment to tell her what he thought, so she made sure she was never alone with him.

'I'll get on with the autopsy then. Has anyone got any questions before I start?' Seeing a few heads shake and after Cadema said she had none, Julia began to examine the victim's outer garments. She removed and scrutinised each item. When she noticed something out of the ordinary, her voice rose with excitement, as the students craned their necks. Seeing nothing to reward their curiosity, they returned to their usual posture. After she had finished with each garment, Brown placed them into forensic bags and labelled them. One student shuffled from one foot to another as if he were trying to curtail the urge to vomit. As the stench in the room and the heat intensified, the student's eyes began to roll. Brown responded by turning the air conditioning to a cooler setting.

The naked body, with numerous puncture wounds, was now displayed for all to see. Julia measured the length, width and depth of each wound as she dictated her findings into her mobile microphone. On several occasions, Brown adjusted her head band magnifier so she could examine even the smallest blemish on the skin. She then turned to her audience.

'I know some of you have never seen an autopsy before,' she looked at the students. 'Now I've completed my external examination of the body, I'm going to open the torso and then the head. If any of you are still feeling squeamish now's the time to leave.'

'I'd like to stay,' Sarah said with some hesitation in her voice. The other two students nodded in agreement.

'If you're sure, I'll continue. But if you have problems, just slip out as quietly as possible. I don't want any interruptions.' They all nodded this time.

Once the y-shaped incision had been made in the torso, all the internal organs were examined and weighed. After numerous swabs and samples had been taken, it was time for the head.

Peeling back the scalp Julia examined the gash with the same precision as she had with the body. After the skull was opened and the brain exposed, one student raced out of the door. Julia continued with the examination and the recordings she had made during the procedures.

With the autopsy concluded, Julia turned to the remaining students.

'I'm pleased that two of you are still here. If there are no questions you may leave.' In unison they said an almost silent 'think you' and left. Julia smiled.

'Typical of students, they long to be in here, but can't wait to get out. This was their first time, when they come back I won't be able to keep them quiet.'

'It's similar in the police service with young officers,' Cadema mused. Then, thanking Julia, she said she looked forward to the official report and particularly the results from forensics.

Later that evening, Julia settled down in her lounge to read her draft report on the autopsy. Her findings were as she expected. She read a synopsis of her report out loud to make sure it sounded clear and succinct.

The body is that of a female, aged twenty-two years of age with auburn hair matted with blood. She was one-hundred and sixty-three cms tall. Blood group A1 RH positive. Skin is clear except for one mole two mms in diameter and situated four cms below the right eye.

There is a ten cm tattoo of a leopard over the right scapular.

There is a ten cm long by 1.5mm wide, longitudinal cuneiform wound running in a right medio-lateral line from the parietal to the occipital portions of the scalp, underlying tissue and bone, shattering the line of the sagittal suture and severing the sagittal sinus. The force of the blow penetrated through cerebral hemisphere resulting in a massive cerebral trauma and haemorrhage - with death almost instantaneous.

There are no defence wounds, and no bruising anywhere else on the body. There are eight, 1.5 cm stab wounds, each one measuring 2.5 mm in depth. Six of these are on the right intercostal margins, the other two are just above the right axilla, but are too superficial to have caused death, and were probably inflicted post mortem.

The Fourchette, labia and hymen are intact, no sexual injury and no rape occurred in any orifice. Body temperature 18 degrees centigrade.

Clothing, body fluids and tissue samples have been sent to pathology.

Other samples of tissue and a dried white substance, found on the back of the jeans, have been sent for DNA analysis.

Signed: Doctor Julia Lilly. And dated.

Julia sat back in her armchair, took a sip of Merlot and sighed. *That's it,* she thought, *but Cadema's work has only just begun.*

CHAPTER SIX

Travelling on the tube towards town, I happened to look up over my newspaper, and there she was. The woman fitted the image of Margaret perfectly, except she was a little younger. But there was the same dimple on her cheek, and the same girlish freckles. I guessed she was about twenty-six years old. She wore a pale green suit which contrasted well with the richness of her auburn hair. That was it; I had to follow her.

There were at least ten people separating us as she alighted from the carriage. Running along the platform, and colliding with fellow commuters, I could see her hair swaying across the back of the jacket in tune with her step. I wanted to get closer, but managed to restrain myself. Once outside, I hoped the area would be less populated, then I would be unlikely to lose her.

As the sun emerged from the single cloud, I knew it was going to be another hot September day; the global warming lobby had got it right yet again. The dry weather enhanced the smells of London. Tar, dust and smoke belched from cars, busses, and taxies, hijacking the oxygen particles and burning millions of throats as it settled on virgin lungs. As eyes stung and noses ran, I imagined these organs were trying to wash away the pollution that had accumulated over many decadent centuries. And of course, there was the lead in the air; it was believed this had caused the riots some years ago. I wondered if there would ever be peace in the city, peace from the traffic, peace from the pollution and above all, peace from its millions of inhabitants.

My world stopped. Without warning the woman in the pale green suit vanished into an office block in Baker Street. I rushed along the pavement, my eyes firmly fixed on the door she had entered. Having dodged several people, and narrowly missed being knocked over by a car; the driver gesticulating some obscenity at me as I passed. Finally reaching the door of the building, I opened it and stepped inside.

The grey dismal lobby was empty. All I could see was the security camera and an intercom device on the far wall. Walking over to the intercom, I made a note of the names on the labels, and left the building. I was frustrated and angry with the result, but at least I knew where I could find her again.

Walking around, I wondered why she had gone to the building in the first place. I speculated for some time, then remembered the furtive way she looked around just before she entered the building. As if she were a private detective or something. Then it struck me, it was quite obvious when I thought about it. She was having an affair. She was there to meet her lover. Yes of course, that was it. Dressing in a pale green suit would make her look more like a business woman, when indeed she was cheating on someone, either her husband, or someone else's husband.

Whatever the reason, I knew she was a good victim. The thought of extinguishing her life made my whole body tingle. I needed to find out where she lived. She could live in the area, but on the other hand she could have travelled into London from any one of the suburbs. These thoughts troubled my mind. *What should I do if she didn't come out soon? She could be in the building for the whole day, what was I to do then?* As the tension of my thoughts built up, I felt my head might explode. So mindful of London's CCTVs, I visited the nearest toilet and donned my second disguise. Then spent the rest of the day mingling in the soup of the metropolis, pretending to sightsee.

Many times during that day I felt the urge to follow other women with auburn hair, but I couldn't get the woman in the pale green suit out of my mind. So, by a quarter-past three I was back in Baker Street.

My suspicions were correct. She appeared from the lobby into the street just after four-o'clock. She looked tired. Her hair untidy, and her suit crumpled. Not what I would have expected from a business woman. Still, I supposed people just don't have the same standards as I have, so I should make allowances.

I watched as she walked swiftly along the pavement, brushing her hair from her face as she disappeared down the steps into the underground. Quickening my pace, and reducing the gap between us, I almost knocked over an old man. Then, brushing aside others who dared to dawdle in front of me, I moved like a sidewinder, dodging everyone in my path. But she made greater progress than I did. As if sensing her urgency, the sea of bodies parted and let her through with impunity, while they barred my path with contempt.

'For Christ sake hurry up will you,' I snarled under my breath at the man in front of me as he fumbled in his pockets. 'Can't you see I am in a hurry; stupid man?' I knocked the man's arm, and sent his Oyster card to the ground as I pushed past and sprinted down the passage way. In my haste I nearly caught up with her. I had to hold back. Not too far though, as I wanted her closer to me. So close that I could almost reach out and touch her. I resisted, hoping to have the opportunity sometime soon. Until then I was another faceless commuter. The woman swiped her pass at the barrier.

Seconds later I followed with mine, and then travelled down the escalator towards the platforms for the Metropolitan line, several steps behind her.

The crowd on the platform made it difficult for me to see her without drawing attention to myself. As I eased my shoulders through ever decreasing gaps in the human line, I thought I might lose her. But being no stranger to the underground, I managed to keep up; then stopped a foot away from her. The urge to kill her there and then was overpowering. Just a little push from the back of the crowd, just a little push; that was all it would take to send her into the track of the speeding train. *But not now*, I reasoned, *it was too easy*. Besides she had to go the same way as the others, there was no alternative. I had to follow my plans in every detail.

After what felt like an hour as opposed to the two minutes displayed on the gantry, the train arrived. It was so packed with people that I wondered if I, or anyone else for that matter, would ever get onto it. The doors screeched open. A recorded message warned everyone to 'mind the gap.' Sweating bodies of passengers fell out determined to reach the exit, as if they were being chased by the same fire ball which had engulfed people in the King Cross fire some decades before.

The woman seemed anxious as people pushed her from the back, edging her forward, while others pushed from the sides, until I completely lost sight of her. Then I spotted her again as her pale green suit oozed into a carriage, followed by people clutching their Nikon cameras, and by a couple of tailored pin-striped suits. As the guard called to everyone to move further inside the carriages, and mind the doors, I managed to slip in, just as they closed.

Steaming bodies smelling of garlic, curry and cheap perfume, belched out breath of overindulgent lunches. Together with the jolting and swaying of the carriage, I felt sick, but kept my eyes fixed on my target despite the oppressive atmosphere and the lack of cool air.

Tourists in their ragged jeans, t-shirts and trainers clung with white fingers to the stainless steel poles. Children, dressed like miniature adults, clutched the hands of their impatient mothers. And, together with the pin-stripes, we swayed to and fro with the canter of the train as it sped through tunnels like a ferocious Moby Dick, full of humans it was unable to digest. It would spit them out at the next station, only to take on more indigestibles.

Three people alighted at Great Portland Street; six oozed in. Squashed more than before, it was a relief when many forced their way out at Euston Square. At the third stop, Kings Cross and St. Pancras, the woman in the pale green suit pushed through the passengers and alighted. I squeezed out just as the doors slammed shut behind me. She was heading for the Victoria Line. Perhaps she would get off at Euston and on to the main line station? I didn't know. As I walked along the platform people gave me disparaging looks, as if they could see the invisible reins I had attached to the woman in the pale green suit.

The train was much less crowded than the previous one. The woman walked towards a couple of empty seats as two young boys, dressed in faded jeans, slid into them. As they did so, a military looking man gave the boys a stern look and offered the woman his seat. She gave a flicker of a smile and a nod of a thank you in appreciation as she sat down and closed her eyes. Shutting off the world around her, she only opened them as the monotonous taped voice announced 'the next stop will be Euston ...'

Just as predicted, I thought, as she left the train and took the escalator to the main line station. I, in pursuit a little distance away.

The concourse was the usual mêlée of people, the smell of coffee mingling with the odour of unwashed bodies. Half-clad people dragged their belongings in over-indulgent suitcases, while others wrestled with bored children who seemed to be looking for an escape route. The noise from a police siren, and screams of young children, mingled with the voice on the loud speaker telling passengers where they could smoke, and not to leave luggage unattended, all mixed in an overwhelming cacophony that sent my senses reeling.

Neck craned, and with her high heels lifting off the ground, she studied the departure board. Then the voice on the loud speaker announced:

'The train now standing on platform four is the 17.06 bound for Glasgow, calling at...'

Before the announcer had time to finish, the woman weaved her way through the crowds of people as if her life depended on getting to platform before anyone else could. Clutching her briefcase, and nearly tramping down a small child, she turned and mouthed, 'sorry' to the mother, then scampered on.

My mind raced, *was she travelling all the way to Glasgow, or was she going somewhere in between?* But there were so many places in between that I could hardly think. She could get off anywhere, and I needed to know where, but had no way of finding out. I could hardly go up to her and ask. And there wouldn't be time for me to buy a ticket at the kiosk. I could have paid on the train, but where to? I didn't want to buy one for the whole journey. That would be wasteful, especially if she were only going as far as Milton Keynes or Birmingham, which were miles away from Glasgow.

Why did everything have to be so complicated? I thought. *I should have picked someone local then it would have been easy. So why did I have to choose her?* I cursed myself. Then my thoughts mellowed. The woman in the pale green suit had the right features and the auburn hair. I had to follow her; I had no choice especially as the voices kept nagging at me.

It was then I remembered that she only had a briefcase with her, so she couldn't be going too far. Perhaps there was still the opportunity... At that moment my heart shrivelled. My blood stagnated in my veins and the world became an inert noiseless vacuum, as I saw the man. He was about six feet tall, with blond and slightly greying hair, and was heading towards her waving his hand. The woman reciprocated with the same gesture. I was devastated.

He, at least ten years her senior, dragged a suitcase big enough to serve two people for a long weekend. It was all over. My heart beat so fast it felt as if it were going to burst out of my chest. I felt cold, clammy, bitter, angry and frustrated. I had been so close, so very close. Close enough that I could almost taste her.

Seeing her disappear into the train with him reminded me of why I was there in the first place. It brought back all the memories of something that might have been; a love from the past, lost to the future. The woman had been whisked away. I felt cheated and dejected, but my anger only helped to fuel my determination to go on. I may have lost my intended victim this time, but there were others. And just because the woman in the pale green suit had escaped from me this time, she wouldn't do so again. No, my urge to kill was stronger than it had ever been.

As I walked slowly out of the station I hailed a cab to take me back to where I had left my car. Telling the cab driver where I wanted to go, I gave specific instructions on the location as I didn't trust taxi drivers, or anyone else for that matter. People were always there to outsmart me, so I had to show them I was in control.

CHAPTER SEVEN

The reports Julia had given Cadema on the three murders were just as she expected, thorough and succinct. Cadema concluded that the perpetrator of the first two murders, Jane Gaunt on the thirty-first of August, and Sophie Millburn on the eighth of September, had used the same modus operandi. They had both been bludgeoned to death with a hammer, stabbed, and ejaculate had been found on their bodies. Although the one on Jane was too degraded for DNA analysis. In contrast, the perpetrator of Madeline Belton's murder, on the fourteenth of September, was different. She had been hit over the head with an axe and no ejaculate was found.

Having noted these discrepancies, she asked Julia to come to her office to clarify the findings. Tea was ready when she arrived.

'Have I got this straight? Are you telling me you didn't find any other tangible evidence on the first two bodies except the ejaculate?' she asked Julia as they simultaneously took a sip of tea.

'Yes, that's all. You're right of course; it's odd that the murderer should go to the trouble of keeping the area spotless, and then leave that,' Julia sounded concerned as she shrugged her shoulders. 'But those are the facts.'

'Why do you think he did such a thing? Do you suppose he thought he could nonchalantly wipe the semen off, and we wouldn't be able to identify him from the DNA he's undoubtedly left us? I can't believe he's that naive, or stupid, can you?' Cadema examined Julia's face for signs of doubt, but there were none.

'It is not up to me to speculate,' she shuffled in the chair. 'I am not the detective. But if you want my opinion, the forensic evidence speaks for itself. He planned the murders well, but probably lost control and worked himself up into a sexual frenzy, then had to relieve himself,' she flushed and brushed a strand of blond hair from her face.

'Yes, that could be one possibility. But I need to know what his motives were. Was it murder for its own sake, or for control, or is there a sexual one? Or perhaps a combination of all three?' she shook her head while studying the photographs of the last crime scene again.

'I am sorry I can't help you there. As I said, you and your team need to find that one out. You're not questioning my methods are you?' Julia frowned—her voice slightly angry.

'You know I wouldn't do that; although it all seems very unusual to me. If there's no other physical evidence, I'll just have to accept it. Especially with the first two murders.' Cadema grimaced, then drained her cup.

'Well, must go now, good luck; thanks for the tea. You know I'm happy to help with anything you need.' Julia pattered Cadema's arm in a comforting gesture, said goodbye, and left.

***

It was the thirtieth of September when Cadema's telephone rang informing her of another murder. The body of a young woman had been found in Richmond Park by someone jogging. Doctor Lilly had been sent for and had just arrived.

Calling for Ryan and Marriott to follow her, Cadema headed out of the building to her awaiting car. Twenty minutes later they were at the scene where the usual assemblage of personnel were carrying out their professional roles.

With a nod of the head as a greeting, Julia began to give her report.

'From my preliminary examination, this looks similar to the first two murders,' Julia sighed and she shook her head as they walked to where the body was. Ryan and Marriott walked away examining the terrain.

'I'll take a look,' Cadema's voice quivered as she slipped on the protective clothing over her suit and then peered inside the police tent. 'I expect you'll want the body removed as soon as possible?'

'Yes, I don't want any delays, or contamination. If I can get samples off for DNA analysis quickly, then you'll have a much better chance of finding the perpetrator.' Julia nodded at the photographer as he moved around in his quest for various viewpoints.

'At least if you can give me a short brief of what you've found, that will do for the time being. We can catch up later on the finer details.'

'The time of death was probably about eleven thirty last night. As you can see there's the auburn hair. The scalp wound, indicates the use of a hammer. The stab wounds are superficial. And there's, what appears to be ejaculate around the pubic area. The hallmarks of the first two murders.'

'Yes, I see. I'll organise for the body to be removed.' Cadema beckoned to Marriott.

'Thanks, I must get off. I've got an important meeting soon so can't delay. No doubt I'll see you at the PM.' Julia rushed to her car and drove off.

Once the scene had been secured, and the body removed, Cadema left CSI to complete their work as she headed back to the station with Ryan and Marriott.

By late afternoon the body had been identified by her parents as Frances Cole. Consoled by Johns they eventually went home with a PC to piece together their daughter's last movements.

***

Cadema had all the reports she needed, so précising these in her mind, she headed for the briefing room with Kasson, the office manager. Her team looked attentive as she outlined the cases.

'So there you have it. We now have four murders. Three, we believe, were committed by the same perpetrator: Jane Gaunt and Sophie Millburn on Wimbledon Common, and the latest one, Frances Cole in Richmond Park. The fourth, Madeline Belton found near Putney Heath, we now believe is by a different killer.

'Doctor Lilly says the first three sustained fractures to the skull, probably by a blow with a hammer. They were then stabbed superficially, and as you know the ejaculates we found were sent for DNA analysis. All four murders were committed during a weekend and around the same time of the night. And I'm not surprised that the Press are taking great delight in calling them "The Common Murders",' Cadema explained as the virtual reality screen buzzed into action.

'Now let's see,' she looked at the screen waiting for the first photograph to emerge. Her team of officers sat in a semi-circle on chairs.

'It is estimated that the latest victim…' Cadema cleared her throat.

'Frances Cole,' Evans smirked, stretched out his legs, folded his arms and looked around the room at his colleagues.

'Thank you, Evans,' Cadema noticed his arrogant attitude. But she had to admit that, on the surface, he seemed smarter than the average DI. And it was no secret that he believed they couldn't manage any investigation without his expertise. Perhaps this would be true in the old days. Now he could never manage without HOLMES-two and the Major Investigation Team. No, it was far too complex, and Evans must know this. Anyway, she wouldn't endorse his attitude. He may be intimidating to some, but she realised that when a curl of his hair slid across his forehead, it was a danger sign to any self-respecting woman.

Nevertheless, she believed he respected her as his senior officer, so decided to put up with his idiosyncrasies, at least for the time being. Especially since he had done what she asked after the last murder on Wimbledon Common. He managed to examine the whole Common in the five-day timeframe she had given him. Although his team didn't find anything, his succinct and thorough report was on her desk on day six as instructed.

Cadema took a deep breath.

'It's good to see you're all looking smart and taking notes, now let's get on with things.' Cadema's voice was deliberately patronising. 'Frances Cole was last seen at about twenty-two fifteen hours heading for the park. She passed the CCTV, but it was turned off at the time, for maintenance I understand. Make a note of that,' she gestured to Evans.

'Yes Ma'am. By the way, I've found out that the CCTV camera was not working when Jane Gaunt was murdered. So there's definitely a connection with these two murders.'

'I remember, so we need to find out whether they were off when the other murders took place. When were they turned off, and who may have known they were not working? If the killer knew they were out of action it would have been an ideal time for him to strike.'

'Yes, but he could be the person who turned them off, that is if he worked for the company who maintained them,' Evans's chest expanded as he spoke.

'That's a good point. Everyone make a note of that.' Cadema scanned the other officers. 'So there could be a connection. We need to know, not when, but who knew about the CCTVs and why they were not working. We also need to find out who has the maintenance contract and how they are maintained.' Cadema turned to face DI Johns. 'You can deal with these questions. If you need any help then ask Evans.'

'Yes Ma'am.

'Now you have all the facts as they stand at the moment. Here are the Actions and the questions I need the answers to,' she handed out note paper containing many more questions than had been raised in the session. 'I want to be the first to know when you find the answers. Any problems, ask Evans.'

There were nods of heads, and scraping of chairs on the solid floor as the officers stood up and began to leave the room.

***

Back in her office Cadema gathered all the evidence together again. Then, as always, she focused her mind as if she were hovering above the crime scenes. *Jim's helicopter approach*, she reasoned. Now, as she held all the threads, even the small ones, she could see the whole picture. She began to rearrange the evidence under specific headings. The auburn hair. The victims. The ejaculate. The superficial stabbings. The locations. The time of day. The days of the week. The weather. The CCTVs. The probable profile of the killer. This, she realised, would form the basis of her ten-point action plan. It would help her to get the job done effectively and efficiently: *the way Jim always did*. Nothing would be overlooked.

She reflected on how she had done this at the last briefing. But she had not collected enough data, especially about the CCTVs. Nevertheless, she managed to pick up the threads and weave them into the Actions for her team. *This time was different*, she had given each officer the ownership of a small thread to work on. She believed this would enhance their self-esteem, encourage productivity, and ultimately prevent more murders. And she knew who she could trust, who would need extra support, and who she needed to keep on tight reigns.

With her support, her officers would meet the tight deadlines she had set. Some being even tighter than necessary; not just to keep them working hard, but because she needed results. Besides, no member of her team had ever complained about the deadlines before, and believed they enjoyed the challenge.

Evans was the one she had to watch. While he seemed to do a good job, she found many errors with his paperwork. He would appear efficient but had recently upset some of the lower ranked officers by undermining their abilities to do the job. While they were pedantic about sticking to the rules, he ignored the rules whenever he could. And on one occasion she had to reprimand him about this. Lately she noticed he had begun to change, probably because of the forthcoming promotion board. Not that he was ready for promotion. But now was not the time to speculate, especially during complex murder enquiries.

CHAPTER EIGHT

Julia was sitting in her office at home when her telephone rang.

'Evening Lilly,' a strong masculine voice, with a slight chuckle said, as she answered it.

'Bagley, is that you?' she replied 'I was just thinking about you. You seem excited, so am I right in thinking you've found something?'

'Yes Lilly, you're right as usual. But this time I have, and yet again I haven't,' he chuckled.

'Come on, let's have it. Either you have or you have not.' she emphasised each word light-heartedly.

'Well Lilly, you know the sample you sent me from the back of Madeline Belton jeans. Well, it was dried semen after all. So I did the usual PCR and managed to obtain enough DNA to do a profile. But this is the crunch; it's not same profile as the one from the other murder victims. So there are definitely two different killers.'

'Great Bagley. Just what we suspected. Superintendent Sharma will be very happy with that news. I'll tell her myself.' She was just about to turn the telephone off when she heard Bagley's voice again.

'Hi, you're still there?'

'Yes, sorry Bagley, I'd thought you'd hung up.'

'No. I expected you to ask me who's DNA we've got. I can't answer that at the moment as its being checked against the national database. I should find out soon, as long as the person is on it, that is. I'll let you know when I have any news.'

'Thanks Bagley. By the way, how is the baby?'

'Just great, thank you for the advice, it worked perfectly.'

'You're welcome, any time. Bye.' Julia waited for the phone to click, then gave a little chuckle as she thought how sanctimonious professionals were in calling their closest colleagues by their last names. But she felt turned out to be just wind.

The DNA profile was a different matter, so instead of sending the information to Cadema, she decided to phone her. In this way she would be able to find out how the investigation was going. She could also offer her some help if she needed it, even though it was not in her job description.

***

'Hi Cadema, I'm ringing to let you know how things are going,' she said dropping the formalities when no one was around.

'It's good to hear from you. I'm afraid everything's so slow at present. Hopefully you've got some news for me?'

'Just a little, but I'd rather not discuss it over the phone. Can we meet and I'll fill you in on things? Anyway I expect you're a bit lost now your mother's gone back to India for her holiday.' Julia sounded concerned. 'And I'd like to talk about a job I've seen in one of my journals.'

'Great. Come over for tea or something stronger when you're ready.' She hesitated as she heard a faint sigh.

'I didn't think you drank?' Julia said.

'Not officially, but sometimes… On second thoughts, it would be better if I came to see you. Then you can have a drink and I can drive home safely,' Cadema said. Julia offered a hum…, but she did not give her time to respond further. 'Okay, it's settled then. I'll see you soon.' With the press of the off-button on her phone, Cadema donned her coat and drove the half-hour to Julia's address.

The house was situated in a formation of identical Victorian terraces in a quiet tree-lined residential area. Most of the two-story buildings in the street had hanging baskets. The wrought iron fencing and gates looked as if they were all newly painted with the same dark-brown paint. *Looks as if they were all done by the same decorator with a paint job-lot.* She smiled to herself.

Julia was standing on the pavement with her arms folded watching Cadema manoeuvre her car into the one available space, six-houses away. Straightening it in line with the pavement, and ignoring the parking sensors, she managed to squeeze in without bumping into the car behind her. Stepping out she just missed falling over a cat as it scudded in front of her. A little out of breath, she reached Julia who greeted her with a smile.

'Sorry I took longer than expected.'

'That's not a problem, come on in out of this awful wind,' Julia sounded less enthusiastic than her friend. Silently they entered the living room.

'Tea or coffee?'

'Oh tea please, not too strong though, otherwise it will keep me awake, and I've been having enough trouble getting to sleep as is it these days, what with mother away and since Harry…' Cadema stifled a tear. Julia nodded as if she understood, then, after taking her coat, left the room.

Cadema walked into the space created by the bay-window. From here she looked out onto the whole street. A curtain moved in the opposite house just as the wind took a branch off a tree and smashed into the road. A plethora of brown, green and orange leaves responded, swirling around the branch while the cat she had seen earlier sniffed at the rubble.

She turned from the scene as the door behind her swung open and Julia stepped in carrying a tray.

'Here, let me help you,' she said as Julia put down the tray.

'It's okay, I can manage,' she poured the tea into a white-china mug. 'You don't mind if I have a gin and tonic, do you?'

Cadema offered a shrug.

'It's your house. Anyway, I thought that was the point of me coming here, to give you a chance to have something stronger than tea.' She took the mug of tea with a smile and sat down on the green leather settee facing Julia.

'I didn't want to say too much when you arrived, but you don't seem your usual self.' Julia's voice sounded concerned.

'I'm okay really. It's just now and again,' she took a tissue out of her pocket.

'Oh I'm sorry, I didn't mean to…'

'No, that's all right, really. I should've got over Harry's death by now. But you know how it is. We see lots of tragedies in our business, but it only really hits you when it's so close to home. It's been four years today, and I still expect him to come home. And then there was Jim, I don't think I can cope with any more tragedies in my life.' She dabbed her eyes with a tissue. 'Sorry…'

'Don't be. I didn't realise…' Julia said compassionately.

Cadema gave a grimace of a smile and tried to control her emotions. After all Julia hated having to console anyone; it was beyond her nature to do such a thing.

'I'm sorry, but now and again it all comes back.' Her words tapered off, thinking of the car accident and then the miscarriage. But it was her mother's words which, less occasionally now than before, reverberated in her mind. "No one will want you now, especially since you're working in the police service. No self-respecting man will put up with that." Cadema knew what she meant, but to argue with her mother was certain suicide. One thing she was certain of though, even if her mother never mentioned it, was that she would have gone down a notch or two on the marriage eligibility scale, according to her criteria. Despite this, her mother still wanted her to give up her job and go to India. Cadema refused as usual, causing the rift between them. She was lost in her own thoughts for a while until she eventually heard Julia speak.

'That's okay, talk to me if you want to,' Julia coughed and sounded concerned.

'No, that's all right, I'm fine now thank you,' she shuffled in her seat feeling guilty at being upset.

'Good.' Julia sat upright in her chair and took a sip of her gin and tonic. 'Well, as I said, I have some news for you. You remember the jeans Madeline Belton was wearing?' Cadema nodded in response. 'I noticed a minute particle of something on them, so I sent it for testing. It turned out to be semen. Bagley examined it for me and managed to extract some DNA.'

'That's wonderful, so does it match the DNA from the other murders?' she bolted upright in the chair, then leaned forward in eager anticipation.

'No it doesn't, it means we're right about there being two killers. By the way have you managed to trace the owner of the DNA profile from the other murders?'

'We haven't unfortunately, the perpetrator doesn't appear to be on the database.'

'That's a pity, these things do drag on. Hopefully you'll get the results one way or another.'

'Yes, but if we'd found the first murder victim earlier, we might have had another sample,' Cadema said as she sat back in her chair again.

'Don't worry over that. The latest one from Frances Cole, is fresh enough. Bagley will do his best there. And he's still working with PCR on the first one. So I haven't given up hope on that just yet even though the sample is degraded.' Julia sounded excited, but Cadema did not miss the scepticism in her voice.

'PCR, I mentioned this to my team, but I'm still not entirely sure what it actually means. Something about fragments of DNA, to create more DNA so it can be analysed?' Cadema frowned as she tried to remember a lecture she had been to where she hadn't really understood the concept.

'That's the idea. Polymerase Chain Reaction. Yes, it can amplify the DNA if it's there and not too degraded,' Julia sounded as if she were giving lecture.

'Even if there isn't a profile for the first murder, the MO is the same as the other two. So let's hope we can trace them and make an arrest,' Cadema surreptitiously fished for more information.

Julia didn't take the bait. Instead she responded by talking about her work.

This was the trait with many of her colleagues whose sole conversations were about work; even during social events. Work was all they really had in common, so colleagues never became friends. And if, by chance, they did, the friendship usually petered out after a couple of months.

At this point, Cadema realised that Julia needed to escape the mundane ritual of her daily life; as she also needed to do. Then, hopefully, they would form a friendship that would fill the void in both their lives and last well into the future.

'By the way, what about the new job you mentioned? Where is it based?'

Julia blushed, wishing she had not mentioned it.

'It's a bit awkward really. I've not told you this, but I've been looking for some time now.'

'I'm not surprised as I noticed you seemed a bit frustrated with the work at times.'

'That's the detective speaking.' Julia smiled. 'But seriously, I did apply for a job some time ago, but some spotty young thing got it.' Cadema noticed some bitterness in her voice, so did not pursue it. 'I know the timing isn't right, with all these murders, but this one looks promising. Here read the advert if you want to.' She handed the cut-out to Cadema.

'A professorship, ay?' she read on. 'Well looking at this, you fit the bill perfectly. But do you really want to move away from here. What with all the work you've done, won't you miss your colleagues?'

'Obviously I've thought of that. But I've done the usual pros and cons, and I think I fill the specification.' She handed over the job application documents she had received from her perspective employer.

'You've certainly done your homework. And if you're so determined, I wish you all the luck in the world. But I'll miss you, so will my team.' Cadema fingered through the papers.

'Thank you, but sometime in one's life you have to make decisions. I've been determined to find a position like that for over a year now. So as you can appreciate, I cannot let it go without trying my best to get it.'

'Yes I agree, as I said, I hope it goes well.'

When they finally said goodbye, Cadema hoped, if Julia got the job, they would not lose touch. After all Julia had been at her bedside when she had been shot and was recovering in hospital. Recently they had talked about Julia's cancer scare which turned out to be a false alarm. Surely this was what friendship was all about?

Now there was the DNA to consider. Opening the door to her car, she stood for a moment and waved at Julia, hoping that she would not apply for the job, but knowing that she probably would.

CHAPTER NINE

Bagley was as excited as a boy with a new toy at Christmas as he picked up the phone and dialled Doctor Lilly's number.

Please let her be in, please, he danced as he spoke to himself, his blood rushing through his body in tune with the adrenaline surge. *Come on, come on. Pick up.* He heard a faint click and then a voice saying please leave a message.

'Hi Lilly, Bagley here. Just to let you know that the database has come up with a match for the DNA from Madeline Belton's jeans. It belongs to a Bernard Franklin; Superintendent Sharma has gone to arrest him. Speak to you latter.' He replaced the phone on its station. *Answer phones, I wished they'd never been invented.* He had thought about using the mobile phone number that Doctor Lilly had given him, but he liked those even less, so the answer phone was the better of the two evils.

He turned to walk out of the office as his phone rang.

'Bagley here.'

'It's Doctor Lilly.' She paused, as if waiting for an answer phone to start.

'I'm here. Did you get my message Lilly?'

'Yes, thanks Bagley.'

'I could take that as being patronising, if I didn't know you better.' He laughed and heard a faint tutting sound.

'That's great news. Thank goodness something's happening, even though it's not the serial killer, at least it may lead to the closure of one chapter.'

'Yes, but I hope everything goes according to the rules, we don't want to lose this one just because of red tape.'

'You're right Bagley, but Cadema knows what she's doing, so I'm sure it will all be okay. Anyway thanks for everything. It's good to know about the progress you've made to this case. Well done.'

Bagley smiled to himself as he replaced the receiver and headed for the laboratory.

***

It was four in the afternoon on the twenty-sixth September when Cadema arrived with Evans and a PC, at Bernard Franklin's semi-detached house. Its peeling painted door and overgrown garden matched most of the other houses in Governor Court.

As soon as the bell rang Bernard opened the door as if he were expecting them. His heavy frame oscillated backwards and forwards when he said hello, giving the impression that his legs wouldn't hold him if he went further than twenty degrees from the vertical. His nearly bald head and the ruddy appearance of the capillaries marked his otherwise unblemished face. She thought he looked older than fifty, and either a heavy drinker, or he had high blood pressure. But rather than reply to his name, Bernard just listened as he examined the two police identity badges that she and Evans displayed in front of him. With the nod of his head, he peered past the doorframe and glanced up and down the street with fear in his eyes; then beckoned them into his house.

'Are you Bernard Franklin?' Cadema asked again; wanting a verbal assertion that he was, and wondered why police always had to state the obvious. As he did not answer, she decided he was considering the question in greater depth than necessary. She waited. Evans fidgeted.

'Yes...,' he replied as if he were unsure. 'So what's this all about officers?' He straightened; his voice polite and assertive.

'Can we go into the living area Sir? Then I will explain everything to you,' she gestured for him to lead the way.

'Okay, but I haven't done anything. I suppose something happened in the area. And even though I've a spent record, you lot always come round when there's trouble. But you've got the wrong one; I haven't done anything not since coming out of prison.'

'We will see about that, Sir,' she sounded condescending. Evans raised his eyebrows.

Walking into Bernard's sitting room, they stood in the turmoil and stench of his unkempt and sparsely furnished abode. Fearing that, if they were to sit, as requested, on the torn brown sofa, their clothing would be contaminated by something that smelled like rotting cheese, and by the probable infestation of lice and other fauna that could not be seen, both officers remained standing in the middle of the room facing Bernard.

'What were you doing on the thirteenth and fourteenth of September last between eleven PM and one o'clock in the morning?' Cadema asked; holding back the nausea she felt.

'I know my rights; I don't have to answer your questions. Anyway, how the hell should I know? Judging by the time I was probably in bed. I don't keep a diary you know. One day's the same as the next to me,' Bernard replied in an anxious tone while scratching his head.

'Okay, if you do not answer my question, we will arrest you and then we can question you at the station, Mr. Franklin.' Cadema said, her voice sounding frustrated at the lack of his cooperation.

'Now let me see,' he scratched his head again and looked up at the ceiling, as if the answer were written there. 'I did go out that evening, but I don't have any witnesses. I just went out for a drive, nothing else.'

'I think you are talking crap,' Evans butted in. 'You know very well where you were, you've got guilt written all over your face. That's why you looked at the ceiling. Now, come on and tell us where you really were.'

'No, I've just told you. That's my final answer. I don't know why you're picking on me. What have people been saying about me? It's all a pack of lies whatever you've heard.'

'Well Sir, we have come to arrest you.'

'Arrest me? For what? I've told you, I haven't done anything.'

'Mr. Bernard Franklin, I am arresting you for the murder of Madeline Belton. You do not have to say anything. But it may harm your defence if you do not mention when questioned something which you later rely on in court. Anything you do say may be given in evidence. Do you understand the caution?' Evans looked into Bernard's dark eyes and shuddered as if he had seen the very soul of hell looking back at him.

'Of course I f...ing understand. But why are you all picking on me?' he shouted, his face red as if every capillary under his skin would surely burst.

'We haven't picked on you, as you put it. We have linked you to Madeline Belton, the girl who was murdered nearly three weeks ago. Did you know the girl?'

'No, I've never heard of her.'

'Come on, don't lie to me. You must have heard her name. It's been in the newspapers, and on all the major news programmes since then. And I can see you have a TV,' Evans smirked.

'I don't buy papers,' he snatched. 'Nor do I watch the bloody TV, so I wouldn't know that, would I?'

'Come on, you don't expect me to believe that, do you? So let's go.' He moved towards Bernard as the uniformed PC clipped on the handcuffs and led him out of the front door towards the waiting police car, followed by Cadema and Evans. They had hardly reached the car when a mob of some ten people appeared and blocked their way.

'We knew you were shit when you first came here,' a woman in a green and yellow striped jumper, showing her punctured navel, shouted.

'Yer, yer,' the rest of the crowed jeered as they punched at the air with their clenched fists.

'Thank God you've got him. He needs putting away forever, he does,' the woman in the green and yellow stripes continued. The crowd edged forward.

'Now everyone, please keep back, so we can put this man in the car. Then I would like you all to disperse without any trouble. The law will deal with this,' Cadema said in her official but calming voice. Her heart was pounding, she tried to swallow but her mouth was far too dry. *Is there a sniper*, she thought?

'Yes, the superintendent is right. We will deal with this.' Evans moved across in front of Cadema as he shouted and waved his arms for them to disperse, as if herding cows. The crowd continued to jeer but with less enthusiasm.

Evans had seen this type of behaviour before on similar estates. He believed that it would not take long before the situation escalated, especially where unemployment was as rife as the crimes in the area. The drug taking, and people's imagination fuelled their animosity against any man on his own. The gossip would escalate until they metamorphosed him into a monster. The residents would believe they understood what was going on. Then they would gather, each fuelling the others' rage, until some poor innocent citizen was ridiculed, attacked or even murdered. If you kept your head low in a place like this, it was sure to be metaphorically decapitated.

Now everyone was on edge about the murders and when they saw Bernard as a loner, they had put two and two together, and decided he was the serial killer.

Evens continued his negotiations with the crowd until they heard the police sirens in the distance.

'Bloody f...ing hell, their bringing in the cavalry,' the woman in the green and yellow stripes shouted. The crowd began to disperse. She followed.

Evans, Cadema and the PC, shielding Bernard, continued their walk towards the car. Evans glanced back twice but after a couple of minutes the street was clear, as if nothing had happened. Two marked police vehicles screeched to a halt as Bernard, along with the PC, moved into the back seat of the car. Cadema gave a short briefing to the newly arrived officers before leaving for the police station escorted by the two marked police vehicles.

Bernard continued to protest his innocence on the way to the station. He still believed they had picked on him because of his criminal record. He rambled on about his girlfriend, Sue. He only saw her when she phoned him on his pay-as-you-go mobile. She was always such a very busy lady so there was never a hint of a routine with her. He said he couldn't remember things. He'd seen Sue, recently, but couldn't remember the date. He never kept a diary, but if he had he would never remember to record anything in it. Sometimes he could hardly remember what he had for breakfast. How could he remember something that happened weeks ago? Perhaps it was old age, but he was too young for that and was too scared to visit his doctor to find out.

Arriving at the police station, Bernard was taken immediately to the custody Sergeant who authorised his detention, booked him in and escorted him to a cell.

'Before we interview you. I need to know if you would like a solicitor present,' Evans said.

'On a charge like this, what the f... do you expect? Of course I need one. I'm surprised you had to ask, anyway I repeat, I'm innocent. I have never murdered anyone in my life,' his voice shook.

'Okay Mr. Franklin, I will inform the custody sergeant who will organise a solicitor for you,' Evans said and then left.

Bernard had always felt intimidated by the police, ever since he was convicted of theft. His eighteen months in prison had been hell to him especially as he also lost his home, his job and eventually his wife. Since then he had never broken the law, nor caused trouble with his neighbours. So he was shocked when he saw the police at his front door, then terrified at his neighbours' behaviour towards him. They had always been polite before today. Now he realised they hated him, and always had.

The cell where Bernard was waiting for his solicitor was similar to the ones he had been in before. And as he expected, the police officers portrayed the usual belligerent attitude towards him. *They don't believe I'm innocent, so they'll go out of their way to convict me,* he thought. Sitting quietly in his cell, Bernard made up his mind he was waiting for some young solicitor to arrive with the sole purpose of using his case as 'experience' towards a better paid career in the future.

***

The desk clerk in the lobby of the police station watched as a young man, with dark-brown hair, clad in a blue pin striped suit and bright yellow tie, approached.

'Hello, I'm Julian St. Justin, the solicitor from Nicholas, Jones and Nicholas. I've come to see a Bernard Franklin.' Julian flashed his business card at the Sergeant.

'Sorry Sir, but I need to see your formal ID.'

'Oh yes of course,' he replied. 'This is my first visit to the station, so you will have to guide me on your protocols.'

'That's no problem, Sir. I'll just get a constable to take you to the cell block. She will introduce you to the Custody Sergeant. He will ask you to wait until a detective arrives. You'll then be taken to an interview room, briefed and then you'll see Bernard Franklin. Does that seem okay, Sir?' The clerk's voice was condescending.

'Splendid, just as I expected,' Julian said as he gained his usual military posture his father had insisted he used whenever he talked to someone in authority. "It always brings instant respect," he recalled his father's voice.

Evans had just finished briefing Julian as Bernard was ushered into the room by the police constable. Following the initial introductions, all the police officers left the room so Julian could talk to his client.

Julian sat facing a man who resembled his father. He took a deep breath and loosened his collar and tie a little.

'Good afternoon, Mr. Franklin, I'm your Solicitor, Mr. Julian St. Justin. As you know I'm here to discuss your case, give you advice, and help where I can.' He offered a half-smile. Bernard fidgeted in his chair.

'My case, I don't have 'a case' as you put it, I'm innocent. I couldn't have done it. I wasn't there. I have an alibi. It wasn't me,' Bernard babbled on with such verbosity that Julian sat perfectly still. 'They have arrested me for murder. They think I murdered four young women, but I never did.' Bernard's face contorted and wrinkled at every word. His eyes portraying innocence as they drooped like a puppy's when being reprimanded by its owner.

Julian shuffled in his chair, cleared his throat, and took a deep breath.

'Excuse me Mr Franklin, you need to calm down and tell me what you really know. All as I can tell you is the police are going to interview you about *one* of the murders, not all *four*. So try, if you can, to remember where you were as it will help us both to focus on the real issues and sort these thing out.'

'One you say, I thought it was four. Okay I'll do my best, but my memory's not as good as it used to be.'

'We can deal with that first if you like. Would you like to see a doctor?'

'No, I am okay, thank you. As I said I'll do my best to put you in the picture,' Bernard sat still for a moment trying to think what the 'picture' really was. He began to explain about his girlfriend and about being arrested, but that was all he could remember.

'Bernard, please do try to concentrate. Do you remember anything about the fourteenth of September? Anything at all will do. It was raining and you were driving,' Julian prompted.

'They said it was raining that evening and I must have been driving, but I can't remember,' Bernard said as he leaned on the table and rubbed his head with both hands.

'Please try your best, anything will do. Just think please.'

'Okay I'll try. All as I can think of is that it must have been the night when I saw Sue; it was definitely raining that night. So Sue could be my alibi if I could only be sure. I know she will say I was with her if I was.'

'So if you did see Sue that evening, can you remember what time you met her and what time you left her?'

'Yes, it was about nine thirty, when we met and about eleven when she left.'

'Left where? Can you remember where you were?'

'Oh yes, we were in my car.'

'I know you have already told me. So where did you go.'

'We didn't go anywhere, we never do. We were just in my car.' Bernard fidgeted.

'Look Bernard, I think you are keeping something from me. Something that is probably vital to the case.' Julian's voice and posture were deliberately confrontational.

'No I'm not. That is the truth. I don't know anything else.'

'Nevertheless, this is not helping your case. If I am going help you I need to know exactly what happened that night. So please be open with me and tell me what you were doing in the car with Sue?' Bernard fidgeted again, his neck reddened.

'We just sat in the car, that's all I am prepared to say. But I didn't kill anyone, you have to believe me. I've never hurt anyone; ever.' He wiped a tear with his finger and sniffed.

'Look Bernard, I'm just trying to help you. Perhaps we should concentrate more on Sue.'

'Yes, perhaps you're right.'

'Can you tell me Sus's full name and where she lives?'

'No I don't know, so I can't answer your questions. I only know her as Sue and she always phoned me. She had her business to see to. We always meet in the same place and always stay in my car. And that's the truth.' He blew his nose on a tissue he took from the packet on the desk.

'I believe you. Do you want me to tell the police about Sue?' Bernard agreed to this.

***

Cadema had her own methods of finding things out, so when Bernard finally decide to agree to an interview, she was ready.

Once settled in the interview room, Evans turned on the tape and asked everyone to say who they were.

'Bernard, can you tell me where you were on the night of the thirteenth, and the early morning of the fourteenth of September last?' Cadema asked as she looked straight into Bernard's blood-shot eyes and cringed at the thought of him as a killer. Although she wasn't sure whether he was, the evidence was overwhelming.

'I saw Sue; she will say she was with me. Have you found her yet?'

'How can we possibly do that when we don't know who she really is.? We've done some initial enquiries in the area you mentioned, but can't find anyone called Sue. Therefore, it sounds as if Sue is a figment of your imagination,' she looked straight into his eyes again. 'Bernard, Sue does not exist.'

'No, she does exist. She's my girlfriend, she does exist; she does,' he pleaded, looking from one officer to the other, then at his solicitor.

'Well if she does exist, where did you go with her?'

'Nowhere, she was in my car.'

At this Evans was given a nod from Cadema to ask the next question.

'Why was she in your car Bernard? What did you do there? Did you kill Sue, Bernard?' Evans asked.

Bernard sat staring at the wall, and said nothing. After a couple of minutes he asked to be taken back to the cell. Julian interrupted:

'I would like to speak to my client alone and without the tapes,' he looked at Cadema who agreed with his request.

Alone with his client, he moved closer: 'Listen Bernard, the police are unhappy. They think you're keeping things from them, and they don't like that. What is the problem Bernard? You can tell me; that's what I am here for. Who is Sue and where is she? Could you have killed her? You need to tell me for your own piece of mind.'

Bernard said nothing. How could he talk to people he didn't trust? And he decided he didn't trust his solicitor. He was far too inexperienced to take on such an important job. And much too young to be told what he had done with Sue, in private.

Later, in his cell, Bernard began to think about Sue. He loved her; that was a fact. She was alive when he last saw her—that was a fact. But he could not understand why they couldn't find her. Was she really a figment of his imagination?

CHAPTER TEN

Bernard's arrest took me completely by surprise; I had to find out what was really going on. After all Thomas had jeopardised everything and now he was sulking, so I had to take charge again. I decided the best thing to do was to find Julia Lilly. Not a difficult task since the media coverage had identified exactly where she worked. All I had to do now was to wait for her to come out of the building and then follow her home.

I'd not been waiting for more than half an hour when she appeared. Knowing her from before, I immediately noticed how strained she looked. Her normal short blond hair was beginning to show strands of white and its unkempt appearance gave me the impression she must have been too busy with work to keep hairdressing appointments. She used to be so particular about her appearance back in our university days. I sighed.

As she walked closely past me I saw furrows on her brow. Despite only being in her late thirties, the years since I had last seen her had taken their toll.

Thank goodness she didn't recognise me as she walked on. The last thing I wanted to do was to meet her in the street. I needed somewhere much more private, so I could talk to her and ask her the questions that festered in my brain. I had to know how the investigations were going. What was happening about the DNA profiles, and if they were any nearer to identifying the murderer. And then I would inadvertently, she may suppose, give her my theories. Some of which would be unrealistic. Ones which would entice her into discussion and contra arguments, hoping she would eventually furnish me with answers I needed without suspecting any improbity. In her naivety I expected her to enjoy our debate.

After following her home and waiting for about a minute, I rang her door bell. She didn't recognise me at first and said she wasn't interested in anything I was selling. She was just about to shut the door, when I saw a frown on her face, then her startled look.

'Hi Julia,' I said excitedly. 'I was just passing and as you went into the building I thought it was you. It took me a while before I decided to ring, just in case I was mistaken. But now I can see it really is you.'

'Yes, and after all these years. How are you? Do come in. Would you like some tea?' Julia went on, hardly giving me the space to answer.

'I'd love tea, thank you. But I don't want to disturb you. I just wanted to see if it were you and then be on my way.'

'Nonsense, you sit just there and I'll go and make tea,' she gestured to a green leather chair in her living room. I obeyed. After she had gone, I looked around the room which, judging by the rest of the furniture, had either been an inheritance, or was furnished from a second-hand shop. The sideboard, matching coffee tables and fire surround were all dark brown; oak I presumed. The stained and polished floor boards matched the furniture, while the gold, red and brown rug and the curtains brightened up the whole room, which was otherwise depressing.

'Let me help you with that,' I jumped up as she brought in a tray containing two mugs of tea and the usual accompaniments.

'No, it's all right. I have some cake if you would like some,' she carefully lowered the tray onto the table.

'The tea will be fine. Anyway, how are you?'

'I'm okay, and you look very well. It's been such a very long time since
. . .'

'Must be nearly fifteen years at least since we last met?' I noticed Julia
fidget in her chair as she stirred her tea with the spoon. 'So what are you
doing these days, Julia?' I asked innocently. She was silent, as if debating
the answer.

'This and that, you know how it is. Busy as usual. But what about you?
Are you still . . . well, you know what, I can't remember what you were
doing,' Julia gave a nervous giggle.

'After we graduated, I went to Canada for a while. Came back and
started working at Brooks and Co. the chemical firm. I'm still there,' I lied
as I didn't want her to know where I was working now. 'But tell me what
you are doing these days?'

'As I said, not much really. My work is quite demanding, and keeps me
busy, so I don't have much time for socialising.' Julia fidgeted again.

'That's the problem, employers want their pound of flesh these days.
No wonder people get burn-out. Anyway if you don't want to talk about
your work, that's fine by me. I'm in the same boat, never have the time to do
much, only work.'

'You never married then?' her question came out of the blue, I was
stunned. *How could she ask me a question like that, as if it's any of her
business?* I thought as I sat in silence thinking of how to answer. 'Are you
all right? I didn't mean to pry,' she sounded concerned.

'No, I'm fine thank you. No, I'm not married, nothing turned up for
me.' *Well at least that was the truth.*

'Me neither,' Julia replied, then changed the subject. 'Anyway with
these recent murders, I never have the opportunity to go out much.'

'You mean the Common Murders? You're working on them? My goodness that sounds challenging,' I said trying to quash my enthusiasm.

'Yes, and I must remember not to get too engrossed in these things. It's only when I speak to people like you, I realise how intense my work really is. My team are great though, and very enthusiastic.'

'So are you in charge then?'

'No, but people tend to think so from time to time.'

'That's good, so how's the investigation going?'

'Well it is and it isn't. You know I cannot talk about it—but you've no doubt read the papers and heard the news about Bernard Franklin?'

'Yes, and I expect he committed the other murders, too.' I tried not to sound too interested. 'Anyway, that's what I've heard on my travels.'

'We cannot be too hasty on that. We must look at all the forensic evidence not just the DNA.'

'I agree, but at least they caught the bastard. Now everyone will feel safer. Even my assistant is afraid to go out on her own. Her boyfriend has to collect her from work now, even though it's ten miles out of his way to do so.'

'Wait a minute, I didn't say the police had arrested the serial killer,' Julia sounded angry.

'Sorry, so why have they arrested him then?'

'I can't say. It's confidential, but of course we always need to keep an open mind and find as much tangible evidence as we can.'

'Like fibres or blood, or something?' I was trying my hardest to sound as if I didn't really know anything.

'Yes, that's right. But you sound as if you have been watching too much television. Some of the so called forensic evidence will only be circumstantial. We will need much more than that to make a case.'

'Well, good luck. Anyway I think this Bernard guy will turn out to the serial killer.' I hoped she would take the bait.

'You might be right, but we will have to see.' Julia gave a stifled yawn.

'What do you mean; you will have to see? Do you have anything else in mind?' She looked at me incredulously as I spoke. I knew then, she was not going to say anything else about the case.

We spent the rest of the time reminiscing about the old times at university and sharing what we had been doing recently. Obviously I left out the bits about Thomas. Then she told me about her work and the new job she was searching for. She had seen a job but hadn't got the time or the energy to apply for it. She said she was in a rut with no way out but when I tried to offer solutions to her problems she just discounted them saying they wouldn't work.

Exchanging contact details and saying goodbye, we agreed to meet up again soon. I would certainly make sure we met sooner rather than later as I needed to keep abreast of what was happening. And at the same time focus on the murders Thomas had committed and the ones he was still considering. To do this, I had to make sure Julia and her team focused in the right direction.

CHAPTER ELEVEN

Cadema took a deep breath, exhaled and then whispered 'thank you God,' as she replaced the telephone onto its plinth on her desk. It had been over two weeks since the ejaculate, found on Frances Cole's body, had been sent for analysis. Now she had a suspect. Wasting no time, she picked up the telephone and pressed Chief Superintendent Grimes's number.

'Sorry to disturbed you at home, Sir, but I thought you would want to hear the news.'

'Well, it must be urgent for you to phone, especially at...What time is it?' She heard him stifle a yawn.

'Sorry Sir, its eight o'clock on the sixteenth of October.'

'I know that, I only asked for the time.'

Ignoring his outburst, she began to explain about the findings.

'Yes Sir, we have a probable match from the DNA database. It belongs to someone called Edward Mason from twenty-two Broad Green. We intend to arrest him as soon as possible. I'm just getting my team ready for the briefing,' Cadema said.

'That's excellent news. You'd better handle it then. But don't forget, I need regular feedbacks, and don't take any undue risks.'

'I've already done a risk assessment, so there's no need to worry about it. As soon as I have any news I'll let you know.' As she said goodbye she felt the tension in her whole body relax as it always did after she had spoken to him.

The team briefing only lasted long enough to allocate officers to their appropriate Actions. An hour later they were all ready, much later than she would have liked. Dawn was her favourite time for arresting suspects, but it had passed. Nine O'clock would have to do.

Two unmarked police cars slid into spaces, their engines silenced. Just around the corner was Broad Green, a cul-de-sac south of the Thames off Putney Bridge Road. Cadema slipped out of the car and braced herself. Shuddering, she pulled the scarf tighter around her neck and did up the top button of her coat. As the officers assembled on a patch of waste ground, she reiterated the instructions she had given earlier.

'Marriott, you go round the back with Barry. Ryan and I will go to the front door together. And remember, keep quiet and no heroics please.'

Cadema lead the way to a row of prefabricated bungalows, which looked as if they should have been demolished years ago. Sheltered behind the privet hedge which lead to Edward Mason's garden, she waited for Marriott to confirm his position. Neighbours were up. She heard one shouting for a Masie several times; *presumably a cat. That's all I need, a group of nosey neighbours getting in the way,* Cadema thought.

Then she heard the noise of a lawnmower which produced a flurry of feathers from a nearby ash tree. She tensed. Stifling a scream, she felt sweat trickling down the back of her blouse. Her head ached. The birds swerved towards her. She clenched her teeth, closed her eyes and held her breath for the next wave. *I mustn't make a sound.* She opened one eye, then her other one. The birds had gone. She let out a slow breath; now she was in control. They were ready.

'Right, let's go,' she shouted, in a loud whisper, into her radio. Then, standing erect, both Cadema and Ryan began their journey.

Lichens had almost taken over the concrete path which lead to the door of number twenty-two, except for the tram-like furrows. The door, at one time white plastic, was now streaked with tears of brown stains. The bell, held by masking tape, swayed in the light breeze.

Cadema leaned forward, stabled the bell with her left hand, and then pressed the button with the index finger of her right hand. There was no sound. Letting go, she knocked the door with her keys in a groove that had obviously served the same purpose before. Nothing. She knocked again, this time much louder. She took a deep breath, pushed open the letterbox, looked inside, and then shouted.

'Mr. Edward Mason this is Superintendent Sharma from the Metropolitan Police. We have your home surrounded. Can you open the door please?' She put her ear to the letterbox but there was no sound from within. She knocked again. There was a twitch from the curtain. 'Mr. Mason can you hear me?' She knocked again. 'If you don't open the door, I'll be forced to open it. Do you understand?'

'Yes,' a shaky but loud male voice replied from behind the door. 'What the hell do you want?'

'We want to talk to you. So please open the door.' Her voice was calm, almost sympathetic.

'What about?'

'I will tell you that when you open the door and I can see you face-to-face. So open the door, please Sir.'

'Are you armed?'

'No, I'm not but don't try anything. Just open the door.' After waiting for a couple of seconds, and hearing no movement from behind the door,

Cadema spoke again: 'If you refuse to open the door, my officers will break it down. So it's in your best interest to open it.'

'How do I know you're police? Push your ID through the letter box so I can see it,' a voice snarled.

Cadema took the ID from around her neck and dangled it through the letter box. Seconds later the noise of a chain rattled across metal. A key in the lock turned, but the door remained closed.

'What are you waiting for, you can come in now.' The voice was some distance away from the door now.

Cadema slowly pushed on the door. Both officers moved slowly forwards and stopped. The man sitting in a wheelchair was about forty years old, had dark brown hair with a streak of grey over the left side of his temple. Both officers took startled breaths, then swallowed. Cadema managed to speak in a controlled and precise manner.

'Are you Mr. Edward Mason?'

'Yes, but what the bloody hell's going on here and how dare you come into my house like a herd of elephants,' he looked at Marriott and Barry who had just come in through the front door.

'In that case I must ask you to come to the station with me. I need to ask you about the recent murders in the area,' Cadema said, ignoring his outburst.

'For murder, you must be joking. You've made a mistake. Look at me, I have MS, that's multiple sclerosis. I've been in this wheelchair four years now. That surely discounts me as a murderer? And if I do go with you, how do you suppose I get there when I can't even walk?'

'Can you stand?'

'I can weight bear, if that's what you mean.'

'In that case you can wheel yourself to the police car and these officers will help you to get inside.'

'I see, so you don't intend to bloody charge me then.'

'Not yet, Mr. Mason. We need to question you before any charges are made.'

'Then question me here, I refuse to go to the station unless I am bloody charged.' Mason's voice shook in tune with his whole body as he wiped a rivulet of sweat from the side of his cheek with his sleeve.

Cadema wondered if she was out of her depth with Mr Mason and his disability. She tried to recall the policy about people in wheelchairs. Should she do as he requested and interview him in his home or take him down to the station? If she were to take him to the station, what mode of transport should she use? Whatever she decided to do, she felt it would probably be against the Disability Discrimination Act.

Nevertheless, she decided to caution him and then arrange for appropriate transport. After all, his DNA was found on a murdered victim and therefore she had reasonable suspicion to arrest him. He must have had something to do with the murders despite his MS. She recalled what Jim had once said.

'Get them to the station. You can find out what they can physically do when they've been seen by a police surgeon. Anyway, some people with MS are not in wheelchairs all the time, they have periods of remission.' She wondered why Jim Logan knew so much; much, much more than she would ever know.

'I don't want to question you here so I'm going to arrest you and arrange for you to be taken to the station.'

'So what the bloody hell are you going to charge me with?' Mason said as he scudded across the living room in his wheelchair and tried to confront Cadema who believed he would stand up and hit her. Marriott must have thought the same as he stepped forward, preventing Mason's advance.

'I'm not going to charge you. But I am going to arrest you. I also need a swab from you for DNA analysis.'

'I refuse to have a swab taken. That's my right isn't it?'

'You can refuse. But we can arrange for one to be taken at the station. Anyway, if you don't cooperate it may indicate you have something to do with the murders.'

'Do as you like then,' he snarled and crossed his arms.

Cadema took a deep breath. 'Mr Edward Mason, I am arresting you on suspicion of murder.'

'You are out of your bloody mind. How could I possibly commit a murder in my bloody condition? I refuse to be arrested.'

'You can't refuse. I am arresting you on suspicion of murder,' she cautioned him and asked if he understood.

'Yes,' he snarled. 'I do, but its bloody ridiculous, that's all I can say, bloody ridiculous.'

Leaving Ryan and the two officers to deal with Mr Mason, Cadema turned away and pressed Grimes's number on her mobile phone.

'Yes sir, I need a van to transport the suspect to the station; one that will hold a wheelchair. No he can't walk, anyway he's causing too much trouble to get him into a police car. I definitely need a van. And when he arrives he will need a doctor. I'm in the middle of arranging one for him so he can be seen as soon as possible.'

'Okay, but when you get here I need to have a word with you before you question him.' Cadema raised her eyebrows, anticipating what he was about to say.

Grimes always seemed to undermine her authority and her integrity at times like this. Having chosen her as chief investigating officer, he didn't appear to have confidence in her ability to cope with such complex cases anymore. Deep down he was probably still angry about Jim Logan's death, and perhaps felt responsible. At least that's how she reasoned with herself about his behaviour towards her.

***

Cadema shuddered as she entered the police station and went to the front desk to report Edward Mason's arrest, which she was feeling uneasy about. If he were confined to a wheelchair on a permanent basis it would be impossible for him to murder anyone. He might be able to stab someone who was asleep. But he would never be able to stalk anyone, then bludgeon them to death while they were awake, strong, and able to fight. Despite these doubts she still needed to interview him. He was hiding something, and, God willing, she was determined to find out what it was.

To be on the safe side, she had ordered a discrete enquiry into the DNA from the murder scenes to see if any errors or contamination could have occurred either at the scenes of the crimes or in the laboratory. She knew there was more than one in a billion chance that two people could have the same genetic fingerprints; and identical twins shared the same genomes. This was the extent of her knowledge of genetics despite having discussed it with Julia.

The CSI team, Marriott and a uniformed officer were left searching the bungalow, when Edward Mason was transferred to an awaiting police van. Grumbling all the way to the station, the van arrived three-quarters of an hour later. After his name had been entered into the station's admission book, Mr Mason was informed he would be seeing Doctor Frank Kenworth, the police surgeon. Still protesting, and escorted by DC Barry, they entered the doctors' room. It was sparse and cold. Remnants of spilt coffee were visible as were the marks where someone had made a feeble attempt at removing them.

Dr Kenworth glanced at the anxious face of a man who looked ill-kempt and whose body was stuffed into an undersized wheelchair. From his thirty years as a doctor, he knew the man had multiple sclerosis by his posture, the exaggerated flexion of his right foot and the slight intention tremor of his hand as it stretched out to shake his.

'Good morning, can you confirm you name and date of birth?' Edward Mason replied and confirmed everything as requested. 'Thank you. I'm Doctor Kenworth. The police have asked me to see you as they need to know whether or not you are fit to be detained and interviewed.'

'Of course I'm not fit. I have MS.'

'I realise that, but the police have their protocols that they, and I, must follow. All you have to do is sign a consent form for me to see you, then I can carry out my examination.'

'If I'm not fit, will they let me go?'

'Sorry, I cannot answer that,' he said then turned to DC Barry and asked him to leave the room. On leaving, he reminded the doctor to use the call system should he need it.

Alone with the doctor, Mason leaned forward in his wheelchair and began to speak quietly:

'I am happy to speak to you as long as what I say to you is in confidence.' He eyed the doctor with some caution. 'I don't usually trust anyone in authority, but I hope I can trust you.' He looked around the room as if searching for some hidden camera.

'Let me put you at ease Mr. Mason, everything we discuss in this room, about your health, is strictly confidential. I will only tell the police about your condition if you give me permission to do so. Do you understand?'

'Yes I do, and it sounds fine to me.'

'Good, but before I do I must also say that if you mention anything about the case that somehow incriminates you, I have a duty to report that.'

'What do you mean, report it?'

'For instance, if you tell me you murdered someone, then I cannot keep it confidential. Is that clear?'

'Yes, of course. You can see I'm incapable of murder in my condition.'

Doctor Kenworth nodded with some hesitation.

'Anyway, before I can categorically say you have MS, I need to take a history and then examine you to see if you are fit to be interviewed.'

Finishing his examination, Dr Kenworth concluded that Mr Mason definitely had MS. Later he intended to verify all the points raised in the examination with Mr Mason's GP and his consultant whom he knew well form his days in the local Hospital.

Having left Mr. Mason, he gave his brief report to Cadema.

'I can confirm Mr Edward Mason has been using a wheelchair for the last four years. He has some periods of remission, but he has never fully recovered from each episode. He can weight bear for a limited period, probably for a minute or two, but could certainly not walk or drive a car. In my opinion, he is fit to be interviewed.'

'Thank you doctor, but has his MS affected his memory?'

'Sorry I'm not in a position to answer that. But he sounds as if his cognitive reasoning is sound. But you need to ask his consultant about that. All I can say is, he's fit for you to interview him.' Doctor Kenworth then left the building believing that Mr. Mason was undoubtedly innocent.

The custody Sergeant was given the signed report confirming Mr. Mason was fit to be detained. Having said he wanted a solicitor, he was then committed to a cell.

Cadema considered what Doctor Kenworth had said to her, and realised she could not really remember the whole report on the DNA analysis. Furthermore, she wondered if she were making a mistake. Not just because of Mr Mason's arrest, but because she had misgivings about his ability to carry out the murders. She needed tangible evidence, and needed to know whether the DNA could belong to someone else? A brother maybe? But Mr. Mason had said he was an only child. How could she be sure of that? She knew what families were like. There could be a family secret. The only solution was to investigate the family and find out if there was a history of twins in the family, and find out if Mr Mason was a twin. If he was, then the records should show this. She would assign Evans to set up an investigation into this theory.

***

Edward Mason fidgeted in his wheelchair in the cell as he waited to be interviewed. He had told himself that he couldn't possibly be charged with murder. Nevertheless he was worried they didn't believe a word he said. But that was not all he was worried about. It was the thought of his house being searched. He was always a private person, keeping himself to himself. And the thought of the police snooping into his private things angered him. But his main concern was the secret business he had there. So, although he tried to put a brave face on the arrest, underneath he was determined no one would find out how he really felt.

***

Now, with fatigue after his arrest, Cadema decided to let Mr Mason rest before he was interviewed. She took this advantage to brief her team.

'Okay, are you all listening?' speaking above the noise, everyone went quiet. 'Good, so let's examine the evidence. As you know, Mr. Edward Mason has been arrested and will be interviewed soon. But as he has MS he most probably did not commit the murders despite his DNA being found on the victims.' There was a buzz of voices. 'Quiet please. Now, this is what we've got so far,' she began to list the items on the board.

'One, we have the DNA that matches Edward Mason's DNA, or it matches some unknown person's DNA.'

'Do you have any ideas on who the unknown person might be, Ma'am?' DC Barry asked.

'No, but when we interview Mason, I hope he will be able to help. He may have a brother. DI Evans is following that Action. If there are no more questions I'll continue,' she looked round the room. No one else spoke.

'Two, our prime suspect is Edward Mason, but according to the Doctor Kenworth, he could not have committed the crimes because he has advanced multiple sclerosis.'

'Could he have been involved somehow, but not actually commit the murders?' Barry asked.

'That is a possibility we need to keep in mind.' Cadema nodded and turned to the board again.

'Three, we don't know if the samples of DNA were contaminated, and if so, where this might have happened,' she took a sip of water.

'Four, the forensic team have just finished their work in Mason's bungalow. According to their preliminary report, they haven't found any tangible evidence to link him with the murders. But they have taken several samples and there may be something in these.'

'Let's hope they do find something,' Ryan said with some enthusiasm.

'Yes, maybe they will, but I doubt it.' Cadema shook her head and continued with her list.

'Five, we have not found any weapons which could have been used on the victims. There are no fingerprints. The only forensic evidence we have is the DNA linking Edward Mason to the murders. Indeed, it appears all the victims were murdered by someone who knows about scenes of crime investigations and as such most probably wore protective clothing.'

'Do you think the murderer could be a police officer?' a DC Galke shouted from the back of the room.

'It means we cannot rule anyone out, not even ourselves,' she answered. 'Right everybody, we need to know more about Mason's condition. We need an expert opinion on his abilities and inabilities. The best person to answer this is his consultant.'

'What about his GP, Ma'am?' the DC Galke resumed.

'His GP is not an expert. We need to talk to his consultant. So let's examine the things we need to do now. Some of you can tell me what questions we need to ask.' She looked around the room. No one spoke. 'Come on, one of you must have some burning questions. It doesn't matter how silly or incredulous they may sound, let's hear them. I'll put them on the board.'

'I think we need to find out where he was he born and whether or not he has a twin brother.' DCI Ryan said.

'Yes,' she said and turned towards the board. She had just finished writing when another question was raised.

'We need to identify his nearest relatives and see if we have their DNA on file, if not then we need samples.' Ryan continued.

'That's correct. It means we can eliminate everyone as possible. Are there any more questions?' No one spoke. 'Well there is a very important one. We need to know if Mr Mason is capable of having sex.' She did not see who sniggered but the hairs on her neck began to rise. Slamming the marker pen on the table she scowled at her audience.

'Look, some of you may think it's funny, but I assure you it's deadly serious. And so am I. I don't expect any officer on my team, irrespective of rank, to be so puerile. Anymore sniggering, or derogative comments of any kind, and the culprit will be disciplined,' she watched as her officers went pale and fidgeted. 'I like my officers to have ownership of the cases we investigate. I want them to think for themselves, not be led like children. That's why I asked you to contribute to the questions. Having ownership will help to boost your self-esteem and enhance team work. This is a management theory, I know, but its application here, I believe, will lead to crimes being solved sooner, rather than later. So I don't want to see, or hear any more inappropriate or unprofessional behaviour, is that clear?' Cadema imagined she could hear their hearts beating as they all nodded their heads in unison.

'Right, now that's clear you need to be aware some people with MS may have physical problems with erections. If Mr Mason does, then he may not be able to ejaculate. If this were the case it would have been impossible for him to leave ejaculate at the murder scenes. That's one of the reasons why we need to visit his consultant, who will be able to give us much more information than we have at the moment. So if there are no more questions, let's get on with the work. Ryan will allocate your workloads.' Cadema said, but remained in the room,

'Thank you Ma'am,' Ryan faced the offices and handed them their Actions. Turing to DC Barry and DC Galke, she said they could work with DI Evans when he returned from his current enquiries. As the officers left, another officer entered the room.

'Excuse me for interrupting,' the officer said as he cleared his throat. 'But I've been sent to tell you that, before the officers finished searching Mr Edward Mason's bungalow, they came across an extension at the back, disguised as a garden shed. It has no windows and has a securely locked door. When they managed to force it open, which was apparently very difficult, they found cannabis plants growing inside. There was all the equipment for hydroponic cultivation, as I understand it's called. Looking at the amount, they think he was not only growing it for himself but for others. Well that's the message, Ma'am,' he finished reading and put his notebook in his pocket then turned to leave.

'Wait a minute officer, who sent the message?' Cadema asked, puzzled that the information appeared to come from another team.

'It came from DI Evans, Ma'am.'

'I see, but why didn't he contact me directly?'

'Apparently DS Marriott tried to contact you but there was some technical problems. Eventually DI Evans picked up the message and relayed it to the main desk.' Cadema looked incredulous but decided not to say anything else. She then thanked the officer as he left the room.

'That explains a great deal,' she said under her breath.

'Sorry Ma'am, I didn't quite hear what you said?' Ryan asked.

'I was just thinking to myself, but as you're still here I'll explain.

'As you may remember, when Edward Mason was arrested he was very protective of his bungalow. If you recall, he had insisted, even after his arrest, that we could not search his home.'

'Yes I remember, but I thought he had some mental problem or he was just naive and didn't understand the law,' Ryan recalled.

'He did give us that impression, but how wrong we were. Now I understand why he was so agitated when we arrived. And why he had insisted in reading the search warrant word for word before he accepted it. He never mentioned the shed, but when I saw it I wondered why there were so many solar panels on it. But thought he was just being environmentally friendly. It now appears he is growing cannabis. So let that be a lesson to us.' Cadema reasoned.

'It certainly is Ma'am,' Ryan sighed.

'Yes, so he may be hiding something else. In that case, I'll send another couple of PCs round to help Marriott to do a thorough search. They can take up the floor boards, and search the loft. I'll let DI Evans know as soon I can.'

'That's great; I'll tell the custody sergeant that we're about to charge Edward Mason with possession of an illegal substance.' Ryan said cheerfully as she left the room.

***

Cadema was elated, knowing she could at least charge Mr. Mason with something more tangible than she had before. When she entered the cell Edward Mason evaded her eyes. She ignored this and walked straight up to him.

'Edward Mason, I'm going to charge you with possession of an illegal substance. You don't...'

'I knew it, I knew it. You weren't bloody satisfied in hauling me here under some ridiculous charge. And now you've realised your mistake you've had to come up with another charge. You searched my f...ing bungalow, so why did you have to search my shed,' he took a breath.

'We had every right to.'

'You have no right to. You had a search warrant for the bungalow, not for the bloody shed.'

Cadema realised it was no use arguing with Mason at this point. Instead she told him his solicitor was on his way and he would be taken to the interview room soon. Besides, for the first time in her life she actually felt annoyed with a suspect. But, instead of showing her anger, she told him he would be interviewed later. He gave a grunt in reply. As she walked up the corridor, she could still here him cursing and swearing

Pleased that the investigation was gaining momentum, Cadema was sure Chief Superintendent Grimes would be happy with the progress she had made, and as usual she was about to brief him prior to the management meeting. But entering his office, she tensed.

'I hear you're making some progress now,' he said as she lowered herself into a chair facing him.

'Yes Sir, but not as good as I hoped it would be at this time. But at least I have many more leads to follow up.'

'You sound a bit despondent to me. Are you sure you're all right?' he sounded concerned.

'I'm fine Sir. Everything's under control. I was just considering these preliminary reports from my team and forensics.'

'Good, so let's hear what they have to say.' He moved his chair closer to his desk.

'Yes, of course. One thing I'm disappointed with is that there is no evidence on the premises at the moment to link Mr. Edward Mason with any of the murders. That means...'

'I know what it means, you have made a mistake.'

'If you put it like that, then yes I have. But the DNA was a match with Mason, so the mistake is somewhere else. I'm perusing that line of enquiry from all angles. And will let you know the results as soon as I have them.'

'Them? You said them.'

'I did.' She took a deep breath and explained about the DNA from the crime scenes. And then said she was looking for close relatives of Mason, to examine their DNA. She did not mention her twin theory.

'That's sounds a reasonable strategy, just be careful with the budget.'

'I will, Sir.'

'So what's this I've heard about cannabis?' He leaned back in his chair with a frown.

'It's all here in this report. The shed where the cannabis was found looked like a normal wooden one from the outside. However, it was lined with breeze blocks and then with silver insulation cladding. The cannabis was of high quality and was certainly used for some commercial purposes. To support this, they found some sales records in a filing cabinet in the shed.'

'That's excellent police work. Tell your officers well done for discovering it.'

'Not really, Sir, we would have searched it anyway, it was just routine.'

'Nevertheless...' he sat still as if thinking of what he should say next.

Cadema continued with her report.

'Anyway, Mr. Mason had some income from his cannabis business, which supplemented the social benefits he was claiming. So in effect he has committed benefit fraud, evaded tax and was found in possession of an illegal substance.' She stopped speaking and looked at Grimes. He remained quiet. 'Are you all right, Sir?'

He shook his head, his eyes flickered as if he had been startled from a sleep, then looked at her.

'Are you all right,' she repeated.

'Yes, of course. It sounds as if you've got a lot more work to do.'

'Yes there is, and hopefully I can find out who the perpetrator is without any further delay.'

'Good. So I'll expect progress reports.'

Leaving the room, she heard him sigh, but was not sure whether it was a sign of relief or frustration on his part.

Nearing the end of the day, Cadema decided to delay interviewing Mason until the next morning. This would give him time to rest and she would still be conforming to the twenty-four hour deadline before needing an extension or letting him go. She planned to interview him about the murders first, then hand him over to the drug squad, hoping not to breach the deadline by then.

Eight-thirty the next morning, she entered the interview room together with DI Johns. They sat facing Mr Mason and his solicitor, John Bradbury-Stokes.

'Mr. Edward Mason, I am going to record the interview, so after I have turned on the tape I will ask you to state your name clearly.' Without waiting for a reply Cadema turned on the machine, said her name and rank as did DI Johns. When asked, Edward Mason spoke almost in a whisper, so she asked him to speak up, and he did so. His solicitor, spoke next followed by a PC who was standing by the door.

'Mr. Mason, I have arrested you on suspicion of murder. Do you understand?' Cadema looked into Mason's dark cavernous eyes which showed no signs of emotion.

'Yes I do, but I don't know why you've bloody arrested me, I haven't done any murders. How the hell could I in this state? And you have asked me to state my name, but don't forget I'm in a wheelchair and am unable to walk, and that I've bloody well been like this for the last four years.' She ignored his outburst and maintained her upright posture.

'From what Doctor Kenworth said, you have had multiple sclerosis for ten years. Is that correct?' she portrayed no emotion or concern for his feelings. Mason stared at her in contempt as he answered:

'Yes, of course I bloody well have,' he stared at Cadema, his pupils wide, his face contorted.

'Good, then if you will tell me what I need to know, this interview will be over and you can get some rest. But if you decide not to cooperate, we may be here all day.'

'Okay, I'm ready to cooperate as much as I can. But I firmly believe this is discrimination and you're picking on me because I'm in a wheelchair. You can't keep me here all bloody day. I suffer from fatigue and need my rest. The DNA evidence you say you've found doesn't belong to me. Anyway, how the bloody hell do you think I'm responsible for that when I can't even walk, let alone drive. Doctor Kenworth must have told you that. So it can't possibly be mine, can it?' Mason was almost pleading now.

'As you know, I'm aware of your fatigue, so if we clear this up we can get onto the much less serious business. Do you have any brothers or sisters?' she waited for any signs of response, there were none, only a puzzled face appeared back at her. She coughed. 'Do you understand the question Mr. Mason?' Before she could finish, he interrupted her.

'Of course I bloody well understand, I'm not stupid. So you don't think the DNA is mine then, do you?' he looked her in the face, beyond her eyes as if undressing her mind.

'Just answer the question please.'

'No, I don't have any brothers or sisters, I am an only child, but you know that already.' He turned to his solicitor.

'My client has been asked this on several occasions, and has given you the same answer. To his knowledge, what he says is correct. I request you refrain from asking this question again, and move on.'

'Yes, of course, But this is for the tape, I would like him to answer.'

'Very well.' Bradbury-Stokes said and instructed his client to speak.

'Thank you. Now Mr Mason, can you tell me where you were on the nights of the thirty-first of August, the eighth of September, the fourteenth of September, and the thirtieth of September last?'

'Yes, I never go out at night, so I was at home on all those dates. I may even have had company, but without my diary I can't be sure.' At this, Cadema produced his diary and asked him to explain the coded entries in it on the dates in question.

'Yes, that's bloody easy, the 'I' means I was in. The 'g' means I had a guest and the 'c' means—well I suppose you know what that means seein' as you're going to charge me for it.'

'So 'c' is for cannabis, is that correct Mr. Mason'

'If that's what you think, then it's right.'

'Who were the guests you mention. We need to know to be able to verify you alibi.'

'Oh, that's simple, it's Mabel Brown, my friend. Not my girlfriend you understand, I was never that way inclined. Now I'm not inclined at all, if you get my drift.'

'What do you mean by saying you're not inclined at all?'

'Okay, so I'm gay, it's not a bloody crime, is it? I've never fancied women in that way, but I have never had sex with a man either. Just because you're gay, people always think you have to be having sex with all and sundry. But no, I was happy to be in male company but I have always remained celibate. I suppose I never really found the right person.' He was showing another side of his character now and Cadema realised that under the tough facade there was a man with some feelings. He broke into her thoughts. 'And I don't hate women if that's what you bloody think.'

In some way she felt sorry for him sitting in his wheelchair having to admit he was gay. It obviously troubled him. But she needed to find out more about his relationship with the woman. And, now she knew he was gay, it would have significant bearings on the investigation. Was he a misogynist, was he capable of murder or of planning murders for someone else to carry out, she had to know? But how could she ask him without divulging her suspicions?

She listened without interrupting him. And as he talked she was convinced he wasn't a killer. So she could have released him from custody if it hadn't been for the cannabis issue. She stood up.

'Well, thank you for your cooperation, that will be all for the time being.' She said then switched the tape recorder off.

'My team will follow up the information you have given Mr Mason. You may go back to your cell. The drug team will interview you about your cannabis business.'

'Oh, so you're bloody letting me go on the murder charge are you? Well, it still doesn't bloody change anything. You bloody coppers are all the same, no matter what colour you are, or what sex, for that matter,' Edward Mason said as he turned his wheelchair around and headed for the open door, followed by his solicitor.

CHAPTER TWELVE

Cadema's teams were busy carrying out their allocated Actions when she made her way to see Philip Crown, the Media Officer, to brief him about what was happening. Saying hello, she noticed his condescending grin that he always had when he met her.

Having once been a DCI, Crown had left the police service following the loss of his right eye. He earned the George Cross for this after he tackled a drunken man with a knife which cost the man his life. He was particularly proud of that, especially as he had saved the county millions of pounds that would have otherwise been used to keep the villain in jail. Being an ardent supporter of capital punishment he couldn't see why the death penalty had been scrapped decades ago. He believed he had done the country a great favour and was proud of his achievement.

Now he had returned as a civilian, he still acted as if he were an officer. But as the Press Bureau did all the work on the statements, he wasn't even allowed to tweak them to suit himself, as he used to do. No. Bureaucracy was the name of the game these days, so he was getting bored. 'Even another murder would liven things up,' he had commented to a senior officer.

Watching Cadema was not enough for him. He wanted to be there, in charge and with the energy the role needed. Besides if there was something he couldn't stand, it was women giving orders in a man's world. Cadema should never have been given the promotion, especially when there was a serial killer lose in London. When Frances Cole was murdered he knew he could have done a better job than her, and he resented this.

Nevertheless, he made the most of his post despite the lack on hands-on policing. It gave him what the police service would never have given him; prestige and fame. And, although he was no longer a young man he believed he was still good looking enough for the media. Okay, so he had a few streaks of grey in his otherwise blond hair, but they hardly showed. Neither did his encroaching pendulous paunch that hung over his belt, especially if he breathed in. When he stood in front of the television cameras he was a Hollywood movie star. *Someday they would recognise my talents, from the media perspective, and offer me a job,* he thought to himself.

Crown stood in front of Cadema. His remaining eye, just visible under his greying bushy eyebrow, viewed her suspiciously as she wondered how he could possibly see at all. Following the contours of his body, she noticed how his sedentary role was increasing his weight. But no one would dare mention it, as he had become more unapproachable with everyone these days. Anyway, there were comments he was in the same lodge as the Commissioner, while others said he was from the 'old school'. There were of course the rumours about his health, but she didn't listen to rumours, she was only interested in facts.

'Please take a seat, it's good to see you.' He gave what he considered a welcoming grin as she sat opposite him. 'Well, from what I hear, you seem to be doing pretty good.'

'Thanks. As I said when I phoned, you will probably need these for the press release,' she handed him two sheets of A-four paper. He began to scan through them.

'Yes, of course but you could have e-mailed them to me.'

'I realise that, but there's something I need to ask.' She threw him a half-smile.

'Ask me?' he said incredulously as he sat upright in his chair, his chest expanding. 'I thought you had everything under control.'

'I have, but I'd like to be involved in the media coverage. So next time, when you give a press statement, I would like to accompany you.' Her request sounded more like an order.

Crown sank into his chair, rubbed his chin and began to laugh quietly.

'You're having me on. This is my job you're talking about. Surely your time would be better spent catching this monster.' He stopped laughing as he wiped his brow with his handkerchief.

'I would like the experience. Besides I could give a different angle on the cases, from a woman's point of view.' As soon as she had said this, she knew her argument was lost. Why should he agree, when it was, after all, his domain?

'If you put it like that, I suppose I could give you the opportunity sometime soon. Not today though as I've already rehearsed what I'm expected to say. But I'll keep you in mind for the next one.' He edged forward. 'Well, you seem to have things under control, so I'll get back to my work; the press conference is in half-an hour,' he looked at his watch. 'But I'm here if you need any help, you just need to ask.'

Cadema thanked him, then left in the knowledge that Crown would never help anyone, unless he had to. And she was the last person he would willingly assist. But she hoped to be involved in the next press conference.

***

Philip Crown could hear the cacophony of voices as he entered the hall from a back door. Climbing the two steps onto the stage, he held tightly onto the podium and eventually found enough breath to speak to the audience of reporters.

'Good day ladies and gentlemen. This is the press report you've all been waiting for,' he held up two pages in his right hand.

'Have you arrested anyone for them yet?' a journalist said as the flashes of light stung into Crown's retina, leaving their impressions much longer than any had done before. *This is what the work should be all about*, he thought as he stood to attention and then turned to look at the person who had spoken.

'As you know, we have an excellent team following up leads as we speak and arrests are imminent,' he said hoping this information would satisfy the crowd. Then, hardly stopping for a breath he continued. 'I would ask you to respect the work they do and ask you all to remain quiet while I read out this report. Once I've finished, you can then ask me questions which I will do my best to answer.' He scanned the faces knowing that some of their questions he could not, would not, or even be allowed to answer. He coughed and stretched his six foot six frame as much as he could.

'Thank you, thank you,' he gestured with his arms for them to be quiet, as he faced the sixty or so reporters with their cameras, dictaphones and tablets at the ready.

The room went quiet. Crown stood proud, sentry-like in his well-pressed suit, precisely matched shirt and tie, and shining black shoes. The two medals proudly displayed on his left lapel.

'Ladies and Gentlemen, as you know this is our fourth press statement and you will find I have much more information for you this time. As you are aware, four young women have been murdered. The first two were Jane Gaunt and Sophie Millburn murdered on Wimbledon Common, on the thirty-first of August and the eighth September respectively. The third was Madeline Belton on fourteenth of September, on Putney Heath. The most recent is Frances Cole, found on the thirtieth of September in Richmond Park. Obviously these are terrible tragedies, and my sympathy goes out to the four families involved.' He lowered his head as if he were in mourning for the people he did not know.

'As you can see, the murders were spread over a wide area but with current policing practices and technology we should be able to catch the perpetrator as quickly as possible. We expect to make arrests soon.'

'I understand you have made two arrests so far. Are you going to charge anyone?' a man's voice from the middle of the room shouted.

'Yes, we have arrested two suspects. One has been released pending further enquiries, while the other has been arrested and charged for an unconnected offence,' he shuffled from one foot to the other and took a sip of water.

'Do you mean you've had to let them go, through lack of evidence?' the man continued as another stood up at the back of the room and shouted something inaudible to the people at the front.

'Yes and no. As I said, we arrested two men, and now we are continuing with further enquiries. That is all I can say at the moment.'

'Were any of the women raped?' a young blond woman sitting in the front row asked. She must have been a new reporter as he had never seen her before.

'None of the women were raped but may have been sexually assaulted,' he continued, not wishing to give out too much information.

'What do you mean, 'may' have been sexually assaulted? Surely you should know if they have or haven't?' the woman said in a slightly threatening tone which made him wonder why the woman was really there, and what kind of paper she worked for. She was wearing an identification badge, but even as he squinted, he could not read the name from where he was standing.

'Yes, we can tell sometimes, it depends on how long the person has been dead, and many other factors. But we are not ruling out anything with these murders.' He shuffled again, took a drink of water, cleared his throat and quickly finished reading out the report. Stiffening, he then announced that the briefing was about to end.

'What makes these murders different then?' the woman continued her interrogation while some listened and others buzzed in the background. *Different from what?* he thought but decided not to enter into the debate.

'I am sorry but I cannot answer any more questions as everything else is confidential and may jeopardise our enquiries if I continue. I will be in contact with you as soon as we have completed our enquiries; good day to you all,' he turned to leave.

'Are you going to do a re-enactment on Crimeview soon? You could at least tell us that before you go?' a man in the third row wearing a yellow shirt shouted.

'We are thinking of doing that sometime in the future but not yet as we are still gathering forensic evidence. When we have done this, then it will be discussed at the highest level.'

As another hand was raised behind the man in the yellow shirt, Crown headed for the steps at the back of the stage. Some of the audience had already left while others were packing up their equipment. Disappearing behind the curtain, he heard some reporters raising objections about the shabby way they had been treated on such serious matters.

Five minutes later everyone had left the hall except for the young blond woman in the front row who was busy with her laptop. She typed away at the speed of light and listened to the echo of two voices coming from somewhere behind the stage. One of the voices belonged to Crown. The woman stopped typing, tilted her head, and listened.

'I really don't know what they expect. We haven't got a magic wand. Anyway Sharma is keeping this one close to her chest, or should I say breasts,' Crown sniggered, then gave a loud laugh in harmony with the laugh from an unknown person he was talking to.

'Anyway, I didn't want to tell them any more in case they start to interfere with police business and upset the whole investigation. You know what reporters are like. And who was that bloody prat on the front row? Who does she think she is, asking stupid questions? I know we haven't really given them anything they didn't know already. But I bet they didn't know about Mr Mason's arrest and the cock-up there with his so called MS. It's obvious to me a man confined to a wheelchair couldn't possibly murder anyone. And let's hope they don't find out about the cannabis, at least not yet anyway. You know what the press are like. Really I don't know what Sharma is playing at.'

Someone muttered 'I agree,' and as the voices faded away the woman left the hall unobserved.

***

Chief Superintendent Grimes read the front page of the newspaper, then picked up the telephone and pressed the button for his secretary.

'I want you to locate Superintendent Cadema Sharma and Phillip Crown and tell them to come to my office immediately,' his voice bellowed.

'Yes Sir,' an assertive voice answered.

Half an hour later, Cadema and Crown stood outside Grimes's office door.

'Do you know what this is all about?' Cadema asked. But Crown just looked at her, shrugged, and then knocked at the office door.

'Enter,' Grimes's shouted. They did and then stood facing him.

'What do you think you are playing at?' he slammed the newspaper down on his desk.

Crown took a quick glance at the headline and shouted his reply:

'How dare you speak to me like that, I'm not one of your subordinates who you can order about? I only ever tell the press what has been agreed.'

Cadema picked up the newspaper and began to read it. Shaking her head, she turned to face Crown:

'I was not aware of this, but it's outrageous. What on earth have you done Phillip? I need you to explain how the press got hold of this information. This has compromised the whole investigation,' she prodded the newspaper with her index finger. Crown snatched it from her and turned towards Grimes. He opened his mouth to speak but Grimes interjected:

'Listen you two, I'm not prepared to sit here and let you shout at each other. Just calm down. Sit down and tell me how it happened,' Grimes's said in a calm authoritative voice. They quietly obeyed, and slid into the two chairs facing him. 'Good, so now explain.' Crown began to speak:

'I know nothing about this. I don't always have time to listen to the news, or read any newspaper for that matter,' he clenched his fist but dare not mention he had been far too busy booking his holiday for next year. As he read further he began to sweat. 'Look,' he continued. 'I can see how angry you both are. I'm angry too. I never said any of this. And I don't believe any of the team would do this either.'

'Someone has Phillip, and I won't rest until I find out who did,' Grimes said as he noticed Crown was reading the text over and over again, while his whole body shook.

'Surely you must know something about it?' Cadema said accusingly.

'I assure you both, I do not. But I intend to find out.' Crown gave a wry smile as he turned towards Cadema. She watched every twitch of the expressions on his face.

'They must have got it from some internal source. And I'm determined to find out who it was. Then they will be in for disciplinary action, no matter who it is or what rank,' Cadema said.

'Good, so both of you find out and report back to me later today.' Grimes stood up and watched them leave his office.

As Cadema walked off in the opposite direction to Crown, she could hear him muttering to himself, but could not hear what he was actually saying.

'It can't be, no. But yes that's what I was discussing with Ross after the press report yesterday,' Crown said under his breath.

Chief Inspector Jordan Ross was Crown's friend from X-division. He knew Ross would never speak to the press; it was more than his job and his pension were worth. So he decided not mention their discussion to anyone until he had spoken to Ross. Then together they would find out who had written the article.

***

After reaching her office, Cadema organised for her team to meet her in the briefing room. There she intended to read the newspaper article out loud so they could all hear it. When she arrived, Crown was standing at the back of the room. She ignored him and began to read.

Police Blunder on Common Murders: The press statement given by Philip Crown, the Media Officer, yesterday left everyone with the impression that the police were still following up leads on suspects. However, a reliable source had said that they have arrested two suspects so far and then let them go. It turns out that one of those arrested, a Mr. Edward Mason of Putney, is confined to a wheelchair with multiple sclerosis. Police arrested him without a shred of evidence. When they realised they had the wrong man they had to let him go with an apology. Mr Mason said he would take his case to the Police Complaints Authority and accused the police officers concerned with harassment, breaking and entering, verbalised assault and wrongful arrest. A spokesman from the local MS Institute said that Mr. Mason was a pillar of society and that being accused of murder has devastated him so much that he now needs professional counselling. Another man has also been arrested and is about to be charged with one of the murders but will not be charged with the other three.'

'Right,' said Cadema, 'you can all get back to work now. But I intend to investigate this breach of security, and when I find out who informed the press about this, you know what will happen.' There were mutters from the team as they left.

'Bloody press,' Crown said under his breath, as he began to leave the room. *They must have had some listening device in the back room, or someone must have been listening to us, but who?* He tried to think who it could possibly be.

His thoughts were interrupted as Cadema said they could go to her office and discuss the matter further. After entering her office, she closed the door.

'As you know this article has caused us a lot of embarrassment, so we must find out who wrote it. Do you remember anyone else in the hall when you left?'

'Mm… Well yes, now you come to mention it. There was the young blond woman wearing a light green suit under a black coat sitting on the front row. But I assumed she had gone before I spoke to Ross. In my opinion she was a little overdressed for a journalist.'

'So this all stems from gossip you shared with DCI Ross,' Cadema said with some exasperation as she stomped towards him and crossed her arms. 'What were you thinking of, discussing my cases with him in the first place? You had no right to do that. Now you've jeopardised the whole investigation?

'Don't get stroppy with me. I didn't know she was still there. Beside we spoke almost in whispers, so I cannot imagine how she could have heard anything.' Crown dabbed his brow with his handkerchief several times.

'But she must have done. It's all here. Anyway, who was this woman and what was she doing?' Cadema asked.

'I haven't the faintest who she was. She sat down after I spoke and was typing something or other on her laptop when I left. I thought she was typing what I had said so she could send it to her paper. I'd better get Ross in right away.' He said as he walked towards Cadema's desk and asked to use the phone. Cadema nodded.

'Hi Jordan, have you seen the article in the newspaper?' Crown waited for a reply. 'Good, then you'll know what this is all about. So can you come to Cadema's office as soon as possible as we need to discuss it with you?' Crown nodded a couple of times, then looked at his watch. 'Yes, I make it a quarter past. Shall we say about half an hour?' He nodded. 'Good, see you soon.' Replacing the phone, he looked at Cadema but said nothing.

'I'm just popping out for a minute,' she said. 'You may stay here if you wish but while I'm out I'll arrange some refreshments.' Cadema turned on her heels and headed for the door. 'I'll be back when Ross arrives.'

Exactly half an hour later all three were seated in Cadema's office.

'What do you know about this Ross?' she asked as she placed the newspaper on the table in front of him.

'I'm not really sure. I can't understand how they managed to find out about this.' Ross fidgeted in his seat, took a gulp of tepid coffee, and then replaced the mug back on the table.

Crown cringed as Ross spoke. 'Look Jordan, I've already explained to Cadema that we discussed this at the back of the stage. So after I left, did you speak to anyone? A reporter perhaps?'

'What are you suggesting? I never spoke to anyone. You know me better that that.'

'Do I?' Crown frowned. 'So how the hell did this get into the papers? I know there was a woman in the front seat, but she couldn't have possibly heard what we said. So did you speak to her later?' his face contorted as he spoke.

'No I did not. And to be honest, I don't like the frame of this questioning. If I'm being accused, I think you'd better stop now and give me time to speak to the Federation.'

Cadema turned to Ross with anger in her eyes. She took a deep breath then slowly released it:

'We are not accusing you of anything. We just need to know the facts. If you didn't speak to anyone, then we may reasonably assume that this woman must have overheard what was said.'

Ross nodded. Crown coughed, stood up and walked across the room as if examining the floor for the answers he was looking for.

'Despite what you've both said, you were wrong discussing it in a public place, and I'm not going to let that lie. But we could go around in circles about this. If neither of you spoke to this woman after the press conference, then she did overhear your conversation. So find out who she is, and ask her. She may have nothing to do with it. Could it have been someone else?'

'I don't think so,' Crown answered.

Ross shook his head and then agreed to find out who the reporter was.

'I expect it will be difficult though, especially as her name had not been printed in the newspaper.'

As they left Cadema's office, they agreed to meet again as soon as the woman reporter had been located. Then they would all go to see Grimes and fill him in on the details.

Ross believed that ever since the newspaper businesses had moved out of Fleet Street things had not been the same. Before, it was much easier to know who was who. There was always someone who knew someone, but now they were scattered all over London, no one really knew what was going on any more, especially with the escalation of freelancing. Information about specific journalists was difficult to obtain, unless of course you were on official police business. And this was definitely official.

After making an appointment with the editor of the *Implant News* publishing company, he arrived there an hour after leaving Cadema's office.

Built during the 1770's the four-story terraced building was situated just off Mansfield Street. It was accessed directly from the street by an oversized bespoke brown-stained oak panelled door with a large ostentatious brass door knob. To open the door, Ross had to ring the bell and state his business into the intercom system.

On entry, he climbed the wide marble staircase, only touching the elaborately carved wooden banister occasionally. Arriving on the second floor, he entered the door to the publishing company. The clerk, a young brown haired girl who looked like she had just left school, gestured for him to take a seat and said she would call Miss Baker to see him. A minute later Miss Jane Baker, a blond woman of about thirty, wearing a red knee-length dress, with shoes to match, smiled as she shook hands with Ross and escorted him to her office.

'As you know I'm here on official police business,' he showed his ID. Miss Baker glanced at it and then asked what it was all about.

'I need to know who wrote this article in your paper today,' he demanded as he reached into his pocket, took out the paper and placed it on the table. Miss Baker shrugged her shoulders.

'Yes, this is the article we published this morning. But I don't know who wrote it. It was sent in by an agency who supply us with stories. I suppose he might be found at Smith and Co, the Consortia of publishers. We get a lot of articles from them as they deal with a plethora of freelancers.'

'Why no "by-line"? Isn't that unusual?'

'Not that unusual. It's cheaper without a "by-line", the writer doesn't get paid as much by the agency and they don't charge us so much for publishing the story.'

'Didn't you think that this was a bit strange?' he asked.

She shook her head:

'That's how business is these days. And if it's from a reputable source, then we will publish. Otherwise an article is rejected. This one was verified and I accepted it. Is it a problem?'

'Not exactly, but I need to find out who the author is so I can speak to him or her.' With reluctance, Miss Baker gave him the address of Smith and Company and said goodbye.

When Ross reached the address in Baker Street, he entered the foyer and took the lift up to the first floor. Speaking into the intercom on the outside door of the office, he explained who he was. A cheerful female voice said 'Come in' as a buzzer sounded. He later discovered her name was Melanie, the receptionist. A blond girl around seventeen, but the heavy make-up made her look much older. Her dress matched the greyness of the shuttered room. After a quick phone call she escorted him into a Mr Connor's office.

Ross was surprised how quiet it was in there considering the noise of the traffic in the street below. He reasoned that the thickness of the walls, together with the heavy curtains, accounted for this. The room was warm, and Mr. Connor's handshake firm. The dimpled smile, and the cherub-like face of the man, and his whole persona, gave Ross the impression that he had known him all his life.

Glancing at the ID, and telling him to call him James, he asked how he could help. After being told about the article, James leaned back in his chair and smiled.

'Oh yes, Natalie Taylor. She's a freelance journalist. Sometimes she writes under other pseudonyms, which I cannot recall at the moment,' he smiled again.

'Thank you, but do you know where she lives?'

James ran his fingers through his thick dark hair.

'Sorry I can't help you there, either. And I don't know when I'll see her again. She just turns up here sometimes for lunch, a chat or when she has a story.'

'How often does she do that?' Ross sounded exasperated.

'I suppose I see her, on average, once a month.' James reached into his pocket, took out his wallet and gave Ross a photograph of Natalie. 'That's the only one I have of her.'

Ross looked at the face of an attractive woman of about twenty-five years old smiling back at him. They were mischievous blue eyes, inquisitive ones that looked as if they could follow him around the room. Half-hidden by the auburn hair which seemed out of place on her pallid complexion, her eyes smiled back at his. He wondered why James had a photograph of her, not her business card.

'I took that in the summer, she had auburn hair then, but she washed it out and now has natural blond hair again,' James said with a matter of fact tone in his voice.

'Why did she change her hair colour?'

'I really don't know. Anyway, I didn't think it was my business to ask. But between you and me, I think it was the murders. She was interested in them. Had her own theories on them. Not that she said much to me, but I could sense the excitement in her voice whenever she mentioned them.'

'How tall is she?' Ross's voice intentionally butted into the narrative.

'Oh, let's see. Yes, I would say she's about five feet six inches tall, and, as you can see, she has blue eyes,' Ross stared at the photograph again. He wanted to keep it, not just for police business though, but for some personal need.

'Would you mind if I took this with me?' he asked, keeping hold of the photograph.

'Yes I do mind. It's the only one I have of her and I don't want to lose it.'

'Why, is she your girlfriend or something?'

'No she is not; I just don't want to lose it that's all,' James answered impertinently at the surmise in Ross's comment.

'I'll see it doesn't get lost,' he said as he placed the photograph into a plastic bag to put it into his pocket. James protested, saying he thought he should ask Natalie for her permission first.

'Well, Sir, you keep it if you like, but I can get a warrant, then you will have to give it to me.'

'A warrant, are you serious. Natalie's not mixed up in anything illegal. She would tell me if she were,' he protested.

Ross gave a twitch of a smile; happy to have an animated reaction from James at last.

'Oh is that so Sir, well I thought you only saw her once a month.'

'That's right, but she always tells me what she does.'

'Always?' Ross frowned as he considered whether he should ask James to accompany him to the police station for questioning, but decided not to.

'Yes, she does when I see her. I suppose if the photograph is so important I'll give you a copy.'

Ross retrieved the photograph from the plastic bag, handed it to James who took it and then walked out of his office and handed it to Melanie. Ross could hear him tell his secretary to scan it into the computer and to do a colour printout.

As soon as he had the photograph, he said goodbye. Speaking to Crown on the telephone, he said he did not have Natalie's address, but was prepared to go with him to see Grimes and hoped that Cadema would not be there. Later Ross stood in front of Crown.

'It certainly looks like the journalist I saw on the front row, but now she has blond hair it's difficult to be sure,' Crown said. 'But with everything that's going on at the moment, I think we can safely ignore it for now. If Cadema wants to peruse it, she can, but I know she's too busy at the moment. I'll handle Grimes if necessary.'

'Thanks, but let that be a lesson to us both and move on.' Ross said, then left the station and headed for his division.

CHAPTER THIRTEEN

Natalie Taylor was happy to have her natural blond hair back again. It wasn't that she didn't like the auburn colour, she simply believed it was not right for her. She was too pale and only experimented with the change of colour after her last boyfriend persuaded her. When she discovered he was married and had a couple of kids, she finished the relationship and changed it back.

In the wake of her new freedom, she now concentrated on her work. When she discovered that all the murder victims had auburn hair, she decided to do some investigations of her own.

Spending a week, both at peak and other times, on the London underground she discovered there were very few people with actual auburn hair. So why had the murderer chosen women with auburn hair? She debated this in her mind for some time, but there were many more things to investigate before she would be able to answer that question.

She phoned her friend James.

'Hi, just though I'd thank you for getting my article published. You're very good to me.'

'You're welcome. But did you know the police are trying to find you because of that.'

'You've got to be kidding. Why should they want to talk to me?'

'Don't know,' he said. And then told her about the photograph, and that he had given her name to the police.

'Oh James, James. You're such a softie. You didn't have to do that. You poor darling, I suppose they put pressure on you.'

'Not really. But you know how it is. I thought they needed to know. Anyway I expected them to find out sooner or later.'

'I suppose you're right. But I'm a bit cross with you for doing it.' She brushed her fingers through her hair and sighed. 'But now you've got me intrigued on what they want me for.'

'Let's hope it's nothing serious. And I hope you're not going to do anything stupid, or put yourself in danger.' James sounded concerned.

'Not at all,' she whispered down the telephone and said goodbye.

Deep down she didn't really blame James, as she knew how intimidating the police could be. And James, seeming on the surface to be strong and assertive, was more like a lamb than a lion. Anyway, the police were the least of her worries. Her career needed boosting, and with the rivalry between her fellow journalists, she decided to do some more investigations without anyone knowing, except James.

These murders were her first real job as a freelance. Everyone wanted to get involved, to do undercover and illegal detective work, and then get into print before anyone else. She hadn't realised how cut-throat they could be. University had never prepared her for this, neither had her last four years as a journalist.

Perhaps she should have listened to her parents when they disapproved of the profession she had chosen. But their opposition only made her more determined to peruse that career. Even when she was grown-up and independent, they still thought she should have studied for a degree to give her a 'real job'. Journalism, to them, was demeaning. That was their opinion, so she stopped trying to please them. Now, since her mother's death a year ago, she just made her dutiful visits at Christmas and birthdays.

She used to have friends who were journalists, but they had moved on, unable to cope with the competition. James O'Connor was the only one who had the tenacity to stay. She appreciated this; sometimes believing he only stayed because of her. But she knew differently. He liked the buzz of the world and the excitement of every story he managed to get.

When James went to a Buckingham Palace Garden Party as a guest of Ruth's, his friend, who was heavily involved in voluntary work, he raved on and on about his experience for weeks. The Royal Family and the ease with which they accepted everyone, the pomp and ceremony, the sandwiches and tea, the whole ambiance of the day had been wonderful to him. The world was wonderful especially when there was something new. Natalie believed he was like a child who had discovered the most magical gift in his Christmas stocking. He seemed mesmerised by everything others took for granted.

Then there were the train crash and the bombings, and through these events she realised how happy James was with high-profile work. So when she needed him, especially with something like murder, he was there for her. He managed to get Natalie's three articles on the Common Murders published without any problems. But she knew, for all his boasting, James didn't really have any money to his name. So when she was finally paid for her articles, she shared the money with him as a 'good will gesture'.

There were just a few more things she needed to investigate and decided to discuss these with James. And with his help, she hoped to find the killer.

'So let's see what we have,' Natalie said as she began to write on the paper on James's desk. 'Four murders, all on or near common ground,' she looked at James and smiled, remembering she was the journalist who had first termed the phrase, *The Common Murders.* She thought it was uncanny, as if she had known all the murders would be committed on commons. Except the one with Madeline Belton, and she didn't believe she was murdered by the same person. Neither did she think Bernard Franklin had murdered her, despite discovering he liked entertaining prostitutes in his car. So leaving Madeline Belton out of her investigations, she concentrated on the other three.

'So why three?' Natalie asked James who shrugged and said he had no idea. 'Maybe there's more than three, but the others haven't been discovered yet.'

'Look Natalie, we've enough to think about at the moment, so don't speculate. We need to stick to what we know.'

'You're right of course. So why women with auburn hair, and what about the dates, and why weekends?'

'Maybe you should just stick to one question at a time?'

'Okay, so what do you suggest we focus on? We don't want to be slow like the police have been, especially as women are beginning to panic?'

'We need to know what the police are intending to do now. I'll look into this if you like, especially with the contacts I have,' James boasted.

'While you're doing that, I'll see what I can find out about the DNA, there must be some explanation as to why it matched Edward Mason's,' Natalie jumped up, looked at her watch and said she needed to get home.

'Just be careful Natalie, I don't want you to be his next victim,' James shook his head, gave her a peck of a kiss on her cheek and walked her to the lift.

'Oh don't worry about me. Everything's going to be all right.' She laughed as she disappeared into the lift.

CHAPTER FOURTEEN

I was beginning to get desperate, not just because one of my victims was not found early enough, but with the blunder with the DNA samples. How was I to know they wouldn't find the right person with the DNA match, especially as there are very few people with the same DNA in the world?

'Thomas you should stop now,' I heard one of the voices in my head say. I had no intention of stopping, and certainly not when I was in control. Originally I felt indifferent towards my victims, who were just the means to an end. But after Sophie Millburn, things had changed. I started to enjoy myself with the excitement of both the stalking and the final kill.

October the fourth in London was warmer than I had expected. Remembering the woman in the pale green suit, I hoped to find her again; if not, there would be others to choose from. But she was still on my mind. Would I be able to recognise her? Nevertheless, I had to find her, the urge to do so was overwhelming.

Walking past Euston railway station, the inclination to go in was so strong, I only hesitated for a moment before succumbing to my predatory instinct. I supposed I might be fortuitous, if I waited long enough, to eventually see the woman. Then laughed at myself for being so ridiculous. For a start there were far too many people in the foyer. I was overwhelmed with the hustle, bustle and shove of the crowds. And, even if she were there, it would be difficult to recognise her in such a mêlée of faces. No, I would have problems enough recognising her if she were close up, as her features had blurred in my mind since I'd last seen her. All I could remember was the auburn hair and pale green suit. Now she could be wearing something completely different. It would be impossible to find her there. I headed for Baker Street instead.

Waiting around the area for as long as I could without drawing attention to myself, I eventually decided to check into a local bed and breakfast place. It was the sort of establishment where no one asked questions. After changing into my city disguise, I nonchalantly sauntered down Baker Street.

The sign to Madam Tussaud's in Marylebone Road caught my attention and for one moment I thought of visiting the place again, but decided against it, especially when I saw the queues. Anyway, I couldn't see the benefits of the Chamber of Horrors, not since I had experienced the real thing. So on I walked, my eyes keenly looking at every female face, some of them turning away as I stared at them.

The day was good to me. When I entered the lobby of the office block, I could see nothing had changed since my last visit. It was empty as before, and, as I scanned the list of corporate names near the lift, I ignored the noise of a door opening behind me.

After scrutinising the list of names etched into the new brass plaque, I decided to leave. But turning round, I faced a man. Where he came from, I didn't know.

'Can I help you?' he said.

'No thanks, I think I must have the wrong building,' I averted my eyes believing he was trying to remember if he had seen me before. Rather than stand around, I left and walked slowly along the road, looking up at buildings now and again, as if I were searching for something. I felt as if the man from the lobby was still watching me as I turned the corner into Marylebone Road again.

As I walked, I remembered the man the woman in the pale green suit had met at Euston station; he was much too old for her. I imagined the type of man she would prefer. He would be handsome, tall and slender with a whiff of arrogance that would be intriguing and attractive to her. He would dress in a manner which pleased her. Savile Row suits sprang to mind. Yes, he would have money, otherwise how could he take her out to restaurants unaffordable to the majority? And she liked dining: good food, good wine and definitely good company. She would only choose someone who matched her specifications.

The man from the lobby was stocky with an unkempt appearance, giving me the impression he had slept at least one night in his somewhat threadbare and unfashionable suit. His dusky looking hair didn't look as if it had been combed all week and his beard definitely needed trimming. No, he could not, in any way, be connected to the woman in the pale green suit.

As I hurried along the road I became somewhat melancholy at the thought of not seeing the woman ever again. Was she just in my imagination? A trick of light perhaps; I wasn't sure any more.

My body had taken over my mind and was taking me further and further away from where I needed to be. I stopped to reassess the situation. It wasn't easy. The voices played with my thoughts, some wanting me to go on; they knew how I felt. Others wanted me to leave, to get away before I was caught. I argued with them, despite knowing, if I lingered too long, I would draw attention to myself. But the urge was too great, I had to go back to Baker Street. The sceptical ones would have to endure that, there was no other alternative.

From my vantage point on the edge of Regents Park, I could see Baker Street and thought of what the famous Detective would have done if he were here now. It pestered me; how would He find out who committed the Common Murders? And as I stood there, I imagined He were there, looking at me through his window, observing me from a distance. The distance of over a hundred years or so, deducing who I was. He would realise I was in disguise. Why would I need to do that? Was I, like him, a private detective solving crimes as He did? No, he would see through that. His eyes would penetrate my very soul and He would deduce that I was a sinister character, in disguise. Therefore I must be someone who could be recognised easily; someone who was known to a lot of people. A famous person perhaps; known to people in higher places. It showed by the clothes I was wearing. And He would believe I regularly changed my disguise, so it would become more and more difficult to discover who I was. People would give descriptions which contradicted other descriptions. But could He recognise me through a million disguises? Would He, could He, see my eyes? See their colour, see what I could see, know what I knew and identify who I really was? He could, I was sure of that. His eyes would penetrate any disguise. Yes He could see me; naked, barren of clothes with a soul of iron which would never melt; even in the jaws of hell. Yes, he knew who I was. And as I turned and walked back down Baker Street passed the Guru's museum, I could not help thinking He was still there watching me, he always would, and after all I was in His territory.

It was now Thursday, I had been waiting to see the woman for four days and believed she would never materialise. The small dingy hotel I had moved to after the bed and breakfast place, was cold and damp with mildew creeping along the walls from the faulty shower room that hadn't been cleaned all week, and most probably all year. I could smell the odour of bodies from centuries ago and imagined it penetrating into ever crevice, and clinging to the, now threadbare, curtains. It mingled with the smell of stale tobacco and ammonia, preventing me from sleeping. So I sat instead in the recliner by the window, as my half-consumed takeaways, crammed into the waste bin, added to the stench.

Of course I could have chosen a better hotel as I had the money, but this had one advantage. It was opposite the office building. If the woman appeared, I wouldn't miss her. I could vacate the room at a moment's notice and be in the street in seconds thanks to the Government and their insistence on easy access for people with disabilities back in 2004. Not that I was disabled, but it served my purpose admirably.

Boredom began to set in as I waited at my window, scrutinising the street below. The voices in my head were getting worse. They tormented me so much, I felt like jumping out of the window just to get some peace. In fact, some of them tempted me to do just that. So I tossed and turned in the recliner, trying to snatch even the smallest wink of sleep.

The waiting clawed at my patience. I began to doubt whether she would ever show up. Perhaps she was on holiday? Perhaps I'd picked the wrong week? When the morning finally arrived, I decided to go back into the lobby to see if I could find out which office she had visited. Staring at the list of names I had seen before, nothing was obvious. Jones, Jones and Jones were the solicitors on the sixth floor, Martin and Keys on the fifth, Frank and Allan Nicholas, Logistics on the fourth, Blue and Son on the third and Smith and Company, consortia of publishers on the second. It appeared that the first floor was vacant. I shook my head but as I turned to go, I felt the presence of someone behind me.

'Can I help you, Sir?' a soft friendly voice echoed in the empty lobby. I turned and looked into ocean blue eyes. It was her, the woman I was waiting for, but as I expected, she was not wearing the light green suit. Neither did she have auburn hair. Her hair was blond. It hung in strands below the red knitted hat which pedantically matched her gloves, scarf and boots. I could see the black tailored pin-striped trousers and jacket, were bespoke. *This woman*, I thought, *dripped taste*; I could almost feel the nectar of her on my tongue. The seconds seemed like hours, as I struggled for an answer to her question.

'No thank you, I think I've got the wrong building. I'll try next door,' I needed to get out of the building fast and think of what to do next.

'Who are you looking for?'

'Weaver and Walker the architects,' I hoped it sounded genuine.

'I'm sorry but I've never heard of them as I don't work here, and don't know the area. But my friend might know. He's on the second floor. If you wait here I'll see if he knows which block they're in.'

'Oh no, please don't go to so much trouble, it's not urgent. I'll try next door'

'Don't be silly,' she insisted.

I mumbled something. She had just put the first screw in her coffin. She was too open, as if she had known me for a long time; *just like Madeline Belton*, I thought. But she will not get away like Madeline had? No, I'd spent far too much time tracking her down.

'Well, if you insist,' I half-smiled.

As she disappeared into the lift to the second floor, my feet hardly touched ground as I ran out of the building, across the street and up into my room. I stood panting and looked through the window.

She had seen me—seen me close up. I needed to change and change fast. She would be able to recognise me, perhaps in any disguise? She saw the real me. My face. My complexion. My nose. But most of all my eyes, and therefore my soul.

My room was cold as I stood at the window and inched the curtains for a better look with my theatre binoculars. In the time it took for me to leave the lobby and reach my window, she had met with Him. They were now standing in the street below eagerly looking up and down the road, no doubt hoping to see the man she had met moments earlier.

She was more attractive than I remembered. Her round full face with two well defined dimples, the blue eyes that had quizzed at my features, were now smiling at Him. I could almost tell what she was thinking as she stood in the street below. Her thick pink lips speaking words I could not hear. I imagined feeling the vibrations of invisible wires that travelled through the gap between us; neurons firing upon neurons. We, that is, the others within me, felt the electricity between us as it arced in fury across the resistance of the aura which surrounded us. We met in the space between, gained the energy to penetrate the resistance of our flesh and entered into each other's minds. Oh, yes, she knew who I was, and I knew who she was—not by names, as names meant nothing now. I knew her and she was with Him, the friend from the second floor. He was not the man I had seen her with when she took the train out of Euston.

This man was a meek twenty-five year old or there about. He had a gaunt long face with dimples mirroring hers. They could have been siblings if she had not referred to him as her friend. He looked like a good friend, protecting, caring, anxious to meet the person she had met in the lobby. He stood there scratching his thick dark hair, as if the answer lay buried in the dandruff that probably littered his shoulders. They stood miming together, his body towering a foot above hers as his pin-striped trousers revealed his socks; defying any tailor. They almost looked comical together, he in his short sleeved shirt ready for the central-heated office, she in her thick designer winter trouser suit.

Second floor, I whispered to myself; second floor. I closed my eyes to visualise the plaque in my mind and then searched the list of names; yes, yes of course the Consortia of Publishers. Was he a publisher and she a writer? But she hadn't been carrying a manuscript. No, I believed she was meeting Him because He was her friend. She needed to talk to Him about something personal. They would go to lunch, and then she would go home. But I couldn't follow her now, she had seen me. So I waited until they disappeared back into the building. Then I escaped knowing I would meet her again under different circumstances.

It had begun to rain, and it, together with the noise of bustling traffic smothered the sounds of human feet. The spikes of dripping umbrellas prodding at my head like a million beaks as I headed for the sanctuary of the underground. As I clutched my Oyster card, the thought of the woman still lingered in my mind. But the frustration I was feeling was so great that the voices began to argue again.

They said, the police had all the evidence they needed and would make an arrest soon, so I should go home and be happy with the work I had done. I was not satisfied, I had to go on, as the urge for killing had taken over. Thomas was in full charge now.

CHAPTER FIFTEEN

After looking up and down the street, Natalie and James decided the visitor from the lobby had vanished. Why he hadn't waited for James to arrive they couldn't imagine but guessed he was in the wrong street. After returning to the office to get James's coat, they went out for lunch and sat in a quiet spot at the back of the café.

'I haven't found out much about the murders,' Natalie said. 'What have you found?' She sipped at her cappuccino.

'You've got,' he gestured with his index finger across his upper lip to mime she had froth there. Natalie wiped it away. 'I've not found much. Only that Superintendent Sharma was furious with your article. But I don't think the police have much more than we have.'

'Well, I have a theory,' she bit into the Danish pastry and then took the last gulp of her coffee. 'I think the perpetrator has a grudge against women with auburn hair.'

'If he has then why leave his DNA as a calling card?' James swallowed the last part of his smoked salmon and cream cheese sandwich.

'I believe he wants to be found. Anyway the DNA will give him away sooner or later,'

'Yes, but how much later? Every passing minute means that someone else is in danger. And so far the DNA has proved useless. You only have to look at the fiasco with Edward Mason. He's no killer,' James argued.

'No, but his twin brother could be.' Natalie smiled as James nearly choked on his black coffee.

'Twin brother? He doesn't even have a brother, let alone a twin. Or have you found something no one else knows?' James leaned across the table.

'No I haven't, but I think he must be a twin. And what's more, I believe they may have been separated at birth for some reason, most probably because his mother could not cope with two babies at the same time.'

'That's pure speculation and I am surprised at you for thinking such a thing when you are normally quite rational.'

His condescending tone made her recoil.

'You're surprised? What about your attitude? You know how analytical I am, so don't judge me. I was only verbalising my thoughts, so we can discuss all the possibilities. Anyway you don't usually criticise me for divergent thinking. So why are you being obnoxious now?'

'I'm not being obnoxious as you put it; I am mealy being objective; looking at the facts,' he smiled.

'I've done that too. The facts are all there. They have DNA. The DNA belongs to someone in the Mason family. It matched Edward's. So there can only be one other explanation.'

'But when you spoke to Edward and afterwards wrote the article about him, did he say he had a twin brother?'

'No.'

'Did you get the feeling he has one and he is hiding this fact?'

'No.'

'And if the police believed he had a brother, wouldn't they be pursuing him?'

'I suppose so, but I believe...'

'No matter what you believe, it isn't fact. So get real Natalie.'

'Don't laugh at me,' she fidgeted. 'But going back to the DNA, he must have a twin brother and I intend to find him.' She leaned further over the table and whispered. 'That's where you come in James,' she fluttered her eyelashes and gingerly smiled.

'No, Natalie; definitely not, not this time. I don't think it's a good idea. What if there is a twin, and I don't suppose there is. But if there were, what would we do if we found him and he turned out to be the killer? He could easily kill us; he'd have nothing to lose,' James frowned, sat back in his seat and folded his arms.

'Oh don't be so melodramatic. Anyway, I wasn't expecting to meet him, just to make some enquiries and find out where he lives, that's all.'

'So what's the point?'

'The point is that we can then go to the police. And we would have helped to solve these crimes.'

'Mmm...,' he leaned further forward and whispered. 'You've got a good point there. I don't like the idea, but if you are so determined I suppose I'll have to go along with your plan. Besides I don't want anything to happen to you. But you have to know that I don't like it one little bit.'

'I know, you've said it often enough. Nevertheless, you're a star James, a real star,' she bent across the table and gave him a kiss on his forehead. 'A star that's great,' she continued.

'That's a matter of opinion, anyway you can have the scoop, I don't want anything to do with it, it's too dangerous.'

'Oh, come on James don't be such a spoil sport. You used to say the fun is in the chase. I remember when you were eager to find the pseudo Kray twins. And your methods paid off. So much so that when you phoned the police with the information you managed to prevent a shoot-out with rival gangs long before any of our other colleagues knew what was happening.'

'Yes, and look how they all ostracized me, it took me ages to get back into journalism again and even now they are suspicious. Mark my words Natalie, they will treat you in the same way.'

'I'm not bothered about me. But I was proud of you, so please help me now. Together we'll find the answers. I do really need your support on this. Besides, I bet you're broke again,' she searched his eyes, looking for the answer.

'I'm okay at the moment. Had a win on the horses earlier this week, so my bank manager has given me some reprieve; at least for the moment.'

'That's great,' there was some disappointment in her voice at him gambling again.

'I can see you disapprove. And I always know when you're trying to butter me up. Especially when you flirt, like you are at the moment. And I know it's part of your fun before I make the final decision in your favour Natalie. So yes, I will help you. But this one's yours baby,' he said in a *James Cagney* accent and gave a smile which emphasised his dimples.

'You're a darling, James,' Natalie said kissing him again with her usual exaggerated peck as James shrugged with a little embarrassment as other diners looked on.

'Okay that's enough, just promise me you'll be careful,' his hand reached across the table and kissed hers.

'Oh, go away, stop teasing,' she giggled.

'Well I'll find out all I can from the birth records of the time and see what transpires, but I'm not promising anything. You keep your head low and don't do anything without telling me first, promise? I'll phone you in a couple of days.'

'Okay,' she said as the chairs screeched across the tiled floor when they both stood up together. With a kiss on the cheek, they said goodbye and headed down Baker Street in opposite directions.

***

Natalie recalled that when she had interviewed Edward before, he was happy for the press to splatter his details about his MS over the tabloids. But when she asked him about his mother, he had changed the subject. This made her believe he would disapprove of any media coverage surrounding his birth. So she decided not to tell him what she had in mind. Instead she hoped James would be able to come up with the answers she needed.

Having discovered Edward Mason's date of birth, James renewed his membership to several online ancestry archives. After spending many long hours trawling through these, he managed to discover many entries for the date in question. Eliminating those which seemed unlikely he was left with one which sounded plausible. It referred to a Miss Connie Mason recording the birth of Edward Stuart Mason. When he told Natalie, they decided to find Miss Mason and somehow gain her confidence before asking her about her son's birth.

James managed to find Connie Mason a couple of days later, after he had spoken to a close friend who said Connie Mason had been in the court room when her son was charged with possession of cannabis. Not only that, but he knew where she lived as he had followed her home just in case he needed to find her again in a hurry. James, although concerned to realise how vulnerable older people were in London, nevertheless thanked his friend and made a note of the address.

***

Natalie and James were let into the building by an unsuspecting resident. The four-story tenement building, on the edge of Camden, had been built not long after the last world war and now looked unkempt. As they scanned the area they could see why Edward never visited his mother. There was simply no access for wheelchairs despite the current legislation. It was obvious to them the local authority had neglected the place which was confirmed by the 'for demolition' notice on the side of the building.

'That explains a lot,' James nodded at the sign as they walked towards Miss Mason's flat. They waited without saying a word for a reaction to their knock on a door which, at one time, had been painted green. James knocked again. Now they could hear a muted low voice, and the shuffle of feet on the surface behind the door, giving the impression there were no carpets. At the sound of the chain slipping into place, James knocked again and said who he was. The door creaked open a little.

'Are you Miss Connie Mason?' Natalie asked in a loud whisper.

'Yes,' she confirmed in an anxious and angry voice. 'Who are you and what do you want?'

'Sorry to disturb you Miss Mason but we need to talk to you about Edward. I'm Natalie, the woman who spoke to your son and wrote the article in the paper.'

The slamming of the door was the only noise that broke the cacophony of voices, traffic, hooters, sirens, the thud of the underground and some children happily screeching somewhere in the tenement. The door remained shut, but the fumbling inside gave the impression the door was about to open. When it did, a woman of about seventy, dressed in designer clothing and wearing high heeled shoes, stood before them. Connie's dark brown hair showed no signs of grey, but the complexion of her skin and grey eyes, said she was usually fair and had not made a good choice of hair colour.

Natalie stood without saying anything for a few seconds. It was only the sound of Connie's voice, asking her who was with her, that jogged her to react.

'Sorry, this is James, the editor of the article I wrote.'

Connie eyed him with suspicion.

'How do I know I can trust him?' her eyes scanned James from top to toe as she spoke.

'I've known him for such a very long time, I can vouch for him, he's totally trustworthy.'

'Well if you say so, you had better come in. The neighbours are nosey here, don't miss anything,' Connie said. As they entered, Connie walked past them and peered out along the balcony to see if anyone was looking; and then came back and slammed the door.

Asking them to follow her, they entered a small over-furnished living room where even the odour of lavender failed to hide the fusty smell. An accumulation of a lifetime of once smart furniture, which for some reason could not be thrown out, greeted them. On the mantelpiece a collection of memorabilia suggested a fondness of trips to Spain, but from Connie's pale completion, Natalie guessed it had been some time since her last visit there.

Seating herself into a large leather reclining chair, Connie nodded to the settee of ageing leather, indicating that they should sit there. She continued to eye James with suspicion and asked him somewhat abruptly:

'So what do you want? Stirring up more trouble for my poor son, hey?' she snarled.

'No, we hope this may benefit him. But thank you for agreeing to see us without an appointment, Mrs Mason...' Natalie was halted in mid-sentence by Connie.

'Miss, if you don't mind. I've never been married. Never thought it was necessary. Okay, so it was a stigma getting pregnant in the seventies if you weren't married. But that's life isn't it? Water under the bridge. So please call me Connie.' She tugged at her short skirt to hide the mark of a recently repaired varicose vein. Natalie opened her mouth to speak, but Connie interrupted her again:

'So you're the one who wrote the article about him?' she looked at Natalie whose pose could have been considered confrontational if she hadn't leaned backwards with her hands together resting loosely on her lap. Added to this was the caring and sympathetic look she gave to Connie.

'I'm afraid I did...' Natalie started to say.

'Why are you afraid girl? I thought it was a good article. Told the police a thing or two, that's what they need. Think they can do as they like, they do. It's about time they were told some home truths.'

'Yes I agree, and thank you for saying you liked my article.'

'And Eddie liked it too.'

'Eddie?' Natalie asked with a frown on her face.

'Yes, Eddie. My son Edward. He gave me a description of you. As soon as I saw you at the door, I knew who you were. So what do you want to know?' Connie smiled and sat relaxed into her chair.

James cleared his throat in his usual manner when he was uncomfortable about what he was going to ask. Natalie did the same, as if James had given her an unwritten cue.

'This is a very delicate matter Connie, and if you would rather not answer we will understand. But before I ask, there's one thing that's been puzzling us. It's the DNA which matches your son's DNA. We don't believe for one minute Edward is a killer, though,' James said in a quiet reassuring voice.

'Thank God for that. But the police told me as much yesterday. So what have these murders got to do with my son?'

'The police called on you yesterday?'

'Yes, a Detective Inspector Evans. He left me his card.' Connie stood up and retrieved it from behind the statue of a bull in full fighting mode on the mantelpiece and handed it to James.

'What did the chief inspector want to know?' Natalie interrupted gingerly.

'He just asked me about my son and said they were still looking for someone else. That, if I had any information which would help with their enquiries, I was to let him know,' she said curtly.

'And do you?' the question rebounded like a reflex action from Natalie before she had time to think. Now she seemed uncomfortable in her chair as she looked at Connie.

'Do I what?'

'Know anything else?' Natalie blushed.

'Of course I don't. Is that why you've come to talk to me? If it is then I've nothing else to say on the matter,' there was anger in Connie's raised voice.

'Sorry, but I need to ask you this.' Connie's eyes narrowed as Natalie spoke. 'Did the police ask you if you had another son?' Natalie shuffled in her seat and coughed. 'I know it's difficult and realise how you must be feeling, but it's important. Does Edward have a brother?'

At this question, Connie rose to her feet and stood with her hands on her hips looking down at Natalie, and with her voice raised another pitch, said:

'A brother? What's going on here? A brother? I don't have another son.' Her eyes narrowed as she examined Natalie's face, who was now standing in front of Connie. 'No. I've only been pregnant once.'

'I'm sorry but I have to ask another question and I know how it may sound; but was Edward a twin?'

'How dare you! No, he was not a twin, but I know what you are thinking. You think I had twins and gave one of them away at birth. That's what the police think too. But no. No, I would never do such a thing. I assure you I did not give birth to twins. I think I would have noticed! Now get out and don't ever call on me again,' Connie turned and raced along the hallway. Natalie and James followed, but before they could say anything Connie opened the door to let them out. They tried to say sorry as they left, but Connie was too upset to listen. She slammed the door behind them.

***

Connie stood with her back to the door, her mind transfixed in thought. She had denied giving birth to twins, but now. . . In a flash, she was back in the labour room where she had given birth to Edward. She remembered going into labour hours after her waters had broken.

No one had told her what the birth was going to be like. She imagined she would have stomach ache and the baby would be born when it was ready. It would be simple; a natural phenomenon. All she had to do was to take the gas and air when she felt a pain, and the pain would go away; it didn't. It kept on, and on, and on. She had screamed and twisted with each contraction, trying to wriggle out of the situation. She arched her back, and gritted her teeth. It felt as if her abdomen would burst. She begged the midwife to give her something stronger, something she could not remember the name of now, but that she had read about in a leaflet another midwife had given her when she went to her local clinic. The midwife at the clinic was reassuring and sympathetic, as if she knew what Connie was about to go through.

But the labour room midwife, Sister Pearson they called her, was indifferent to her needs, hard and unsympathetic. Connie remembered she gave orders which would impress a commandant in a concentration camp. She gave Connie the impression she hated unmarried pregnant women. 'The girlies,' Connie remembered her and the others being called.

Sister Pearson had refused to give her anything stronger, besides she was in a cottage hospital, not a big hospital, therefore there were no facilities; she would just have to manage with the gas and air. Anyway it was considered to be too late to give her anything stronger, she had said.

'The baby is coming soon; you don't want to distress the baby now, do you?'

But how soon was soon? The thought of how long Connie had to wait terrified her. So she took deep breaths of the gas, taking every last breath of what was left in the cylinder, until it was empty. The second cylinder soothed the pain a little but by that time she was exhausted so between her contractions, she fell into what she thought must have been a deep sleep.

She remembered the midwife roughly examining her; the dreaded 'internal' and muttering everything was okay. She said the baby would be born in the next couple of hours. That everything would be all right. But the next pain and the one afterwards were overwhelming, until Connie could stand it no longer and inhaled so deeply into the mask that she felt the gas burn as it drifted like fog around her body. She was limp but conscious.

In her dream-like state she remembered the rustle of aprons, rattle of surgical instruments against stainless steel bowls; the smell of anaesthetic. The release of tension when something slithered out of her—when birth has surely happened, only to experience the same feelings moments later. But she was too exhausted to move or even open her eyes.

The eerie silence of the room and the muffled voices emanating from the sluice, where she knew the midwife took the afterbirth, soothed her. She was unafraid, relieved and sleepy. Then the reality awakened her senses; there were no hearty cries of a new-born, there were no cries, no slap of a hand on an unsuspecting bum. All Connie could hear was the running water, muffled voices and the grunt from the bottom of the bed as the doctor put the last two stitches into her perineum.

The midwife returned, 'all done doctor?' she said as Connie's legs were taken out of the stirrups. It was then that she had been told she had a baby boy weighing six pound four ounces. That he was all right but had been put in an incubator, 'to warm him up,' and she could see him the next morning.

She remembered someone saying how well she had done, but that wasn't Sister Pearson. They said what a handsome baby she had, but she must rest and stay in bed. If she needed the toilet she should ask for a bed pan. The pain was over. The overdue sleep engulfed her.

She was grateful another midwife had brought the baby to her at six the next morning and hoped she would not have to see Sister Pearson again; she never did.

When Connie took hold of the little bundle of white string blankets she had to forage inside, like a child peeping at a present before she was supposed to, and expecting to be reprimanded at any moment. Her smile turned to a grimace when she saw the contents of the bundle. Her 'big baby' as the midwife had called him in the antenatal clinic, now looked like a withered old man, half-starved at the gate of life.

Even her GP had said it was going to be a big baby, so she had expected something different and wondered if there had been a mix up at birth. But with all her faults, she could not imagine Sister Pearson mixing anything up, let alone a baby; why the very thought of her being accused of such a thing would have been a death sentence to any accuser.

There wasn't a mix up; it was Connie's baby all right, its labels said as much. Anyway it looked just like its father. It smelled just like her. There was no mix up, but she couldn't help wondering why her baby was so small.

She was still standing by the front door in her hallway when the telephone interrupted her reminiscences. By the time she had reached the sanctuary of her living room, it had stopped ringing. But the scene of the cottage hospital was still fresh in her mind. Connie remembered how proud she was of Eddie, who had thrived so well and grew into a healthy and loving child. When he was diagnosed with MS she was devastated, especially as there had never been any hint of a disability in her family. Suspicion entered her mind again, but she couldn't confide in anyone, least of all Eddie. So her doubts were hidden until today; now they would never go away.

Could Eddie have been a twin? Could the second baby have been stolen from her at birth? If there was a second baby, perhaps it had died at birth and they had hidden it from her. But what if she had had another son and he was born alive and healthy? Was he given to someone else? Did he become a killer? Is that why the DNA at the murder scenes matched Eddie's? If he were alive, where did he go when they took him away from her? He must have been raised by another family, so did they believe he was their son. Perhaps their son had been born dead and they swapped the two babies at birth? Who could have swapped them? Not Sister Pearson, the regimental tyrant. But suppose she had ordered them to do it? Surely the staff at the hospital would not support such a practice. Anyway if she had had twins, wouldn't Eddie's brother have MS too? If he has MS, then he could not be a killer either.

She went cold, recalling there were two sets of twins in her family. When she finally went to bed that night, the cascade of questions kept her awake. It was like a court room full of accusers; and she in the dock being cross-examined.

**

Natalie and James did not speak as they walked to the car. They were still shocked and felt numb as they fastened their seatbelts and James turned on the ignition.

'Do you believe Connie?' James asked as he drove off.

'Yes and no is my answer. She may be telling the truth as she sees it. She could have given birth to twins, felt that she could not cope with two babies, especially in the seventies, when unmarried mothers did not have the support they have now.'

'I know what you mean; they were stigmatized in those days. So she could have decided to give one away secretly.'

'She could have. People used to do that quite a bit. I read about a woman who was going to give her unborn baby away, although she was married. There was a hell of a public outcry at the time. But she ended up keeping it. The press at the time had a field day with that case.'

'God, you do read some things Natalie. I expect it would have been much worse if she hadn't been married.'

'Not really, if you were unmarried you would never have brought media attention to yourself.'

'Of course. So she could have given the baby away and no one would have known outside the hospital.'

'That's right, James.'

'And if she had done, then legally she was not the parent.'

'Right again,' she said condescendingly as James smiled. He was out of his depth with the conversation, but willing to show his ignorance in front of Natalie.

'So she isn't lying, only evading the truth.'

'Yes, you saw how she fidgeted when I asked her the questions, a sure sign something was amiss. That means we'll have to dig deeper to find out what's going on.'

'Dig deeper, but she won't let us in again?' he said credulously. 'So how do we dig deeper?'

'Oh stop whinging, James,' she said in her usual light hearted way. 'There are other ways to find out what we want to know.'

'I'm not sure I like the sound of 'we', so what do you have in mind?' he turned a corner and just missed knocking a cyclist who was wobbling in the road. 'Damn nuisance,' he whispered under his breath. Natalie decided not to answer as he hated driving into London and was only doing it as a favour to her.

'Hospital records, the staff at the hospital at the time, Registers of Births, courts for adoption, there's plenty to choose from, it's just making the right choice and finding the right documents, that's all,' she boasted.

'There you go again with your 'told you so' attitude. You know it irritates me. All I need to do right now is to get back to my office and finalise the day's work. So you make the priority list and I will help you when I can.'

'No problem. But let's hope we can find all the answers before the police do.' Natalie replied as they reached their destination and said goodbye.

CHAPTER SIXTEEN

Cadema was unhappy when she heard what Evans had to say about his visit to Miss Connie Mason.

'I know it sounds incredulous, but she doesn't appear to know anything much about her son's birth at the Wayford Hospital,' he said.

'How could she not know anything? She was the one who had been pregnant and had Edward. I think she knows everything including the fact that she had another son and had him adopted. There's no other explanation for it.'

'I agree Ma'am. I think she is lying through her teeth and we need to put pressure on her.'

'That's not my method. But I'm determined to find the truth. We need to find the relevant birth records and registration documents. These should provide us with evidence to corroborate this.'

Cadema was doubtful about her own theory; something she resorted to when things were not going well. Not only that, but she couldn't even apply Jim Logan's philosophy. She could not see the whole picture. So perhaps Jim was right when he said she needed more experience in the job before being promoted. Was her inexperience beginning to show? And if so, how long would it take for her colleagues to notice?

After thanking Evans and assigning him to other Actions, she did some online background research on the Wayford Hospital, then contacted Julia.

'Hello, its Cadema here,' she sucked at her lip.

'Hi, what can I do for you?' Julia answered.

'I know its nine thirty, and you're probably getting ready for bed, but do you have a couple of minutes, I need your advice.'

'You mean you need at least an hour to confirm what you are thinking, I know you too well,' she gave a little laugh.

'You're right as usual. I need to get the records of Edward Mason's birth from the Wayford Hospital. But before I do I want to make sure I don't miss anything out.'

'Told you so, you've probably identified all you need to find out,' Julia replied with some sarcasm.

'Maybe, but am I right in thinking that, now matrons are back in hospitals, they do the same role as they did in the 1970's?'

'The answer to that is yes and no.'

'Please stop teasing me Julia—I'm not in the mood. Just tell me. I haven't got time for quizzes, or your dry sense of humour.'

'Sorry. Yes, the title returned some time ago, but they don't have overall responsibility, not like they used to have in the past. They used to practically run the whole hospital. No doubt you've seen the *Carry On* films?'

'No, I haven't.'

'Just as well, because it's not like that these days. They mainly manage the nursing staff, teach and do research now.'

'But would they have managed midwives in the seventies?'

'Oh yes, they would have done.'

'Thanks Julia that's all I wanted to know.'

'Are you sure there is nothing else,' Julia probed as she yawned. She knew Cadema had a way of avoiding things when she was investigating delicate matters. Besides, she could tell by the hesitation in her voice she had something else she wanted to ask.

Cadema cleared her throat. 'There is something.'

'Go on, I'm listening.'

'I've found out that the current matron at the hospital is Stephanie Granger. I haven't interviewed her yet, but Stephanie's mother, Jessica North, was matron when Edward Mason was born.'

'So are you going to interview Jessica?'

'No, unfortunately she died four years ago but apparently she kept copious records of her experiences in the sixties and seventies. I'm going to examine the archives and at the same time take a look at the notes she made.'

'Well, good luck, you'll certainly have your work cut out. But if you have any problems with the medical terminology, I'll be happy to help. No need to worry about the cost, I'll do it from pure interest.'

'That's great. I'll see what I can find out first, then, if I have any problems, I'll let you know.'

'Good, I look forward to the update soon, bye.'

***

Back in her office next morning, Cadema picked up the telephone. A male voice answered.

'Sargent Marriott, come to my office as soon as you can I have some work I need you to do,' her tone sounded like an order rather than a request.

'Yes Ma'am,' he stood to attention and replaced the telephone. Taking the last swallow of his bacon sandwich, he smothered his hair with his fingers and headed down the corridor. Standing outside Cadema's office, he tapped on the door:

'Come in Marriott,' she shouted. He entered and stood facing her. 'Good. I want you to organise a warrant to search the maternity records at the Wayford Hospital for nineteen-seventy-five. And here take this,' she handed him a sheet of A-four paper. 'These are the questions I want you to find the answers to as you search through the files.'

'Thank you Ma'am, but it sounds quite a task.' He glanced at the list.

'Oh don't worry, I'm not expecting you to do it all on your own. You can organise for a couple of PCs to help.'

'Thank you Ma'am, will do,' he said goodbye and left the room.

Although Sergeant Marriott didn't really know what Cadema wanted, he wasn't going to ask. Instead he would read the list she had given him in the hope that his mission would become clearer. Besides Cadema preferred officers who could use their initiative. Instead of having problems, they needed to have solutions. Once he'd found solutions he could report back to her. So, before he took any action, he returned to the main office and read the whole list.

1. Who was in charge of the hospital at that time?

2. Who was working there in the 1970's – names and addresses of all staff in the maternity unit at the time?

3. Are they all still alive?

4. What were the names and addresses of the patients who were in the maternity unit during the time Connie Mason was there? – and up to date ones if they have moved.

5. Exact dates of birth of all babies delivered when Edward Mason was born, including any stillbirths.

6. If there were there any stillbirths; what were the mother's names?

7. How many babies were born to each mother; were there any record of twins being born?

8. How long were mothers in hospital? – exact dates of admission and discharge

9. Were any babies put forward for adoption?

10. What were the rules about adoption? Did the babies stay with the mother while adoptions were being arranged?

11. Did mothers have to personally hand over their babies for adoption?

12. Are there any documents that look suspicious? For example, are pages missing, are there crossings outs, use of codes; that sort of thing.

Marriott had to admit to himself that the plethora of questions were quite daunting. He could see the logic in some of them, while others were a bit nebulous. What were the rationales for some of the questions? And especially about the process for adoptions during the nineteen-seventies. He decided to ask her.

When Cadema explained that legislation on adoption had changed since then, he was happier about it. And with a good team to help him, he expected to find the answers from the patient's notes and records in the hospital's archives. So armed with the warrant, and with the two police constables, he was ready for the next morning.

Cadema reported to Chief Superintendent Grimes, who said he was happy with the work she was doing. Philip Crown was a different matter. He seemed annoyed about something. Was it to do with the fiasco about the press conference, or was it more personal? For some reason he wanted to know, in the smallest detail, what was going on. When challenged, he said he needed to keep abreast of the media coverage, just to keep them happy. What he meant by 'keep them happy' she didn't really know, but hoped that Crown would be more discrete with the press in the future.

The urge to discover what had been going on at the hospital had robbed Cadema of the sleep she needed. By morning she had decided to go to the hospital with Marriott and speak to the matron herself. When she called at his home, before he had had time to dress himself, she knew he was annoyed with her even though he did not say as much.

'I know it's early, but I thought we could get there before the rush-hour,' she said as the Sergeant took a bite of his toast and then a gulp of his coffee.

'I'll wait in the car.'

She didn't see his scowl as she turned to leave.

'There's trust for you,' he muttered to his wife. 'Gives me a job then muscles in on it, it's like she doesn't trust me to do it properly,' he groaned. Dressing quickly, he gave a peck of a kiss on his wife's cheek and then left.

***

Picking up the two constables on the way, they arrived at the cottage hospital just before nine o'clock. It was not the Victorian-type building Cadema had expected. Instead, she was faced with a prefabricated, end of World War Two add-on, which she considered to have long passed its demolition date. As she, with the others in tow, walked down the ever-sloping maze of corridors which groaned from the pain of its scuffed surfaces, she expected to end up in the dungeons of the building. But after ascending and descending flights of stairs, that didn't appear to have any function except to hinder the traffic of patients, she faced two opaque polythene overlapping doors with smears of what looked like excrement on them.

The pungent smell of stale anaesthetic lingering in the air brought back her fears of the dentist. While the fumes from the boiler room and the tang of festering blood and dressings, emanating from the bins of rubbish, nauseated her. As they emerged from the add-on building and entered a courtyard, she took a deep breath. But in the stagnant air, she could still smell the remnants of anaesthetic which had probably seeped into the very bricks of the building over the decades. She looked at Marriott, but he seemed unaffected, *probably because he smoked*, she thought. Then she became aware of a figure facing her. The woman was tall and stout, dressed in a smart blue striped suit, standing century like, baring her entrance to the gothic building that was flanked by the add-ons.

'Hello, I am Superintendent Sharma.' She held out her police identification badge, then turned and introduced Marriott and the two PCs.

'Pleased to meet you, I'm the Matron, Stephanie Granger we spoke on the phone. Did you have any problems finding the place?' she said holding out her hand and giving a grimace of a smile at Cadema, ignoring the rest of the team.

'No not really, I knew where the hospital was, but I expected to find something quite different.'

'Yes, I know what you mean, it's very old and we are in the process of moving out to a new wing at the general, four miles away.'

'Oh I see, so that's why the place is so sparse? By the way, how old is the hospital?' Cadema said trying to sound interested but she really only wanted to know about the records.

'The original part was built in 1858 by families and friends of the local community. It was handed over after the 1944 Act and became part of the NHS in 1948.'

Cadema grunted and gave the necessary polite 'mmms,' as she listened to the history of Wayford Hospital.

'It was a great hospital then, but as the population grew, especially after the War, it had to be extended in 1956, just before my mother became Matron here.'

Stephanie's voice went on and on so much, Cadema decided to change the subject before Stephanie could recite the whole of the hospital's history. With a bluff of an apology for being early, Cadema asked about the archive room.

'Oh yes, of course, do forgive me. I am sorry I do go on a bit. But as you can see this hospital is part of my heritage. Especially as my mother was here, I'm sorry it all has to go. But look at this. The glass in this door has been here since it was built, and although the wording has faded a bit, you can just make out 'Wayford Hospital, 1858' engraved on it. And I am pleased to say they have had the sense to preserve it. So it's going to be restored and will be fitted to the front door of the new wing,' Stephanie said excitedly.

'That's great,' Cadema tried her best to appear interested. 'I hope it all goes very well. But I know how busy you must be and I don't want to keep you from your work Matron.' She showed her the search warrant. 'Now if you will take us to the archive room we will get on with our investigation.'

Stephanie glanced at the document: 'Yes, that looks in order. I'll take you there. No idea what you'll find though. I am very busy, as you say, but I have made arrangements to stay with you. I hope you don't mind, but after all the archives are hospital property and I have responsibility for them.' Cadema was just about to say she appreciated her concern, but Stephanie didn't give her the chance. 'In any case, I know how the archives work. You won't be able to find anything without my help.'

'That's not a problem to us, we expected someone to be there anyway. But please remember, this is all confidential.'

'Oh don't bother about that, our Nursing and Midwifery Council would have me struck off if I breached confidentiality. And I would then lose my job in the Trust. So you can count on my integrity. But I'm a bit concerned, as the archives had not been touched for many years. But I trust you'll find what you're looking for,' Stephanie said, hoping they would not find anything to incriminate her mother.

Leaving the add-on, they entered the older building. The winding and undulating corridors eventually led them down tread worn concrete steps of a cellar, and into, what resembled, an ancient crypt; *as cold as death itself,* Cadema thought and shivered.

The height of the ceiling meant even Cadema had to bend her neck to avoid scraping it as she brushed away numerous cobwebs which tenaciously gripped its surface.

From the metal-clad doors and the padlock, it was obviously a secure place that had not been opened for decades. Stephanie continued her mutterings as she had done during the whole journey. Cadema had not been listening before, now she had tuned in.

'Yes here we are. As secure as a bank, all as I need now is the right key.'

Cadema ignored Stephanie, instead she concentrated on the questions she would ask her when they were alone in her office.

'Here we are,' she began to pull on a chain deep within her hip pocket. The bunch of keys gave a protesting clang as she extracted them. Like a jailer, she examined each one in turn until she found the oldest, then forced it into the padlock. After a couple of turns, the lock gave way and its top sprang open. The metal doors grated and groaned as if in agony as Stephanie pulled them apart along the grooves of some unkempt tracks. Finally, they came to a halt, leaving just enough room to enter, one at a time.

Each person shuddered as they entered the musty, damp and dismal room. Marriott was the last. Bending his head, he had squeezed through the gap. Gradually standing upright he began to smile when he realised there was at least two foot of space between his head and the ceiling.

'I think you'll find the files are in alphabetical order,' Stephanie said as she pulled the switch to the only light in the area. And then pointed to the left where the first set of shelving, stacked with files, could just be seen in the gloom.

'Please don't be put off by the way they are piled on top of each other. They were excellent at keeping records in the past, not like nowadays, when many a case is lost to the plaintive because some midwife or doctor couldn't be bothered to keep contemporaneous records, and trusted everything to memory.'

Marriott shook his head and tutted as he walked over to the shelving, followed by the two PCs. *This is going to be a daunting task*, he thought. Cadema's eyes followed him for a moment, then she turned to Stephanie.

'It all looks a bit overwhelming, but are the birth registers also kept down here as we will need to see those, too.' Cadema said as she silently thanked Julia for telling her about them.

'Yes, of course; how silly of me. They'll tell us what we need to know including the names of the midwives who were involved in the births. I don't know where they are at the moment as I haven't been down here for a long time, but I will have a look for you.'

'Will they give details of births, deaths and still births?' Cadema said, wondering why Stephanie had managed to get the matron's job, considering she was so forgetful. At least it was what she appeared to be.

'Yes they will. I'll try to find the ones you need,' Stephanie turned and walked towards a chipped metal cupboard that could just be seen in a recess across the room.

Searching her bunch of keys again, she took one out and opened the padlock. The double doors groaned as Stephanie opened them. Peering inside, Cadema could see several shelves crammed with mottled dust-covered ledgers which didn't appear to be in any specific order.

'I'm afraid we'll have to go through all of these. You see, some years ago they were brought down here by the porters who didn't have a clue about filing. I was going to have them archived properly, but . . . Well you probably know how difficult it is to get staff these days, especially on NHS salaries. Besides, you cannot let any member of staff down here until they have been properly trained and then they have to be supervised.'

'Yes, I understand. It's the same in the police service, but at least we have a properly managed and secure filing system for our records. And the PNC is wonderful, but we still have some very old files which have not been entered into the system. And you never know when you will want something from a case that took place years ago,' Cadema tried to sound sympathetic, but was agitated about the time it was taking to deal with what she though should have been a straight forward matter.

Doing a quick calculation of the number of shelves in the cupboard, and counting the number of ledgers on one shelf, Cadema estimated there must be at least 100 of them there. They were much bigger than any ledger she had seen before and none were in order. So after sending for another porter who assembled an old trestle table, Cadema reluctantly helped Stephanie to empty the contents of the cupboard. By the time they had reached the third shelf, Cadema was just about to summon Marriott to help when Stephanie handed her the ledger they had been looking for.

'That's great, so can we go to your office to read it?' she asked.

'Yes, of course. The light's better there and it's more comfortable. But if your officers can't manage on their own, we could stay here.'

'They will be all right,' she looked over to where a couple of the files had fallen on the floor. 'Be careful with those,' she called to Marriott.

'I will. But we'll need more light if we're to spend a lot of time down here,' Marriott looked around and took shallow breaths as if trying to avoid inhaling bacteria that may be lurking in the dust. He jumped and gave a quiet screech as a mouse ran across his highly polished shoes. *I hope the plague isn't spread through dust*, he thought as the mouse left a trail behind him.

'Don't worry, we have some bait down here somewhere. We don't want them eating our files do we?' Stephanie said as her eyes trailed the creature. 'And I'll get them to fix up another light. When you find the files you're looking for you can sit at the table at the far end; I'll see to it that they put the light there,' she pointed to a corner of the room which could just be seen.

He nodded a 'thank you' as Cadema walked gingerly across the floor leaving tracks which any police officer would be happy to follow in pursuit of a villain.

'Now, you wanted to look at Mason,' Stephanie said as she reached the shelf labelled 'M' and pointed to the ceiling. 'There' she said, and then quickly corrected herself. 'Oh, silly me, that's the 1930's, we need to go forward a few years.' She chuckled in a reprimanding way and marched on crossing isle after isle until she stood looking at another 'M' for 1975.

'Here we are. I think you'll find what you are looking for here.' She pointed again.

'Thank you, that's great, Matron,' Marriott said as he deliberately squinted in the dimness.

'Oh yes. The light; I'll get it organised right away Sergeant.'

By the time Stephanie's footsteps had faded away, Marriott had taken several M files off the shelves and placed them into the arms of the constables.

'Let's see what we can find in that lot. I'll see if there are any other interesting ones at the top. Thank goodness for these steps or we would be here all day trying to reach them,' Marriott stretched upwards.

'Be careful Marriott,' Cadema shouted as the steps began to wobble.

'No problem,' he steadied himself. 'But do you think we should have some protection, we could all be allergic to dust mites, or whatever there is lurking in here?'

'Nonsense, you get on with it, the sooner we can get out of here the better. When Stephanie comes back I'll leave you all here. If you need anything, just call me on my mobile.'

'That's if it'll work down here.'

'Well if it doesn't, there's an internal phone back there, use that. Stephanie's extension is 197, and if you need an outside line just add nine before the number.'

***

By the time they heard the footsteps and muffled voices of the matron and a porter, the small table was almost covered with files. Once the light had been connected, the porter said they could call him again if they needed anything else.

'You've certainly got your work cut out here. I recon there are over 1200 files, reflecting the number of births the hospital had in that year. Are you going to go through all of them?' Stephanie sounded sorry for the officers.

'Not all of them, but we'll go through as many as needed.' Marriott replied not wishing to mention the list of question he had.

Cadema gave a nod of approval and picked up the birth register that Stephanie had given to her.

'Well I'd better leave you to your work. As I said before, if you need...'

'We'll be fine Ma'am, anyway we've got the telephone number if we need anything.' Marriott was eager to see her go.

***

As Cadema followed Stephanie along the corridors they had travelled an hour earlier, Stephanie continued to talk.

'When I first came here I used to get lost, even for meetings,' she chuckled. 'Now I could find my way blindfolded.' Cadema nodded in a couple of places.

As they climbed a set of stairs, Stephanie stopped, took a deep breath, shrugged and then moved on.

'Not far now, just through these doors and up a couple of steps and we'll be there.' She trudged on, then pushing open the door to an office marked '*Matron-Private*' she gestured for Cadema to enter. 'There, now I'll arrange a cup of tea and then answer your questions.'

'That will be good, so will the tea,' Cadema said as she sat in a chair and placed the birth register on the table as Stephanie went in search of tea.

***

The office looked as if it had been converted from a patients' delivery room in the original hospital building. It was as cold and oppressive as the dungeon she had just left, with the exception of the daylight which streamed through grimy sash windows.

Skeletons of the rails on the ceiling, that had once held the curtains around a bed that was no longer there, were still visible.

Cadema sat thinking about midwives and the jobs they had to do. Looking round, she wondered how many babies had been born in the room where she was now.

She could almost hear the echo of the cries of women emanating from its four corners. The walls splattered with unseen blood from many deliveries. She thought of the pain and the suffering of hapless women in childbirth.

Then her own miscarriage flashed across her mind. Although half-conscious, she recalled the pain, the blood and then the loss of a life so precious... At a noise outside, she jumped back to the present.

She thought of the women in the hospital again. The ones who had waited years to conceive, finding themselves in the same room with others who didn't want their baby. The women, who had planned their pregnancy with minute details, while others, for many reasons, some beyond their control, had conceived without much thought.

Women who were too young, others too old, while some were worn out through years of childbirth. Women who had perfect babies while others had given birth to deformed or dead ones.

The women with loving husbands; ecstatic at being parents. Mothers with their newly decorated and well equipped nurseries, with their new layettes, new cots, new prams and new toys, waiting for the arrival of the precious child, welcomed into the family by doting Grandparents. While other mothers made do with second hand clothes from jumble sales and charity shops, hoping no one would notice as they swaddle their new-born babies.

The unmarried mothers that no one dare visit; whose babies were looked on as burdens, to be rid of as soon as possible. The averted, unsmiling eyes of people passing their crib, not daring to look inside or to say 'what a lovely baby'. The mothers, some suspicious of their offspring who had the audacity of being born alive, were then rejected and became the consolation prize for some adoptive parent, who would nurture it and, in time, come to love it.

The mothers who reinvented themselves after giving their babies away. Becoming wives and mothers as if nothing had ever happened. That is until twenty years later, when the image of themselves walked up their garden path.

Yes, there had been sad times as well as happy times, and the walls knew, they always would.

Cadema wondered if this were the room where Miss Connie Mason had given birth to Edward and maybe his brother; the room that had heard the first cry of a serial killer? The room where he had been given away to unsuspecting parents? The room where Stephanie's mother had delivered women of their babies and had made her records that others, years later, would find interesting.

***

The rattle of teacups and saucers startled her for a moment.

'Milk and sugar?' Stephanie asked as she placed the tray on the table..

'No sugar, thank you, just milk,' Cadema replied, pulling the birth register nearer to her. It was a huge A-two sized, bound and embossed ledger. 'It's very heavy and I'm finding it difficult to handle,' she opened it.

'Yes they are rather cumbersome, that's why we kept them in the staff quiet room. Midwives could fill them in there without interruptions.'

'I'm not surprised at that.' With further effort, she turned to the first full page. The pages were divided by vertical and horizontal lines. Each vertical column had a different heading. She traced her fingers across the register from left to right as she read the headings which were relevant to her. The mothers' name, date of birth and address, the time and date of the delivery, the number of babies born, the condition of each baby, including the weight, length and head circumference, the sex of each baby, stillbirths or perinatal deaths. The column headings went on, but by this time Cadema felt she had read enough as she looked up and spoke:

'It seems to contain what we are looking for. My goodness, it even states the type and the amount of drugs that were given, and whether the woman had Entonox and if they had an episiotomy.' Cadema had problems reading the last word and had to be prompted by Stephanie. 'What's Entonox?

'Oh that's gas and air to lay people. You could even call it laughing gas, but mothers know it as gas and air, it's used for pain relief.'

'Gas and air; mm-mm and it also gives the number of babies born, whether it was born alive, a stillbirth, or whether it was a perinatal death.'

'Yes as you can see everything is recorded, so you should be able to find what you are looking for.'

'I assume there are definitions for all of these terms? Can you explain what a stillbirth and a perinatal death actually are?'

'Stillbirths are babies who are born dead from twenty-three weeks gestation. It was different in the 1970's, back then it was twenty-eight weeks not twenty-three as it is now. A perinatal death is a baby who is born alive but dies within seven days of birth. Stillbirths are included in perinatal death statistics.'

Cadema thought again of her own baby. She had been fourteen weeks pregnant, now she knew why is was called a miscarriage. But she had heard the doctor call it a natural abortion. How could they call it that? It had been alive, fully formed. She had felt it move inside her. It was definitely a real baby. She shuddered.

Now Stephanie was going on about statistics and she was getting confused. Despite this, she had to concentrate as much as possible on what was being said as it would have an impact on the case. So she decided to ask as many question as possible, and make as many notes as she could.

'That's interesting, but how would you know if it was going to be a perinatal death, if it was born alive and then suddenly died.'

'You wouldn't, you are right, that's why you will see that part is mainly blank.'

Stephanie pointed to the register and turned a couple of the pages. Cadema noticed the defensive tone in her voice, as if she resented being questioned. 'If a death did occur, the midwife concerned would enter it into the register, it is their duty to do so. They would have done it back then as my mother was fastidious with record keeping.'

'But some midwives may not have filled in that part, especially if they didn't know a baby had died?' Cadema continued with her questioning so she could understand every detail. Besides she didn't want to appear ignorant on the matter when she briefed her team.

'It was every midwife's statutory duty to follow up all the women she delivered for up to twenty-eight days. In fact, we still have that legislation but we're more inclined to hand them over to the health visitor nowadays.'

'I see they identify the sex of each baby, its weight, its length and whether there were any abnormalities, which I would expect them to comment on. But why did they have to add the placenta and membranes, type of placenta, its weight and whether there were any abnormalities?'

'Oh that's just for professional information, nothing more.'

'Please don't be condescending; I really do want to know what professional information you are talking about?'

Stephanie shuffled in her seat and began to explain about the formalities surrounding childbirth and the statutory responsibilities midwives had.

'For example,' she said. 'If twins were delivered the midwife would be able to tell, not just from the sex of the babies, but from examining the placenta and membranes if they were identical. The placenta would be much bigger than in a singleton. There would be one placenta rather than two, as in non-identical twins. There are usually two membranes in identical twins. In non-identical ones, there may be at least three or even four. I can give you a book to read on this if you would like one.'

'No, that's okay, I think I understand but if I need one in future I'll let you know.'

Cadema had lost her concentration now. So, saying she would have to go, she thanked Stephanie for the information and for the birth register, which she promised to return as soon as possible. Although she knew the 'soon as possible' would most probably be several months from now. By which time she hoped to have found the killer she was looking for. Somehow she felt the mystery would be solved with the register she held tightly under her arm. Before leaving the building she telephoned Marriott who said his was still busy with the files.

'Just keep me informed,' she said, then left the building and headed for the police station.

CHAPTER SEVENTEEN

Cadema had been told at the last minute to appear on Crimeview as Philip
Crown was unavailable. There had been no time for her to prepare anything.
But nothing could have prepared her for the scenes she witnessed when she
entered the television studio. It looked more like a battlefield than the calm
she expected. Five cameras loomed, either above or in front of everyone like
menacing interlopers towering over intimate life scenes, witnessed by the
strategically placed television sets around the studio. Presenters, Producers,
Porters and Make-Up mingled with coffee cups, scripts and debris that
littered the floor.

Something shattered in a screened corner followed by whispering angry
voices. Props scratched the floor as they were dragged into position by
young men looking like schoolboys. Voices rose and fell like the chest of a
giant snoring in its sleep. The clock ticked on as if anxious to reach its
deadline.

When the television presenter and the producer spoke to Cadema it
seemed as if the scene had calmed itself. Now all she could hear was a faint
buzz of voices in the background. She hoped the briefing she'd had would
give her the confidence to look into the camera and be clear and assertive.

Her heart gave a flutter as she recalled what Grimes had told her.

'Remember, you'll be watched by millions of people. If you make a
mistake, or came across unsympathetic, or wooden even, the public will

judge us all for your actions. To them, the viewers, you are The Police Service.'

So, as she stood anxiously waiting for her turn with the cameras, she was tense and sweating, but hoped she would feel better when facing the camera.

'Now we have the most brutal crimes which have happened this century. Many of you, our viewers, will know them as 'The Common Murders'.' This was the cue for Cadema to move into the camera's view. As she did so, her mouth was so dry she could hardly swallow. 'To tell you more about them and to ask for your help in solving them, we have here in the studio Superintendent Sharma who is in charge of the investigation.' The presenter half-smiled and looked towards Cadema.

Cadema looked at camera number three, and cleared her throat for the second time. She was still nervous and wished Crown was there instead of her. But for some reason, which she was not privileged to know, he had telephoned Grimes and said he had other, more urgent business to attend to.

Typical of him, always sensationalising everything, she thought as she gave another short cough. She wondered what could be so urgent. She could hardly desert a show that had been planned and scheduled for this evening to find out. But she believed he was definitely up to something. After all it was he who said the murders were not opportunistic. That the killer planned each one, then stalked his victims before killing them. The killer knew the areas very well, so why not his victims? Perhaps that's how he managed to lure Jane Gaunt into that field. Yes Crown knew so much, perhaps too much, she thought. Was he the perpetrator? She didn't think so. The DNA matched Edward Mason's, fact. Edward Mason had been interviewed and eliminated, fact…

Something flashed across Cadema's face. The lights and the cameras brought her mind back to her current task. She lifted her head and smiled into the camera.

'Superintendent Sharma, will you take us through the murders and then explain to the audience how they can help to solve these terrible crimes?' The presenter said in a soothing voice, putting Cadema at ease for the first time that day.

'I will do my best.' She looked into the camera again and gave the accounts of the murders. Although she didn't want to mention the murder of Madeline Belton, she did say it had been solved and was not related in any way to the other three.

'So, before we show the reconstruction of the crimes to the viewers, will you explain where the murders took place?' the presenter spoke again.

'Yes, certainly, the three murders took place on Common ground. All areas were well used by members of the public so the murderer took a chance on each occasion.' Cadema hadn't wanted to mention the next part as she was worried about the response she would get. But she had been asked to include it at the briefing. 'All three victims were bludgeoned to death, probably with a hammer then left so they could easily be found. In the case of Frances Cole, the murderer used his victim's mobile phone to tell us where she was.'

'Thank you Superintendent.' The presenter turned to the camera. 'Well you can see how dreadful these crimes really are. Now we are going to show you the reconstructions. You may find the scenes disturbing, but we feel they are necessary. Hopefully they will jog people's memories of the nights in question.' The details of the murders were shown on the air.

'Terrible scenes of carnage, and if any of you remember anything suspicious around the times of these crimes, please phone, we are waiting for your call. The police desperately need your help. Is there anything else you can tell the viewers to jog their memories Superintendent?'

Cadema gave a twitch of a smile and looked into the camera again.

'As you may be aware, all these women had auburn hair. They were most likely murdered by someone they had never met before, but who probably came across as very plausible. They must have trusted him. Especially his second victim, Sophie Millburn, whom we believe he met over the internet. So if you can tell us anything, either about the women, or if you saw any of them on the nights in question, please call us.'

'Thank you Superintendent Sharma. The telephone numbers are on your screen now. And don't forget the lines will be open all evening. If you have problems getting through please keep trying. If you want to call the police station involved, then do so. We look forward to your call.' The presenter read out the telephone numbers. Once the programme was off the air, Cadema relaxed, believing she had done a reasonable job and hoped she would get the response from the public which was needed.

'I wonder how many calls we will get,' Cadema said turning to the presenter who was just about to speak to her.

'We usually get thousands, but there are a lot of false leads. Some people only phone in to get their names in print. You'll find at least a dozen will phone in and confess to the murders. Sometimes we get written information from the supposed murderer. I remember when the police were looking for Sutcliffe, mind you that was probably before your time, we had over ten thousand suspects, and two hundred letters confessing to the murders. The ones who were caught were prosecuted.'

'Yes I do remember about a tape recording in that case. It turned out to be a hoax. And some twenty or so years later the hoaxer was arrested and convicted.' Cadema said.

'You're right, it appeared the killer came from a place near Sunderland, and a dialectologist said that he definitely had a Geordie accent. The whole incident delayed the investigation for over a year, put lives at risk as they were concentrating their search in the wrong area. The public thought the tapes were genuine, and forensics even managed to link the tape to the other evidence at the time. Anyway I hope we don't have any hoaxes this time,' the presenter said.

'We are much better at dealing with those sorts of incidents nowadays, what with satellite technology, HOLMES-2, and things like that. And of course we have facts which are only known to the killer. Anyone pretending to be the perpetrator will have to give us a lot more information. And the DNA, of course, is helpful,' Cadema said although thinking it had not been much use in these cases.

'Mm, that's true. One other thing, we may get people phoning in with ideas. They tell us how the crime should be solved. They identify people they suspect in their area. Some of them even make notes when their suspect is away, and then try to fit them in with the dates of murders or other incidents.'

'Is that so? I didn't know.'

'Yes Superintendent, I remember a woman who thought her husband was a rapist. You may remember the case. He had a job which took him out of town. She collected enough circumstantial evidence on him to convince the police he was guilty. But it turned out she was having an affair with someone and wanted a legitimate way to get rid of him. When the case was investigated the police saw through her story and she was arrested along with her lover.'

'Oh yes, I remember something about the case, but it was such a long time ago. Back in the sixties I believe.'

'That's right. But what I'm saying is, don't be too worried if we get cranks like that.' The presenter smiled condescendingly.

'I won't worry, I'm used to it, and as I said, we have our ways of finding out the truth.' Cadema turned to walk out of the studio for a well-earned break. When the phones had stopped ringing around midnight, she said goodbye and left for home.

The night had been longer than she had expected, so it was two in the morning when she went to bed. As she drifted off to sleep she imagined the killer had watched the programme. Had he seen her on the television and gloated over the work he had done? She wondered if his ego was so overwhelming, he would have to phone the studio and either confess or incriminate someone else. But he wouldn't be that stupid especially as most calls could be traced.

By the time her radio-alarm woke her at seven in the morning, Cadema had met with Jim Logan. He told her again to look at all the issues, as if she were on the outside hovering above everything.

'Judge everything with fresh eyes; as if you were the murderer,' he had said. And, by dawn, she had already caught the killer. He turned out to be someone who hated women with auburn hair. Apparently, his mother had auburn hair and she used to beat him as a child. He decided to have his revenge. The last thing she remembered from her dream was Jim saying the DNA evidence was the hoax this time.

It was eight o'clock the next morning when Marriott congratulated her over the telephone and said he had found something interesting in the hospital records. He would bring them to her office when she arrived for work.

'By the way Ma'am, what time will you be there?' he asked.

'In forty-five minutes, just give me time to get ready. If you arrive before me, tell the rest of the team to get ready for a briefing.'

CHAPTER EIGHTEEN

They just wouldn't let me sleep. The voices in my head had kept me awake for nearly a week. Night after night they went on, mainly about Bernard Franklin. I was desperate to get some sleep and resorted to taking sleeping tablets to help me drop off.

That night I was exhausted and took three. I drifted off to sleep immediately.

The trial of Bernard Franklin had taken such a short time to get to court. It was in its fifth day when I stepped into the public gallery at the Old Bailey. I was determined to get a glimpse of the man who was certainly not a killer, but who would inevitably spend the rest of his life in jail for the murder of Madeline Belton. It was his fault he'd picked her up in the first place. God knows why he dropped her off.

So there he was, sitting with his head to one side, with a hint of a shave being done much too early in the morning. His thin hair looked much greyer than it had done in yesterday's newspapers. With his hooked nose and gaunt features, he reminded me of Fagan. Everyone thought he must be guilty.

'Guilt was written all over his face; the face of evil' as one tabloid had written. While others had said they were 'stereotyping Bernard' and he was being 'tried by the media' as different newspapers gave their own version of events. By the end, everything was being so distorted and disjointed that no one would know which version was fact or which one was fiction.

The jury of six men and six women looked attentive and alert, capturing every word, every movement and every blink from Bernard as witness upon witness floated in and out of the courtroom like ghosts. But they didn't falter as they sat hour after hour listening to the evidence like cloned wooden statues that matched their surroundings. The courtroom had an aura of oak-lined panelled walls dripping with the blood of murders like Crippen and Christie; where judges once donned their black cap and sent criminals to the gallows. But those were long gone days, Bernard would live, even though he would spend the rest of his days in the most secure jail they could find.

When the video surveillance tape was played, it showed Madeline leaning over into Bernard's car, and then opening the door and getting inside. It was there for everyone to see. Unfortunate for Bernard, and fortunate for me, there were no cameras at the spot where he had dropped her off and where I had picked her up ten minutes later. To everyone, including the jury, this meant one thing. That Madeline was with Bernard all the time and therefore he must have killed her. This was corroborated by Bernard's DNA, and by fibres and mud from his car. Oh yes, Bernard was definitely guilty. He had the opportunity, he was at the right place, at the right time and the forensic evidence was overwhelming. But no one could establish what his motive really was. Madeline was not raped. There was only a very small amount of semen found on her jeans. And there was no sign of the murder weapon.

I sat in the courtroom listening to all the evidence itching to say something. Should I tell them I'd picked Madeline up after Bernard dropped her off? Should I tell them that Bernard was not the killer? Should I tell them or leave them to determine Bernard's fate?

These thoughts were swarming round my head. And, as *the voices* inside me argued about what I should do, I felt like screaming for them to stop. On several occasions, I just managed to prevent myself from shouting out loud as *the voices* went on and on.

'If you tell them you were there then they will suspect you. It will put you in the right area, at the right time. And you don't have an alibi,' the gruff voice of number one said.

'If you don't tell them, then an innocent man will be sent to prison,' the soft pleading voice of number two added.

'Who cares about him being innocent? Look after yourself that's what you need to do,' the angry voice of number three interrupted.

'Sod that, innocent my foot, he picked her up didn't he. Well then, let him go to prison, who knows what he would have done if she had not insisted on him letting her out of the car. He could still have killed her, he had the opportunity,' said voice number one.

'Yes, I agree. How do you know he didn't go back and murder her after you dropped her off, Thomas?' voice number three said.

I put my head down and covered my ears, unable to stand the banter any longer:

'Oh, please stop, I cannot hear myself think, let alone answer your questions,' I said as I looked around the courtroom, hoping I was not giving any external clues on the torments I was having with the people within. But the voices continued on and on until I couldn't stand it anymore. And, although I wanted to run, I got up and began to walk out of the courtroom. I was too bewildered to look back, but I heard the sound of the people stand up and sensed the court was being adjourned. But instead the jury went out.

According to the clock in the courtroom it was twelve midday. Thirty minutes later, they returned.

I could feel the immense tension in the courtroom as everyone held their breath for the verdict. As the guilty verdict was read, the whole court room shook with excited bodies. I was ecstatic knowing Bernard Franklin was now doomed forever.

I don't remember saying anything, only thinking of it. But the jury, and Bernard Franklin, all looked up at me, pointing their fingers with anger on their faces.

'It's him' the jury shouted—Bernard followed, his voice echoing around the court. At that the judge put on his black cap and pointed at me.

'Thomas you are guilty as charged and therefore you will be taken from here to a place of execution ..., where you will be hanged by the neck until you are dead.'

'No, no, no,' I shouted, 'this isn't justice. I haven't had a fair trial. I will appeal. It wasn't me, it was him, it was him…'

I woke up in a sweat as my alarm went off. But the dream lingered on in my conscience for the rest of the day. And despite waking unrefreshed, I decided to go out and find the woman in the pale green suit.

***

My detective work had paid off. I discovered the woman was Natalie and her friend, in the Consortia of Publishes, was James. It's surprising, even in these days of confidentiality, secretaries will tell you anything if you ask in a nice way. James's secretary was no exception.

It was the eleventh of October when I booked into the hotel I had used before in Baker Street. The manager didn't recognise me as I completed the usual paper work and he handed me the key. How could he with such a great disguise? And even though Natalie had met me before, she wouldn't recognise me now. So I resumed my place at the window in the same dingy room and waited behind the faded curtains for my next victim.

I had the feeling Natalie would appear soon. Then I could get on with the job I'd waited so long to complete. This was my last chance. I had to do it now.

James was probably right for her. It was fortunate to find out her name and who she really was. I didn't know the names of my other victims, until it was announced in the press; except of course Sophie, who had been so stupid to meet me.

Natalie was different; I felt as if I knew her. She would come to me, not the other way around. Like a victim stalking the killer. She would come closer and closer, until I could hear the clicking of her heels as she hurried up the road to meet me. I was waiting, and somehow I believed she knew it.

I was ready, and although I sensed Natalie didn't appear to have a routine in her visits to James, I was prepared to wait for her, for as long as it took. I didn't have to wait long.

As she reached the building, her blond hair caught the first ray of sunlight that had managed to filter through the otherwise cloudy sky. When the wind ruffled it, I saw the whole of her neckline. Blond or not, she had had auburn hair once and that was all that mattered.

The door of the office block closed behind her. I sat wondering what she was doing. Would she emerge with James and be taken to lunch? But it was too early for lunch and too late for breakfast. So I waited. She emerged from the building with Him at around twelve thirty, just like she had done before. This time I hoped they would have a quick sandwich and say goodbye.

The long hour seemed like four as I went over and over the plans I had made, just to make sure I hadn't missed any details. It was all going to happen like clockwork. I would follow her onto the underground and stand in the next carriage to hers so I could see her through the glass. I would get off when she did, but would keep ten paces behind her no matter how slow or how fast she went. I had my new Oyster card so could travel to any zone in London.

I would follow her home and wait outside to make sure she was alone. It didn't matter what type of building she lived in, I was sure I could get in without any problems, knocking on the door or ringing the bell would be the best solution. She wouldn't recognise me and I could talk my way in.

I thought of the Boston Strangler who had used this direct approach to get into the apartments of the women he had killed. I would do the same. It was just a matter of time, patience and trust. I had all three. I knew, once Natalie opened the door, she would never expect me to be a killer. And, once inside, it would be easy to kill her then do what I had to do, and leave.

The second the clock struck one, I dashed into the street and waited on the corner, pretending to examine my London A to Z. If anyone saw me with the book they would suspect I was a tourist and pay no attention. My position was secure, and as I waited page after page of my A to Z caught the drips of the ceaseless rain.

'Are you lost?' the small figure of a boy, donned with an attempt at dreadlocks, said.

'No thank you, I'm fine. I don't need any help'.

'Suit yourself,' he replied with an air of authority as he rode off on his skates.

'Are you lost?' someone else asked. I shook my head, turned up my collar, and slid the book into my pocked. As I looked up I could see one figure, under an umbrella, running past the building. I was right. She was back, and to my delight, was alone. She hurried along the street. I overtook her on the opposite side of the road knowing she was heading for the underground. My coat was getting wet on both sides. The outside from the rain and the inside from perspiration. But I couldn't take it off, it was part of my disguise.

Waiting on the concourse at Baker Street, she arrived. She stood for a moment, then headed for the Bakerloo line as the announcer said there would be a five minute delay. I followed. 'Keep calm,' I whispered. 'Keep calm it's all going to plan.' But the gruff voice I knew too well butted into my thoughts.

'It doesn't look as if you're going to kill her tonight, does it? The train's late and I know how you hate being delayed,' the *Voice* inside went on, there was no respite. It liked tormenting me. It was jealous of what I intended to do. It was jealous of me being in control. And as it laughed at me, I just stood there looking down at the track, the electric track, the track that could end it all for her. One little push at the right moment; that was all it would take. Natalie would just be another suicide statistic.

I kept my cool. I was still in control despite the voices, as the others joined in. They wouldn't get the better of me, I was going to succeed this time and they knew it. The *Voice* was right; it would be easy to do it here, but that was not the point. The kill was not the point; it was deeper than that. It had become a ritual. I had to follow my plan to the letter, there was no room for deviation. It had to be done one way, and one way only. There would be no errors, nor changes or modifications. But I couldn't deny it, the track was tempting.

When the train pulled in, she got into the carriage, as planned I followed her. There were too many people for me to do otherwise. The train sped through the tunnels at, what felt like, the speed of light. I could see her holding on, swaying, reading the graffiti covered advertisements, too embarrassed to meet the eyes of others in the carriage.

Everyone looked down, as if their shoes were covered with newsprint of a thousand years which had to be read before the next stop; as if they would learn the meaning of life. Some mindlessly peered through windows pummelled with the grit of Victorian tunnelling. She was free in her world, I was free in mine. Locked in a battle to complete the journey; the journey of life.

I wasn't expecting her to alight at Marylebone station as she did. So I feared she would head for the main line station and catch a train before I had the time to buy a ticket. She sped into the tunnel then ran up the steps. I followed with great difficulty from the burden of my coat. Not wanting to draw attention to myself, I kept calm and walked as swiftly as possible with the rest of the crowd.

When I reached the escalator, which I imagined was the steepest and the longest in London, she was half-way up. I ascended quickly, despite the pounding of my heart. Twice I stopped to let the escalator carry my ailing body. Stepping off at the top, I stood for a second or two to regain my strength.

She had disappeared. I walked around to see where she had gone; craning my neck, but to no avail. I had lost her, but at least I would know which station she would be heading for in the future. So with a steady exhausted and defeated pace, I went into the mainline station and stood panning the scene. The concourse was crowded. Natalie was nowhere to be seen.

Scanning the times of trains on the board, I sensed a familiar perfume. Glancing round to my right, I saw her. She stood so close I could have stabbed her there and then. Instead, I slowly turned and walked away towards the ticket office.

'A return to Birmingham please,' I said, waiting to find out how much it would cost.

'When do you intend to return?' the man's voice replied.

'I don't really know. Can you give me an open ticket?'

'Yes of course, it's no problem. That will be…'

But before he had time to complete his sentence, I handed him some money, hoping it would cover the journey.

'If you want an open ticket, one that will let you travel back to London at peak times, I need another twenty pounds please.'

I handed him the money without saying a word, grabbed the ticket and mingled with passengers on the concourse.

She was obviously early, or her train was late. Standing there with a coffee, she looked at the circular metal bench, then sat down next to a man who was eating a burger. Sipping her coffee, she shuffled and stood up.

She looked so helpless waiting for the train that I struggled with the urge to go and talk to her. But when she sat down again, far away from the burger man, she started to read her newspaper. Well, she looked as if she were reading it, but instead she studied the people around her. I noticed how she smiled at a young girl who was playing on the floor near the bench.

Natalie tensed every time the girl got into someone's way; as if she might get injured. Where I believed Natalie would give the girl a great big hug, I would have resisted giving it a smack and telling it to be quiet. Children had too much of their own way these days. I even saw a child hit its mother the other day, but rather than slap her in return, all the child received was 'you shouldn't hit mummy like that.' And the matter was closed.

I think children need to be taught the difference between right and wrong. And not given so many choices. They choose what to wear, when they eat, what they eat. How the bloody hell does a child know what it should eat? What is good for them and what isn't? So they eat junk food, sweets and drink high calorie fizzy drinks, sit in front of the TV or computer and eat and eat, until they almost reach bursting point. So, when they are in their teens and beyond, they will be fat, have diabetes and suffer with heart conditions. Coupled with either drinking, taking drugs or smoking, and what have we got, unfit young people, who die early. In this situation the older generation has to look after them. So when the older generation need care, there will a deficit of fit younger people to look after them. The whole human race will be defeated by self-indulgence. Okay, so the Government tried to change things a few years ago, and it worked for a while, but people resorted back to their old ways of life. Nothing seems to be permanent these days.

Natalie took her eyes off the child and stared at the display board. As the announcer said 'the next train is for High Wycombe' she stood up and began walking towards the barrier to the platform. Quickening her pace, she joined the short queue. 'Not Birmingham,' I said under my breath.

Before I could gather enough speed to catch her up, and bumping into fellow travellers, some of whom shouted abuse or asked me to watch where

I was going, she disappeared through the barrier. I felt the panic of other passengers as they bustled passed me. As if it were the only train they could catch that day. Or if they were left behind, they would perish at the hands of a terrorist in the capital.

This urgency to escape was not their fault. I believe Londoner's have been in escape mode ever since the Black Death and the Great Fire of 1666. And each subsequent disaster reinforced their urgency to escape. Escape mode was now a way of life, innate in their minds with neurons switched on, and ready. The fear was always there, the hurry intense. And I knew I was right as I followed with the same urgency.

The queue to one of the carriages stopped her, enabling me to catch up. She looked irritated, not at all like the woman I imagined; serene and cool in any emergency. And Natalie, I believed was fuming from within, fighting against the urge to shout at a man who pushed her from behind. The man, so close that I thought she must have been able to feel his hot breath on the back of her neck; feel his body tense as it got closer, invading her space and raping her mind. She knew what he was doing but may have been too embarrassed to protest. Everyone was so close, so she had to endure the torment.

I sensed the CCTV examining the scene as I pulled my collar a little further up my neck, averting my eyes from the prying lens. I knew it would not have mattered if I were seen, but I preferred not to give my disguise away.

Pushed and shoved forwards, I still managed to keep my distance. Hoping someone would sit next to Natalie, I looked for a seat as far away from her as possible. I always found it difficult when perusing someone on public transport, because it is too easy to bring attention to yourself. If everyone were seated, the last thing I wanted to do was to have to sit next to a victim. But if it were the only seat available, some Good Samaritan would offer me the empty seat. That would result in people looking at me to study my reaction. To avoid this, I waited before settling down into a suitable seat three rows up, but facing Natalie.

From my vantage point I could see most of the people in the carriage, but of course, this meant they could see me. But instead of looking at me, they read newspapers, books, magazines, e-books, did crosswords or the Sudoku, used their laptops, spoke to friends, dozed or looked out of the window. I was pleased it was still light outside, otherwise they might have seen my reflection in the window.

Men were dressed for the office as some appeared safe enough to loosen their tie. Women were dotted about; Natalie was one of these dots. Her eyes resting, her mind probably lost in the day's activity. I was alert to everything. To the man who crunched on crisps, the one whose coffee dripped onto his while shirt, while another gave me the impression he should cut down on fats and carbohydrates. The woman with the laptop looking important while completing her second game of backgammon. But Natalie never faltered from her sleep and, I expected, even the Prince in *Sleeping Beauty* would not waken her until, by some instinct, she became alert when she reached her destination.

She was peace itself, cocooned in her world, almost death like. At that moment, I decided she wasn't going to die today. My plans had been changed. Tonight I was going to find out where she lived, and then return home.

I was resting my eyes when the train stopped at South Ruislip. To my amazement Natalie jumped up; she was not going to High Wycombe after all. Slipping into her dark coat, she headed for the door. She had obviously listened to the forecasters and seemed prepared for whatever the weather threw at her. Although it had been raining earlier, it was supposed to get colder than expected for early October. Then I remembered that, some ten years ago, people said we were in for global warming. That the ice caps would melt, and, as a consequence the sea would rise and the south east would totally disappear. But of course this never happened.

As she waited for the door to open, I was there. Natalie alighted from the train and ran along the platform as if being chased by someone unseen. 'Excuse me please,' I said passing through ever decreasing spaces created by bodies acting as guards. But before I could catch up, she had disappeared completely. And, as everyone left the platform and queued at the gate, she was nowhere to be seen. Then I noticed her huddled in a corner, she was talking to someone on her mobile phone. But rather than wait, I went to the exit and mingled with the other passengers. She returned quickly, slipped her ticket into the automatic exit to the station, and headed for the car park.

My heart sank, if she had a car I would be unable to follow her. So I held back and waited to see which type of car she drove.

As I waited the voices started arguing again. They poked fun at me, telling me how pathetic I was. I told them to shut up.

When Natalie finally emerged, I was surprised to see she was driving a four-wheel drive car, something like a Discovery. I expected her to drive a sports car, or something much more suitable for her character. Now I was seeing a different side of her. There was much more to her than I realised. And although I didn't know my other victims, I wanted to find out about Natalie as I felt she was different.

***

When I arrived back in London, the weather had indeed turned colder, so I was glad I'd worn the coat. Reaching my front door, I could see the milk had been tampered with by the birds again. Perhaps I should have stopped having milk delivered years ago, as my neighbours had. But I liked tradition, and was determined to keep this one going as long as possible; my last hold on my English heritage.

Cameo, my cat, liked the pleasure of fresh milk, even though I knew it wasn't good for her. But I usually mixed a little drop with a lot of water, which seemed to fool her.

Wrapping herself around my ankles and dribbling saliva over my shoes, I couldn't help wondering how it was, that no matter what disguise I wore, she always knew who I was. But conversely, I was pleased humans had lost their sense of smell, otherwise my disguises would be useless.

Then I began to speculate; crimes would be easier to solve if human pheromones could be analysed. Police could collect pheromones from the scene of crimes, analyse them, and compare them with a database they would have in place to identify suspects. It would be better than fingerprints, and probably as good as DNA. There would be teams of pheramonologists who would work with others to solve crimes. But I supposed we would have to wait for this technology to be developed. Nevertheless, I was sure that one day someone would do it, they always did.

I recalled the time of Jack the Ripper, in the 1880's. Someone decided that the image of the last person seen by a murder victim would be etched on the victim's retina. So at least one of Jack the Ripper's victims had her eyes

198

removed, but nothing was identified. Forensics still had a long way to go from there, and still have.

Cameo purred louder as I picked her up and opened the door. Standing in the hall, I could hear the faint sound of the telephone ring and dashed, with cat under my arm, into the living room just managing to pick up the receiver as it stopped. It infuriated me when I dialled to find out who it was. But the caller had withheld their number. To my mind, there was no reason for a person to phone unless they wanted to speak to someone, and, if they didn't leave their number, then they were not worth speaking to.

After feeding Cameo, I picked up the paper and began to read the article about the murders again. As I did so, I wondered how I could covertly change the enquiries the police were making in order for them to find the perpetrator. It wasn't really me, I was just there so they could find him. So when killing Natalie, I would leave plenty of forensic evidence there so the police would be able to identify him and make an arrest. Yes, I would make it happen this time.

CHAPTER NINETEEN

Cadema had just taken her coat off when her office phone began to ring. Picking it up, she recognised Marriott's voice.

'Hello Ma'am, I've been a bit delayed, but I'm on my way. Will be there in about half an hour.'

'What are you doing?'

'Driving with hands-free, so I thought I'd fill you in on some of the details,' he stopped at a red light. 'As I said, I've found something interesting in the archives which was overlooked before.'

'It must be exciting from the sound of your voice, hopefully it matches up with your expectations.'

'We shall see. Anyway, I went back to the hospital and Stephanie Granger let me into the cellar again. I had a hunch...'

'Yes, I know your hunches; go on,' she sounded sceptical.

'Anyway. Whoops, just turning the corner Ma'am. That's better, on the straight now. Where was I; yes. I wondered if there were any more files that may be helpful to the investigation. So looking again, I found one filed in the wrong year.'

'Not by mistake, if I know the hospital and the meticulous records that Stephanie keeps there. But spare me the preliminaries, just get on with the main issues. I don't want to wait for ever for you to tell me something which should only take a couple of minutes.'

'Yes, sorry Ma'am,' he cleared his throat. 'Well it looks as if we have some more evidence, this time it involves a Mrs. Mary Buxton, she had a baby on the day Connie Mason gave birth to Edward. There's something fishy here in the notes. I'm not an expert, but it seems she had a baby, and it looks as if it died. Ten days later she left the hospital with a healthy baby boy.'

'Well done Sergeant, but ten days seems an awful long time to be in hospital.

'Not necessarily, apparently ten days was the lying-in period following delivery. And some mothers stayed for ten days, some even longer if their baby could not be discharged for some reason,' he boasted.

'It sounds as if you have something there, and you've certainly done your homework. See you in half and hour then.' She replaced the telephone.

Cadema had been suspicious that something was going on at the hospital. But with Stephanie Granger always being there, she had not found any proof. Nevertheless, she would not be surprised if Stephanie had something to hide. Not directly though, but relating to her dead mother. Somehow she was protecting her and she needed to find out why. And the term, "Problems with filing" also fuelled her suspicions. Now she believed Stephanie must have misfiled the records in the hope they would never be found. But couldn't understand why she hadn't destroyed them; that would have been the most obvious thing to do. *Thank goodness I put Marriott in there when I did,* she thought.

Marriott appeared on time. By then she had almost recovered from her lack of sleep; the coffee had also helped.

'Tell me exactly what you've found,' she asked, with a breath taken after every word as they rushed towards an interview room. Here she would have the privacy she needed. Grimes, or anyone in the team, would not find out what was going on. Not until she had all her facts and was sure the records would make a significant contribution to the investigation.

As they peered over the notes, Marriott pointed out that a Mrs. Mary Buxton was having her first baby and had booked in at the hospital. When Cadema turned the pages she discovered the woman had been admitted to the hospital on several occasions and the baby, or 'fetus' as it was called in the notes, was classed as 'small'. And, according to the records, Mrs. Buxton's baby was delivered at twenty-three week gestation. Ten days later she had been discharged from the unit with a baby boy weighing 2.5 kilograms. *That would be around six pounds*, she thought to herself. Immediately she realised, on the surface everything looked feasible, but as Marriott pointed out; a baby born at twenty-three weeks could not possibly weigh six pounds. He said he knew because his sister had a baby who was born at twenty-four weeks a couple of years ago, and that the baby only weighed two pounds two ounces. It could not breathe for itself, and died in a specialised intensive care baby unit after three days on a ventilator. Since then his sister had had a full-term baby who weighed seven pounds.

After going through the notes several times, Cadema realised she needed expert advice as there were many technical terms only a midwife or obstetrician would be able to understand. She needed an interpreter so she, and her colleagues, would be able to identify the significance of the information.

She thanked Marriott for his work, and told him to put the briefing on hold. Leaving him to pick up the documents, she headed for her office to telephone Julia for advice. Julia was unable to help her, saying midwifery was not her field of expertise. Instead she referred Cadema to the Director of Midwifery Services at the local university hospital.

***

Cadema was on her way to see Malcolm Burley, the CEO in the Trust. She intended to explain the situation, and ask him to identify an appropriate professional who would be able to help.

The hospital was the usual NHS establishment where hygiene was the priority, but where superbugs could flourish if indifference to this prevailed. Entering the hospital, Cadema instinctively took short shallow breaths to prevent any lurking infections from reaching the depth of her lungs. Walking over to the hand cleaning dispenser, she smeared her palms and fingers. In the couple of seconds they took to dry, she watched in disbelief as visitors walked straight past without even a second glance at the request to use the dispenser.

A few minutes later, she had reached the CEOs office and was shown in by his secretary. Before Cadema had time to say anything Malcolm began to speak:

'From what you said on the telephone, I've taken the liberty of asking Janet Hooper, our head of midwifery to sit in.' Following polite introductions, he gestured for Cadema to take a seat facing them both.

'Well Superintendent, I know you're working on a murder enquiry, as I saw you on TV a couple of days ago.' Cadema fidgeted and felt the heat creep across her face at being recognised from her television appearance.

After she had explained about the file, and the need for it to be interpreted by someone with the appropriate qualifications, and integrity, the CEO turned to Janet:

'You should be able to find someone who has the prerequisites the superintendent is looking for.'

Janet looked at Cadema and gave a motherly smile giving the impression she would be compassionate to women in labour. She took a minute of deliberation before she said: 'Yes, of course, Samantha Bowler is the best midwife for your needs. She is already an Expert Witness and has been for the last five years. She's on duty today, so I'll go and ask her. You can come with me if you like.' Janet was by the door before Cadema could answer.

Reaching her office, Janet entered the security code and entered.

'If you don't mind waiting in here Superintendent, I'll go and ask Samantha to come and talk to us,' Janet said with an air of authority. When she left, Cadema looked around. The desk was obviously a relic from the old hospital that was demolished a few years earlier. A photograph of two children, who looked like miniatures of their mother, sat on the desk. They had the same hazel eyes and black hair. She looked for more family memorabilia, but none existed. The lack of a father for the children puzzled her until she remembered Janet did not wear a ring of any description. So she had either never been married or was divorced.

Cadema had been thinking of Jim Logan's Hospital phobia, when Janet returned. If Jim were still alive, he would not be where she was today, he would have sent someone else. And for the first time since his death, she was in her rightful place. He would definitely have delegated the task to her.

Janet introduced Samantha. She had light brown bobbed hair, a short fringe, and was wearing a Sisters' uniform. Explaining what she wanted Samantha to do, Cadema looked sternly into Samantha's hazel eyes.

'As you can appreciate, this is a delicate and confidential undertaking,' she spoke softly, but emphasized the confidentiality.

'Look Superintendent,' Samantha's face blushed. 'I'm a midwife and have been for the last ten years. Integrity and confidentiality is engrained in my profession. And I adhere to this whole heartedly. If a midwife breached the rules on confidentiality, or any of her code of practice, she or he would be reprimanded or even struck off the register.' Her voice echoed in the room.

'I wasn't trying to undermine your profession. It's the same in ours. So I'm sorry if I have offended you.'

'Apology accepted,' Samantha huffed. 'I am free on Thursday morning, about ten. Can't come when I'm on duty, my patients come first, no matter what.'

'I'll see you at ten o'clock on Thursday then,' Cadema said, wishing it were sooner. 'At the police station. Just ask the desk clerk for Superintendent Sharma, and she'll call me.'

'I look forward to it. And you never know I may exceed your expectations,' Samantha gave a smile.

***

Samantha was exhausted after her long shift. But, once home, she organised her usual after-school childminder for Thursday, just in case she was home later than usual.

By Thursday she had postponed her hairdressing appointment, and made another one hoping her grey hairs would not be too obvious by then. But she thought she had forgotten something, and no doubt she would remember it again when she was engulfed in paper work. It always seemed to happen that way; senior moments, she called it. And she smiled at the thought as she entered the police station.

'Good morning, Samantha,' Cadema sprang up from a chair in the lobby, walked up to her and held out her hand. 'You look so different out of uniform,' she said.

'People always say that, and that I look taller. But the uniforms make me look more than a size twelve. Never flattering. People only see the uniform at first, and not the real person. It must like that in the police service.'

'Yes, that's right. But we have a very different image from you where the public are concerned. Anyway, thank you for coming in, especially at such short notice.'

Samantha smiled back at her: 'You're welcome. But I didn't expect you to meet me,' she sounded excited as if she couldn't wait to get started on the work.

'Oh, yes, I'm always early and a little impatient. So I decided to meet you here rather than wait for the desk clerk to call me from my office.'

'I know what you mean, I was up at five o'clock. I think it's the shifts you know, and sometimes it's difficult to adjust,' she said as she followed Cadema to her office.

On arrival Samantha hardly took any time to settle when Cadema gave her a file containing the notes. Opening the file and then turning the pages in the notes, Samantha took a deep breath: 'This all looks very interesting.

Whatever you want me to do Superintendent, I'll be as through and as succinct as possible. I sense you need this urgently.'

'You're right, but please call me Cadema. What I would like you to do is go through the notes piecemeal. Tell me what all the professional words means, and give me your opinion as to whether or not the information in the notes is correct.' Cadema looked straight into Samantha eyes waiting for her reaction. The nod of the head and the mm, told her that she understood what she wanted.

During the next hour, she noticed Samantha had a much deeper personality than she had expected. She was quiet, intense, private and reluctant to share anything unless she was certain of her interpretations. On occasions she referred to the midwifery text book she had brought with her just to confirm her diagnosis of the facts. With this knowledge, Cadema decided she could trust her implicitly, despite her initial misgivings at their first meeting.

Watching Samantha work through the notes, Cadema noticed the similarities between their personalities. She recalled the time when she had thought of becoming a nurse. Now she could see herself in Samantha and wondered if they were at the same rank in the general scheme of things. Perhaps she could be sitting where Samantha was now, understanding the medical language and giving advice.

After an hour or so, Samantha looked up from the notes:

'I think there is definitely something amiss with these records. I'll go through them with you and explain,' she frowned as she turned a page.

'That's interesting, but can you wait a couple of minutes for my Sergeant to come in?' she picked up the phone from her desk.

Marriott arrived five minutes later. Introductions over, he picked up a chair and joined Cadema. They both sat very close to Samantha, where under other circumstances, it would have been considered an intrusion. But at that time it was necessary as they needed to see the notes being referred to.

'You see here,' Cadema and Marriott moved to the edge of their chairs and began to follow Samantha's finger as it moved across the page. 'Mary Buxton was admitted three times early in her pregnancy. She had Hyperemesis Gravidarum at that time. And she was admitted later with antepartum haemorrhage, or APH as it is written here.'

'You've lost me already. So what does it all mean?' Cadema asked as Marriott nodded in agreement.

'It means she had severe sickness in early pregnancy, the type that is pathogenic, rather than the normal morning sickness. It can make women very ill. There are several reasons for this, but I will spare you the details because they may not be relevant. Anyway, she left the unit after four days, so she must have recovered, but was admitted later with a bleed.'

'I see, but can you spare us the Latin words if possible?'

'Certainly. Now let me see, yes she was seen by a midwife at twelve, sixteen, eighteen and twenty weeks. Although that's unusual in normal circumstances, but as she had an APH, sorry a bleed,' she looked up at Cadema and received a nod of understanding. 'It could have meant she had a low-lying placenta. That is, if it was over the cervix, it could cause a sever bleed as the baby grew. So she was seen more frequently. Now let me see,' Samantha turned to the back of the notes. 'Yes it's here, the scan. Although they were not always accurate in those days, depending on who was doing them.'

'I didn't realise they were available then.'

'Oh yes, they were first used in the fifties in Glasgow. And by the seventies they were being used in large maternity hospitals. And look at this, as I suspected—she did have a low lying placenta, but it didn't cover the cervix.' She pointed to the scan result, Cadema and Marriott looked closer. 'These records are useful to us in many ways. But mainly because she was seen early and was frequently followed up, so we can be sure of the accuracy of her dates and the growth of the fetus,' Samantha sounded excited.

'I think I can see what you are getting at. But can you elaborate on the significance of what you have just said?'

'Yes, if her dates are accurate, the growth of the fetus can be monitored against these to see if it's growing at a normal rate. The data can then be added to a special chart, percentile chart it's called. It's then easy to detect any deviation from what is expected.'

'Oh I see, thank you. So if the baby, sorry fetus, was small it would obviously weigh less than it should when it was born?' Cadema asked, as Marriott nodded and shuffled in his chair.

'Yes, it's very significant and my next bit will explain why. When Mary Buxton went into labour at twenty-three weeks, she was admitted to the hospital when the cervix was five centimetres dilated. This would be far too late to prevent delivery. And in my opinion she should have been transferred to a hospital with a Special Care Baby Unit, (SCBU) as it was called then. Not that it would have done much good in those days as a baby born at twenty-three weeks was not viable, and therefore it was not expected to live once it was born. Or it could have died, in utero; that is before it was born.'

'It seems a bit complicated to me. Are you saying she was not transferred to another hospital because the baby had died? But what if the baby was born alive? What would they have done then?' Cadema frowned and sounded angry about the situation.

'If it were born alive and was expected to live they would have called the flying squad. Both the mother and baby would have been transferred to the nearest well equipped maternity hospital. The baby would have been taken to the SCBU, assessed by a paediatrician, and no doubt put on a ventilator and nursed accordingly.'

'But you said earlier that the baby was not viable at twenty-three weeks. But if the baby was born alive, it was viable.' Cadema moved forward on her seat.

'That was the statutory definition of a baby born before twenty-eight weeks gestation and was not expected to live. Obviously if it were born alive, then everything possible would have been done to keep it alive, in the hope it would survive. Nowadays, because of technology and the advancement in neonatal intensive care, the age has been lowered, but in those days it was twenty-eight weeks.'

'So are you saying they knew she was twenty-three weeks pregnant and they expected the baby to be born dead?'

'Yes and no. The baby could have been born alive but it was probably born dead. The dates of the pregnancy were, as I said before, correct, because she was seen so regularly. But the midwife who examined her did comment that the fetus was "small for dates". So not only was she in premature labour, the baby was much smaller than expected.'

'So she should have been transferred to a consultant unit. My God, is that what you're saying?' Marriott said angrily.

'Don't get annoyed, this happened in the seventies and there's nothing we can do about it now,' Cadema said, as she remembered Marriott's wife was twenty-three weeks pregnant. 'Anyway Sergeant, will you go and organise some tea please. I'll fill you in on anything relevant when you come back?' Marriott left the room with an audible grunt.

Turning the pages of the notes backwards and forwards incredulously, tutting as she did so, Samantha said she believed there was some information missing.

'The birth is recorded on the Partogramme. That's a document used to chart the progress of labour, and record the delivery. Sometimes there is a mention of the baby's Apgar score, there is no mention of it here, but it was not always standard practice to record it on the Partogramme.'

'What is the Apgar score?' Cadema asked.

'It's the assessment we apply to the condition of a baby at birth, and subsequently if necessary. A good score is ten, five in intermediate and so on. There's no mention here, but I'd expect to see it recorded in the baby's notes along with the sex, weight and length and any other relevant information. But the baby's notes are blank. Not only that, but the baby is not mentioned in the Kardex; the document where the progress of the mother and baby was usually recorded.'

'How unusual is that?' Cadema asked, realising it sounded serious.

'It's extremely unusual. Midwives always add all the details of the delivery and the baby in the notes before she leaves the labour room. Then there should be ongoing reports on the progress of the mother and baby in the Kardes and where applicable, in the notes too. Looking in this file, I think the information was deliberately omitted.'

'Why do you think that was the case?' Cadema shuffled with impatience in her chair.

'It may have been that the baby had something wrong with it. Or it could have been born dead. They may have recognised there was something wrong with the baby before the birth and that is why they didn't send the mother to a consultant unit.'

'But how could they tell something was wrong with it?'

'Initially by the clinical history, by amniocentesis for Downs's syndrome. By scans, and they would have taken the bleeds she had in pregnancy into consideration especially as the fetus was 'small for dates' as they called it then. I could speculate that there were other things wrong, but as there's nothing in the notes, it is not worth considering. What I am certain of is that the baby she took home could not possibly have been her own baby.'

'What makes you so sure?'

'I think...' The door opened and Marriott entered with a tray of tea and biscuits for all three.

'Thank you Sergeant, now please be quiet as I think we are on to something. Samantha has just said Mary Buxton probably took home the wrong baby.'

'Not exactly, I inferred she may have been given a baby which wasn't hers. You see a baby of twenty-three weeks would never have weighed six pounds. And it would certainly not survive out of an incubator. If it had survived, it would have taken much longer than ten days at that gestation for it to breathe on its own. As there are no records of the baby in the notes, I can only conclude that her baby was probably still-born. And if it was only twenty-three weeks gestation it may have been classed as an abortion, or a miscarriage to lay people, and therefore not legally born. That means it wouldn't need a birth certificate or a certificate of burial. In those days women would not have been given the opportunity to see their dead baby as it would have been removed from the room as soon as possible after it was delivered.'

'My God,' Marriott said almost choking on his tea.

'I can hardly believe that something like that could happen.' Cadema said.

'I must admit I've never seen anything like this before and have never read about any cases.' Samantha sat shaking her head.

Cadema's mind was racing. There was definitely a loophole in the birthing system at the time which someone had taken advantage of. She wondered what their motive was, *probably financial* she reasoned. No matter what, the whole thing could, and possibly will, have a huge impact on the current investigation.

'I think that's all I can do for now,' Samantha said as she handed the file back to Cadema. 'If I can help you with it in the future, I will be happy to do so.'

Without any further speculation, Cadema thanked Samantha for the excellent work she had done, asked her to produce a written report on her findings from the notes, and said goodbye. Leaving Marriott to clear things away, she made her way to brief Grimes and discuss her suspicions with him.

'I am serious. It has to be right. This Mrs. Mary Buxton had a baby that was born dead and took home another woman's baby. And I think the other woman's baby was Miss Connie Mason's second baby; the twin brother of

Edward Mason, our suspect.' Cadema pleaded with Grimes to understand the circumstances as she sat on the edge of his desk, waiting for his reaction.

'No, Cadema, it doesn't make sense. She couldn't just walk out of the hospital with another woman's baby without someone knowing. No, I'm not having it. It seems to me you've taken what information there is from the notes to justify this twin theory of yours. There isn't a twin, and that's final. And don't be so melodramatic with your hair brain ideas.'

'But Sir,' she bit her lip and took a deep breath. 'I know I'm right. And if I'm going to solve these murders I need your support. Will you back me on this if I bring you more information? All I need is to search the hospital records for more information.'

'You can if you like, but don't forget you'll need some tangible evidence, which I don't think you have at the moment.'

'I'll get the proof. In the meantime, I've asked Samantha, the midwife who went through the records with me, to send me her report. I've got some of the records I need from the hospital. And, as Evans has been looking into the registers of midwives from that time, I intend to send him to interview the retired midwives who were working in the unit. Thank goodness they had to register their intention to practice. If it were nurses we're looking for, it would be much more difficult.'

'Well if you know what you're doing, you had better get on with it. But whatever you do, I don't want any of this to get into the press.'

'I assure you that will not happen this time Sir. My officers will only be told on a need to know basis, and they know the rules and the consequences should any leak occur.'

As she left Grimes, she began to devise an action plan hoping it would lead to the information she needed, and as she walked she made her imaginary list.

Track down Mrs Mary Buxton and find out when and where she registered the birth of the baby.

Find out who signed the birth notification; Samantha had said either a doctor or midwife could have done this.

Talk to Connie Mason again and find out if she ever met a woman called Mary Buxton. She may have given her baby away willingly to Mary, hoping no one would ever find out.

Interview Stephanie Granger again and find out more about her mother and the records she kept.

Identify all the other midwives who were practising at the hospital at the time, and interview them if possible.

Examine the Birth and Death register for the time to identify babies who were registered at the same time as Edward Mason.

Determine what the murder victims had in common.

Her list was incomplete, and probably needed adjusting, but at least it would do for the time being. In her mind she had already designated her team to the various Actions, but she would personally interview Stephanie Granger.

CHAPTER TWENTY

I was unable to sleep all weekend since seeing Natalie get into her four-wheeled drive and leave the car park at South Ruislip railway station. I needed to return there, this time in my car with false number plates. I intended to wait near her car, then follow her to see where she lived. I wasn't going to kill her then, but once I'd found out about the area, I planned to return and carry out my final plan.

It was six thirty on the seventeenth of October before I had the chance to go. Arriving much later then I wanted to because of the heavy traffic and the road closures, the whole journey put my sat-nav into overdrive. I had only just parked up when she walked past my car and got into hers.

I watched as she climbed into the driver's seat, drew the seatbelt across her chest and drove off. When she neared the exit, I kept my distance. Her ticket was quickly snapped up by the machine and the barrier lifted. She sped off as I thrust my ticket home, then set off after her. I kept close behind, but not too close to cause suspicion. She vanished, my heart fluttered. There were no clues as to where she had gone. I slowed to a crawl, turned left, looking everywhere. That's when I saw her turn right at the traffic lights.

'Don't change, please don't change you bastard,' I shouted, but in defiance, they did. I had to wait.

As the traffic lights changed, I darted out like a missile, beating the oncoming car headlights as they drove towards me. Driving on, I thought I'd lost her again, but no, she was there, waiting for me at the next set of lights. Creeping up behind her, we waited for the lights to change again. We moved off in unison, as if she were towing me, knowing that, if she braked, we would collide. Her driving was immaculate, slow but determined; oblivious to my presence.

The avenue of trees seemed to bow as if we were royalty as we continued in convoy. When she signalled to turn left, I kept my distance. I could see her head bobbing to some music playing in the sanctuary of her car not knowing that everything she was doing now, would soon be her last time.

The dull street lamps were perfect as I glided into the parking space several meters from where she had parked at number 48 Grosvenor Road. After she disappeared into the house, I got out of my car and walked around. It seemed as if nothing had changed there in the last fifty years or so. The blue paint that had once clung tightly to glistening railings, hung like sobbing potato peelings while the hinges creaked at the slightest breeze. Bricks on the walls had crumbled, littering the ground with their dandruff. I wondered if the people from the fifties were still inside, frozen in the time they had created for themselves. Still sitting in wood-wormed chairs; meals untouched. The chipped ceramic sink, stained with the years of leached lead as the tap dripped in tune with the clock on the mantelpiece. The metallic tainted food, entering their rotting mouths. They had loved the place, but when the last of them were gone their houses decayed as sure as their bodies in the graveyard. City dwellers, waiting for another house-market boom, replaced doting relatives who looked on in dismay.

Natalie, was living among them, like an orchid in the midst of thistles. When her key entered the lock on her front door, she looked around and then walked into a world where she didn't belong.

I waited for her to switch a light on. Then, getting back into my car and driving off, I noticed that number 63, was empty. And from the unkempt front garden, it had been like it for some time. Thinking of my final plan, I headed for home.

Next morning I was at the estate agents. He agreed to show me around number 63 Grosvenor Road outside the normal block viewing times. He told me all the properties in the street had been built around nineteen-hundred. That they all had the same layout, but some of them had been modernised. Several had open plan configurations. But number 63 had not been altered much, although it did have central heating and some double glazing had been added.

'Even though it's a terrace house,' the agent said as we stood in the hallway, 'you won't hear anything from the neighbours. You see,' he said tapping the wall. 'It's not hollow; these partitioning walls are at least two bricks thick. Not the usual breeze blocks mind, but solid bricks. They knew how to build them in those days. An Englishman's castle and all that; well these houses were built like castles and are sound proof. Give me an old house any day.' He went on and on. I didn't interrupt him but just put the odd mm and a nod in on occasion, just to let him know I was listening. Having said I would think about the purchase of the house, we said goodbye.

Heading away from Grosvenor Road, I decided to stay in the area rather than go back home as I found the journey from London was too stressful for me. Instead I would visit the Victoria shopping centre I'd heard about. There

I would mingle with shoppers, have lunch and return to Natalie's address in the early evening. The prospect of killing her excited me much more than I expected. She had to go; I had promised myself as much over the last month—waiting was not an option now.

Parked near her house again, I waited. On time, she pulled up outside number 48 and went inside.

As soon as she disappeared I was there, looking around, wondering. No curtains twitched as I climbed the foot-worn steps up to her front door, rehearsing what I was going to say. I pressed the door bell. The door slowly opened. I could see I hadn't even given her the chance to remove her coat. The suspicious look on her face made me feel like turning around and walking away; apologising that I had somehow gone to the wrong house, the wrong street or something.

'Can I help you?' her voice was soft. Caring. What could I say? In an instant I heard my voice reply:

'Sorry to bother you, but I saw you pull up. I've just moved in to number 63 down the road and wondered if I could use your phone as my lights have just blown,' I said, trying to sound anxious.

'Yes, of course. By the way, I'm Natalie. Don't you have a phone then?'

'Yes but BT cannot connect it until tomorrow, and my mobile's flat.'

'Number 63 you said, oh it's been empty for ages. We were only saying last week, it's about time someone moved in there. When did you say you moved in?'

'Today; by the way, how are the neighbours round here?' I said trying to sound interested.

'Today, well you must be exhausted. The neighbours are very good, but I don't see them much. They all work in the city and don't come home until late. It's a good job I work too; otherwise I'd never see anyone.'

'I know what you mean, but you said you spoke to someone about number 63.'

'Oh yes, that was my next door neighbour. I'd introduce you to him, but he's away in Frankfurt until Sunday. Do you have a telephone number for an electrician?'

'No,' I said. 'But if I can use your Yellow Pages, I can find one if that's okay with you?' I hoped she would ask me inside so I could get on with what I had to do.

'That's not a problem. But do come in while I look for the number of an electrician I know. He's good, and doesn't charge the earth.' As I entered the hallway, she closed the door behind me. 'If you contact him he'll be with you in less than half an hour,' she said walking down the hall, then stopped as she pulled a card from a box on a table. 'Here's his number, just mention my name. Coffee?' she said with a spring in her voice.

'Oh, that will be really nice, thank you.'

'You can sit in the living room while I make you one if you like,' she gestured towards the door at the end of the hallway. 'Milk and sugar?'

'I hope I'm not putting you to any trouble. Just milk, please,' I said as I half-entered the living room.

'Not at all. I know how it is when you move house, can never find the kettle,' she giggled.

My disguise had totally fooled her. She hadn't recognised me from our brief encounter in London, probably because our meeting now was out of context.

As she turned towards the kitchen, the first blow of my hammer struck her head. Its strength was so powerful her blood splattered the ceiling and walls of the tiny hallway as she fell unconscious onto its flagstones. Fearful she should wake at any minute, and worried about forensics, I dressed as quickly as I could into a disposable suit, over-shoes and gloves. Now I was ready for the night of hell I had promised myself, and that the world would read about in a couple of days whilst enjoying their toast and marmalade.

When I picked up the hammer again it seemed to have a mind of its own as it struck out at her features time and time again, leaving her splintered skull looking more like pulverised summer pudding rather than anything human. Hell had begun.

She was heavier than I had expected as I dragged her into the living room; giving me more space and light to work in. Then I immediately set to work on her body. Undressing her was a real problem as my gloves hindered my progress. But once it was done I went straight for her abdomen, the knife tearing at her flesh without hesitation. I was powerless to stop its momentum; the fiend, Thomas, had taken over. And as the hands, his hands, my hands, foraged around inside her, I felt the fast beating pulse of another life stop. And, just for a microsecond, I felt remorse. The semen was ready, and, as it penetrated her, I felt proud with a job well done.

The shower was as perfect as the 'Fresh as a Mountain Spring' gel I used; so were Natalie's clothes. As I stepped out through her front door I squinted as the early morning sun was just rising. Making the call, I knew it wouldn't be long before she was found.

Her mobile phone shattered as it hit the ground, just before I drove off. In the distance I could hear the rumblings of the new day mingled with the faint sound of a siren. But the certainty of the police being there in a few minutes didn't bother me. Even if our paths crossed, they would never suspect me, they never did. But I hoped that by the time they found her, the washing machine would have finished its cycle.

CHAPTER TWENTY-ONE

With the search warrant firmly gripped in her hand, and without any formal notification, Cadema entered the Wayford Hospital. Stephanie Granger hardly had time to stand up from behind her desk as Cadema barged in. For a moment, no one spoke, as if each one was waiting for the other to react. Cadema gave a shiver as she felt the icy stare from Stephanie who then opened her mouth:

'How dare...'

'Stephanie Granger, I have a warrant to search this hospital and your home, and seize anything I think is important. That includes your late mother's memoirs. Detective Inspector Evans and Sergeant Marriott will do the search. You and I will go to the station where I can take a statement. I need to remind you that you are not under arrest; you are just helping us with our enquiries. Do you understand?'

Stephanie bit her lower lip and nodded, but didn't question Cadema's actions. Instead she asked if she could call someone to be with her when she was interviewed. Cadema agreed to this and informed her of her rights to have a solicitor present if she wished.

'I know what my rights are. I also know what my duty is. I cannot possibly leave the hospital without cover. So you'll have to wait until I've arranged this. That will take me about an hour or so to do. And yes, I'll want a solicitor present.'

'That is not a problem, I'm prepared to wait. And as to the solicitor, one will be arranged for you.' Cadema watched the puzzled look on Stephanie's face.

'On second thoughts, I have nothing to hide. So I'm happy to talk to you without anyone being present for the time being.' She picked up the phone to organise cover for the hospital.

Stephanie had already removed the incriminating evidence her mother had left. So the officers wouldn't find anything, no matter how thorough they were. And even if they did, no one could be prosecuted. Stephanie smiled as she looked at the photograph of her mother, as if to say; *thank goodness you aren't here anymore.* Now all she had to do was to protect her mother's good name.

'Do you have any records of your mother's qualifications?' Cadema asked, knowing what the answer would be before she even asked it. Besides, if she concentrated on the mother, the daughter would be more relaxed and hopefully more willing to say what she knew.

'Yes of course. I keep them in that cupboard,' she pointed, 'as a record of the work my mother did for this hospital. Indeed, we have a memorial lecture on her behalf every year. And then there's the scholarship midwives can apply for to help keep them up to date. My mother was extremely well respected for all the work she did for this hospital.' As she spoke Stephanie's demeanour changed into something resembling an authoritarian old-fashioned matron.

Probably the image of her late mother, Cadema thought and gave a twitch of a smile. 'Very commendable,' she said and changed the subject, bored with the glowing reports from the daughter. Besides Stephanie seemed to be deliberately delaying the investigation by talking.

Stephanie snatched up the receiver the moment the telephone rang. A quick conversation with the caller, she told Cadema the senior midwife, who had agreed to cover for her, would be there in ten minutes. She then moved to the back of her desk, opened a draw and took out a bunch keys. Choosing one, she walked over to the shoulder-high oak cupboard and opened its double doors.

The inside looked like a shrine to a goddess. On the top shelf there were candles, photographs in gilded frames, framed certificates which bore the name of Jessica North, State Registered Nurse 1952, and State Certified Midwife 1954. But it was the inscribed photograph that interested Cadema the most. It read; *'Jessica North, Matron 1969 to 1977.'* And, as those dark eyes looked back at her with the contempt of a matron from that era, Cadema gave a shudder, thinking how Jessica must have terrified even the bravest of mothers.

Cadema ignored Stephanie's protests as she began to search through the items. Moving several photographs and ornaments to one side she discovered, half-hidden at the back, a large ledger. Extracting it, she realised it was a photograph album. On opening it, some of them cascaded onto the floor. Stephanie raced to scoop them up.

'Please be careful with those. Mother cherished them and always kept them in order. I don't know what she would say if she could see this mess.' She gave Cadema an angry look, then sank to her knees and began to retrieve them.

'The album's bulging so much with photographs that they won't even fit back into it,' Cadema said as she looked to find the spaces where the photographs might fit into. There did not appear to be any empty spaces.

Nevertheless, she thought, *they came out of it so they had to fit in it somewhere.*

'Let me do that,' Stephanie's voice was calmer as she held out her arms for the album. Cadema handed it to her. 'Oh yes I can see what the problem is. My mother did have a lot of photos, and it looks as if the glue's become brittle over time, and they've been dislodged.' She began to put them back into the album, explaining that the photographs were of the babies her mother had personally delivered. 'Look you can see she made a few notes on the back of each one.' Stephanie pointed, sounding helpful.

'Yes I can see the name, date of birth and type of delivery written on the back,' Cadema replied. Stephanie handed the album back to her with trembling hands. 'Is this the only photograph album your mother had?'

'As you can see she delivered many babies and the photographs of them are all there. She put them in chronological order and numbered each one. My mother was an excellent record keeper.' Cadema ignored the banter as she carefully turned the pages and nodded when she saw the old glue. She expected the album, with its black and white photographs, to help with her enquiries despite some being damaged or faded. She took extra care with those ones as she did with the ones of dead babies, where someone, supposedly Jessica North, had written the reasons why they had died on the back.

Realising it would be impossible to examine the album in detail while Stephanie was present, Cadema said she would take it to the police station. With some reluctance, Stephanie agreed to let her 'borrow' it, saying it was the only photographic record she had of her mother's work as a midwife. Cadema did not believe the cold dark eyes which looked back at her when she slid the album into one of her forensic bags. No, there was more to Stephanie and she was determined to find out what she was hiding.

Not wanting to remove the photographs of her mother, and the certificates from their frames, Cadema initially decided to take photocopies of them. Then hesitated, thinking there may be evidence hidden behind the frames. She turned to Stephanie:

'I have decided to take all these to the police station, along with the album, so they can be examined in more detail. We will go to your house and if necessary to the police station later.'

Stephanie's body stiffened on hearing this. 'I would prefer to go to the station with my mother's belongings rather than to the house.'

'That may be the case, but I've now decided to go to your house first.'

'Why?'

'I don't have to tell you why I've made that decision.'

'So you'll be taking me to the station later,' Stephanie's voice shook.

'Well it depends on what we find in your house. So when your replacement arrives, we'll go directly there and make a start.'

'There's nothing in my house that warrants this intrusion, but I have no choice than put up with it. You'll have to wait for me though, while I hand over before we can leave.'

'That's fine, I can wait.'

While she waited, Cadema arranged for the contents of the cupboard to be bagged, labelled and taken to the evidence room at the station. An hour later they left the hospital, flanked by two uniformed officers, and headed for Stephanie's house.

The terraced house was smaller than Cadema had expected and before the grey peeling door was opened, she hoped the search would be swift. But, stepping inside she had to negotiate several boxes, journals tied with string, old furniture and other family memorabilia which was stacked everywhere. She estimated it would take at least a week to go through everything. *Grimes will be furious*, she thought as she followed Stephanie into a lounge as cluttered as the hallway. The two police constables followed just as Evans and Marriott arrived. Marriott asked to see Cadema on her own for a minute and told her he had not found anything else relevant to the case in the archives.

Following the allocation of tasks, the two police constables were directed to start work in the loft, overseen by Marriott. Evans would assist Cadema with the other work she needed to do. She told Stephanie to sit in the lounge, while Evans searched the cupboards there. Returning to the hallway, Cadema reached into her bag and pulled out her mobile phone.

'Yes sir, the job's much bigger than I expected. No, I won't keep the two PCs any longer than necessary. But it will take about three days, probably until Thursday, to do a thorough search of the premises.' She heard Grimes grunt as he always did under such circumstances. He told her she could only keep the PCs until Wednesday at the very latest.

'Anyway you're supposed to be investigating the murders, not some bloody baby-swopping scam or some non-existent twins. I'm only going along with this because of your reputation. Anyone else…'

'I appreciate that Sir.'

'You'd better. So when you've finished what you are doing there today, I want to see you in my office. Is that clear?'

'Yes Sir,' she protested. 'But I think we have some proof on that now. When I come in, I'll show you.'

'Have you? Well, it had better be good, I can tell you. Just get here as soon as you can.' Cadema imagined he would explode at any moment. She smiled as she pressed the 'call ended' button on her phone.

She knew he would not yield to her wishes and cursed herself for misjudging the amount of time the investigation would take. It would all be in her records. Everyone knew Grimes was a misogynist and also prejudiced against non-white people. One day she would have proof of this, it was just a matter of time. But she was annoyed with herself too. The more she seemed to do, the worse it became for her to judge the workloads; *a self-fulfilling prophecy*, she thought. But as for the baby-swopping scam, she almost had the tangible evidence to prove it.

Calling Marriott to see how he was getting on in the loft, she hoped it would not be as cluttered as the rest of the house.

***

Standing on a ladder one of the officers had found in the spare bedroom, the constable pushed at the loft door. With the groan from the rusted hinges, he managed to push further until, just past vertical, he let it go and heard it crash on the loft floor. Fumbling in the dark, he caught hold of a cord, and pulled. There was a flash.

'Damn it,' the officer called out.

'What now?' Marriott's exasperated voice called from below.

'Bulbs gone, got a torch Sir?'

Marriott handed him one. 'Always be prepared.'

'Yes Sergeant,' the officer said as he turned the torch on and climbed into the loft shuddered, and then sneezed.

'Be careful when you come up, everything's covered with dust.' He called to the other two.

A couple of minutes later, all three were standing in the cold, dusty and eerie loft.

Marriott recalled what colleagues had said about finding mummified bodies in these places. He shuddered, fearing the worst. But after a new bulb had been fitted, it seemed the same as all other lofts he had been in, except this one was empty apart from an old large brown trunk. Marriott wondered why some of the clutter in the rest of the house hadn't been put up here, although he was glad it hadn't. *Maybe it would have been too much trouble for Stephanie to keep coming up to the loft,* he thought.

'A good place for a body,' he jested to his colleagues; none spoke but he noticed them shiver.

The trunk looked as if it had been dragged across the battle fields of the two world wars. Lowering their heads to avoid the low beams, they approached it. A bell sounding in the distance made them all recoil. They stood in silence for a moment and held their breaths, as if waiting for the trunk to explode. Then jumped at the sound of Evans's voice shouting up the stairs.

'It's just the mail. Don't forget, if you find anything important up there, we need to take it to the station so it can be thoroughly examined.'

'Will do,' Marriott shouted back.

The padlock was opened easily. One of the officers prized the lid open, and immediately stood back. Marriott held his breath and moved forward. He could see some old books inside and realised Jessica North had kept more than just photographic memoirs Cadema had told him about.

Underneath the books he found several diaries, some of which looked as if they had been damaged, *probably by mites,* he thought.

'I think we've found what we are looking for. It's all in a big trunk, so we're going to bring it down once it's been secured,' Marriott shouted down to whoever was listening.

'Just hold on a minute, I need to see it for myself before making any hasty decisions,' Cadema said as she quickly mounted the stairs, leaving Evans below.

Entering the loft, she did a quick examination of the contents. The more she looked the more her heart raced. 'You're right Marriott, these seem extremely important. But the trunk is much too heavy to manoeuvre through the hatch, let alone struggle with it down the stairs. No, we need to think of health and safety. Do a risk assessment and then we can remove it safely,' she scowled at him.

'Yes Ma'am. But we could empty the contents and take them down bit be bit. Once the trunk is empty, it can be lowered down safely, so no one will get injured.'

'That sounds like a good plan to me. Just organise a van so it can be taken to the station, and then get on with it.'

'Yes Ma'am,' he replied as she disappeared through the hatch.

When Evans realised what was happening, he decided to go and supervise the activity, and help where necessary. He ordered Marriott to stay in the loft with one of the officers and the other to join him on the landing. Half an hour later the contents of the trunk lay in piles in one of the bedrooms, the trunk was then secured by Police investigation tape.

'One, two three,' Marriott said as he and the PC lifted the trunk and manoeuvred it, with difficulty, through the hatch. Evans and the other PC caught hold of it and carried it down the stairs to the awaiting van. Once filed again, Evans watched as it was driven off to the police station, then turned to Cadema:

'I haven't found anything significant to our investigation in the lounge yet. Do you want me to continue with the search now we've found the trunk?'

'In light of that, and the need to get on with the rest of the investigation surrounding the murders, I think we can hold off searching the house for the time being.'

Explaining this to Stephanie, she told her that she would not be required at the police station until the trunk and all the other items had been examined.

'So I can go back to work, can I? Well I'm not happy with this toing and froing and I intend to make a complaint about the way I've been treated.'

'You are in your rights to do that. But for the time being we don't need you to assist in our enquiries.' Cadema said and then called for the rest of the team to leave as she headed for the door leaving Stephanie to the turmoil of her house.

***

'I think I've found what we've been looking for Sir, so there's no need to search the whole house now,' Cadema's excited voice echoed in Grimes's office.

'What's your rationale for your decision to call off the search? And for that matter, what have you done with the two PCs I let you have for that very purpose?' his voice was raised to almost shouting point as he towered over Cadema.

'We have found a trunk in the loft containing diaries, ledgers and notes Jessica North made when she was matron at the hospital,' Cadema's voice was calm and assertive.

'So you're still perusing the twin theory? I can't see how it's relevant to the investigation?' he shouted, his face red.

'I've thanked the two PCs and sent them back to their divisions. And as for the twin theory, it is relevant. How else could the DNA match Edward Masons unless he has a twin?'

'But you interviewed Connie Mason, and she denied having twins. Anyway it doesn't explain why Edward Mason's DNA was found at the murder scenes, does it?'

'Not yet anyway, but I think the whole mystery can be solved from the photographs of the babies we found, plus the hospital birth records and now the content of the trunk. The proof is there somewhere, and once we have cross-referenced all of those, I hope to have the answers.'

'Hope, you're always hopeful. But hope will never get the job done. I need something tangible. Real evidence. And I needed it yesterday, not tomorrow.'

'I'll give you all the tangible evidence you need once I've analysed the content of the trunk, Sir.' She reiterated her point as she headed for the door.

'Just do that. And as regards to the two PCs, it won't be easy for you to get any more from other divisions in future. I had enough trouble getting them for you this time. Is that understood?'

'Yes sir,' she walked out of his office and closed the door.

***

Cadema sat in her office thinking about what Grimes had said to her. Earlier he had told her that, at her rank, she should be able to determine the number of police officers she needed and for how long she would need them. That she should never change her mind halfway through an investigation, or deviate from it. But the most damaging thing he said was that if she went on the way she was going, he would inform the deputy commissioner that he had no confidence in her. Now she believed Grimes was collecting evidence on her to support his incompetence theory.

Reaching the examination room where the trunk had been taken, she saw Marriott had already begun working on its contents. He told her Evans was doing some other investigation, but he did not know what it was.

'Well, Ma'am, there are twenty-five diaries here, and I've stacked them in chorological order. One for each year Jessica North worked at the hospital. And there are five more photograph albums, similar to the one found in Stephanie Granger's office,' Marriott said excitedly.

'That's great, but have you had time to view the contents of these?'

'I have done on some of them.' He stood to attention, with his chest forward. 'As you know the albums contain photographs of babies Jessica North delivered over the years. I've only managed to examined two so far, but it looks as if they correspond to the dates in the diaries.'

'Good work, Sergeant, now let's see if we can match the diaries for 1975, with the photographs,' Cadema's voice sounded excited and urgent.

Marriott quickly searched through the items on the table.

'If she was as immaculate at keeping records as her daughter said, it should be easy to identify whether babies were born full term, premature, still births or whatever.'

'You're right,' Cadema said. 'So let's see what we have here.'

Examining the diary for 1975 when Edward was born, several pages were missing before and after the third of March. In the corresponding photograph album some of the photographs were also missing. But after they had been placed in the right order, according to the number written in pencil on the back, they were all there.

The photograph of Edward Mason identified him as a full term baby weighing six pounds eight ounces and his mother had had a normal delivery. But there was something odd about the photograph. After the number and the date on the back, someone had written, A and B. There was no explanation about the letters. When Marriott showed this to Cadema, she realised there was something significant about them and asked him to keep looking to see if there were any other photographs labelled in similar ways, then left the room

Two hours later, Marriott had found six with dates and the letters A and B. When he examined the corresponding pages in the diaries they, too, had been torn out. He telephoned Cadema.

'Excellent, now I know there was something significant going on. I'll be with you in a couple of minutes.'

Arriving in the room, Marriott showed her the photographs.

'You're right, it looks as if it happened about six times in this one year. And it won't surprise me, if we look back over other years, we would see similar patterns.'

'Yes, Ma'am, but I haven't found any photographs of a baby with Mary Buxton. In fact, it appears from the records, that she didn't exist.'

'Not really Sergeant, don't forget those are only the records of Jessica North. Another midwife could have delivered her baby. And there's also the birth register we can check to see what is recorded and if there's any discrepancies.'

'Yes I know, but it recorded what we needed to know, now it looks as if the birth register was falsified.'

'Your right, but we need to concentrate on this new evidence now.'

'Yes Ma'am, and I recall, Jessica North was at Mary Buxton's labour and Mary was eventually discharged with a full term baby.'

'Yes, so it confirms my suspicions that Jessica, and at least one other midwife, must have separated the twin babies at birth. They gave one to the real mother and the other to another mother who had lost her baby. They must have done this several times over the years. And that would account for the A and B on the back of the photographs. I think it represented a code for twin births.'

'I agree, but surely a mother giving birth to twins must have known something was wrong when she was only given one baby?'

'Not necessarily, they may never have known they were having twins. You remember Samantha saying that if they had too much gas and air, nitrous oxide she called it, then they could get disorientated. Similar to being drunk she said. Anyway they could have given her other drugs; who knows. Therefore the mother may not be able to remember everything about the birth. So what we need to do now is find this Mary Buxton and discover what happened to her in labour. Find out about the baby she took home. It is the same age and probably the image of Edward Mason, his twin brother.

That is, if they were identical twins.' Cadema said, making her usual mental notes.

'But what about Connie Mason, Ma'am?'

'Oh, I don't believe she knew anything about what had happened. And has no idea she is a victim of a terrible conspiracy, the same as other women if I am not mistaken.'

'But the husbands, or partners, they would surely know.'

'No, I remember Samantha saying that in those days most prospective fathers were left pacing the corridors and were hardly allowed to be with the woman during labour, and certainly not at the birth. The only people who would be in the room, apart from the mother of course, would be the midwives. Unless they were in a consultant unit, but we're talking about a cottage hospital here. A woman may see her GP at his surgery, but, as Samantha said, they may not examine her if she had recently been seen by the midwife and everything was satisfactory. A GP would probably be called in, at the hospital shortly after the birth. But no one else would be needed unless there was an emergency.'

'That's terrible, so anything could have happened,' Marriott shook his head.

'Yes, but as Samantha said, these women were considered to be low risk. That's why they were there and not in a consultant unit. They had a system called shared-care between the GP and midwife. Generally speaking they each saw a pregnant woman alternately. It seemed that some GPs were more thorough, or experienced than others. So some GPs may have agreed to let midwives do all the examinations. Samantha didn't know, but said it was feasible especially as GPs were always so busy. Therefore, if midwives looked after the women throughout their pregnancy, they would be the only ones who knew if a woman was pregnant with twins. And in those days women would have believed everything a midwife told them. If the midwife said she was delivering the placenta, the woman would believe her. So I think each second baby was most likely taken away while the first one was crying. Then the noise from the second baby would be overshadowed by the first, or muffled by the midwife as she left the room. And the placenta was probably delivered soon after this.'

'Good God,' Marriott exclaimed then clasped his hand across his mouth. 'Sorry but I didn't mean to offend you. I know you don't like us swearing, or blaspheming in this case, but it was just a reflex action,'

'Don't worry Marriott, I've heard much worse than that, even from my own team. Anyway, I'm too engrossed in this to worry.'

***

Cadema asked Evans to go to the address found in the hospital records to see if anyone could recall anything about Mary Buxton. She didn't expect him to find much, but believed he would do his best. *Besides the rest of the officers don't call him 'The Ferret,' for nothing,* she thought, although he was unaware of that.

'Before I go,' Evans said, 'what if she had given a false name and address to the hospital.'

'I know she didn't, as the community midwife visited her at home on at least two occasions. And you can be pretty certain she used the right name.'

'Fine, I'll go and see what I can dredge up.' As he left the office he asked DI Johns to accompany him. He didn't really like working alone, and out of everyone else, he preferred working with her. She could be relied on to talk in her usual soothing tones. When she asked questions, most people, especially other women, would talk to her. On one occasion, a woman suspect she was interviewing confessed because she wanted to please her. *Women*, he though, *are most illogical and fickle.*

Johns said she was happy to help. Besides, with such a sensitive subject, her expertise was paramount to the investigation. Cadema agreed. The case was gathering momentum each day, and as other officers were busy, she had planned to enhance Johns' involvement. Evans had unwittingly helped with this plan.

***

Having called at the last known address of Mary Buxton, to no avail, Evans and Johns visited the immediate neighbours in the street. No one knew her or her baby as it had been too long ago. Most of the people had moved into the area eight years ago when the last business was relocated to Edinburgh and the houses were sold to their current occupiers.

One of the residents remembered a woman called Carol Kershaw who bought her house off an old woman who had lived there in the nineteen seventies. The old woman had given Carol graphic details of everyone who had lived in the street. But Carol had sold up some time ago. Nevertheless, she thought the estate agent would probably know where Carol had moved to.

The two officers went to visit the estate agent. They discovered the agent only kept records for five years. After which time they were destroyed as they took up much too much space. He named a solicitor who dealt with the sale of houses in the area and said they kept records far longer than he did. Evans thanked him for the information and set off with Johns to the solicitor's address.

The chambers were situated on the upper floor of a new development. Messrs Bradshaw and Son was written on the shiny brass plaque screwed to the wall. The bell was answered by someone who looked like a butler. Evans swallowed, stood to attention, and then, showing his identity badge, asked to see Mr Bradshaw, saying that the matter was extremely urgent. They were ushered into a traditional oak-panelled office which contrasted to the modernity of the building. Waiting just a few minutes, they were introduced to Mr Bradshaw. A stout man with a pendulous middle, and round doubled-chinned face, greeted them with an outstretched hand.

'Do take a seat Chief Inspector, and the Sergeant,' he said without any noticeable eye contact. 'I hate it when people tower; inspector. That's better. Now what can I do for you?'

'I am Detective Inspector Evans and this is Detective Inspector Johns.' He reinforced the names and ranks to show they were as important as the letters on Mr Bradshaw's name plate. 'We have come to ask you about the sale of number six Hawthorne Road. We need to know the name of the woman who sold the house to Carol Kershaw, and where she went to.'

'The vendor you mean?' Mr. Bradshaw said in a condescending manner. 'When did you say the sale was?'

'I didn't, but it was about eight years ago.'

'Now let me see. I seem to remember something but I will need to get the file out to be sure.' He flipped the switch on his intercom which looked almost as old as he did. His secretary answered.

'Miss Morgan, will you get me the file for Number six Hawthorne Road?'

'I know you may find this impertinent, Mr. Bradshaw but why do you want the file?' she asked.

'I just do, so get it will you?'

'I can get it, but I may be able to tell you something important if you let me know why you want it. We don't write everything in the files you know,' she replied indignantly.

'Yes I do know, just get the file and I am sure the chief inspector will find the information you have interesting. But I need the file and I need it now.' His voice sounded angry as he fidgeted in his chair.

'Yes Sir. Right away.' And no sooner had she answered than she was at the door with the file. Her red nails contrasted with her blanched fingers as she held the file tightly to her chest.

'Good, Miss Morgan. We want the file to find out the name of the person who sold the house to Carol Kershaw. And also the address where she moved to.' Mr. Bradshaw said, his head nodded with every word as if he would bite off his tongue if he continued to chew as he spoke.

'Oh, that's an easy question to answer. You should have asked me first then I wouldn't have had to go and get the file. You see, my mother knew her.'

'Well that's remarkable Miss Morgan. Tell the Inspector how she knew her.'

'My mother was her friend; well that is, she visited her.'

'It's all right Mr. Bradshaw, we will ask the questions thank you,' Evans said. He had tried to speak earlier but Mr. Bradshaw ignored his covert attempts.

'A friend of your mother's. So what was her name?'

'I'm afraid she died seven years ago.'

'I am sorry to hear about your mother,' Evans continued with indifference in his voice, unable to cope with emotive outbursts. 'But what was the old woman's name?' he insisted.

'Oh my mother is still alive; she was only in her twenties then. The woman she knew died.'

'Can you tell me the woman's name, please?' Evans tried hard not to show his frustration as he spoke.

'I think her name was Mary Fletcher, mm, yes that's it. And Mary sold her house to a Carol... somebody, I believe.'

'Yes, we know, Carol Kershaw brought the house. But did Mary Fletcher have any relatives?'

'Not that I can remember, but what did you want to know?'

'We want to find out what happened to a Mrs Mary Buxton who lived at number twenty-two.'

'Oh I can tell you that. Apparently Mary Fletcher used to baby sit for her from time to time. That is until the family emigrated to Australia. They said he was a lovely boy. Robert I think his name was. My mother mentioned him from time to time. Australia, I always wanted to go there. Have you ever been there Inspector?' Miss Morgan's eyes sparkled as she spoke.

'No. Please, Miss Morgan,' his voice sounding exasperated. 'Please tell me about Mrs Buxton.'

'Well, they said she just left in a hurry. The baby would have been about three years old then. You could ask my mother about it if you like, but I don't think she will be able to tell you much else.'

The disappointment showed on Evans's face as Johns silently stood up. He sat there wondering if they would ever be able to solve the mystery as each day grew more incredulous. Thanking Mr Bradshaw and Miss Morgan for their cooperation, they left the building without speaking to each other.

As Evans drove back to the police station, he was pleased Johns had kept quiet. He wanted to think. So he did as he usually did when he was feeling exasperated. He created an aura around him hoping people would sense it was fruitless to talk to him when he was in such a mood. He felt so defeated and knew Cadema would not be pleased with the result of their investigation.

CHAPTER TWENTY-TWO

Cadema was annoyed when she heard about Mary Buxton. After gaining her composure, she reminded Evans and Johns that Australia was only twenty odd hours flying time away and that Australia House was almost up the road. So she instructed them to go there to find out if she, and her son could be traced through Australian Government channels.

As the two officers stood before the steps of Australia House the rays from the mid October sun glistened on the marble pillars of its portly facade, while pigeons circled above them like vultures waiting for their prey to die. Walking up the steps, they entered through the front door. Being greeted by one of his retired officers, Evans said he had an appointment with Mr. Allan Marsh in the emigration department. They were immediately escorted up to the second floor and were shown into a capacious office.

'Good morning, you must be Inspector Evans and Inspector Johns, it's good to meet you,' Marsh said as his lean body stood up towering over them like a military officer. His handshake greeted Evans as if he were Doctor Livingstone.

'Please, do sit down,' he gestured to the two Queen Ann chairs in front of the desk. 'How can I help you?

'We are here on a serious police matter. The person we need to interview may have emigrated to Australia, probably around the early 1980's.'

'Can you be more specific with the dates Inspector?'

'I am sorry but that's all the intelligence we have at the moment.'

'Very well, so what can you tell me about the person?'

'We are looking for a Mrs. Mary Buxton. Her last address was twenty-two Hawthorne Road. She had a son aged about three years old at the time, we think his name was Robert but we can't be sure.'

'At least it's a start. There are many ways of tracing people who have emigrated. One is through the immigration records at the time, one is through employment records in Australia and the other is through the schools, or other educational establishments. And of course, there's also the penal system. Unless, of course, the names have been changed; either through marriage or by Deed Poll.'

'How long do you think it will take for you to find them?' Johns asked.

'That depends on how urgent you want them and how long it takes to locate the year they emigrated.'

'It's extremely urgent; we are following leads to a suspected serial killer,' Evans said somewhat irritated that Johns had butted in.

'Do you mean the 'Common Murders'? Well, it really is important then. I'll set the wheels in motion right away. I should be able to tell you something by tomorrow at the latest. Our technology is spot on these days.'

'What about later today? As you can appreciate, any delay could put lives at risk.'

'That's a tall order, but I will do my best,' Marsh said, then stood up as they began to leave. 'Remember, it's the end of the day in Australia now. But I'll set things in motion so that it is looked at first thing tomorrow.'

Saying their good-byes, the two officers headed back to the station.

'I got the impression you were angry with me back there, Paul,' Johns said.

'I was when you began to take over. I don't like interruptions when I'm asking questions.'

'So why did you ask me to go with you if you didn't want me to get involved? I can't sit there like one of your appendages and say nothing. And at my rank, I need to be involved as much as possible.'

'Okay, I get the drift. But next time…' he stopped, not wanting to get involved in a petty argument and decided he would not ask her to accompany him again. The rest of the journey was made in silence except for him cursing at other road users.

***

As Evans and Johns entered the police station they were surprised and saddened to hear another murder had been committed. Finding the address, and forfeiting lunch, they turned, ran to the car, and headed for Grosvenor Road, South Ruislip.

When Cadema reached the address, the area had been cordoned off by the local police. The CSI team were already there. An Inspector Murray greeted her.

'We think this may be another victim of your serial killer and it's not a pretty sight Ma'am,' he said.

'It never is, but we have had to get used to seeing such things. Is Doctor Lilly here?' Cadema dressed into a forensic suit as she spoke.

'Yes. As she's been involved with all the other murders, she was called to this one. I think she has completed her initial assessment.'

As they walked to the tented front door, Julia was standing there; Cadema offered a silent nod.

'When they called me, I was sceptical at first. But now I've seen the body, it looks like the same killer, despite the lack of auburn hair. My quick assessment is that the victim, has been dead for at least twelve hours. She was obviously struck repeatedly on the head with a blunt instrument, most likely a hammer. But it's hard to tell anything else from her wounds. There are no signs of rape but there was a large amount of something that looks like semen, both on the genitalia and her upper pubic area. For some reason the killer opened her abdomen, but all the contents are intact. I noticed she was about eight weeks pregnant but I can tell you more when I do the post mortem.'

'That's awful. I wonder why he chose her then, and here of all places? It's a long way from where the others were murdered.' Cadema shook her head as they walked into the hallway.

'Like the others, he struck her on the head, the first blow must have felled her. See, the scattered blood stains on the hall ceiling and walls,' Julia pointed. 'That shows she was hit more than once. Then for some reason he dragged her to the lounge. That's when he obliterated her features and mutilated her body. But as you know I won't be able to swear it's our serial killer until we do a DNA test on the ejaculate he left.'

'I'll treat this as if it were the same killer until we discover otherwise,' Cadema said. Following Julia, she placed her feet, one at a time, onto the stepping plates and entered the living room.

The scene was chaotic, with hardly any difference between blood and other matter scattered on the floor and walls. Even the photographs on the mantelpiece were blood spattered. She moved towards one of a young woman with blond hair. Turning it round, she read out the name 'Natalie Taylor.' For some reason the name rang a bell, but she couldn't remember why. She suspected that the person on the floor was Natalie but it was impossible to identify her from the photograph. Nevertheless, as all the identification in the house pointed to the victim as Natalie Taylor, a freelance journalist, Cadema surmised it was probably her; that she had been murdered by the same person as the others had, despite the hair colour.

Three hours later Cadema and her team were back at the police station for a briefing, and an update on the investigations. But before she had time to talk to her team, Grimes called her into his office and asked her what was going on.

'Yes Sir,' Cadema said. 'The victim in this case was killed in her own home and has blond hair, not auburn. Her body was also mutilated, revealing that she was pregnant. These things are different to the other cases, where all the victims were killed in the open air. However, the fact that she was bludgeoned, possibly with a hammer, and the fact that a large amount of semen was left on her body suggest it might be the serial killer.'

'My God,' he exclaimed as his body shuddered again, then he quickly composed himself. 'So what does it tell you, Superintendent?'

'Well Sir, it tells me the person had plenty of time to do what he did, he even tided up after him. But we won't know if it's the work of the same killer until we get the DNA profile. Bagley is working on it at the moment.'

'Good. So what's this about Mary Buxton?'

Cadema explained what Evans had found out and said she hoped there would be some news in a couple of days.

'At least you are making some progress there.'

'And another thing, Sir, we have found records of Stephanie Granger's mother suggesting she was the leader in a baby swapping scam at the hospital. It looks as if she substituted dead babies with live ones taken from women who had given birth to twins. The records we've collected appear to show she did this on at least six occasions. We may unearth other information as we track the people down.'

'Good grief. Do you mean mothers gave their babies away without the proper authorities knowing?'

'No, that's not the case Sir. It appears that, when a woman was having twins, the midwife, in this case Jessica North, told her she was having one baby. So when she went into labour and the second baby was delivered, it was given away to another woman who had recently had a still birth. There is no record of this but from what we've found it looks like the case.'

'Bloody hell,' Grimes lowered his head. 'But how does all this fit in with the current murders?'

'One of the babies involved was probably Edward Mason's twin brother. He was given to a Mary Buxton; that's where the Australia link comes in. If this brother, whom we believe is called Robert, came back to England, then he must be our killer. That's my theory anyway,' Cadema said trying not to be too presumptive in the matter.

'Your twin theory again, hey. Well, you may have a point there after all. So it looks as if you have it all under control. Now let's hope you'll make an arrest soon.'

'Yes, I hope to once we've found Robert Buxton and done his DNA profile.'

'Good, so you'd better get on with the investigation.

'Thank you, Sir,' she said leaving his office.

Cadema felt drained of the energy she needed for the accumulating workload she had. After briefing her team, and Actions had been allocated, all she really wanted to do was to go home to bed. But as it was only three in the afternoon, this was not an option.

Now, sitting at her desk, she tried to think logically about the killer's motive. What troubled her the most was why the killer had chosen to murder his latest victim in her own home. She had obviously let him in, which meant she could have known him. She sat at her desk mulling over the photograph which Marriott had left, when her eyes began to close. She didn't know where the last hour had gone when the telephone startled her.

'Hello is that Superintendent Sharma?' She yawned, and heard a male voice:

'Yes, who am I speaking to?' she said, because for a moment, she could not recognise the voice.

'It's Bill Watson, manager of the emergency services. Can I come over and see you; I've found some more information which may be useful for your murder enquiries.'

He'd better have a clearer recording than the ones he had last time, she thought. She remembered the last time he visited. The recordings of muffled messages from the last two murder victim's mobile phones, proved useless to the investigation. And it had never been ascertained whether they were the victim's voices or the killers. She hoped this would be different.

'So what have you got this time?' she sounded indifferent.

'We definitely think we have the voice of the killer on tape, and this time it's very clear.' Cadema's fatigue seemed to vanish in a flash as she sat upright in her chair.

'Great, when will you be here?'

'I'll be there in half an hour.'

Fifteen minutes later Evans and Johns sat with Cadema in her office waiting for Watson to arrive.

'If the tape is audible and genuine, then this may be the breakthrough we are looking for,' Cadema said optimistically.

'I hope you're right Ma'am, look at the time we wasted on the other two,' Evans said.

'Yes, even after they had been analysed, both by the dialectologist and forensic psychologist, they could not be deciphered. I hope this one will be different. And by what Watson says, it is.

'I'm not prepared to share your optimism Ma'am until I've heard them.'

Johns nodded at the conversation, but as she had not heard the other tapes, she remained quiet.

Bill Watson was a small meek man with a touch of a beard that might be expected on a teenager. But when he spoke his voice of authority lingered in the air like the reverberations of a loud speaker on a factory floor.

'We have recorded a nine-nine-nine call which came in from the mobile phone owned by Natalie Taylor, a freelance journalist; last known address was 48 Grosvenor Road. But as soon as the voice stopped, the phone went dead. I will play it to you,' Watson said like a child eager to please a parent.

'That's great,' said Cadema 'when did you receive it?'

'It was received at 07.29 hours on the eighteenth of October. The police responded to the call at 07.52 hours but there were no signs of a disturbance at that address. Indeed, the house had been empty for some time.' He said as he switched on the tape.

'Police service; I want to report a murder at 63 Grosvenor Road, South Ruislip. You need to go there right away.'

'And that was all that was said?' Cadema asked, trying to identify the voice and thinking she would get the recording analysed as soon as possible. Asking for it to be played again, she sat mesmerized as the voice sounded like a female. It was obviously disguised, and it could not have been Natalie's as she was dead by then. But there was something else about the voice, but she was unable to identify what it was.

'Where did the satellite place the caller?'

'Right outside number 63 Grosvenor Road. But the person must have known we could track him.'

'Yes, so he either took it with him or threw it somewhere. The former is the most likely scenario, as nothing was found by my officers when they searched the area. But thank you for bringing the tape to us. I will keep it as it could be the voice of our killer,' Cadema said.

'I certainly hope so. You can keep the recording for as long as you like, we have a copy for our records.'

'Thank you,' Cadema said and then asked Johns to organise an officer to escort Mr Watson out of the building. As soon as he had gone she asked Evans to assemble the team so they could listen to the tape.

Reaching the briefing room. She turned on the tape.

'Pay attention everyone. This is most likely to be the killer's voice, despite him trying to disguise it. If it's genuine, then it's the first piece of tangible evidence we have,' Cadema said as the officers listened attentively to the recording. When it had finished playing, she stood and waited for their response but no one spoke.

'I know you have already searched the area, but at first light I want you to go back and look again. Speak to the neighbours again. Jog their memories for the day before the murders or even before that. See if anyone found anything resembling a mobile phone, or even a phone itself as someone may have unwittingly picked it up. Find out if the neighbours saw anyone in the areas that they had not seen before as it appears that the victim may have been stalked by the killer. That's all for now, and don't forget you need to be here early tomorrow.' Cadema's eyes panned the audience of officers, then she looked back at Evans.

He coughed and looked flushed.

'We will all do our best Ma'am, but this killer is very cunning, and it appears that he only leaves the things he wants us to find.' Evans said as he arranged the time they were to start in the morning.

Cadema didn't comment. All she wanted at the moment was action and evidence and despite the scepticisms, she believed they would no doubt find something. She left the room saying she hoped she would not be disappointed by their efforts.

***

As she stepped out of the station, the press were waiting.

'We understand there has been another murder. Can you tell us who it is Superintendent?' a man said thrusting a microphone towards her face, almost catching her nose.

'No sorry, you'll have to wait until the press statement is given.'

'Is it another 'Common Murder'?' a female voice yelled out three rows back from where Cadema was standing.'

'I cannot say at this stage, only that there has been a murder and that the victim has not been identified yet.'

'But is it the same killer as all the others?' another journalist at the front yelled as cameras flashed, while the crowd jostled.

'I am unable to say at this time. Now please leave me to get on with the investigation,' Cadema said as Evans and Marriott, who had just arrived, pushed aside the crowd. All three got into separate cars and sped off.

Journalists, Cadema thought to herself, *why do they always act like vultures when faced with 'sensational cases' as they call them?*

She wondered if the body was Natalie Taylor, the journalist. If so, was she like the ones she'd just encountered? After all she knew journalists were tenacious when researching a story. She may have discovered something about the killer. He may have found out, and that's why she had been murdered.

She could have known him beforehand. Or she was collecting evidence about him and was planning to go to the police? He then stalked her, as she probably stalked him. He'd won; killing her was his prize, even though she didn't fit the profile of his other victims. His MO may have been slightly different this time, but somehow she knew she was dealing with the same killer. Now all she wanted was for his voice to be recognised. *But whose voice is it?* she thought.

CHAPTER TWENTY-THREE

Cadema was on her way, with Marriott, to break the news to Mr and Mrs Taylor, who she believed to be, Natalie Taylor's parents, and arrange for them to identify the body.

The Tailors lived in the wealthiest part of Enfield in North London.

It was early evening as they reached the tree-lined street, punctured by the occasional driveway that was the only indication the area was inhabited.

Halfway up, on the left-hand side, a driveway with a sign inscribed with '*The Moor House*' could be seen as the car's headlights illuminated the tears of rain that fell onto its golden letters. Marriott turned the car into the driveway where weeping rhododendrons seemed to bow as they passed. The cat's eyes, lining the drive, squinted as the car crunched its way towards, what appeared to be, an empty house.

Cadema felt her heart sink at the thought of having a fruitless journey. But her fears were alleviated when, after pulling the bell rope, she heard the sound of footsteps on a wooden floor. The ornate old oak door creaked open on its weary hinges.

'Good evening,' a middle-aged woman, dressed in a floral woollen dress half-hidden by an apron, said as Cadema held up her identification badge.

'Who have you come to see?' the woman asked as she squinted at the badge.

'Are you Mrs. Taylor?' she enquired and then introduced Marriott.

'Oh good grief no, I'm the housekeeper, Miss Marshall. There's no Mrs Taylor, but Mr. Taylor is in the drawing room. Please come in and I will tell him you're here.'

Their step made the polished ebony boards creak as they followed the housekeeper along the corridor. Cadema was intrigued by the opulence of the place, its oak panelled walls and doors smelling like an old church, with the dampness of age. Before she had time to contemplate further her mind was distracted by the chimes from the Grandfather clock towering menacingly above her, as if in protest at her intrusion.

As the door at the bottom of the hallway opened the brightness of the light dazzled her so much she could hardly see the figure standing just a couple of metres away from of her.

'Hello, I am Mr Taylor, how can I help you?' he said holding out his hand to greet them as they entered the room. Her eyes adjusted, and Cadema could now see a man in his fifties, standing in his tweed jacket with his back to an enormous marble fire place. The flames lit the room much better than the light from the crystal chandelier.

'We are very sorry to call on you so late. I am Superintendent Sharma and this is Sergeant Marriott, we're from homicide command in central London.'

'Homicide, well this must be serious. Where's P.C Gordon, our local constable?' Mr Taylor looked beyond the two officers as if searching for the PC.

'We have come directly from London. The local police have been informed.' It wasn't really a lie, they had been informed, but only after she had arrived at Mr. Taylor's address. This was her way of getting a head start on the investigation.

'Please do sit down. We used to see our local police much more often than we do now, what with the cutbacks. But we see PC Gordon as he likes our honey. And it's nice to see a familiar face if the police have to call.'

'I am sure it is, Sir. But please, we need to speak to you on an urgent and very serious matter,' Cadema noticed the family photographs on the piano, one of them resembled Natalie.

'I'm all ears as they say,' he gave a hint of a smile.

'I understand you have a daughter named Natalie?' Marriott asked.

'Why? I hope she hasn't got into anything too outlandish,' his said flippantly.

'No sir, please; **do** you have a daughter called Natalie?' he continued.

'Of course I do, I have just said so haven't I?' the smile went from his face and eyes.

'And does she live at number 48 Grosvenor Road, South Ruislip?'

'Yes,' he frowned.

'We are very sorry to say this, but we have some bad news to tell you.' Cadema said softly.

'Bad news, what bad news? Go on Superintendent, I can take it.'

'Well sir, I think Natalie has been murdered.'

From the back of the room the housekeeper made a gasp and almost fell to the floor. Marriott rushed to help her into a chair.

'Oh no, not my daughter. How did she…? I told her not to get involved and to leave the detectives to do their work. Was it that drugs ring she was investigating?'

'We don't think so, Sir. It's nothing like that. We think she may be the latest victim of the serial killer we are investigating.'

'What—oh no, not the so called 'Common Murders'? But she wouldn't go anywhere near a common. We discussed that the last time she visited. She told me then she would never put herself into a compromising position. No, it could not possibly be my daughter. No I don't believe it. You must have made a mistake.'

'I am very sorry, Sir, but I don't think a mistake has been made.'

Mr. Taylor got up from his seat, staggered across the room to the piano and picked up one of the photographs. 'Look, this is my daughter,' he clutched the photograph to his chest as if his arms would break if he let go. 'This is her, take a good luck and tell me she isn't the person you have found. Take a closer look.' The photograph of a young woman with blond hair was thrust into Cadema's face. 'Now tell me you have made a mistake.'

'Sorry Sir, I don't think there has been a mistake. A young woman was found murdered at your daughter's address. We believe that person is your daughter. Nevertheless, we need you to come back to London with us so you can identify the body.'

'Body, how dare you. If she is dead, which I doubt very much, she is my daughter and always will be. I don't mind seeing the body of another person. But I assure you my daughter has not been murdered. I just know she has not.' He took a handkerchief from his pocket and blew his nose.

Cadema spent the next half hour persuading him to travel with them to London and identify the body. There wasn't a Mrs Taylor, she had died of breast cancer over a year ago. All he had to comfort him now was his housekeeper, who went with him to the police car.

***

The journey to London was strained, not just because of the atmosphere in the car, which was subdued, but because of the heavy rain and the numerous small accidents Marriott encountered. Still Mr. Taylor protested. The only deviation from this was when they stopped for a break near Tottenham. He said Natalie had dyed her hair an auburn colour just before the murders started. But she reverted back to her natural blond colour when her colleagues said it looked as if the killer was choosing victims with auburn hair.

As she listened, Cadema thought about what she was going to say to him when they reached the mortuary. She wished the legislation, to identify bodies through DNA testing rather than identification by relatives, had not failed to get through Parliament. But it had, so she still had to deal with the devastating Dickensian consequence.

At least morticians always tried to make bodies as presentable as possible to the family, despite some of the conditions they may be in. She hoped they had achieved this with Natalie Taylor. However, she did warn Mr. Taylor about the condition of the body and that he may have difficulty identifying her. But when she saw Natalie she realised they had done the best they possibly could.

Mr. Taylor confirmed it was his daughter, so Cadema took him and the housekeeper to the quiet room to interview him.

As they entered, he took out his handkerchief and began to sob into it, the housekeeper followed suit. Quietly asking Marriott to order tea, she tried to comfort the couple. Failing to do so, she sat in silence until, after a few minutes, Mr Taylor wiped his eyes, blew his nose and sat upright in the chair.

'There Superintendent, please ask all the questions you need to,' he said authoritatively then looked at his housekeeper who immediately stopped crying and dabbed at her eyes.

Marriott returned and gave two cardboard mugs of tea to the couple.

'When you're ready Mr. Taylor, I'd like you to tell me as much as you can about Natalie,' Cadema said quietly.

Mr Taylor took a sip and looked at her.

'She should never have dyed her hair,' he shook his head. 'I told her it looked ridiculous, but she did it to please her boyfriend at the time. When she finished with him, and also when she heard about the murders, she changed it back to her natural blond colour. But I don't understand why she was murdered in the first place, let alone why it happened at her house.'

'That's what we are trying to find out. Do you know if she had any friends in London?'

'She didn't have a boyfriend but she was friends with James Connor who works in a publishing office in Baker Street in central London. You don't think it's her old boyfriend, or James do you?' he gave a sniff into his handkerchief.

'I am unable to answer that at this moment. But do you know their actual addresses?'

'No, she kept her work separate from me, and from her mother when she was alive,' his focus went to the floor. 'And I don't see her much these days. Maybe at the odd weekend that's all.'

His housekeeper took hold of his hand.

'That's right she's only been twice in the last two months,' she said.

Mr. Taylor snatched his hand away.

'Do you know of anyone who may wish to harm Natalie?' Cadema asked, somewhat abruptly.

His eyes narrowed as he look up:

'I certainly do not know who would want to harm her. But I swear if I find out who did, I suggest you are not around when I do. My ex-military experience is the only thing I will need then.'

'I realise you are upset, Mr. Taylor but taking the law into your own hands is not the solution.'

'Why should I care if I spend the rest of my life in prison, if I can get justice for Natalie?'

'I can appreciate how you may be feeling, but hopefully you will reconsider what you've just said and let us do our work and bring the killer to justice.'

He nodded. Cadema nodded in return, knowing that anger was one of the first responses to the news that a loved-one had been murdered. But she also knew that threats towards the perpetrator were seldom acted upon.

As Mr. Taylor seemed more relaxed, she explained they would keep him informed about the investigation. After transport was arranged for the couple, she said goodbye.

***

The team was waiting as Cadema entered the briefing room.

'Right, what have you been doing?' she looked at Evans. 'Hope you've found something this time.'

'Well ma'am, there's nothing new at the scene,' he tried to hide the twitch in his left eye which he put down to too much time spent looking at HOLMES-two.

'So the second search was fruitless?'

'Afraid so, but I did find out that someone was shown round the house at number 63 Grosvenor Road. However, the estate agent didn't take the person's details. All he remembered was the woman seemed very interested in the house, that she drove a white Peugeot and never came back.'

'Woman, did you say a woman?'

'Yes I did. It was definitely a woman, one with blond hair.'

'That means it could have been anyone, including Natalie Taylor. She may have a friend who was looking for a property.'

'But Ma'am, Natalie Taylor does not match the estate agent's description. He said the woman was about five feet eight inches tall, and was probably about thirty-five years old. Much too tall and old to be Natalie. Besides Natalie drove a four-wheel drive and she had done so for the last three years. So it couldn't possibly have been her.'

Cadema listened with caution. Evans, although very thorough, was capable of leading his colleagues down blind allies. But on this occasion she had the feeling he was right even though the woman probably had no connection with the case and said as much to her team. Despite this, she asked him to find out who the woman was.

'Yes, Ma'am, I'll organise it. In the meantime, I'm following up on Mary Buxton.'

CHAPTER TWENTY-FOUR

'Hello Ma'am, it's Paul. I've just left Allan Marsh's office at Australia House. It sounds as if we're in luck. Apparently Mary Buxton, Robert Buxton's mother, did emigrate to Australia. They settled in a place called Frankston, which is one of the suburbs on the south east coast near Melbourne, Victoria. She divorced her husband, and he returned to England, but Marsh cannot tell me where he lives. Anyway, she goes off and marries a guy called Jones, but it didn't work out. So after another divorce she went up to the Gold Coast.' Evans spoke excitedly into his mobile phone.

'Look Paul, I wish you wouldn't go round in circles. Just get to the real issues please. All I want to know is where Robert Buxton is right now, and not everything he'd been doing since he came out of nappies. If you continue the way you're going, it'll take a couple of hours to get to the point.'

'Yes Ma'am,' he tutted.

'Better still, don't tell me any more over the phone, come to my office and we can discuss it here.'

'Yes Ma'am, I'll be there as soon as I can,' he said then Cadema heard him mutter 'That's a bloody nuisance,' under his breath.

'Good, by the way I have another lead which sounds promising and Grimes is pressing me for an update. How long do you think you'll be?'

'Half an hour. I just need to drop Joanna off. She asked me to tell you that her mother is ill again and the matron at the home has asked her to go and see them. It's not far out of my way; if that's okay with you Ma'am?'

'Yes, very well. But as soon as you've finished, I want you here.' She sounded less compassionate than she would have liked. But she needed to reinforce the urgency.

Although Evans said he wouldn't work with Johns again, he had no choice when Cadema asked her to accompany him. Now he had dropped her off, he would try to avoid her in future. It was her fault he was stuck behind several cars that moved at a snail's pace. The build-up of traffic had started earlier than usual for the 'school run'. The increase in the congestion charges had done little to deter people from using their cars. It had only gone quiet for a few days, then it was back to normal when the hassle of using public transport kicked in. Not having his usual emergency car, he had to wait in the queue the same as everyone else.

It was an hour later when he arrived. Cadema was already in Grime's office and although the door to his office was closed, his bellowing voice could be heard.

'You mean to tell me Superintendent, you haven't found anything else at the murder scene?' Grime's voiced vibrated in the room.

'No, despite the area being searched twice, there was no sign of a mobile phone, so we must assume he took it with him,' she answered quietly. Not that she felt intimidated, but she was determined not to lose control and shout.

'Well it's not good enough; you know how urgent this investigation is. And the press are having a field day now they know one of their own has been murdered. And especially when they found out she'd been doing investigations of her own.'

'I am aware of that. But at the moment I'm about to find out where Robert Buxton is.'

'Good, at least that may help. But did you follow up the likelihood of a woman accomplice?'

'It's being done, Sir.'

'Well that's not a good enough answer. Let me tell you something Superintendent,' as his voice exploded Cadema thought he would certainly have a coronary. 'You know we need results now, not next week. Besides, you can't even control your damn officers. If you tell an officer you want him in half an hour; that's what you bloody well want. Not in thirty-five minutes, and in this case with Evans, over an hour later. It just won't do.'

'Sir, my officers have worked extremely hard during this investigation. And we have good results so far. Now I believe we are about to discover who the perpetrator is.'

'Well, I hope you're right. You'd better get on with it then,' he said as Cadema slipped out of his office and closed the door.

'Are you all right Ma'am?' Evans said, showing some concern for her.

'Of course I am,' she lied. 'What took you so long? It's difficult as it is without you being so late.'

'The traffic...'

'I don't want to hear your excuses, just tell me, as succinctly as possible, about what you discovered at Australia House.'

'Apparently when Mary Buxton had first married Jones he didn't adopt Robert so he remained Robert Buxton. This was because...'

'Look Paul, I don't want to know all the history, just give me the current facts please.'

His eyes twitched as he replied: 'This is a current fact, he's still Robert Buxton so it's relevant to the case.'

'Very well, go on then. No wait, on second thoughts let's get the rest of the team together, then they can all hear. You can brief the others who are still out completing their Actions when they return.'

With the team assembled, Evans had the centre stage. He began by giving a brief background on his visit to Australia House. He explained about Mary Buxton and her husbands. Having then given a graphic account of the adoption of children after marriage, he told his attentive audience about Buxton.

By this time even Cadema was interested in hearing the whole story. Besides, as she had already seen Grimes, she let Evans continue.

'Mary Buxton, now called Mary Jones, married in the Gold Coast. That's on the east coast of Australia in Brisbane.' He looked towards Cadema, but as she sat emotionless with her dark-brown eyes looking past him, he cleared his throat and continued.

'Her new husband was an Aboriginal named Smith. So she became Mary Smith. Apparently it was frowned upon for a white woman to marry an aboriginal in those days. But the marriage didn't last long because Smith was killed when he fell from the scaffolding he was working on as a builder's mate.'

'Oh how awful,' an officer exclaimed then looked at Cadema. 'Sorry Ma'am,' he said as she shook her head and mimed at him to be quiet.

'But Mary was pregnant and not long afterwards gave birth to son,' Evans explained.

'So she was able to have children after all?' Cadema asked.

'Oh yes. So she lived with her two children, one with the surname Buxton and one with the name Smith. Apparently the Smith child went to live with his aboriginal grandparents and their extended family.'

Cadema could see the enthusiasm of the group was beginning to wane, including her own.

'Look Evans, we don't need a potted history, just get to the point. If you want to do a biography, you can do this in your own time.'

'Yes Ma'am; where was I, oh yes. Robert Buxton must have been very bright as he won a scholarship and went to Wollongong University in New South Wales where he got a degree in agriculture and business. Then set up a macadamia nut farm in Queensland. He sold it for a massive profit and returned to England using his British passport. He has since married and has two children.'

'That's great news. Did he say where in the UK he is liable to be now?'

'No Ma'am, but at least we know he's here and he has not changed his name.'

'So the perpetrator is probably Robert Buxton after all. What results have you had from the PNC?'

'None as yet, but the incident room team are searching everything, and the IT team are also looking into social media sites and electoral rolls.' Cadema noticed the twitch on his face again.

'Did you find anything else about Mary Buxton as she was?' she asked

'Yes, apparently she died twelve years ago.'

As Evans spoke Cadema felt the blood drain from her face and her legs became weak. To her relief, no one in the room noticed, they were too intent on catching his every word. She decided to interrupt him.

'That's a pity. I was hoping she would be able to throw some light on what happened to her when she was at the Wayford hospital. Now it will be difficult to establish what exactly went on there. Perhaps that's why she went to Australia; on the spur of the moment. Now we know Mary's dead. We need to focus our efforts on her first husband. He must have known what was going on, or at least may have had his suspicions. Now he's on the top of my list as an accessory to that crime. But that will have to wait, as we need to concentrate on finding Robert Buxton,' she said with enthusiasm.

'That's good Ma'am in one way, but I was really looking forward to a trip to Down-Under,' Evens gave a half-smile, Cadema saw the disappointment on his face. She knew he liked a chase before any arrest, and the idea of a chase across continents, would be the ultimate challenge for him.

'Right; I want everyone here to concentrate on finding Robert Buxton. And when we have a photograph of him it will be circulated to all police forces in the UK and to the media. This man has got to be found, and found as quickly as possible.' Cadema said with some caution in her voice. She was worried that once a photograph was circulated of Buxton, it would resemble Edward Mason if they were identical twins. If this was the case, Mason would most probably be accused by the general public, despite his wheelchair.

The briefing finished, Cadema asked Evans to send an officer to tell Mason about the proposed photograph. She also told him to organise DNA sampling so it could be ready for when Buxton was arrested. It could then be matched with Edward's DNA, and compared with the samples from the crime scenes. If there was a match, it would be tangible proof of the baby swapping activity at the hospital. It would also indicate that Buxton was most probably the serial killer they were searching for.

'When we find Robert Buxton, I want you, Paul, to…' Cadema said, making sure everyone else had left the room. '…gather as much evidence on him as you can. Even if it's what he had for breakfast if it's relevant. I need to know him as a person.'

Under normal circumstances Cadema always followed the police protocols. However, on this occasion, she decided on a different tactic which, she believed, even Jim Logan would have approved of under these circumstances. Evans seemed excited about this. After all it was his way of working. But it was out character for Cadema to act in such a way. *She must be desperate*, he thought, then shrugged; *what the hell.*

'This sounds exciting, I'll do that Ma'am. But I think we should consider Edward Mason's safety in all of this. I'll organise a uniform to stay with him while all this is going on, just in case there're any problems.'

Cadema agreed and said she would talk to Grimes and ask him to sanction a place of safety order for Edward Mason.

She stiffened her posture as she entered Grime's office, determined not to show any hint of intimidation following her last encounter with him. But after she asked him about the place of safety, she sensed there was something wrong with him as he stood in front of her without saying a word.

'What do you think about that?' she looked into his steel-grey unblinking eyes. There was no answer. 'Sir, are you all right?'

'Of course I am all right, now go on; what were you going to ask me?'

'But Sir I just have…' she started, but decided to ignore what had happened and asked if he felt she was on the right track. He said she was, and he would support her in what she wanted to do. He then shrugged, and trancelike he walked to his chair and sat down. A moment later he looked at Cadema.

'Yes, but you shouldn't dismiss the knowledge that it was a woman who visited 63 Governor Road, and you should consider her as a suspect until she can be eliminated, after all she may be his accomplice,' he sat back in his chair, yawned and closed his eyes. Cadema stood looking at him as he was now, like a child nodding off, with no sign of aggression.

She quietly thanked him and tiptoed out of his office. As she walked along the corridor she cross-examined the issues in her mind. Yes, she had been too close for the obvious. If the killer had an accomplice, it would explain why women were killed but never made a sound. If a woman were involved it may have given the victims a false sense of security. This probably happened with the last murder. Natalie had certainly let her killer into the house. If a woman had knocked on the door, she may well have let her in, even though she didn't know who she was. And according to her father, Natalie would never let a man in she didn't know. So yes a woman could be involved, but not in the actual murders. Besides there was the ejaculate, and that couldn't be attributed to a woman. No, she was sure it was a man, and that man was Robert Buxton.

***

Fifteen minutes later Grimes telephoned Cadema and said they needed to go to see the Assistant Commissioner, Duncan Mander, in the Specialist Crime and Operations Directorate, at New Scotland Yard.

The usual pep talk, Cadema thought as she prepared to leave the station.

The room, although airy and filled with the aroma from the flowers arranged on the desk, felt oppressive to Cadema. After exchanging reminiscences with Grimes, Mander remained standing for a time, as if on parade. Then, towering a good three inches above Grimes, he asked them both to take a seat and gestured to two arm chairs. He sat on the third.

'Thank you, Sir,' Cadema said. But looking at Grimes she got the impression she had committed a sin; as if she had spoken to a monarch without first being introduced. Grimes grimaced and continued speaking. Mander's eyes were fixed on Cadema.

She sat to attention.

'I understand you have everything under control and that you are about to arrest the perpetrator?' he sat facing Cadema.

'Yes,' Grimes answered in response. Then, in a natural pause in Grimes's oration, Mander told him to let Cadema answer the questions directed towards her. Grime's face contorted.

'So what are you up to at the moment, Superintendent?'

Cadema's face was hot.

'We think we have found Robert Buxton, whom we believe is the perpetrator of all four murders, Sir. He lives near Kingstone-upon-Thames. We've just got to verify this.'

Grimes looked at her incredulously, took a gasp of air, but remained silent.

'That's excellent work. How long do you think it will take?'

'We expect an arrest is imminent, but certainly within the next day or two.'

'That's great, just as we thought. So I won't keep you any longer. And tell the team from me, to keep up the good work. Chief Superintendent

Grimes will keep me abreast of any further news.' He turned to face Grimes, who gave a twitch of a smile.

Cadema was in no doubt Grimes was furious with her for not telling him about Robert Buxton's whereabouts. That wasn't deliberate though. She had only just found out herself and he had not given her time to tell him before seeing Mander.

Grimes did not say anything as they travelled back to the police station. She felt his anger though, but was it just at her or was it also with the Assistant Commissioner? Had he gone down in Grime's estimation, despite his rank? But at least he had given her the opportunity to speak, and seemed happy with what she had to say. Besides she thought Grimes was beginning to sound like Evans with his waffling. It was at that moment she realised, faced with upper ranks, Grimes showed his subservience.

CHAPTER TWENTY-FIVE

With the work of the IT team and the tenacity of his own officers Evans discovered where Robert Buxton worked, his home address and something about his family. Compiling this information together, he arranged to meet Cadema in her office. She smiled as he entered carrying a handful of papers, and gestured for him to sit.

'Looks as if everyone's been busy. So let's get to work on this.'

'Exactly, Ma'am.' He sat upright and placed the papers on her desk in the order he wanted. 'It was easy to find Robert Buxton after all as he has his own web-site, he's is on Facebook and Linked-In.'

'That's very good, how do you know there's no mistake?'

'Trawling through the photographs, examining profiles, we eventually found him,' he sounded smug. 'I didn't need any DNA as the moment I saw the photograph I knew it was him,' he smirked. Leaning forward he took the first piece of A-four paper from the top of the pile and turned it over. 'See, he is the spitting image of Edward Mason, a clone even. There's no mistake. He has the same brown eyes, the same colouring, and even has the patch of grey hair hanging over his left brow. And although Edward looks older, probably because of his life-style and his MS, they are definitely identical twins.'

'That's remarkable, you're absolutely right.' Cadema peered closely at the photograph. 'There doesn't appear to be a mistake. Well done. So what else have you found out about him?'

'He lives in Raven House, Simpsons Way, Kingston-upon-Thames.' He picked up another sheet of paper, this time showing a photograph of a Georgian-style house. 'These run into several millions, Ma'am.'

'Yes, I see. And it's just a stone's throw from where three of the murders were committed. So now we have two real clues. His appearance, and the geographical area, excluding the last murder, of course. All we need now is tangible evidence.' Her voice sounded as excited as Evans's. 'Where does he work?'

'In the city at Sydney, Mark and Company. They are stockbrokers. He is one of the partners.'

'Mm..., he sounds quite respectable. It makes me wonder what his motives are for the murders. What about his opportunities?'

'We're not sure about this. It seems that he works almost every day at the office and leaves for home dead on six in the evenings. We've checked his phone calls and they are clear of anything suspicious. His calls were all made from home, or at work, and all his mobile ones are accounted for. In fact, even if his DNA matches the crime scenes, I think we'll have difficulty developing a case against him. He doesn't appear to have the opportunity for the murders, and probably not a motive either. And his wife has not long had an operation, so he's probably been busy with her. She's home now but still recovering, I believe.'

'Do you know how long she's been ill?'

'No, all we know is she had cancer. I can find out more if you like.'

'That's not necessary at the moment. But I understand Johns was doing something?' Cadema looked into Evans's eyes. He looked back and shuffled in his seat. 'Now Paul, tell me what she's found.'

'She discovered Robert Buxton visits a private sexual health clinic in Harley Street on occasions. She doesn't know why he goes there. But I suspect he may have some fertility problems judging by the name of the clinic. I've asked Joanna to go there and report back.'

'So you didn't tell me first? That's good, at least you're managing on your own initiative,' she smiled. Evans looked relieved.

'Any more news from the Wayford hospital?' she asked.

'Marriott is still investigating. He'll be reporting back to me later today. Then I'll let you know.'

'Better still, when he comes in you can both come to see me, then we can hear it together.'

'Okay Ma'am, will do,' Evans said. Picking up the papers, he left her office.

Ecstatic at the news, Cadema informed Grimes. She also told him she would postpone the investigation at the hospital, and concentrate entirely on apprehending the murderer.

Obtaining a search warrant for Robert Buxton's house, she briefed the team and arranged some of her team to accompany her. She planned to arrive there in the morning, before Buxton set off for work at eight-thirty.

***

It was seven-thirty a.m. on the twenty-fifth of October when Cadema, along with Evans, Marriott, two DCs and one female PC arrived at the house in Simpson's Way.

The house was off a private road, in an area where everyone had their own physical, as well as metaphorical boundaries which no one crossed without an invitation. The Georgian house stood majestically in its own walled grounds. Covered with ivy it seemed to sway in the cold light breeze as the awakening sun's rays reflected, like some huge orange meteorite, onto the windows. Cadema shuddered and pulled up her collar.

The garden, looking like a manicured field, stretching on, seemingly forever. It was silent, not even the rustle of a mouse in the undergrowth could be heard. Then the squawking and twittering of birds startled her as they flew overhead. Silence again. Then the heavy breathing of her officers as they passed, followed by the snap of a twig when a size fifteen boot failed to avoid it.

'How are you doing, Ma'am?' Evans whispered, startling her for a second as she hadn't heard him approach. She had been thinking of Jim Logan. Would he be proud of the decisions she had made, even though she was having doubts about Robert Buxton being the killer? She wondered if Jim was trying to tell her so.

'We are all fine. Is everyone ready?'

'Yes, but I am worried about Mrs. Buxton, his wife. She hasn't been out of hospital very long so we need to be careful what we do.' Cadema showed surprise at Evans's concern. He was normally indifferent in his work with the public. Besides, she had done the usual risk assessment and did not expect any harm would come to Buxton or his wife.

'Yes, I know, but I understand she's a lot better now, so we can go without any problems.'

'Nevertheless, it's a pity we didn't find Robert Buxton sooner, when his wife was in hospital. It would have been much better if he were on his own.'

'I agree, but let's get on. Is the back of the house covered?'

'Yes Ma'am.'

Walking up to the front door with Evans, Cadema took a deep breath and pressed the bell. When no one answered, she pressed again. The door opened but was arrested by the chain. 'Robert Buxton?' her curt voice said through the gap. 'This is the police, please open the door.'

'Can I see some ID first?' a male voice asked.

Cadema obliged. 'I also have a warrant. So please open the door.

Without any further dialogue, Robert Buxton unchained the door and held it wide open. He had seen this many times on the television, but this was real and now he was the one on the screen.

As soon as the door was opened, Evans flew past Cadema and held up the search warrant.

Buxton took it and began to read.

'You must have the wrong house,' he cried out and shook his head. 'I've never been involved with drugs or anything else illegal, so you must have made a mistake.' At this point Cadema explained why they were there and then cautioned him.

'Where's Mrs Buxton?' Evans asked. But before Buxton could answer, a door at top of the landing squeaked slowly open and a woman dressed in pink satin pyjamas emerged.

'It's alight Mrs Buxton, it's the police here, and you're not in danger.' Evans said as he began to run up the stairs. Mrs Buxton now stood at the top like a porcelain statue. She pushed her short scanty hair away from her forehead with one hand as she clutched the ornate banister with the other.

'What on earth do you want entering our house like this?' The frailty of the voice matched her frame, but the high pitched educated accent sounded like a monarch's.

'I'm sorry…' Cadema began, but was stopped by the indignant voice of Mrs. Buxton as she began to slowly descend the stairs.

'Sorry is just not good enough,' Mrs Buxton grimaced at each step she took. Refusing any help, she finally reached the hallway, then stood facing Cadema.

'You have entered this house, our sanctuary, and you expect me not to protest. But to accept your lament with impunity?' she picked up the telephone.

'Please Mrs Buxton, stop where you are. We don't want you to contaminate any evidence.'

'Evidence,' both Mrs Buxton and her husband said in unison. 'Evidence,' Mrs Buxton continued. 'Can't you see you have made a mistake? You have the wrong house. We have never broken the law in our lives,' her face distorted as if she were in pain.

'Mrs Buxton, come and sit in the lounge and we will make you comfortable while we search the house.' Cadema said and asked the female PC to go with her. Mrs Buxton turned without protest and headed for the doorway to the lounge, once inside she sat down on a settee.

As more lights were switched on, Cadema could see that Robert Buxton was indeed the image of his brother. Except his clothes and his manner were completely different. His voice was well educated, from his accent she would never have guessed he had ever lived in Australia. In fact he looked as ostentatious as everything around him. There were oil paintings hanging on every wall. The silk curtains, hung like seas of gold, matching the deep-piled carpets perfectly.

Cadema coughed and then told Buxton he would be taken to the station for questioning. He did not reply, but as he turned he looked at her with contempt in his eyes. At that moment, Mrs. Buxton, finding new energy from somewhere, returned to the hallway. Catching hold of her husband's arm, she clung on so tightly that the two DCs, escorting him, had difficulty separating them. After they did so, Mrs Buxton began to plead as her husband was taken out through the front door. She continued to watch as he climbed into the back of an awaiting police car with one of the DCs.

'Please let me go with him. He's done nothing wrong.' But Cadema said he had to go to help with their enquiries. As the police car sped off, Cadema turned to Mrs Buxton again.

'I'm so sorry about the situation, but we have to make these enquiries. I can see you're not well. Is there anyone who can come and stay with you?'

'No. I'll be all right. The housekeeper is due at nine, she'll be here for the whole day,' she said. Then agreed to go back to the lounge; helped by the female PC.

Seated in an armchair, she began to talk about her husband.

'He's very good to me. And has looked after me very well since I was diagnosed with cancer, then had the surgery, chemotherapy and radiotherapy.'

'I'm sorry to hear about that, but at least you had good support. Mr Buxton sounds very caring.' Cadema talked quietly.

'He is, and I don't know what I would ever do without him.' She wiped a tear.

'That's good to hear.' Cadema did not really know what she should say, but felt silence was not an option.

'Yes, he is also very punctual. He leaves the house every morning at eight-thirty and arrives back here at seven thirty, unless there are problems with the train. But he always phones me if he's going to be late.' She blew her nose on a tissue. Cadema nodded.

'He never goes out socially without me. If I cannot go, neither will he. When I was in hospital he visited me every day and stayed until late into the evening.' Her weary voice rose and fell as she spoke. Cadema asked if she wanted to rest, but she said no as she needed to wait until the housekeeper arrived.

Five minutes later the housekeeper arrived. Cadema thanked Mrs Buxton, said goodbye and left her being cosseted.

Stepping out of the house, she turned and asked Marriott and the two remaining officers to continue with the search. As the CSI team arrived, she left with Evans and headed for the station.

***

Cadema began to wonder if she had arrested the wrong person. There was something about Buxton which made her think he was innocent. She had dismissed the idea almost as soon as she thought it, but it began to nag at her subconscious. She recalled Jim's philosophy; 'Always consider the human element when examining the evidence, and never forget your own intuition.' She was annoyed she had not asked him what he meant by the 'human element.' But now she was sure her intuition was in opposition to her actions.

Back at the station she told Evans she believed Mrs. Buxton was telling the truth about her husband's devotion to her.

'I don't think Robert Buxton has anything to do with the murders,' Cadema said to Evans.

'I don't agree. I think he's guilty.' Evans scratched his head and thought. 'I remember the West case in 1998. The police at the time said he and his wife could be in it together. But the police decided to ignore it. And it turned out to be true.'

'Look Paul, you always seem to cite other cases when you're stuck for a reasoned argument.' He scowled at her. 'Anyway Robert Buxton has telephoned his Gentleman's club and asked for Ernest Fortescue-Smyth to be with him when he is interviewed.' The aversion tactic worked, Evans screamed, as if in agony.

'Bloody typical. Sorry about the language Ma'am. But in my mind it shows Buxton is guilty. One of the top solicitors in the country; why can't he use the Duty solicitor like everyone else? That proves it, innocent my foot? Anyway, how can he afford one? And for that matter how can he afford to live in such a big house? He probably got all that for doing hardly any work. Not like some of us who have to work all hours and work our socks off for a meagre salary. Some people have it too good.' Evans ranted in anger as Cadema listened, hardly believing he could think in such a manner.

'Don't jump to conclusions Paul, especially when you already know the facts. It's obvious where he gets his money from. Don't forget his inheritance; no doubt he used that to set him off. Now he's a partner in a successful stockbrokers business in the city. And of course there was the money from the macadamia nut farm in Australia. As for him not working hard, his wife says he's always working.'

'Well, it doesn't make sense to me. Why did he commit these murders if he had so much money? I know he did, he's as guilty as hell. And now he is hiding behind this opulent facade he has created for himself.'

Cadema decide not to answer but said she wanted him present when she interviewed Robert Buxton.

***

Two hours later Robert Buxton and his solicitor were waiting in the interview room. As Cadema walked down the corridor with Evans, she reminded him to be on his best behaviour, to watch what he said, and to follow the procedures. If Buxton were guilty, which she doubted, she didn't want him to be found not guilty because of a technicality. Evans bowed his head and said nothing. Begrudgingly he followed her into the interview room.

Cadema sat in front of Robert Buxton and noticed he had lost his military stance displayed earlier. Now he looked much older and less self-assured.

His solicitor, Ernest Fortescue-Smyth, dressed in a grey designer suit and public school tie, was slim, clean shaven and smelt of cigars. His piercing gaze penetrated even the sharpest mind, giving the impression he would never allow anyone to challenge him who hadn't, at one time or another, donned an Oxbridge mortarboard.

The interview began with the usual routine that Evans always found frustrating, but had no choice in following. He turned on the tape.

'For the record there are four people in the interview room; Superintendent Cadema Sharma, Inspector Paul Evans, Mr. Robert Buxton the suspect, and Mr. Ernest Fortescue -Smyth, Solicitor.' Evans continued by adding the time and date and hoped they would start the interviews without further delay. Cadema began.

'Mr. Buxton, I want to thank you for cooperating with us and for giving us the samples of saliva and blood.'

'That was no problem, but I'm still not sure what is going on.'

'As I said earlier, we are investigating the murders of four young women. You are helping us with our enquiries into these. I want to know where you were on the evenings of the thirty-first of August, eighth September, thirtieth of September and the eighteenth of October,' Cadema said with emphasis on every syllable, while handing both Mr. Buxton and his solicitor a paper with the dates on. Evans looked on in disdain; Cadema was taking far too much time with the preliminaries.

'I suppose I was at home on all those occasions and will have the proof in my personal Filofax, and on my Tablet.' Buxton shuffled in his chair, but his external persona remained calm. Evans asked the next question.

'Okay, let's take them one at a time. We need to talk about the murder of Jane Gaunt on the thirty-first of August. She was found on Wimbledon Common. Do you know that area Mr Buxton?' Evans looked him in the face, as if peering into his soul. Buxton's spine gave a reflex twitch. But he remained still, as if avoiding the question.

'I take it that you don't want to answer the question then?' he asked, and then repeated the question.

'No, although I may live near to Wimbledon Common; it is not a place I would frequent. And I work in…' His solicitor interrupted:

'There is no need for you to give any more information before speaking to me,' his solicitor lowered his voice and then whispered into Buxton's ear. 'You have been arrested but not charged,' he added turning to the two police officers.

'My client will only answer the questions you put to him.'

'Very well Mr. Fortescue-Smyth.' Evans showed anger in his voice. It seemed the law always favoured villains.

'Good, then can we proceed,' the solicitor replied.

'Yes sir, no problem,' Cadema turned to Evans and asked him to continue.

'Do you know anyone called Jane Gaunt?'

'No, I do not.'

'Thank you, Mr Buxton. Were you on Wimbledon Common on the 8th September last?'

'No, I have never been there.'

'Do you know a Sophie Melbourne?' he continued.

'No, I do not.'

As Evans raised his voice at every question, Cadema believed, given the opportunity, he would climb over the table and throttle the answers out of Buxton if he could. And, as she looked at the solicitor, she could have sworn he was grimacing at his behaviour. So she decided to take over the interview.

'Mr. Buxton, you must have read in the papers about the 'Common Murders' as the press call them.'

'Yes I have, but I do not know any of the details. I am more interested in the financial papers than reports from the tabloids.'

'Do you know Frances Cole, she was murdered on the thirtieth of September in Richmond Park, which is near where you live?'

'I may live near there, but as I said before, I don't frequent those areas.'

'Do you know a Madeline Belton whose body was found on Putney Heath on the fourteenth September?

'No, I do not.'

'Do you know a Natalie Taylor, the young journalist who was murdered on the eighteenth of October?'

'No, I do not. I have said that...' At this point his solicitor interrupted and reminded him to only answer the question, and nothing else.

'Let me ask you something else. Have you read in the newspapers about the speculation on the DNA which was found on the victims?' As Cadema spoke she noticed Evans had crossed his arms across his chest.

'As I said, I did not read the details.'

'Well Mr Buxton, we believe your DNA may have been found at the murder scenes. How do you account for that?'

'Mine, how could it be? I have never been anywhere near those places, neither have I ever met any of the woman you mentioned.'

'You said you don't know any of these women. But do you know of anyone else who may know these women?'

'No, I am sorry I cannot help you,' Buxton swallowed and looked as if he were about to cry.

'Wait a minute,' his solicitor interrupted, 'when did you obtain the DNA samples from my client?'

Cadema shuffled in her chair, and leaned forward. 'We took samples today.' Now she was about to be challenged.

'Well, how do you know the samples you took at the murder scenes match my client's?' Fortescue-Smyth elongated his chin much further than he had before and his stare stung Cadema's eyes.

'Those samples will be compared with samples taken from another suspect. You may have read about him. He is Edward Mason.'

'Yes I recall, and as far as I know he hasn't been charged.'

'No he has not. But his DNA has come under scrutiny, and we believe that something is amiss. Therefore we will not be able to say any more about it until we have the results from the samples your client has given us.'

'I expect that will take quite a while.'

'Yes, usually two weeks, but as it's urgent, it will be done as quickly as possible.'

'In that case, I think my client has answered enough of your questions. And until his DNA has been analysed, I request that this interview be terminated.'

'Before that,' Cadema turned to Buxton, 'there is one more question I need to ask you. Do you know anyone who may have a grudge against you?'

'That is a strange question. Not as far as I know, but why do you ask?

'Never mind. Thank you Mr. Buxton,' Cadema said as she ended the interview and recorded the time on the tape. 'You can go home now, but I will need to interview you again when I have the DNA results.'

Saying goodbye, he and his solicitor left.

Evans stood frowning, his face distorted, as he confronted Cadema in the corridor.

'What on earth was that all about? A grudge? You don't think he has been set up do you? How absurd,' he laughed at her, then coughed. 'Sorry Ma'am, but surely you don't think he's innocent, do you? He has guilt written all over him. His Filofax and Tablet indeed. Anyone can add information to them and say it's genuine. I'm not going to fall for that one.'

'You don't have to Paul, you can carry on with other parts of the investigation and I will call another member of the team to accompany me next time.'

'But Ma'am you can't...'

'Oh yes I can. You're jumping to conclusions. We need to give Mr. Buxton some credibility. Anyway let's see what happens with his DNA sample'.

'Well I don't care about his DNA sample. He is guilty, and I'll prove it. I can lean on him and he will crack,' he said gesticulating as he spoke.

'No Paul it's not the way to do things. To the book remember. Besides Jim always said…'

'With respect Ma'am, I don't care what Jim said, he isn't with us anymore and times have changed. He would probably say something completely different now.'

'Don't patronise me. Just go and find out what you can from all the victim's families. They may have some clues we have overlooked.'

Evans reminded her that nothing had been overlooked. He had all their clothes, diaries and other paraphernalia that would be useful to the investigation. But amongst all this, he couldn't find any tangible evidence linking the victims either to each other or to Buxton. There was nothing else to find out. But she insisted he find more evidence, DNA was not going to be enough.

What other bloody evidence did she want? he said to himself. *A corpse to come back and point the finger at Mr Buxton?* Well, if that were the case he would try to do this, metaphorically speaking. Somewhere in forensics, they had the evidence but it had been overlooked. It had happened before, so why not now?

But something else troubled him. He could not understand why Cadema asked Robert Buxton about the Madeline Belton case as the suspect for this murder had been found and was awaiting trial. Was she holding something back from him or was she on one of her missions again? He had to find out, otherwise it may jeopardise the current investigation.

***

While Evans was engaged with other duties, Cadema decided to question Mr Buxton again. She hoped it would help her identify any anomalies in the current evidence she had. He arrived the following morning with his solicitor. Briefing Johns, they all entered the interview room.

Cadema's voice punctuated the still dank air, but at every question, he had a perfect answer and an alibi to match. When the interview was over, and Buxton and his solicitor had left, Cadema felt she had reached another dead-end. But at least she had his alibies for the dates of the murders and with this she decided to brief the team.

She told them Buxton was on a business trip in Scotland when Jane Gaunt was murdered. He had given a talk on that day to five hundred people. After the conference had finished he spent the whole evening with his colleagues in the hotel bar until two a.m. and didn't return to London until the second of September.

When Sophie Millburn was murdered he was alone in London on business, therefore did not have an alibi. But as his wife had his car, and he didn't have his driving licence with him, he could not have hired one. And without transport he could not have picked Sophie Millburn up and driven to Wimbledon Common. Cadema considered the possibility of his wife being involved, but she was having chemotherapy at the time. Some days she was even too ill to drive, so Cadema didn't think she was involved.

In relation to Frances Cole's murder, he was with his wife at home all evening. Although she was still suffering from the effects of chemotherapy, it was their wedding anniversary and so they had a small celebration, and retired to bed at about eleven.

And when Natalie Taylor was murdered, Buxton was in Scotland at another conference in the same hotel as he had stayed in before.

Cadema was fairly happy with the information Buxton had given her. However, if all his alibis were genuine, it meant she did not have any suspect for the murders. She realised, that in reality, she was back where she started, except there were now four murders to be solved.

When the officers had been given the Actions to follow up the alibis, DCI Ryan agreed to oversee this, she said she wanted the information by the following day.

After dealing with a few grunts and questions, she believed her team would satisfy her requirements and perhaps find some new evidence in the process.

CHAPTER TWENTY-SIX

Cadema had been up all Sunday night working. By three in the afternoon on Monday the twenty-eighth October she had nearly caught up on her sleep, when the telephone rang by her bedside. Even before she answered it she knew it would be Julia; somehow she recognised the ring. Besides, she was just thinking of her, and when she did that, Julia always rang.

'Hi, Julia how are you? It's good to know you're still in the land of the living, even if I'm not at the moment,' she giggled.

Julia smiled to herself: 'Yes I'm still here, but I've been extremely busy.'

'Tell me about it.'

'Fancy another Indian meal, there's something I need to discuss with you and it's easier out of the office,' Julia said trying not to sound too presumptuous.

'Sounds exciting, what's it about?'

'It's official in a way, but it's also a hunch. It's about the murders, I just need to...'

'Oh great, where and when shall we meet?' Cadema interjected.

'Seven thirty this evening, I've booked a table at the usual place.'

Cadema knew Julia never rang to go out for a meal impetuously. She ran her life like her laboratory, fastidious and to the clock.

'Okay, that's fine,' Cadema replaced the telephone and smiled as she got out of bed and saw the time. She had slept far too long. But wasn't too hard on herself considering it was ten in the morning when she finally got to bed after briefing her team and Grimes. So yes, she deserved a rest. Meeting Julia was a great idea, it would wake her up. Then after dinner she could have a good night's sleep, and be ready for work to next morning.

Having showered she was now clean and refreshed, and ready for what the rest of the afternoon threw at her, and later for dinner with Julia.

Spending the rest of the day thinking about the cases, making list of questions and probable answers, then drawing up work plans, it was seven o'clock before she knew it.

Rushing out into the dark, she shivered as the cold air caught the back of her throat. At the same time a flash burnt her eyes. She blinked several times but could still see the bulb's image indelibly stamped on her retinas. Her vision blurred, she ran along the pavement towards her car, the two reporters in pursuit—calling out requests for information, eager to get the latest story. She ignored them, got into her car and set off, relieved that the windscreen hadn't misted up delaying her getaway, but, because of the traffic, she had to drive much slower than she would have liked.

For a moment she wished she were in India with her mother. It was nice and hot there. Never the damp and cold that penetrated into her bones like it did in England. She hadn't heard from her for weeks and hoped she was okay. Refusing to visit her there was probably a mistake, but she didn't want to meet someone her mother thought would be 'suitable for her' again. *Someone suitable indeed*, she thought.

Her mother had become westernised but soon reverted to the social norms whenever she returned home. She had ceased to listen to her daughter when she said she had no intention of marrying again. But she did feel some guilt when she said it was her duty to be married. Now Cadema had to endure yet another cold winter in London where fumes from cars and the damp air plagued her chest. Perhaps her doctor was right when he said she should have an x-ray, but she was too busy for medical things. Anyway, she couldn't stop while the investigation was going so well and about to reach its climax. She believed the discovery of the final clue was imminent and although she didn't think Buxton was the murderer, she believed he was involved somehow. Perhaps Julia would have the answer.

Julia was sitting at their usual table drinking Merlot. That meant she had already ordered their meal; '*very predictable,*' Cadema thought.

'Hi, how are you? You're looking great and not as tired as I had expected,' Julia said as she stood up and gave Cadema a token kiss with an audible 'Mm wa'.

'I'm fine,' she said, feeling somewhat embarrassed at Julia's behaviour in such a public place. *Julia's idiosyncrasies,* she thought, but wished she wouldn't do it to her. One day she would ask her not to, but today was not the right time.

'I've got something exciting to tell you,' Julia said as her eyes penetrated Cadema's while her body looked as if it were ready for take-off.

'I gathered by your ecstatic voice. Something to do with the murders you said.'

'Yes it's got everything to do with one of them. Natalie Taylor's to be precise,' Julia poured a glass of water for Cadema and took a sip of her wine, furtively looked around, then leaned forward in her chair.

Cadema mirrored the posture, then began to speak in a whisper loud enough for Julia to hear above the buzz of the voices in the restaurant: 'Well, come on tell me.' Although excited, she sounded frustrated with Julia's teasing.

'You remember I told you Bagley's got a new DNA enhancing machine?' Julia boasted.

'Yes, I do.'

'Good.'

They both sat upright as the waiter interrupted them with their meal. Placing several spicy dishes on the table, he said: 'Enjoy your meal,' and then hovered, as if waiting for some acknowledgement.

'Thank you,' Julia smiled. He bowed before walking off.

'Waiters,' she said as he disappeared. 'Why do they always have to interrupt at such crucial moments? This looks good and smells delicious, so let's tuck in.'

'Yes, it does, and thanks for ordering it, but please, don't keep me in suspense any longer,' she resumed her previous posture.

'Well, Bagley was working with his new apparatus on the DNA found on Natalie Taylor's body. He'd examined the sample before, but decided to do it again using his new machine. You know what he's like with something new, can't wait to try it out. You'll have to come down to the lab and see it one of these days, it looks…'

'It sounds great; but please—Julia.'

'Sorry, I do get excited with these things. Anyway, he can examine even the smallest molecule with this new machine but I will spare you the technical details.'

'Thanks, but do go on it sounds fascinating.' Cadema tried to be as polite as she could under such tortuous circumstances.

'Yes, but you should… well never mind that now. The apparatus he uses is much better than 3-D as it enhances the image of each molecule of DNA in six dimensions, can you imagine that. Six dimensions, why it's virtual reality. And when you look at it, it's as if you're part of the molecule. It's like waking up your ancestors and looking at them face to face.' She smiled at the metaphor, Cadema grimaced a smile in return.

'So what did he find?'

'It's the same DNA as the other murders, but when this one was enhanced, he found some unknown residues on the molecules.' Julia forked a piece of chicken and popped it into her mouth.

'What's the significance of that?' The silence was overwhelming as she waited while Julia chewed then swallowed the chicken with a gulp of wine.

'It means the sample of DNA was somehow, how shall I put it? Well, contaminated.'

Cadema's fork hit the plate with such a noise, she thought she may have broken it.

'Contaminated; but how could that have happened, my officers were very careful?' she said in a forceful whisper.

'No, you don't understand, it was not contaminated in the way you know. It was contaminated by something at the macro-level. I'd say at about the ten to the power of five hundred thousand.'

'I don't know what you mean by "ten to the power". Really Julia you know it's not my field of expertise, so stop showing off.'

Julia smiled at Cadema's frown: 'Yes, I know, sorry, it's the magnification. So I'll call it macro from now on if that's okay with you.' Cadema nodded and gave a faint smile as she took a sip of water.

'As I said, the molecules have been changed by some agent and in some areas they have burst as if they have been blown up by a land mine. But you have to look carefully to see it.'

'So what does it mean?'

'I'm not entirely sure.' Julia leaned forward across the table again and lowered her voice. 'But we think the DNA has been tampered with. It certainly isn't fresh. In fact, we believe, the only explanation for the damage to the molecules is they must have been frozen at some stage.'

'Frozen? How could it have been frozen? Are you suggesting Bagley froze it, he would never have done that, would he?'

'There you are again, jumping to conclusions. No, if it has been frozen in the usual manner the cell membrane would have ruptured and the DNA damaged. No, we think the sperm have been frozen in a laboratory under Cryopreservation; or storage of sperm in a bank to you.'

'Good grief,' Cadema said under her breath and leaned so far forward she almost head-butted Julia. They both jerked backwards, as the waiter offered more wine.

'No thank you. That will be all we need,' Julia gave a polite smile which told the waiter she didn't want to be disturbed. He retreated.

'Sorry, where was I?'

'In a sperm bank.'

'Oh yes; it could have been kept in the sperm bank and then thawed out and used on Natalie, and most probably the others victims. Bagley is going to check back on that.'

'But how could that happen? I've just been interviewing a Robert Buxton, our new suspect, about the murders. Are you suggesting that he could have stored his own sperm?'

'A new suspect, well that's good. But you're the detective so you have to find out how and who froze the sperm, that is, if that's what happened. I'm only the pathologist,' Julia said believing Cadema would come up with a plausible answer.

'I'll tell you what I think, Julia. This is strictly confidential though, you understand,' she said, knowing they both had their own ethics to follow. 'I have the feeling Robert Buxton is telling the truth especially as he seems to have such good alibis for when the murders took place. They're being investigated at the moment. But I think they will be substantiated. That leaves me thinking someone else did the murders and, for some reason, planned to incriminate him. If it is the case then we're looking for someone else; someone who has access to his sperm and with the appropriate facilities to freeze it.' As she spoke, something in Cadema's brain flashed, but did not understand why at the time.

'I knew you would come up with a plausible answer. So do you have any clues on who the perpetrator might be?'

'Not yet, but I have a feeling the baby swapping cases have something to do with it. I'm not sure what that might be at the moment, but I'll get on to it tomorrow morning,' Cadema was relieved she had Julia to discuss issues with. Besides, she was an academic, the same as herself, and therefore could be much more objective and discuss issues rather than getting emotive. Or, as in Evans's case, try to convict Buxton irrespective of the facts. Now she was reassured that she was doing the right thing.

'I wish you luck. Let me know if I can be of any more help. By the way, I'll let you know as soon as possible if Bagley finds anything in the other samples; you never know what's lurking there to be discovered. Especially now he has his new toy.' They both laughed at the thought and continued to finish their meal as the conversation drifted on to more personal issues.

After paying the bill, and saying goodbye, Cadema got into her car, happy to have a fresh concept of the issues she would face in the morning.

Arriving home, she didn't bother putting the light on as it was well lit by the light from the lamp post outside. She could see everything she needed because everything was in its usual place. Her life was ordered that way. After another shower, she crawled into bed not expecting to sleep.

Lying there, she watched the lights of passing traffic scudding silently across the ceiling. Half an hour later she was sifting through the rubble in her mind trying to think of answers that wouldn't come.

Suspect after suspect emerged out of the labyrinth. But they were dismissed almost as soon as she thought of them. No, there were no answers, but no sleep either. And, as the night drifted into dawn, she began to devise another ten-point plan. So, instead of trying to sleep, she decided to go to the office early and sort out her thoughts before her team arrived.

As she drove, thoughts ricocheted in her brain. Had Robert Buxton's sperm been planted at the scene of each murder? The thought was grotesque, but plausible if someone had access to his sperm and had a grudge against him. So the killer could be a woman after all. Perhaps the woman who had visited the house in Grosvenor Road before Natalie was murdered? Or a woman who he was having a relationship with at the moment? But of course it could be an ex-girlfriend. In fact anyone from his past who he may or may not have had a relationship with. Someone with a motive and who managed to obtain a sample of his sperm and had equipment to freeze it. Credulous as all this was, Cadema believed, a woman would never do such things. But there was something else niggling in her brain. Something one of her officers had said, but could not remember who had said it and in what context. But she was determined to find out what it was.

She shuddered at the thought of a woman carrying out such brutal murders as acid from last night's meal hit the back of her throat. *So premeditated, so well planned,* she thought. She knew not to judge anyone by her own standards, the police service had surely taught her that. Nevertheless, she dismissed the idea. No, it had to be a man; there was no question about it. As she parked her car in her allocated car space, she had already decided to interview Buxton again. She needed to ask him many more questions than she had done before, some of which he would probably be reluctant to answer. But he would have no choice if he didn't want to be tried and convicted of murder and then spend the rest of his life in jail.

***

It was six-thirty when Cadema entered the police station. Heading for her office, she stopped at the coffee dispenser, filling a polystyrene cup, she continued on. Looking into the communal office, she was surprised to see a couple of her officers were already working at their desks. *That's dedication*, she thought as she offered a nod and walked on.

Sitting at her desk, she began to map out her plan; she yawned. An hour and a half later a noise startled her. Opening her eyes, she looked at the squiggles on the paper before her, snatched the page form the desk and hauled it into the bin. *No plan*, she thought as she drained the cold coffee, and headed for the briefing room.

Anxious faces gave the impression they had completed the Actions and she hoped they had the answers she needed.

'Right everyone, gather round and tell me what you've found. Then I'll explain what else we need to investigate.' Cadema turned to Evans, knowing he would be eager to find something new about Buxton so he could charge him. *He's going to be disappointed*, she thought.

All Buxton's alibis had been verified by her officers. The news confirmed her suspicions; he did not commit the murders.

'So what have you found, Ma'am?' Evans asked, believing that, despite the alibis, he was up to his neck in it somehow. He licked his lips and rubbed his hands together as if he were about to tuck into his favourite meal; and to him, anything new about Buxton's involvement in the murders, was his favourite meal.

'I'll let you know as soon as I have some more evidence. In the meantime good work everyone. And don't forget, keep looking and we will surely find something that will give us the answers,' she looked around at each officer as she assigned them to other Actions.

Evans seemed elated when she told him she was going to interview Buxton again, and wanted him to accompany her. But what she didn't tell him was she only asked him because he was the only male officer there with the rank she needed. She definitely wanted a man's presence, and he would have to do.

Leaving the team to continue with their work, she had not mentioned the frozen sperm theory, as Julia could be wrong. Neither did she mention the possibility of the murder scenes being staged as she did not want to lose her credibility, especially with Grimes. She would tell them all when she had much more evidence.

Evans was another issue. On a 'need to know basis' he had to be told about the frozen sperm theory, so he could ask the right questions at the interview. But when she told him, she had not expected such a negative reaction.

'With respect, Ma'am, I think Doctor Lilly's got it all wrong. Buxton's guilty. It is his sperm, his DNA will prove that. The technology cannot be wrong, why you said so yourself. The possibility of it being wrong is millions to one, or there about. No; he is definitely our man.' Evans's eyes bulged, his face almost purple.

'I know it sounds incredible, but you'll have to accept that Robert Buxton may not have committed the murders. Any other thoughts on the subject will cloud your judgement. Anyway you heard the team confirming his alibis. And as you say, technology cannot be wrong. It's just that this new technology is even better. So I want you to support my decision on this, do you understand?'

'Yes Ma'am,' Evans stood directly in front of Cadema examining her face as if looking for some hint of doubt; there was none. Now he had no choice but to go along with her theory even though he was unhappy with it. He had always supported her decisions before, and he would do so now, despite his reservations.

'My theory is that someone else carried out the murders and planted Mr Buxton's sperm at the scene.'

'But Ma'am, that's ridiculous, how could anyone get hold of his sperm without him knowing about it?'

'Just think about the possibility while we interview him. I'll ask the questions, you can do the follow up; and no theories, is that understood?' she was strict with him, hoping it would stop him from deviating and surreptitiously inching in his own theories during the interview.

'Yes, Ma'am.'

Cadema was thinking there was something else she should have remembered, but still there was no answer. Perhaps it was something Johns had said? She would ask her about this as soon as she could.

Cadema thanked Buxton and his solicitor for coming to the station again. Once all four were seated, the tape on, and introductions made, Cadema fidgeted in her chair, then began:

'Mr Buxton, are you involved with another woman?' she coughed.

'Why do you ask?' he replied.

Before Cadema had chance to say anything, Evans sat upright and said: 'We ask the questions, so just answer the Superintendent.'

'No. I'm faithful to my wife,' he looked into Evans's cold emotionless eyes.

'So who's got a grudge on you?' he butted in as Cadema opened her mouth to speak. Before Buxton could answer, she excused herself and asked Evans to turn the tape off and leave the room with her.

'How dare you. You know what my instructions are. You are to keep quiet; I don't want a Starkey and Hutch interview in this investigation,' Cadema said, not knowing who Starkey and Hutch actually were, but knew what it meant to him.

'Sorry Ma'am, but it really gets up my nose when they answer questions with another question. But from now on I'll take your lead.'

'You'd better, so don't forget it this time.' He nodded in agreement.

The interview resumed with the same procedure as before but this time Cadema sensed there was an atmosphere in the room. The first person to speak was Buxton's solicitor: 'My client is not evading answering your questions, but he believes you need to be more direct and keep to the facts.'

'We intend to,' Cadema replied as she turned to face his client again.

'Mr Buxton, is there anyone you can think of who could have a grudge against you?'

'You asked me that once before, so why again?' he replied. Evans bit his lip, glared at him, but kept quiet.

'Please, just answer the question.'

'Well, at last, it sounds you doubt my guilt?' he leaned back in his chair with his hands behind his head, smiling. Evans, remaining quiet, scowled at him.

'As all your alibis have been verified, we have to examine other possibilities,' she explained as Evans looked up at the ceiling, and fidgeted.

Cadema reiterated the question.

'No, I do not have any enemies. And certainly don't know anyone who would carry out such horrific murders.' He emphasised every word as he spoke.

Cadema coughed and turned to Evans: an indication for him to ask the next question.

'Have you ever donated sperm for any reason?' he asked.

'Well, yes I have, but not recently.'

'Where did you donate it?'

'At a clinic in Harley Street, but why do you want to know?'

As soon as Cadema heard this, she remembered what was nagging in her brain. Johns had mentioned that Buxton visited a sexual health clinic. At the time she speculated he must have some sort of fertility problems. Why she had not asked Johns to follow it up, she didn't know. This was certainly a failure on her part. But she dismissed from her mind what Grimes and her team would think.

'In Harley Street. So why did you donate it?' Evans asked, his voice showing a hit of a sneer.

'Surely you don't need to know that? I did, that's all,' he sounded defensive.

'I would like an answer please,' he insisted.

The solicitor interjected: 'I object to you asking my client superfluous questions so unless you can explain why you need to know, my client is not obliged to answer that particular question.'

'Mr. Fortescue-Smyth,' Cadema interrupted. 'We need to know because there may be a connection between the reasons for Mr Buxton donating his sperm and the reason for the murders.' She constructed her sentence very carefully, knowing Evans had a way of judging people and realised he was doing this right now. He would categorise Buxton into his 'weirdo' pigeon-hole because he had donated sperm for no specific reason. This would give him a good reason to ridicule him in the future.

'Thank you Superintendent, my client will answer your question.'

'I did it to help people. I heard the appeal for donors on the radio, and felt I could help infertile couples,' he shrugged dismissively.

Bull shit, Evans thought. He wished he could say it out loud, as he would have done when he first joined the service. But now, with all the political correctness, he had to control himself. However, it did mean Buxton had confirmed his *weirdo* theory.

'Was there any other reason?' Cadema asked.

'No, that's it.'

'Thank you Mr. Buxton. Now can you tell me the name of the company where you donated it?' she asked.

'It's the Hazelbrook Company, but I don't have the address, it's at home. You won't tell my wife will you? She doesn't know, you see.'

'Let me reassure you that what you say here is confidential, it will stay with me and some of my team. We will investigate further, and let you know what we find as soon as we can. And thank you for being so helpful.'

'Yes, but let's hope there's nothing to find,' Buxton replied.

As he and his solicitor left, Cadema hoped there would be something tangible to find at the clinic, otherwise she would be facing yet another dead end.

***

Cadema had been lenient with Evans long enough, so by the time she reached her office she had decided to give him a verbal warning on his behaviour at the interview. However, before doing so she wanted to find out what he was thinking about Robert Buxton.

'Well, there it is Paul, just what I thought; it sounds as if he may be innocent after all.'

'Yes Ma'am, just as I thought, too,' he lied.

'You did not; you still think he is guilty, don't you?'

'To be honest, his story leaves a lot to be desired; donating sperm for the good of humanity indeed. Mark my words; he was just on a big ego trip, a way of raping women within the law. Just shows what a coward he is. All those children and no responsibilities. He's definitely a weirdo.'

Cadema turned and looked him in the face and began to speak: 'Detective Inspector Evans, please leave now and come back to my office in thirty minutes,' she said in an authoritative voice.

'Must it wait Ma'am? I need to get on with this investigation.'

'Thirty minutes, and that's an order.'

'Yes, Ma'am,' he looked at her with contempt. Then stood in front of her military style. Cadema's face was set as stone.

'Thirty minutes,' she said. He turned and left the office.

Precisely on time, Evans returned. Cadema asked him to sit down using the same tone a judge would have used when sentencing a prisoner to death. He remained standing. Not just to intimidate her, but to emphasise his rank; she was treating him like a probationary; he couldn't have that.

'Detective Inspector Evans,' she said in an official tone, 'before I start, this is a management issue and not a disciplinary one or a caution. So you don't need anyone to represent you. Do you understand?'

'Yes, Ma'am. So just say what you have to say and get it over with.'

'That's just it, your attitude. I have noticed you have undermined my authority several times. You interrupt during interviews when I have specifically told you to remain quiet. And your attitude towards suspects is confrontational. You are not a judge, so you need to keep to the facts and be professional. And don't ridicule suspects as you feel fit.

'Although this will not go on your record, I will arrange for you to undertake communication and attitude training as soon as I find a suitable course for you. In the meantime, you must adjust your behaviours. And I will review the situation in three months' time. In consequence, I don't want you to work on your own, so DCI Ryan has agreed to work with you. She will report back to me. If nothing changes once you've had further training, then I'll formally discipline you, is that understood?'

'Perfectly Ma'am. Is that all?'

'Yes, it is for now.'

Hands at his side and pan-faced he turned, muttered goodbye and left the room.

He had received warnings before, but nothing seemed to be effective in the long-term. He just carried on as if nothing had happened. But this time things would be different. He didn't want it on his records. So, for the next three months, he would have to be careful. Anyway, working with Ryan would give him the opportunity to have a go at the pseudo armour she was reputed to wear. Besides, with the sperm bank investigation, he would be able to find out about Buxton.

CHAPTER TWENTY-SEVEN

Evans expected the sperm bank to be in a state of the art, purpose-built building, not the old Georgian building which stood before them. It hardly spoke of high-tech and the area in which it was situated did not, immediately, suggest any prestige. This certainly didn't live up to his expectations. He voiced his opinion to Ryan:

'I hope this doesn't portray what's inside,' Evans said with disappointment in his voice.

Ryan ignored him for a moment. She was too busy gazing up at the majestic looking building with its ornate carvings and sash windows. The late October air mingled with her thoughts. She took in a breath and felt the atmosphere still lingered from a time long gone, despite the constant refurbishments of one of the most prestigious addresses in London. She had loved the area ever since she had been an officer on the beat there.

'So what did you expect, look at the plaque. This building's been here since the seventeen-nineties. And don't be presumptive from the appearance of the outside. I expect the inside to be totally different,' she said having seen the inside of many in the area.

She was right. As they stepped over the threshold into the capacious marbled hallway, they could see the palatial staircase furnished with what looked like its original oak banister, supported by ornate balusters. And despite the age of the building, the inside was crisp and clinical.

'Hello, we've come to talk to your manager; a Miss Gardner,' Evans said.

'Who shall I say is calling?' The refined accent made Evans recoil for a moment, as he had not expected such an educated voice. *Must be a student*, he thought, examining the porcelain face and the blond contours of the hair of a girl about half his age.

'I'm Detective Chief Inspector Ryan and this is Detective Inspector Evans,' she held up her police identification badge in front of the receptionist's face, which looked as clinical as the surroundings. Evans did the same.

The corner of the girl's mouth twitched as she hastily picked up the telephone and spoke. She had hardly ended the call when a Miss Gardner appeared in the lobby.

'You wanted to see me Chief Inspector?' The voice sounded older than she looked. Evans quickly came to the conclusion that Miss Gardner must have had some form of facial reconstruction and as she approached he examined her features closely. He noted the round eyes looked eager but friendly. Her slightly upturned nose, and over-blushed cheeks, contrasted to the pallor of the rest of her face. As she pushed her short dark-brown bobbed hair, it revealed a hint of silver underneath. He looked closer, but saw nothing unusual. She dressed like someone much older, almost 'frumpy' he could hear his last girlfriend say. But at least she has a good figure, Evans observed, and that was all it mattered. After all clothes were just the dressings of something much more tempting underneath.

She took a few seconds to answer; 'Yes, is there somewhere we can go and talk?'

'Of course, no problem. But what's this about?' Miss Gardner asked.

'We will explain in private,' Ryan said.

'Very well, follow me. Tea Maranda,' she called as they left.

As they hurried along Evans wondered how she had managed to get to the reception so quickly. The layout, with all the twists and turns, would have impeded her journey.

'Please take a seat,' she gestured towards two red leather Chesterfield-style chairs as they entered her office. She moved across the room and sat in the executive leather chair behind her desk.

Ryan examined the landscape of the office. It signalled perfection, even compulsion; a behaviour she might have admired if she could afford it. It reminded her of her own mother; sharp, sophisticated and in control. She shuddered when she remembered the reprisals she received from the lashes of those satanic eyes when she was a child.

'Thank you. We have come to ask you about one of your patients, Robert Buxton he donated sperm here,' Ryan said.

Miss Gardner shuffled in her chair and averted her eyes.

'We don't call them patients, they are clients to us. But I cannot disclose any information on our clients; that is highly confidential.'

'Yes we know, but I have a letter here from Mr. Buxton giving his permission for us to see his records. You see it's all above board,' Ryan handed her the letter and waited for the reply.

'Well, that seems to be in order to me. What do you want to know?'

'Miss Gardner, we want to see Mr. Robert Buxton's notes,' Ryan leaned forward, giving no time for Evens to say anything. Besides his diffident attitude was beginning to show, and may jeopardise the responses from Miss Gardner, if he made her feel intimidated.

At Ryan's request, Miss Gardener pressed the intercom button and gave instructions for the file to be brought to her office.

She sat smiling at them. Ryan noticed the tension in her body increase as Miss Gardner sat upright, then jumped as the grandfather clock struck the hour.

The ticking had begun, increasing and increasing. It beat with the rhythm of her own heart, louder and louder. Her fingers strumming on the desk. She smiled again, then cleared her throat.

'We have an excellent service here,' Miss Gardner said, filling the silence. 'Our cryopreservation techniques are the envy of the world. We are a private company, and of course, we have to comply with the law and all the Health and Safety issues. But we do have problems finding donors especially when the law was passed giving paternity rights to the offspring of donors, it nearly killed the industry. Thank goodness there are still some good citizens to help childless couples.' As she said this she turned to Evans. 'I don't suppose...'

He coughed and wriggled in his seat. 'No, definitely not.'

'That's a pity, but your choice, of course,' she shrugged.

'No problems, but we would like to hear about the sperm donation process, please,' Evans said.

'There's not much to tell really. All I can say is that men come along, donate their sperm anomalously and then leave. We send out reminders for donations once a year. Sometimes they donate twice but sometimes only once. You can never tell. And we never push them.' She looked up as the door opened. The receptionist entered the room, put the tea tray on the table and handed Miss Gardner a buff-coloured thin folder. 'Great, thank you,' she said, taking the folder and waiting for her to leave.

The door was eventually closed, leaving the room with a distinct odour of perfume.

'Chief Inspector Ryan, what would you like to know?' Evans fidgeted in indignation as Miss Gardner directed her question to Ryan and began pouring the tea.

'Please do help yourself to milk and sugar,' again these comments were aimed at Ryan.

'I understand you have stored sperm here for the last ten years?' she asked. Miss Gardner nodded the answer. 'And if Robert Buxton donated his sperm here, we would like to know when he started to donate it, when he last donated it, and if you have a sample.'

Miss Gardner produced a slip of paper from the file. 'This is all the information I have at the moment. It confirms he is a client of ours and identifies his personal identification number. But I am not prepared to use this to access his computer file without a warrant.'

'So you are refusing to cooperate?' Ryan continued.

'That is the essence of it. So until I see the warrant, I'm in my right to do so.'

'Very well, but I'd like to ask you some general questions which I'm sure you'll be able to answer before I get the warrant,' she continued.

'I'll try.'

'When clients' donate their sperm, where is it kept?'

'It is frozen until it is going to be used for clients in our infertility clinics.'

As no one was taking any notice of Evans, he started to fidget and stirred his tea noisily. He listened to what was being said and grunted occasionally. Both women continued to ignore him.

'Thank you, so can you tell me how you screen your clients.' This time Evans fidgeted and coughed so much Ryan decided to include him in the conversation. Besides, questioning Miss Gardner had become laborious, so, despite his chauvinistic attitudes, he would at least speed things up. Leaning backwards in her chair, Evans took the cue.

'Yes Miss Gardner, as Chief Inspector Ryan says, we trust you to tell us what you know,' he said in his seductive voice. Ryan cringed.

'Thank you both. But please call me Philippa.'

'Okay; please do go on,' his voice was soothing.

'Of course,' Philippa said with unsmiling and intimidating features. Evans may have noticed this if he hadn't been so engrossed in his own sense of importance. When he finally looked at her, he realised there was more to the woman in front of him than his first impressions of her had portrayed. His senses alert, he listened.

'We have regular clients and also one-offs. Every client is screened for all diseases each time they come in to donate their sperm. It's taken confidentially, so that once it is collected, it cannot be traced back to the source, that is the donor.'

'But you could trace it if you wanted to.'

'Yes, it could be traced in a number of ways. But we have such full-proof methods of storing data, it would be impossible for any one person to access all the information they would need to know.'

'How are the data stored?' he asked as he leaned forward.

'Client's names and PIN are kept as a paper file. Data is added to a computer linked to my office. This is a one-way process, so once it's entered, it is inaccessible to anyone who isn't authorised. A copy of the data is kept in our safe, and no one has access to this. Each client is given a second personal identification number; this PIN is linked to the UMDS; (Unique Medical Data System) which is regularly updated. Anyone wishing to access a client's details would have to have access to the safe, the second PIN, UMDS and then trace it back to the name which is kept on a separate computer. One other way of course would be to have the DNA profile which could be traced back much easier. But an ordinary person would not have access to this, neither would our staff.'

'But it can be traced?'

'Hypothetically yes, especially for paternal reasons in the future.'

'So we will have to obtain a warrant before we can see Robert Buxton's file?'

'Yes, as I said, all our information is confidential.'

'That's a load of old...'

'What Inspector Evans is trying to say is that, when we return with a warrant, we expect you to fully cooperate with our enquiries.' Ryan had never interrupted him before, but believed, this time it was necessary. He could jeopardise the whole interview if he exhibited his usual aggressive ways. And she didn't want to damage the rapport she had established with Philippa, especially as she was cooperating to some extent.

'Of course, that won't be a problem once I've seen the warrant.'

Although Evans didn't like what she had said earlier, Philippa had just gone up a few notches in his mind for doing so. He liked that in a woman, a good spirit that could match his any day. He rubbed his hands at the thought of another exciting challenge as he examined her features more closely than he had done during the whole meeting. Yes, under her tough facade, there was some weakness and he was determined to find out what it was. He contemplated asking her out, but dismissed the idea as a conflict of interest. He would have to wait for a more suitable time. So, resuming his arrogant posture he said goodbye. Ryan followed, wondering if Philippa would be Evens' next target.

***

When Ryan returned to the office she briefed Cadema without Evans being present as she needed to mention his behaviour toward Miss Gardner. Cadema listened, made a mental note of what was being said, and decided to talk to Evans about it when she had the time.

Warrant in her hand, Ryan was happy Cadema, and not Evans, was going with her to the clinic this time.

On seeing Miss Gardner, Cadema took a deep breath and frowned. She had seen the woman, who was now standing in front of her smiling, before. But as she stared at her, just for a couple of seconds, she couldn't remember where she had seen her, nor in what context. The general public would expect a police officer, irrespective of their rank, to be able to recognise a face. Sooner or later, she would remember; after all it was her duty to do so.

Handing her the search warrant, Miss Gardner seemed to relax when Cadema told her they would interview her as Evans was otherwise engaged. In her office, she sat examining the warrant as if it were contaminated by the latest plague. Her head twisted as she read every line, as if looking for hidden meanings. After some deliberation, she eventually spoke:

'Thank you, Superintendent. I will let you have everything you need,' she said and then explained the clinic's procedures. 'As you can appreciate, everything will take a little time. Hope you don't mind waiting here while I make the arrangements.'

'That's no problem,' she replied as Miss Gardner left the office. Cadema continued to search her mind for clues that would help identify her. Where had she seen Miss Gardner before? What was she doing when she saw her? Was it in the police station, a prisoner perhaps? She dismissed this. Somewhere more sociable perhaps? A party, the gym? How long had it been, probably some months ago, certainly not years? She had never heard that voice before, so she had not spoken to her. But she had definitely seen her somewhere.

'Not much longer now,' Miss Gardner interrupted her thoughts as she re-entered the office.

'That's okay,' Cadema answered without taking much notice of what was being said. Her mind was still racing, while the archivist in her brain tried to locate the file which would give her the answer. 'We have allocated plenty of time.'

'This file only tells me he is a donor, and gives me his first PIN number. Now I need to access the computer to find his other details,' she said, pressing a button on her desk. A computer slowly emerged from the interior of what appeared to be an empty desk. 'It's for security reasons. I'm the only one who can access all the data at one time.'

Cadema and Ryan watched in amazement. It was somewhat pretentious to hide computers, the sort of thing that might be seen in a James Bond film not in a fertility clinic.

'You see, the desk looks quite normal and rather fragile from where you're sitting,' her voice rose and quickened with excitement, believing they felt as excited about the technology as she was. 'Great isn't it? It's just a façade. It's built like a fortress—in fact, if we had an earthquake, and the building collapsed, the desk would remain intact; that's the security we give our clients,' she boasted.

'It's a fascinating piece of equipment,' Cadema eventually remarked as the computer sang into life with its voice echoing 'good morning…' Miss Gardner silenced it with a blow to the mute button and with the enthusiasm as if she were starting a nuclear war.

She entered the PIN. 'Not quite there yet, I have to enter a second PIN when it asks. There, now it's here. Yes, Robert Buxton,' she peered at the screen. 'Apparently he donated his sperm on three occasions, and we have his DNA profile on file. Would you like a copy?' she asked officiously.

'Yes, thank you. I also need to know the dates of the donations.'

'Here we are. It seems he began last year, his last sample was given this June.'

'That's great. Can you give me a copy of his DNA profile, on this USB memory stick, if possible?'

'Yes, no problem.' She took the stick from Cadema, pushed it into the port, and eventually pressed copy and paste. 'There all done,' taking it out, she handed it to Cadema.

'Thank you,' was all she said, then coughed and fidgeted. Who was this woman? Was she hiding something important to the case?

'Is there anything else I can help you with?' she asked as she closed the computer and waited as it sunk back into the desk.

'I'd like to know exactly what happens when a client gives his sperm.'

'That's easy. Our nurses take the donor's details, their medical history, and then, as I said earlier, we do some tests. Do you need to know what they are?' Cadema shook her head. 'After the sperm is donated, it is labelled and sent to the laboratory attached with the security number, not the name of the person. The sperm is then screened and Doctor Andrew King does the genetic profiling. It is then frozen in liquid nitrogen at minus 196 degrees centigrade and stored for six months. After that time it is screened for infections. If everything is okay, and the sperm are undamaged, it will be kept safe until it is needed for future use.'

As Miss Gardner did not have access to the sperm, Cadema eliminated her as a suspect. But there were several other people who handled it and they would all have to be interviewed in the search for a motive and the opportunity for stealing the samples.

Having decided who to interview from the clinic, she said goodbye and both officers left the building.

***

Cadema was still concerned about Miss Gardner's identity. She had definitely seen her before, but where?

Sitting in her office, she gave the archivist in her brain one more chance to search for a suitable answer. She made him probe every filing cabinet, every crevice, every recess, and every labyrinth, in case it had been misfiled. But no answer was found.

Returning home, she made herself a cup of cocoa. After changing into her night clothes, she threw on her dressing gown and entered her study. Picking up her diary she began to enter a record of her day's activities as she always did before going to bed. Writing away, she began to think. *What if there is a record earlier in the year about Miss Gardner?* She didn't think so as she had never heard the name before.

She yawned, put the pen down, and began to travel in her mind, through tunnels, along endless corridors, into libraries, discoursing with people; nothing helped. She took a sip of her warm cocoa. Her mind searched every date until she was sure it happened in the current year. Turning back the pages in her diary, she reached the first of January. Her memories of that date came flooding back. That New Year celebration, then Julia's Burns night party, it was all too much, she giggled. And the boyfriend, who had turned out to be married.

February's cancer charity ball, did she really look skinny in her national dress as others had said? But Julia had commented how good she looked; she felt great. March, nothing much—too busy work-wise. But the two curries in April compensated for this, especially as Julia found a great Indian place to eat into the bargain. So much so, that now they had become regulars.

May-day and Julia's attempt at a garden party that was rained off; she smiled at the thought. They compensated later in the month with another meal at their restaurant, as they called it.

Then she sat upright, her senses alert. Yes, now she recalled Julia's reaction to someone sitting at another table. Did she wave, she couldn't remember? But she definitely recognised someone. Cadema sat thinking for a while trying to picture the woman in her mind. The hair, the features. Then yes, now she remembered, it was Miss Gardner; Julia knew her.

In an instant Cadema realised she could no longer confide in Julia or ask for her advice. She would have to deal with the situation by herself and leave Julia out of the investigation. But she would find it difficult as Julia had all the contacts and the forensic knowledge. As she closed the diary, she decided to go to bed and sleep on the problem; hopefully it would be resolved by the morning.

After much self-recrimination, in which she accused herself of being too reliant on Julia, and putting herself into a compromising position, she fell asleep.

CHAPTER TWENTY-EIGHT

By morning, Cadema had decided, against her internal persecutor's advice, to ask Julia some pertinent questions about Miss Gardner. Before reaching her office, she had already arranged to meet Julia that evening. Deciding not to tell her teams about her suspicions, she allocated the Actions.

Ryan agreed to take Evans and question everyone at the clinic, except Miss Gardner.

'Why not Philippa Gardner? Evans asked.

'I'm following up other enquiries about her and will interview her myself when I have done this.'

'So what enquiries are they,' he continued.

'I'm not prepared to say at present. Just do as I ask, and leave Miss Gardner to me.' Evans grunted an agreement and left the room.

'I'll keep an eye on him Ma'am, and make sure he doesn't go anywhere near her.' Ryan gave a reassuring nod of her head and smiled as she left.

***

The day had dragged on as Cadema went over and over the events in her mind. What should she say to Julia when they met for dinner? How would she react and how would it affect their future friendship? She needn't have worried, as Julia was her usual bubbly self.

'Hi, Julia it's good to see you again.'

'Likewise,' she replied. 'But I don't understand why you want to see me so soon after our last meeting. I suppose it must be something serious?

'It could be. By the way have you ordered yet?' Cadema asked.

'Yes, but not the wine. I am trying to cut down,' she smiled.

'That's good, I'm sure you will feel better for it.' Cadema released an audible sigh.

'You're probably right. So why do you want to see me so urgently. You sounded upset about something?'

'Upset, me?' Cadema smiled, pointed to herself and shook her head. 'No, I'm not upset.'

'Well, you sounded as if you were when we spoke on the phone.'

'I'm fine. Just a few things I need to clarify, if that's okay?'

'Of course. But get on with it, the suspense is killing me.' She laughed. 'So what do you want to know?' Julia sat on her hands as she edged forward, cutting off the circulation to her fingers.

'I can't answer that at this moment because I don't really know what I need to know, and that's the problem.'

'Honestly you do talk in riddles at times. Anyway I don't believe you. You're the one who always knows what the problem is. So I'm sure you know, you're just evading the issue to see my reaction.'

'I'm not. But in a way, I am. You see, have you ever thought that you might be the problem?'

'Me-e-e-e,' Julia screeched under her breath, 'you don't really mean that do you?'

Cadema started to torture the chicken kebab with her fork.

'Look Julia, this is a delicate matter and I'm not sure I should be speaking to you about this; well not here anyway.' She gave a clandestine look around the restaurant.

'Why on earth not?' Julia said tossing her head as if throwing away Cadema's comment along with the daily rubbish.

Cadema leaned forward and looked straight into Julia's eyes.

'Do you know a woman called Philippa Gardner? She manages a sperm bank business in Harley Street?'

'Yes I do, but I didn't know she worked there. Anyway, I thought you knew that. I seem to remember you seeing her when we were out for a meal earlier this year.'

'Now you've said that, I can't say any more about the subject. We will have to talk about it at the station.'

Julia sat in silence for a few seconds.

'An official meeting at the station seems ominous to me. What's going on? Why can't you tell here? Have I done something wrong?'

'No, nothing like that. But we cannot talk about it here. I need it on tape.'

'On tape? Well, I can see that's very official. What are you going to ask me about? Should I ask for my solicitor to be present?'

'Don't be so silly, Julia,' she smiled and leaned forward. 'You've done nothing wrong. I just need to record what you say, in our official records. So let's not talk about it anymore. We can finish dinner and meet sometime tomorrow.'

'But can't you give me some hint on what this is all about?'

'Please as a friend, do not ask me.'

'As a colleague what would you say?'

'Sorry Julia, I can't comment.'

'Surely you can give me some idea?'

'As a friend or as a colleague, strictly confidential mind; I need to know more about Philippa Gardner and Robert Buxton.' As soon as Cadema said this she regretted her words. Why didn't she just ignore Julia's insistence? Instead she had conceded to her demands, and was angry with herself.

'Well I don't know anything about Robert Buxton, only that you questioned him. As for Philippa Gardner...'

'There's no need for you to say anything else about her, tomorrow will do.'

By the time they had finished their meal Julia was now a person helping the police with their enquiries on a murder investigation. Cadema was the Chief Investigation Officer. However, before they left the restaurant, they cordially agreed to meet the next morning

CHAPTER TWENTY-NINE

I couldn't understand why the investigation was taking so long. After all it had been over two weeks since I'd murdered Natalie. Now, the first of November, the police were no further forward. Perhaps I should have gone back to the murder scene and left more evidence. Conversely, I was very tempted to get involved in the investigations, but managed to restrain myself from doing so.

It was one of the voices who persuaded me not to, even though the others agreed that I should have done. Another voice said I should never have gone to the estate agents in the first place to look at the house near Natalie's. What was I thinking? The estate agent would remember me and tell the police. Despite the disguise, he would have given them a description of me, and I would be identified. The voice, was angrier than ever, accusing me of jeopardising our identity. I was furious.

'You,' I said. 'You of all people—if you hadn't stood back and let me, Thomas, do all the work, take all the responsibility, then what did you expect? If you could have done better, you should have done it.' But the voice continued to argue; criticising the way I had stalked Natalie, the way I went to her house and the way I murdered her. Can you imagine, it actually criticised me for killing Natalie.

'No I will not take the blame. I was in control then and I certainly am now. You can go to hell for all I care,' I shouted.

I was worried everything was getting out of hand. And with the recent squabbles with one voice and then another, I had had enough especially when they accused me of being careless.

'The police have arrested Robert, that's what you wanted wasn't it? So what are you so annoyed about?' I asked.

'I know, but the police have been asking the wrong questions, to the wrong people. They have interviewed Robert and let him go. So they are still looking for someone else. Why else did you think they came to the clinic? Besides you should never have murdered Natalie; not in her own house anyway.'

'Oh, for God's sake, shut up. Anyway what's wrong with that—the house was perfect, and I wasn't disturbed, so what's your problem?'

'You're my problem,' she said.

At this, my whole body tensed, my eyes widened and I took a deep breath. I could feel my heart, her heart, pounding like a machine which needed servicing just before it was about to break down.

I felt it. The hot blood surging through my arteries for the extra strength I needed now. They felt it too, we all did. Then I felt as cold as the steel of the blade in her hand, my hand.

She had taken over and we fought with the knife, but it was too late. The knife plunged into my flesh, our flesh again. The pain was like a million neurons firing on the battlefield of life, and I fell to the ground. She cried out too, but it was too late, I had won the battle.

CHAPTER THIRTY

Cadema had gone to sleep as soon as she snuggled into her pillow. But what seemed like hours later, she was wide awake. By the time on the clock, she had only been in bed an hour.

One part of her brain was torturing the other. The commotion would not cease as she wrestled with the quilt and tuned from side to side. Every time she did so, she looked at the clock which seemed to be in collusion with her brain. It ticked and ticked louder and louder, until the tick sounded like a gong that would announce meal times in some old Victorian household.

She tried to think of something pleasant, but all she could hear was 'ask Julia, ask Julia'. But ask Julia what? She couldn't think of an answer, so gave up, and started thinking about a plan. The first on the list was to ask Julia, the second point was to ask Julia what? She pressed the button on her bed-side lamp, hoping the light might help her to think. There was the book on the floor she promised to finish reading, but never had time to, so it lay there gathering dust. Picking it up, she sat against her pillows and opened the page where she had left the bookmark months before. She started to read. A couple of minutes later the book startled her as it hit her chest.

She was alert. 'Ask Julia,' her mind continued. There were no other questions in sight, and definitely no plan. The first question was 'ask Julia,' the second was 'ask Julia' and the third...

The alarm woke her exhausted body from the torment of the night. She lay there thinking and realised, for the first time in her career, she could not do a plan. There was no way beyond the first question. After a lick of a shower, she dressed quickly. Reaching the office much too early, she was devastated to hear the news.

***

It was just after eight in the morning when Cadema called Julia's number from the Harley Street clinic.

'Hello, it's Cadema here.'

'How come you're phoning so early? Are you okay?' Julia yawned as she looked at her bedside clock.

'I know, but I thought I would catch you before you went to work.'

'You have definitely done that. So do you want me to come to the station to answer your questions earlier than we agreed? Or has there been another murder?

'Not exactly. But something else has happened. Philippa Gardner has been stabbed so I need you in your professional capacity.'

'Stabbed? Is she alight?

'She's okay, but in hospital. It's not life-threatening. Anyway, I don't need you at the station. But can you get to the clinic in Harley Street? If you don't want to, I'll understand,' Cadema sat with her fingers crossed.

Although it wasn't a murder scene she still needed Julia and the CSI team there. She decided not to tell Julia everything as she wanted her to come to the same conclusion as she had done when she arrived there earlier.

'You should know me better than that Cadema. I can be there in thirty minutes, what's the actual address?'

Having given her the details, Cadema noticed that the clinic was as clean as it was before. No one would have known it was the scene of a crime until they saw Miss Gardner's office.

When Julia arrived, Cadema took her to the scene.

'Well, what do you think?'

'You said the stabbing took place just before the cleaner arrived at six this morning. From the coagulation processes, I would say you're right. But it's all so very neat. See, there are no scatter patterns anywhere on the walls or ceiling, indicating that the knife was not plunged into Philippa. What's more, there aren't any signs of a struggle. So it looks as if she was stabbed at very close range, almost as if she and her attacker were locked together.'

'Mm, that's very interesting but I see what you mean.'

'I'll take some blood samples, just in case the perpetrator accidentally stabbed him, or herself. But all I expect to find is Philippa's blood. By the way how is she doing?'

'She's doing okay. Apparently the knife missed her heart, but her spleen had to be removed. I'm going to see her soon. I know you are a friend of hers, and I still need to talk to you about that. But I must insist you do not go to see her, at least not at this stage.'

'I was going to tell you last night. She's not a friend of mine. You could say I've known her a long time, but that was university. I caught sight of her again when we were dining earlier this year. Then she turned up on my doorstep out of the blue a while ago. So I don't really know her, and certainly not as a friend,' she said indignantly.

'Thanks Julia. I'll still need a statement from you, but it's not so urgent now. I need to focus on why she has been stabbed.'

After agreeing to meet that afternoon, they both left the clinic guarded by a uniformed police officer. Cadema telephoned Ryan and asked her to meet her at the hospital.

***

There were too many people in the hospital's lobby for Cadema to see the information board at first. Hindering her way was the mayhem of half-clad bodies, some with crutches others in wheelchairs.

She noticed a sign directing patient traffic to *Ward Twenty-three*, she headed, with Ryan, in that direction. Walking on past the outpatients' clinics, children with ruddy complexions and runny noses, ran in circles, under chairs and along the corridor shouting and screeching as if another World War was about to erupt. Cries from infant's lungs informed their micro world that they were starving even though they looked as if they were well over the accepted weight for their age.

The two officers walked on, stepping over toys, books, sweet wrappers and a half-eaten sandwich.

A woman at the enquiry desk, dressed in a grey uniform with a badge denoting her as a 'volunteer', told them they were heading in the right direction for the lifts to the third floor. Cadema thanked her and moved on.

As they reached the ward, Cadema felt exhausted by the journey and by the constant chatter from Ryan about the possibility that Philippa Gardner had tried to commit suicide.

'I've already thought of that, but I don't think it is the case?' Cadema said.

'Why ever not? It looks like it to me?'

'So where's your proof?'

'No struggle. Stabbed close up. No defence wounds. She could have easily done it to herself. Perhaps not intending to actually commit suicide, but as a cry for help.'

'I can see your point. But I think Gardner was probably attacked by the person who somehow managed to access Robert Buxton's sperm. Someone who was trying to incriminate him. Who may even be our serial killer?'

'But Ma'am, if he were, why didn't he kill her? No, I think Gardner knows who the killer is but could not betray him so she attempted suicide,' Ryan sounded indignant.

'You may be right. But a suicide usually inflicts superficial wounds on themselves, unless of course, they fall onto the knife. This didn't happen, so I think someone else was there. Someone whom she trusted-hence the lack of defence wounds. Just consider what Jim Logan would have done under such circumstances.'

Ryan raised her eyebrows at the mention of his name. *At least Jim would listen to his colleagues,* she whispered under her breath. Cadema was different, she liked to come up with the answers, and that made it difficult to challenge her views in any way. One day she would have to tell her to bury Jim and move on, but this was not the right moment.

After showing their identification badges, the sister in charge of the ward led them to a side room where a uniformed officer sat waiting for a potential assassin. Showing her ID, and with a polite nod of her head to the officer, they entered a room saturated with the odours of anaesthetic, congealed blood and other smells which brought bile into the back of Cadema's throat. She swallowed fast and approached Philippa Gardner as if she were approaching someone with the plague. The sister nodded to a question which was never asked, and Cadema leaned over.

'Miss Gardner I need to ask you some questions, are you okay to talk?' There was a nod of the head in affirmation. The patient's parched lips opened, then swallowed, as if her mouth were full of sandpaper.

'Can you tell me what happened?' Gardner shook her head; but she did not speak.

'Can you tell me who stabbed you?' Again there was silence, except for a feeble attempt to shake her head. Cadema moved in closer. The smell of anaesthetic was more noticeable now. Gardner muttered something. Cadema leaned closer, her ear almost touching Gardner's mouth: 'Philippa, can you tell me who it was?' Cadema said in an audible whisper.

'T...h...o... T...h...o...' she lifted her head slightly off the pillow.

'Who?' Cadema whispered louder as if she were in an alien world.

'T...h...o...mas,' she murmured, then closed her eyes as her head hit the pillow.

'Thomas? Who is Thomas? What's his last name?' But all Cadema could see was an exhausted patient lying motionless on the bed.

'It's the anaesthetic and analgesic she's had. She'll sleep for quite a while now,' the sister said indicating that they should leave her to rest.

The journey back to the office was filled with questions and counter-questions in Cadema's mind. She switched Ryan off. Now her thoughts ping-ponged across the table of judges in her mind. This case was getting out of hand, and she was nowhere nearer the answers than she had been weeks ago. Not only that, but she was worried Grimes, and most importantly her team, would give her a vote of no confidence. She needed time; time on her own to sort out an action plan.

Reaching the station, she didn't give the usual team briefing. Instead she entered her office and before closing the door, told Ryan she was not to be disturbed for at least an hour.

Fifteen minutes later, the waste bin was almost full of crumpled paper. The knock on the door prevented more deforestation. She shouted 'come in,' and Julia's head peered round the door.

'I know I am disturbing you, but you did say you wanted to see me again, so here I am. How is Philippa?' Cadema tried to smile, but her face displayed a frown at being disturbed.

'Oh, she is all right,' Cadema said, almost dismissively. 'And yes, I do need to speak to you. But I'll have to do it in the interview room on tape.'

'That's fine with me,' she lied, 'but it's unusual isn't it?'

'Not really; I must get everything down on tape as soon as I can and there is no time like the present.' She stood up and led the way down the corridor followed by the six pairs of bewildered eyes of her colleagues.

The tape was switched on and the usual introductions were made.

Julia spoke first. 'As I said before, I've known Philippa Gardner since we were at university together. But while I went into forensics, she chose a different pathway so she went to another faculty. We were never close friends, only students together.'

'Did you ever go out socially together?'

'No. I believe friendship means going out and sharing thoughts and feelings. But it was never like that with Philippa, she had her own circle of friends and I never met any of them.'

'Have you seen Philippa Gardner since you left university?'

'As you know, I saw someone who looked like her, probably in April or May this year.'

'For the tape, please explain.'

'The person was in the restaurant, but I wasn't really sure, as she was too far away and we didn't speak. Then, as you know, she turned up at my address. She did mention the murders but I told her I was unable to discuss them. So if she did know something it was only from the media.'

Cadema listened to every word, nodded in the appropriate places, and clarified parts, but she had no reason to interrupt or disbelieve what her friend was saying until she asked her about Gardner's behaviour. At this question, Julia fidgeted and took a sharp throaty cough as she answered.

'Philippa didn't mix very well with other students. Some of them found her a bit strange, and that sometimes they felt she was untruthful, and could not be trusted.'

'Can you give me any examples?'

'Yes. I recall the time when Philippa had missed several lectures. When we asked where she was, she said she had not missed any of them. On another occasion, at a lecture, she ignored everyone, as if she didn't know us. When we asked her about it later, she denied even being there and could not understand why we were going on so.'

'Anything else you can recall?'

'I remember another time when Philippa wrote an examination paper. Apparently the marker didn't believe she had written it, even though the invigilator was in the room all the time. She was accused of cheating, but there was no real evidence, only the change in handwriting and grammar. So no further action was taken. Anyway, she was intelligent enough to pass all her exams, probably the first time. I later heard she left with a third-class honours degree.'

'Thank you Julia, that's all for now.' Cadema turned off the tape and sighed.

***

After Julia had left, Cadema felt the emptiness in her stomach as her mind whirled out of control. Instead of returning to her office, she left the building and headed for the cemetery. She needed to talk to Jim and clarify her thoughts; he would understand.

The ground was damp and cold as she sat cross legged, wanting to be as close as possible. As people passed by, she assumed they would think she was visiting a close relative, never suspecting she would be visiting anyone else. And as she sat she told him about the problems she was having with Evans, and she didn't really know how to handle him. Then said how she had missed the opportunity to follow up what Johns had said about Buxton visiting a sexual health clinic. She had suspected Buxton because of the DNA results, but later realised that he was probably innocent. The sperm bank and the problem she faced now Philippa Gardner had been stabbed. Could she have stabbed herself, or could she have been stabbed by the serial killer? She didn't know which. She had assumed the killer was a man because of the DNA, now she wasn't so sure. Although Philippa said she did not have access to the sperm, she now believed she was lying and could be the killer's accomplice, or even the killer.

Then there was also the problem with Julia, despite the recent interview with her; she felt she was unable to confide in her as, for some reason, she believed Julia and Philippa could still be friends. Julia might, inadvertently, she didn't believe she would do it deliberately, tell Philippa something about the investigation. She couldn't let that happen, that's why she was confiding in Jim. He was impartial now, he would understand. But everything was such a mess and she couldn't speak to Grimes, or anyone else for that matter.

Sitting there, she felt the shudder of a breeze across her face as if someone had just passed by, although there was no one there. Darkness was beginning to creep across the sky, turning it a murky grey colour. She shuddered again and pulled her coat tightly round her, not knowing whether she was afraid or cold. There wasn't a crackle of a noise. It was if the whole world had gone to sleep, leaving her to talk, and for Jim to listen.

He was there, or at least she thought he was. She could feel his presence. Not the kind people say they feel. She was not cold any more, but warm. And as she talked, the warmth grew and surrounded her like a furnace. She told him how she felt, how the work was not going as she wished, and asked him if he had any ideas. She listened with patience, sitting in the silence, waiting for a sign, knowing nothing tangibly would come to her. But covertly, in some strange way, she knew Jim would give her the answers she needed. All she had to do was to be patient. And, after the hour-long consultation, she left the graveyard. Driving home, she listed the plan in her mind.

CHAPTER THIRTY-ONE

The next morning Cadema ignored the astonished looks from the team as she rushed into her office, closed the door and sat down at her computer. Instead of writing her usual ten-point plan, she began to type the questions she needed answering, and also the answers. This had never happened before. Was some other force helping her? She typed vigorously. Finishing, she leaned back in her chair, smiled, and silently thanked Jim for his help.

Entering the briefing room she faced the team of officers.

'Everyone pay attention,' she said assertively as she looked round the room. 'Good. As you are aware I don't like interruptions during my presentations, today is no exception. So I expect you to leave your questions until I have finished, unless I ask you to speak. Is that clear.'

'Yes Ma'am,' some of the officers said while others nodded.

The team sat mesmerised as she read the ten questions and probable answers displayed on the screen.

'Question one. What was the motive for all these murders? I believe they were murdered because they had auburn hair. Even Natalie had auburn hair at one stage. But one thing we're not sure about is why he chose these women. There is obviously another motive, and we need to find out what it is.'

'But what does that mean?' DC Galke interrupted, then realised he shouldn't have done as Evans shook his head and mimed for him to shut up.

'What I would like to know,' Marriott directed his question to Cadema, 'is...' But she halted his sentence reminding him not to interrupt or speculate unless asked to do so. Marriott mimed 'sorry' and remained quiet.

'Now before the next question, as you know Philippa Gardner was stabbed and is recovering in hospital. When asked who stabbed her, she mentioned the name Thomas. So here is the next question.

'Question two: Who is Thomas and how does he know Miss Gardner? When Doctor Lilly examined Gardner's office where she was stabbed, she said there were no signs of forced entry. That means she must have let her would-be murderer in. Therefore she must have known him. In fact, it looked as if the wound could have been self-inflicted. But there was no doubt Thomas was very close to her and she didn't have any defence wounds. So she couldn't have known she was about to be stabbed. Doctor Lilly believes they were locked together. But of course, Gardner could be our killer's accomplice: Thomas perhaps? They may have argued, and that was why she was stabbed. This is all speculation though, so we need to find Thomas.

'As murderers usually take some form of trophy from their victims. If Gardner is the accomplice she may have trophies hidden somewhere.'

'Do you think there's going be another murder Ma'am?' DC Galke managed to say before Evans stopped him again Cadema decided to let this question go unchecked.

'As we know, serial killers always find it difficult to stop. I think,' she looked straight at DC Gilke. 'This one will be no different from others. Nevertheless, we need to catch him now, before he strikes again. So who is this Thomas and where does he live? It is vital we find the answer as this is now our main priority.'

'Question three: does Miss Gardner have alibies for the dates of the murders?' Cadema addressed the whole team now. 'I believe she doesn't because I think she was there when the crimes were committed. If she was there, she may try to protect the identity of the real killer. So we need to check exactly where she was when the murders were committed.'

She panned the room, everyone sat in silence as if grasping her every word.

'Question four: some new evidence has come to light which I haven't mentioned before. But we believe the ejaculate left at each murder scene had been frozen.' As she said this, there was a loud buzz of noise in the room. Two officers raised their hands to speak. Evans asked them to wait. 'Doctor Lilly said it appears it was frozen sometime before the murders, thawed out, and then left on the victims. I am waiting for conformation on this. If it were frozen, then that leads us straight back to Philippa Gardner's Harley Street clinic.' The audience remained attentive. She could almost hear their hearts pounding away in the twenty chests facing her. 'This question will be answered by Doctor Lilly.

'Question five: Are there any connections between Thomas and the victims? The killer had certainly known Sophie Millburn. He groomed her using the internet café near Marble Arch. But that's all we know about this. I also suspect he met Natalie Taylor before. He probably sent the woman to the address near where Natalie lived. Probably the same woman who visited Natalie, as according to her father, she would never let a man in. But we don't know why the killer chose that area in the first place. And, for that matter, why Natalie was chosen. She could have been the only one who opened the door that night. So we need to find out what the connection was between the killer and his victims.'

Although Cadema had clarified some of the issues, she believed she was going round in circles as there were still too many questions and not enough answers. She noticed a couple of officers were getting restless, so she asked if there were any questions or comments. Marriott raised his hand to ask the question he was going to answer earlier.

'Why didn't we find any other evidence at the crime scenes except the ejaculates?'

'That's a good point. Basically we don't know, but can speculate that the killer made sure he left only what he wanted us to find. It indicates that he was trying to frame someone else, hence the frozen ejaculate.' Cadema answered. 'That leads me onto the next question.

'Question six: If Robert Buxton is not the murderer, and from the above evidence, I believe he is not, then the only explanation is that he has been incriminated for some reason. So who did this, and why was he chosen? We need to find out if anyone had a grudge against him, Philippa Gardner perhaps, and if so why.'

Go on, dig yourself in deep, Evans said to himself. He had his own opinion on this but was not about to tell her she had it all wrong. That Thomas and Gardner were red herrings. That Robert Buxton was the murderer. No, Cadema would have to find out the hard way and be humiliated in the process. She looked at Evans, he smiled and lowered his head.

'Do you think it's likely that Mr Buxton saw Miss Gardner when he visited the clinic?' Ryan asked.

'He said he didn't, but she could have seen him. Conversely she may have recognised his name on the records and could have passed this information on to the killer, anything's possible,' she replied thinking there could also be a motive hidden there somewhere.

'Question seven: we know Robert Buxton's ejaculate was left at the scenes, so why was it there? The answer to this is not very straight forward. It cannot be answered until we know the result of further tests. Doctor Lilly is working on this at the moment. But it indicates that he was being incriminated for some reason.'

'Do you know how long it will take Doctor Lilly's analysis?' Johns asked

'A few days and we should know one way or the other. But let's get on with this meeting. It's taking much longer than I expected,' she watched as some of the officers shuffled their feet, as if they were anxious to get on with their work.

'Question eight: What is the psychological profile of the killer? As you know this was done recently. It's a bit long so I'll precise it,' she held up the document. 'It suggests the perpetrator probably lives alone, and has a grudge against women with auburn hair. He is in his mid to late-thirties, has a good job, most likely works in a medical setting from Monday to Friday. He is neat and fastidiously clean, has very few friends, and most of these are probably not long-lasting ones. He dresses smartly and blends in well. The killer probably lives within a five mile radius of the murders, except Natalie Taylor's of course. That's all we have at the moment, except the results from the autopsies. But again, this takes us back to the earlier question; what is the real motive?

'Question nine: Has any other tangible evidence been found at the scenes? We have already scouted around this question. Nevertheless, we think he wore a forensic suit and gloves at each one so he would not contaminate anything. This also helps to support the theory he was incriminating someone else, and why we only found the ejaculate at the scenes.

'Question ten: How is the baby swopping case related to the murders? This is where the twin theory was derived from. And why we originally suspected Edward Mason. It hasn't got anything to do with the murders but at least it shows that DNA evidence is fallible.' When Cadema had finished talking she asked if anyone had questions or comments to make.

'Well at least you have given us some good ideas. Do you think the killer may work in a hospital?' Galke asked.

'It could be, but remember Gardner runs a clinic, so there is a connection there,' she replied as the others nodded.

Evans coughed and decided to speak. 'That's a tricky one, especially as the profiler doesn't mention an accomplice.'

'You're right, so we need to be more focused on this.'

'But there is something else, Ma'am. As Natalie Taylor lived outside the radius you mentioned. He may have met her before, in London. If he did, the only plausible explanation is that he followed Natalie, found out where she lived, and visited the nearby house to see the layout before he murdered her.' Evans smiled as the audience gasped.

'I have considered that,' Cadema said, not wishing to peruse the hypothesis even though she thought it was reasonable. Somewhere there was a woman involved, and she suspected it was Gardner, or someone she knew.

'Thank you Evans, so let's get on with the investigation as there are many questions remaining and I want the answers to them ASAP.'

Delegating the Actions, she thought about the baby swapping investigation at the Wayford Hospital. This would now have to wait even longer. A visit to Philippa Gardner in hospital would be her next priority.

CHAPTER THIRTY-TWO

When Cadema entered the ward the next day, Philippa Gardner was sitting up and looking as good as she had when they first met. Except for the tenseness in her voice, she appeared as if nothing had happened. That is, until she edged up in the bed, and grimaced.

'Do you need a nurse or something for the pain?' Cadema asked, hoping to get on with the questioning. She just shook her head and grumbled, eventually asking Cadema get on with the questioning so she could rest.

'I will, if it's okay with you, but I can go and come back later if you're in too much pain.'

'I'm fine, just get on with it,' Gardner grunted as she moved herself up the bed again.

'If you're sure,' Cadema pulled up a chair and sat facing her. 'I assume you know about the murders we are investigating?' Her voice sounding flippant, hoping to give the impression she was just making conversation. In reality, she wanted to see her reaction to the question.

'Do you mean the 'Common Murders'? Cadema nodded. 'Well, yes of course I have heard about them. How could anyone fail not to know, it's been on the media enough. But why are you asking me?'

'We think there may be a link to your clinic. We arrested a suspect whose DNA matched the crime scene. He turned out to be Robert Buxton, your client.'

'So he's the murderer, that's great, isn't it?' she frowned. 'As far as my clinic is concerned, no one there would ever be involved in anything like that,' Gardner grimaced again.

'It would have been but we need to do some more work on it before we can be sure. By the way, Philippa, you mentioned someone called Thomas yesterday, so can you tell me who Thomas is?'

'Thomas? You must be mistaken. I don't know anyone with that name.'

'But I definitely heard you say Thomas had stabbed you. So we need to know who Thomas is and where we can find him.'

Gardner edged up the bed again, her face contorted as she shook her head and reiterated that she did not know a Thomas.

'Are you saying you don't know anyone by the name of Thomas even though you said his name yesterday?'

'Yes, that's what I am saying. As far as I know, Thomas does not exist.' With an audible grunt she moved her hand to her abdomen and tried to cough. Cadema decided to stop questioning her. Instead, told her she had a warrant to search her apartment.

At this information, Gardner looked agitated but was too overwhelmed by the pain to say anything. Anyway she had nothing to hide. She knew the police would never find anything incriminating at her apartment, no matter how hard they looked. And, as for the murders, it was Thomas who carried them out, and he would kill again if necessary. But she could never tell the police what had happened, it was her secret.

***

I couldn't believe Philippa had mentioned my name to the police, anaesthetic or not, she should never have done that.

Despite the pain I was in now, my anger grew to boiling point. I had to threaten Philippa again. But she said she hadn't mentioned my name, that police must have misheard, or they had fabricated it all, or something.

Did Philippa really expect me to believe that? How could she be so stupid? She knows she cannot hide from me. It was then I realised that, at the next opportunity, Philippa would have be silenced for good. When she was fit, but not too fit this time. But I expected the police would arrest her as soon as she was discharged. The only option for me was to do it before they had time to interview her. My plan was very simple, she, like many others, would be successful at committing suicide.

CHAPTER THIRTY-THREE

'Is that you Cadema?' Julia asked as a voice answered in the affirmative 'I'm just phoning to say my suspicions have been confirmed. The DNA had been frozen and that it was from the same batch. Apparently the Philadelphia Institute has developed a new technique, and using it, we managed to find the answer.'

Cadema was elated at the news; she could now take one of the questions off her list.

'That's great. Julia, it confirms Robert Buxton is innocent. But I don't know why someone would try to incriminate him or who it might be.'

'I thought you'd know the answer. Isn't that why you are pursuing Philippa? You don't think she is the killer, do you?'

'Sorry Julia, I cannot answer that question, you know better than that. But thanks for letting me know about the DNA, it's wonderful news.'

'You're welcome.'

Cadema heard a click on the phone and the line went dead. She smiled to herself and decided she now had enough evidence to tell Grimes what she suspected. She headed to his office.

'You see Sir; the DNA had been frozen by cryopreservation techniques. This can only be done in a laboratory. The Harley Street clinic where Philippa Gardner works uses that technique.'

Grimes paced the room as if he were trying to understand the significance of what she was saying. He had never been very bright on technology, but up to now he had managed to hide his ignorance from the ranks.

'Mm, I see, do go on.'

'I think Philippa Gardner may be the murder's accomplice and I am about to interview her, that is, when she gets out of hospital.'

'What makes you believe she is involved in the murders?' he asked in a slightly agitated voice at being told something he already knew. Cadema had a habit of doing that. So he decided to tell her not to keep repeating things once the current investigation was over. He didn't want to upset her at this stage.

'Well Sir, when Gardner was coming round from the anaesthetic, she said someone called Thomas had stabbed her. But when I asked her today, she denied even knowing anyone called Thomas.'

'Then you need to find out who this Thomas is. Do you think he is the perpetrator? If so, what proof do you have?'

'It's all circumstantial at the moment. But she was the only one at the clinic who could have accessed the sample by herself once the sperm had been frozen. All the other employees didn't have access to all the PINs and keys needed to do so. I just need to verify that.'

'So that's your evidence is it? I suppose it could be feasible. If you're right, Thomas could have stabbed her; but for what reason?'

'I'm not sure yet, but I intend to find out, even though Gardner doesn't appear to want to tell me.'

Grimes was trying to listen, and not to interrupt Cadema, but his mind kept wondering off into another world. These days he often had difficulty concentrating, so he grunted periodically, giving the impression he was listening. This time, he was thinking of his favourite pastime, when somewhere in the distance he heard her voice again.

'I've got a warrant to search her apartment, Ryan's gone there to supervise the search. I don't suppose she will find anything though as Gardner seems very secretive and cunning.'

'Good, so let's hope she has been careless, and they find something.'

'Hope so, we will have to see. But while Gardner's in hospital, I don't think there will be any more murders.'

Grimes muttered, inaudible to Cadema: *supercilious bitch, thinks she knows everything.* He gave a smile. 'You'd better be right, if you're wrong there'll be hell to pay,' he grunted and said goodbye. As the door closed, he wished he could dismiss her ideas as readily as he had dismissed her. But underneath it all, he had to admit she had some plausible arguments.

Leaving his office, Cadema wondered if he was ridiculing her? Was he thinking of interfering in the investigation? Was he thinking of assigning someone to examine what she was doing and to report back to him? It had been done before, when Jim first started to work with Grimes. He found out before it was too late. She had to do the same or he would take all the credit for the investigation. Not that it mattered, as long as the perpetrator was found.

***

Cadema was still thinking about Grimes when her telephone rang. It was Ryan. She listened for a moment and then said:

'You mean to say you have finished searching Gardner's apartment and found nothing?'

'That's right Ma'am, there nothing there to incriminate her. That is, not to the naked eye. We need forensics to see if they can find anything, so I've asked the CSI team to go and see what they can find.'

'Very good, let's hope they find something.' Cadema didn't mention she was pleased that Ryan had not asked Julia to go there. That would be a conflict of interest on Julia's part. Besides, she didn't want Grimes to find out that Julia had known Gardner in the past.

'As you've done all you can for now, I want you to come back to the station with Evans. I've asked Mr Buxton to come in again for questioning, and I need Evans with me.' Cadema expected to hear some groans from Evans in the background. But there were none. 'I assume Evans is still with you?' her voice sounded accusing.

'Yes he is, we're just packing up. I'll leave a PC here, so expect us in fifteen minutes.'

'Make it thirty, I know what Evans is like, so tell him to drive carefully,' Cadema said knowing too well he liked to speed when he had the opportunity. One day, she feared, he would cause a collision.

They arrived at the station twenty minutes later. Evans was cursing about the problems with the traffic. Cadema didn't mention Julia to him, but said that Buxton had been taken to the interview room, and his solicitor was not going to attend. With the tape switched on, and after the preliminary introductions were completed, she began the interview.

'Mr Buxton, do you know this woman?' she handed him a photograph of Philippa Gardner. He squinted, turned the picture from side to side and answered:

'She looks vaguely familiar to a woman I was engaged to a long time ago. But her face looks different, and her nose is smaller in this picture. So what have these murders got to do with her?'

'I just wanted to establish if you knew her, and it appears that you may, so we can continue with our other enquiries.'

'I only said she looks similar to the woman. But she isn't mixed up in this is she?' he shook his head slowly. 'Come to think of it, it could be her. If it is, she was a bit odd, that's why I broke it off, but I didn't expect anything like this.'

'Broke what off? And like what, Mr Buxton?' Evans snarled.

'We need to know what you mean by that,' Cadema interrupted, she gave a disparaging look towards Evans. 'And what did you expect her to do?'

'Why nothing,' he hesitated as he spoke.

'What's the matter Mr Buxton? It sounds to me as if you expected her to do something. What did you expect her to do?' she continued.

'Nothing really, but Cynthia was unusual.'

'Cynthia, you said Cynthia, was that her name?' Cadema sounded disappointed.

'Yes, it's the name I knew her by, if that is her in the picture. But I'm not quite sure,' he examined the photograph for the third time, looking at it from several angles.

'I'm sorry to tell you the name of the person in the photograph is Philippa Gardner.'

'Well, the Gardner is right, but she called herself Cynthia back then, so it must be her. I suppose you want the whole story about our relationship.'

'That would be a very good idea, Mr. Buxton,' Cadema said hoping his story would identify what she needed to know and that it would establish a motive for the murders.

Buxton took a deep breath, drained his plastic cup of water, sat upright in his chair, and began to speak:

'My relationship with Cynthia was turbulent, but to start with, we were great together. She doted on me and would hardly let me out of her sight. As you can imagine, I was elated about this.'

'I can't imagine, but do go on,' Evans interrupted. Cadema gave him a stern look and shook her head.

'Sorry Mr. Buxton, we won't interrupt you again.'

'Thank you. Well, she brought me gifts, spent hundreds of pounds dining in expensive restaurants. She even helped me to choose my own clothes and then insisted on paying for them. Although I believed she could not afford it, I went along with her actions, worried that if I intervened, she would be angry.'

'Angry? Why would she be angry?' Evans ridiculed. Cadema scowled again.

'I'd seen her anger on more than one occasion. The first was when we were travelling back on the underground from a show in London. A woman dressed in a long black skirt and a high necked black cloak, with wild satanic makeup, giving me the impression she worked in the tourist attraction which recreated London's East End of 1888. Cynthia had taken an instant dislike to the woman in the black cloak. I laughed it off as a joke. When the woman clung on to the pole as the train sped through the tunnels, the woman moved closer to me. Her knee almost touched me as she winked. That was enough to kindle abuse from Cynthia. As her anger surged to the surface, she lunged forward, took hold of the woman's hair and called her a f...ing whore.

'It took three men, including me, to prize the women apart. Cynthia, still shouting abuse, left behind the dishevelled shell of the woman whose face was covered in rivulets of blood. But Cynthia calmed rapidly and within a few seconds she acted as if nothing had happened. It was never mentioned again but I was cautious of her from then on,' Buxton asked for his plastic cup to be filled. He took a gulp, and then continued his narrative.

'The second time was when I stopped to buy a newspaper. As I got out of my car, a woman carrying her shopping accidentally bumped into me. I said sorry, and forgot the incident. But as I went into the shop I heard a commotion and turned to see Cynthia attacking the woman in the same way she had done to the woman on the underground. As I approached, Cynthia let go, then got back in the car as if nothing had happened.

'By then we were engaged to be married, but I decided not to marry Cynthia. Being somewhat a coward, I didn't tell her. She continued to make arrangements for the wedding. This time I insisted on paying for everything. But when the wedding day finally arrived, I was already on a plane bound for Australia to stay with friends I used to know when I had my macadamia farm. And never looked back.

'I supposed Cynthia would think I'd just vanished into thin air. That was eight years ago. I never saw her again.' He drained the water from the cup and sighed. The room remained silent for a while until Cadema finally spoke.

'Thank you for your honesty Mr. Buxton. But that puts a fresh light onto our investigation. So what happened when you were in Australia and why did you return here?' she sounded sympathetic, as if she were counselling him rather than interviewing him as a police officer.

'When I was in Australia I met my present wife Margaret whose family had emigrated there some years ago from Ireland, they had since returned.

'Margaret was the complete opposite to Cynthia. Mild, caring but most of all, even tempered. We were married six months later in a quiet ceremony in Perth. We decided to go to London where I invested in the business I now have in the city. I never gave Cynthia another thought. Margaret worked locally and never ventured into London.'

'Thank you Mr. Buxton, so can you explain why you decided to donate your sperm?' Cadema fidgeted when she asked this question. She was going to leave it for Evans, but following his last remarks, she decided to do it herself.

'Everything was going well for us. Although our twins were born the following year, I wanted a larger family. Margaret was unable to have any more after the hysterectomy she had following complications during the twin's birth. I was devastated. And, although I love my two boys, to compensate, I decided to donate my sperm, but never told Margaret about it. When she was diagnosed with breast cancer, I was pleased I had kept it from her.'

'So where are the twins now?'

'They are in Ireland being looked after by their maternal grandparents. We took them there just before Margaret started her chemotherapy.' Buxton took out his wallet and showed Cadema the photographs of the boys. She smiled and said how they resembled their father.

'Sorry but we need to press on with the questions,' Cadema said as she fidgeted in the chair.

'When you became a donor, you didn't know that Philippa, or Cynthia as you call her, worked at the clinic?'

'No, I didn't. But anyway as the clinic offered anonymity, I felt safe there. All I gave was my name and not my actual address. And I only did that because of the change in the law giving any off-spring the right to trace their biological father. I couldn't have that, it would upset for my wife. But at least I knew that somewhere in the world, I had an extended family.'

Cadema decided not to comment, but thought it was a strange thing to do. And she couldn't see, if he wanted a large family, why he would donate sperm; never to know who the children were.

'Philippa Gardner must have seen you there, or perhaps noticed your name on the database,' Cadema said.

'She must have done something like that. But if she were going to kill someone, surely it would have been me or even my wife. Anyway you said you were looking for a man. No, despite all her faults, I don't believe she is capable of murder.'

By this time Buxton was almost pleading with Cadema to believe him, but for some reason, she knew she could not. Instead she decided to end the interview and not let him know her suspicions. Before the interview was over she asked him if he had a photograph of his wife. He reached into his pocket, opened his wallet again, and handed her a photograph. Cadema didn't know why she asked for the photograph as she had seen his wife when Buxton was arrested. But she was ill then. Now she was holding a photograph of a fit and healthy woman. As she looked closer, she began to realise why the murdered women had been chosen.

CHAPTER THIRTY-FOUR

Although my wound was still very sore, somehow I managed to get out of bed and dress myself. Taking the white coat off the hook on the door, I put it on over my clothes. The stethoscope around my neck, completed my disguise. As I slid quietly out of the room, I could see the police officer, who was supposed to be guarding me, had been distracted by some noisy children along the corridor. He failed to notice me as I walked in the opposite direction to where he was looking.

The urge to do one last murder had overwhelmed me as I walked upright, with difficulty because of the pain, along the corridors, down the lift, and out of the hospital. Just this one, that's all, just this one, then I would stop. But the voices began to torment me again. They were trying to take over, and I couldn't have that. The woman had to go, she was my ultimate aim now. She had to suffer as I had all these years; but they argued with me again.

'You promised not to kill again Thomas, and we won't let you,' one voice said.

'Try to stop me, you cowards,' I said, trying to fuel their anger, hoping for a good argument. 'You've seen what I can do when I want to, and I want to now.'

'We'll stop you, you can't go on, we won't let you,' a second voice said.

'So who's getting a conscience now, you've never stopped me before?' I screamed under my breath.

'I've always tried,' number one said.

'No you haven't, you've always sat back and watched. You're as guilty as I am.'

'We won't let you this time, the police are too close, you've seen the Superintendent, she has a reputation of being very thorough. You can't fool her. Next time you'll be caught. That means we'll go to prison,' number one continued.

'Nonsense, you don't know what you are taking about.' They argued with me again, but I drowned them out with different thoughts as I made my way across town to my other apartment. I hadn't been there for some time and felt like a stranger. But at least the key was still where I had hidden it.

Philippa was ecstatic to be back in our favourite place. I struggled to change my clothes. My anger rose when I thought of the injustice she had been dealt over the years. Robert had been the last straw.

Philippa always had to have everything she wanted, when she wanted it, not when others decided. I remember when she was about to get married. The satin dress clung to her contours as she waited outside the church. And, for the first time in her life she felt like a princess waiting for her prince; the prince who would never come. Was she too early? But the anger inside her rose as the time went on. Then it became my anger; Thomas.

She stood her ground as relatives tried to calm her; trying to persuade her to go home; that Robert wasn't coming. She didn't believe them. He must have been delayed, had an accident or something. She imagined him in his car somewhere, his head splintered against the windscreen; blood dripping from his wounds; calling for her. He needed her. No, he wasn't the sort of guy who would let her down; she knew him too well.

It was midnight by the time she'd left the churchyard. Later she found out Robert had boarded a plane at the very time he should have been saying his vows to her; there in the church where she had waited like a fool. That's when it started, that's when I, Thomas, and the others began to talk to her.

She never forgot Robert. So when he had the audacity to donate his sperm in the clinic, she felt humiliated, violated and unclean, and hoped his sperm would never be used.

But he had the perfect body, no genetic defects. Philippa did some good detective work. She discovered he had a master's degree and a doctorate. This infuriated her, when she was still struggling to get her masters. What's more, she found out he was married and lived in four-bedroomed house in Kingston-upon-Thames, an expensive area in the London suburbs, while she had to live in noisy humble apartments. It should have been her living there. Margaret Buxton had taken everything away from her; the house, the cars, the clothes, children, the lifestyle. They should have been hers, mine; ours.

And to think he had all that, and was legally spreading his sperm around and not through adulterous opportunistic mating, but through the AID process, where he knew they would go to good homes. A home which rightly belonged to us; yes he had deprived us of that.

It was Cynthia, later to become Philippa again, who suggested the plastic surgery. And I, as Thomas, encouraged her when she had doubts. I said it would protect her in the future, and I was right.

So, sitting in our chair, changing our appearance again, brought me back to reality. The plastic surgery had worked wonders. I could be anyone I chose to be, a man, an old woman, a young woman, a tramp, why, just anyone. No one would be certain who I really was, only I was certain. But the person who looked back at me from the mirror was something else. And, for a microsecond, it scared even me. But I was there and we both knew what we had to do.

***

I am Thomas; dressed and ready to kill again, heading for the Buxton household. The house I'd visited many times over the last few months. Robert had never noticed me following him. His wife was so plain, I couldn't see why Robert had married her. But that didn't matter now, I was in control.

I waited behind the hedge, making sure there was no one around. Then walked slowly, but with a sense of purpose, to the front door and pressed the bell. She opened it almost immediately. It was going to be easier than I thought, than I could have ever dreamed of. I noticed how frail she looked. Her auburn hair had gone, now it was patchy, almost grey, and lifeless—half hidden by the scarf; her skin like alabaster.

But I saw someone we both hated, someone we wanted to suffer. The others had gone; given up their arguments; they could never compete with me.

***

I stepped over the threshold, invited in by the woman who would soon wish she hadn't done so. And as we sat there on her green leather sofa in her lounge, I had the feeling she knew what was about to happen. She looked nervous.

Did she really believe I'd moved into the house up the road and was in need of an electrician? I thought my excuses were wearing thin. Had I been convincing, or was she going to give me a cup of tea to keep me there until the police arrived? I had to know, Philippa had to know, but I couldn't ask.

Margaret spoke so quietly:

'I have cancer, that's why I am wearing this scarf.'

I nodded in some kind of acknowledgement and muttered something inaudible; neither of us knew what to say. I began to speak, but thought better of it. Somewhere the chimes of a clock punctured the silence; the tick, tick, tick had begun. She gave a nervous cough and handed me her telephone and the number of an electrician. I dialled a fictitious number. She left the room, shuffling down the corridor. I sat there with Philippa on the sofa; trance-like and unable to move. The voices had left; I was alone with her. We could have been anywhere, we had to do something. I whispered, she listened. I had a plan and there was plenty of time. The cups and saucers rattled on the tray as Margaret returned. We sat there sipping our tea. I waited.

The door opened slowly, quietly. There was movement, hurried, hushed movement. Then the noise of feet scuffling across the floor. There were too many feet; closer and closer they came. We sat there in silence sipping our tea. The Superintendent stepped quietly into the room. We smiled at her in acknowledgement and continued sipping our tea. The officers surrounded us but no one spoke. The tea was delicious.

It was well before then that I had decided not to kill Margaret. She was too frail, too thin, and too ill. Time would be her killer not me. So we just sat there, Margaret Buxton, Philippa, and I, sipping our tea. The two of us waiting for the inevitable arrest.

get his wallet and see the photograph of his wife, who had auburn hair. That was the trigger,' Cadema said. Evans coughed and spoke:

'So there we have the motives; revenge and the auburn hair.'

'Thank you,' Cadema continued. 'She obtained the sample of ejaculate, and left small amounts at each murder scene to incriminate Robert Buxton.'

'How did she manage to get the sample Ma'am?' DC Barry asked.

'We don't know for sure. As you know she's in Broadmoor, and therefore we have not been able to interview her again. Her psychiatrist says, due to her multiple personality, especially her narcissistic behaviour and her psychosis, we will most probably never be able to interview her. Despite this, Thomas became the dominant personality, and as far as Philippa is concerned, Thomas carried out all the murders.'

'It sounds to me that Thomas knew exactly what he was doing. So how did he discover Buxton's address?' Galke asked.

'As we know, he didn't give his actual address when registering at the clinic. Now this is only speculation, but we believe Philippa followed him and found out where he lived. If she could not incriminate him with the sperm she left at the murder scenes, she would try something else. As we know, she went to his house intending to kill Margaret, but for some reason she never carried it through.'

'But surely she wouldn't kill his wife, when it was her husband she was after?' Marriott asked.

'It seems by then, she had lost all reasoning. The psychiatrist said, because of her narcissistic tendencies, she believed Margret had everything she should have been entitled to. Margaret had Robert, the house, the lifestyle and the children. She was deprived of these and blamed Margaret.

'It seemed that when unmarried women were carrying twins, they were told, by a midwife, that they were expecting only one baby. If they went into labour the same time as a woman who had just had a stillbirth, their second baby was given to this woman. Neither women know anything was amiss, each mother left hospital with a healthy baby.

'I don't know how this arrangement actually worked at the time, but there doesn't appear to be any GP involvement.' Marriott exhaled loudly and took another sip of water. 'I hope this all makes sense? Some of it is speculation, but feasible.'

'Thank you Marriott that was excellent detection on your part,' Cadema said and asked if there were any questions from the audience.

DC Galke was the first to raise his hand: 'So have you managed to trace all six of the babies?' he asked as he looked round the room.

'We've traced three. Robert Buxton and his brother was one of them. One of the babies died of 'cot death' at eight months. The other one has been informed. And of course the Buxton brothers are now aware of this, but their mothers would never have known.'

Marriott sat down in his chair.

'Thank you,' Cadema turned to the team. 'So as you can see we have three distraught families from the baby-swopping scam. In Robert Buxton's case, he was given the opportunity to meet his brother, but Edward said he just wanted to get on with his life and not meet Robert. Who knows, they may meet up one day,' she shrugged.

'As for the original Mr. Buxton, Mary Buxton's husband. He may not have known anything about the scam, but we will never know for sure as he died of liver sclerosis ten years ago.'

But he was the main target.' Cadema said as she looked round the room for more questions. DC Barry raised his hand and stood up:

'Although Philippa has not been charged with any of these crimes, are we assuming we are not looking for anyone else? There were rumours that she had an accomplice,' he sat back in his chair again.

'We are not looking for anyone else, and there are no accomplices. This is because Philippa and Thomas were the same person. Although, when Thomas, she dressed as a man but dressed as a woman when it suited her. As she must have done when she visited the estate agent who showed her around the house in Grosvenor Road. Later she went to Natalie Taylor's address, perhaps dressed as a woman. Why she went there we do not know. But we do know that Natalie had auburn hair once. She wrote the article and had questioned Connie Mason. Philippa must have discovered this, and then decided to kill her for some reason.

'When we discovered Philippa's second apartment we found several disguises and theatrical makeup, so she could have disguised herself as any number of people. And, as you know, her car was found in a nearby lockup garage.

'In relation to Madeline Belton's murder, Bernard Franklin was charged with that, and is awaiting trial. Any questions?' No hands were raised.

'Well, if that's all, thank you all once again on a job well done.' Leaving the room, she went to see Grimes.

He smiled as she entered the room and praised her for the work she had done. She offered a thin smile in return, and with some embarrassment waited for the 'but' or the 'well'; she wasn't sure which he would use.

'Well, now that's all over, perhaps you'll take some time and reflect on what you have learned and what you would do differently in future.'

'Yes sir, it's been a tremendous experience and I've learned a lot. Thank you for your support,' Cadema said with some hesitation.

'I'll tell you what you've learned. You've managed a large team, and handled several difficult cases at once. During this time, you've also managed to stay sober, not like some SIOs I've known in the past. However, you haven't managed some of your team as well as you could, especially Evans. And if you had remembered the sexual health clinic which Johns said Robert Buxton frequented earlier than you did, then the cases would have been solved sooner. That means the cost of the whole investigation would have been reduced, instead of the extra thousands wasted. And you're just lucky my girl, that it didn't cost anyone their life. But nevertheless you did the best you could and at least we have a positive result,' he smirked.

'Thank you, sir, I'll keep all that in mind.'

'Good, so let's not keep the SMT waiting any longer,' he picked up his notes and headed for the door with Cadema.

'By the way, what are you planning to do now, a holiday perhaps?' Grimes asked as they walked down the corridor.

Cadema coughed and said she had not given it any thought.

The SMT over, she left the building and headed for home. Now she was ready to visit her mother in India.

CHAPTER THIRTY-SIX

It was nearly two years later when Bernard Franklin and I met for the first time. I was in an ambulance being taken to hospital, as my condition could not be treated in the secure unit I was in. But the ambulance broke down. When another one arrived, Bernard was there, as he too, was on his way to hospital for some treatment.

Although the wire mesh segregated us inside the ambulance, it didn't stop me from whispering to him.

'Do you know who I am?' I boasted.

'Yes, I know. You're the serial killer Philippa Gardner,' he replied.

'You are right in one way. But it wasn't Philippa who committed the murders it was Thomas. I am Thomas.'

'Whatever…' Bernard looked up at me and shook his head. Somehow I felt he was sorry for me.

'I have a secret, do you want to hear my secret?' I was almost growling with excitement.

'No, not really.'

'That's too bad because I'm going to tell you anyway.'

'Tell me what?' Bernard was getting anxious now and was no longer humouring me. He looked suspiciously at me.

'You know I've murdered four women, but I can assure you right now, I didn't murder Madeline Belton. I did meet her though, but the police are unaware of that.'

'Go on,' Bernard said as he leaned his head against the cage.

'I saw Madeline hitch-hiking and stopped to pick her up; she was going to be my next victim.'

'So it was you after all?' Bernard screamed under his breath.

'Keep your voice down and just listen will you? We'll be at the hospital soon so we haven't time to argue. All I did was give her a lift, nothing else. She was alive when I dropped her off. She told me about you, how you tried to touch her up, you pervert. She told me, but I kept her secret.'

'So you know very well I didn't kill her. Why don't you tell the police?'

I smiled and turned my head away. I was not prepared to answer Bernard's question; besides I was having a much better conversation with Philippa.

The End

About the Author

S J Ridgway was previously head of studies in a health related setting. Has a first degree in biology, and applies an interest of genetics in writing crime fiction. Links to a retired police offer in the family is helpful as a resource and for critical appraisal of police procedures. Visits to close relatives in Australia and New Zealand, trigger plots for current and further writing.

She is a member of several writing groups, and has given talks on this crime fiction novel. The second novel in this genre is near completion and a third one is currently being planned.

Has had six non-fiction articles published in professional journals.

Currently works as a volunteer in health related organisations, and uses social media sites for networking purposes.

More from Blue Hour Publishing

Blue Hour Publishing offers an eclectic mix of books for the discerning reader.

Our ever growing list of authors makes it impossible to review all the books and authors here but whatever your fancy from thrillers and occult to human interest books and fantasy check out our website for more details.

Thrillers:
The Blue Hour*
The Penhaligan File
Postcards From Berlin*

Human Interest:
Silent Love*
Shattered Dreams*
Simon's Choice*
Edge of Extinction

Occult:
Shadowchaser*
Angels of Retribution

Fantasy:
The Tower and the Eye: A Quintology*
Snowblind and Other Shocks

Factual:
Licence Reviewed: 50 Years of Bond Movies*

*available as ebooks and paperbacks

7